ETANI

MORE FROM THE AUTHOR

A huge thank you to Andrew for always believing in me, and encouraging me to keep going even when I doubted myself and my ability. Thank you to mum for supporting me during these past months, and thank you to Max, who can't read.

Cover Design by Grace Zhu
twitter.com/gracezhuart

ETANI

N. MALONE

1

IN THE BEGINNING THERE WAS DEATH, AND IT WAS PERFECT

*H*ow long had it been since she reached them? Months? Years? It was time to move them, and yet she couldn't focus on that fact. Her mind fixated on the knot in her stomach as it tried to consume itself. She was emaciated, her fingers trembled, and she needed to eat.

She could feel it, that blackness inside herself that was starvation, and she struggled to push it down and at least mostly remain herself. People died when she was starving, more than just the one or two she needed to sustain herself.

With that in mind, she had ventured closer to a city than she ever intended, and she saw them, all those delicious, tempting souls for her to eat.

She couldn't attack a group; she was too weak for that. She would need someone alone, as even a pair of travellers might overpower her, and then she would be trapped. Getting out of Ceress would be dangerous, and she could easily be tracked that way.

Chewing on her tongue, she did her best to ignore the gnawing in her stomach and simply watched, waiting for someone passing by to be on their own.

When he arrived, she was panting and sweating, though it was growing cooler as the night drew closer. She needed to eat desperately, and if she didn't, she was going to lose control and go on a rampage.

The man barely registered to her, only vague flashes of pale skin and silvery hair, his long ears telling her his species. She knew only vaguely that he was higher ranked, thanks to his smart travel attire, but her hunger-addled brain was unable to fully register the details.

One problem, however, was registering: his mount. Horses and she did not get along under any circumstances. She had theorised with her sisters that horses could smell the predator in her and panicked. It wasn't a good thing when the beast would then alert her prey to her presence.

She didn't much like it, but she settled in to watch the man as he joined a handful of others who didn't aim to enter the city from the main gates; instead, he headed for stables that were closer to the ridge where she stood.

He trailed behind the others, taking his time to dismount and then unpack the beast before handing the creature off to a young, stable boy.

Only once the beast was gone did she finally move, creeping her way around the ridge to come to a slow stop just inside the tree line.

She would need to be careful; if he really saw her up close, he might panic and run—if she stayed shadowed, he would likely get close enough that running would be no good.

Glancing down at the sparse covering of grass, leaves, and twigs around her feet, she intentionally stepped on one of the larger ones—the snapping sound drew his attention.

He stood frozen for several seconds, seeming uncertain of her until she lifted her hand in offering to him, a plea for help or an invitation.

Whichever he took it to be, it worked. He stumbled forward for her and when he was close enough to see her face, she saw his comforting smile fade, could smell his fear as he realised the threat.

The moment he turned to run, she lunged for him, and her world was turned to black as the need to feed pulled at her.

She could taste his blood, smell his panic, and hear his screams.

They were running, her chasing and attempting to bring him down, trying to keep him from escaping when she was so weak.

She was in pain, her shoulder on fire, and yet she knew she could bring him down if only she could get her nails into him.

He was screaming and his blood sprayed the walls, coated the cobblestones, coated her.

She filled herself with his blood, greedy and desperate for more, and finally, the man was dead.

Blood coated her face, and her teeth sank into the flesh of his chest, tearing away at the firm muscle and thin layer of fat.

She was missing an arm and her shoulder burned where the skin and tendons had been ripped.

Swallowing the meat, she swept her eyes over her surroundings but found nothing of note.

Their blood coated the walls of the nearby buildings and the cobblestones beneath them. The ground had been torn and the stone of the building had been cracked during their fight.

Digging her fingers into his chest, she found what she was looking for and, with a wet sucking sound, she pulled the heart free of his ribcage. It was still warm, and it oozed blood as she bit into it, chewing the tough tissue.

Licking the blood from around her mouth, a scuff had her looking up, and she found him there. He watched her curiously as she crouched over the corpse, her hair a tangled mess and her simple brown dress torn from the fight. Her feet were bare, and she was covered in blood, but she did not really care. She would go back to the river she had found earlier and clean off most of the gore.

He was a problem, though, and her eyes narrowed as she considered what he might want.

She knew what he was, and it made her immediately wary of him.

His kind were dangerous and volatile. She wanted absolutely nothing to do with him, and yet, she had to protect her kill or he or any of the other scavenger species would take it and she would be left with nothing.

His hair was long and silvery-white, he was broad and tall with muscles that she thought must have been present before his death, and yet he was still somehow gaunt. His eyes were slate grey and cold as he studied her, and she knew he was assessing her the same way. They were both gauging the threat that the other represented.

She knew instinctively that he was a Lich, one of the dead arcane magic users who was once human and had given himself up to the dark, demonic magic that, once found, was almost impossible for the human to give up again. It was an addiction like no other.

Neither of them dared to move, aware of the other predator that could so easily turn on them. Frozen, she contemplated her choices. She could run, but that would leave her open to attack and would mean abandoning her kill, a kill who had been difficult to bring down.

He had damaged her body, and she needed his meat to recover, or her arm would possibly never grow back.

He had been a skilled fighter, but he was no match for the savage ferocity of her starvation. It had been weeks since she had found food, the lands surrounding the city being almost entirely devoid of life. It had been a risk, but when she found the city, she decided to take that risk.

Normally she would never have dared to set foot in a place like that, there were too many who could feel what she was, too many who knew how to defend themselves, and that made the risk too great. She had her own things to defend, but her hunger drove her into the outskirts of the city, to their encounter.

He had seen her, she knew it. But she also knew that he would not immediately react; the men never did. They caught one look at her and were captivated, enthralled. It made the men easy prey, and she preferred their meat over women's. Men did not have as much fat, lacking the second layer that women possessed; she preferred the leaner meat, as fat did very little to sustain her.

The fight had been brutal, and she thought he was an elf of some description, perhaps a Fae. She did not care enough to look, and, with the Lich watching her, it was no longer wise to try to determine what he had been.

She had no pity for any of them; they were food, and that was all.

THE LICH MOVED and her thoughts returned to him, her fingers tensed on the lump of meat. She needed to make a decision; she needed to choose what she was going to do. Did she run, or did she fight?

Fighting a Lich was not the smartest move. It was impossible to tell how strong they were until the fight started and she did not feel like dying to him.

He tilted his head slowly, and she found her head tilting in the same direction, the mirrored movement bringing a hint of amusement to his dead face, a spark of light to those empty, soulless eyes.

Did Lich have souls? She really had no idea, and the thought made her wonder about him and all of those like him. Liches were rare, so few mages ever survived the transformation. The humans were not designed to own magic, but some of them managed it, making deals with the Fae or demons, or any number of other mythical creatures, for a shred of their magic. That was all it took, and their fates were twisted and warped into something entirely different and completely vile.

Trailing her eyes down his frame. He did not have the usual supply of fetishes and bones that was supposed to be common for his kind, though she had never actually seen one of them before. They were reputed to be covered in runes and skulls. But he wore only a robe. It was black and made of some coarse material she thought might have been cotton, but she could not be sure.

His strength was what gave her the most pause. The Lich could not develop muscle or mass after death, and their bodies deteriorated after the change. So, what was it that kept him from becoming the gaunt, skeletal creature he was supposed to be? She did not know, but the curiosity ate away at her.

The thought had her swallowing the meat that was still in her mouth; she needed to focus, but her mind wanted to meander all over.

His attention dropped to her lips as she licked them and she smiled, amused that even a Lich could succumb to the same trap that every other member of his sex fell for.

He was thinking—just as she was, though if he was afraid of her, he made no show of it. She refused to show fear either, unwilling to give him the satisfaction of thinking he scared her. He did scare her; she had no interest in involving herself with his kind.

Her thoughts turned to escape, and she traced over the path their fight had taken, drawing a map in her mind of the part of the city, slums or whatever they were called, just inside the city wall. Removing the parts in which they had doubled back as he attempted to flee, or she retreated for the next attack—and she had her escape route.

The only problem was, he was standing in it. She would need to go past him to get out, and that was not going to happen.

There was an alternative to going around him, and that was to sacrifice her kill to the Lich and flee while he was distracted. She was no stupid woman; she was not going to fight him. She was missing an arm and in no state to fight.

With the heart still gripped protectively in her hand, she shifted her weight and stretched out her right leg slowly, so very slowly.

Setting her foot down, she moved her weight to that foot and away from the corpse, returning to her crouched position.

His white eyebrows lifted as his gaze took in her movements, his attention going from her to the corpse and back again, though she couldn't fathom what he was thinking.

It was obvious to her, though; an offering of meat in exchange for her freedom. It would have been obvious to most of the predators, but the Lich were a different kind of predator. They were not like her, feline and feral. They were more like vultures, circling and waiting for what was left, waiting for those like her to vacate the area before they moved in to scavenge parts for whatever depraved magic they devoted themselves to.

Would he accept the trade? He seemed to be considering it, and as she repeated the slow, careful retreat, he crept closer to the corpse, his eyes locked on her, wary and alert for any change that would indicate an attack.

Their dance was careful, deliberate and slow. Each manoeuvred the other around until they had traded places, him at the corpse and her near to the entrance of the alley.

He did not immediately go for the meat; instead, he felt around in his pockets for something, a knife or other tool for his need. She did not need a knife; she had sharp teeth and nails.

HE MADE a move just as she was turning away, but it did not seem to be directed at her. Rather, he seemed to be throwing something into the alley. Something thin and gold flashed above her, and she looked up, wondering if it was a shooting star, but it was the oddest thing, a thin golden chain dancing in the air, moving towards the end of the alley where she crouched. She had never seen anything like it, and the shimmering gold kept her attention, fascinated her by its appearance, and then vanished as though it had never been.

Something cool touched her shoulders, and she immediately jerked away, the touch rolling up over her exposed skin as something pulled tight around her throat.

The Lich was grinning, a hugely savage grin as he held something in his grip, and she followed a shimmering line of gold from him to her.

Lifting her hand to her throat, she touched her skin, and she felt the tiny gold chain that pressed into her flesh.

Panic flooded her system with adrenaline, and she yanked on the chain, but that only pulled it tighter against her, making it hard to breathe. She struggled with it, trying desperately to wedge her fingers in between the chain and her neck.

He approached her, winding the other end of the chain around his hand while she tried desperately to pull away, her body straining against the chain. It was like he had tethered her; the thin metal refused to break or even release at her touch, like it had been... enchanted.

The Lich had tricked her, and she gasped for air, gripping the end of the chain and tugging at it to try to get it to break, bending and twisting it, but the links were more solid than any metal she had ever encountered in her life. How could something so thin and delicate be so impossible to break?

Her lungs burned with the lack of air, her head spun, and her heart raced in her chest, desperate terror and that blinding urge to flee.

She had to escape, she needed to get back to them, but she was trapped. He had trapped her, and she could not breathe, rolling forward onto her knees and then onto her backside. Vision darkening, she whined and clawed at her throat, but nothing she did earned her the freedom she craved.

It was not possible for such a simple, stupid little thing to trap her.

She who had been escaping capture for so long, trapped by a Lich? Her body tilted and she caught herself with her hand, her muscles trembling even as she dropped with an ominous thud.

He came to a slow stop above her as she lay on her side on the cobblestones, straining her neck to try to get even a whisper of air into her. But the chain had pulled too tight.

"Don't fight it," he said in a low, oddly scratchy sounding voice. "The more you fight, the more it's going to hurt."

She swiped at him; he only laughed and pulled the chain taut between them, the pressure pulling her upright. She could feel herself fading, her mind struggling to keep up while the lack of oxygen dragged her down towards unconsciousness.

She felt weak, her muscles unresponsive, heard his low exhale of breath as he crouched down at her side, a cool arm sliding against her back as he supported the weight of her torso.

He gripped her jaw, turning her face so that she was looking at him, though she could barely make out any details now, the blackness had crept in until she could only see a tiny circular smear.

"You and I are going to have so much fun together," he breathed.

She expected his breath to be foul, rotten flesh and decaying teeth, but there was no odour at all, not on his breath or from his body.

The Lich were supposed to smell like rotting corpses, were they not? The thought was oddly disjointed as she clung with every last shred of willpower she had to consciousness. She barely felt his free arm slide up under her knees, her body slumping against his chest as he lifted her. She gave herself over to the darkness with a terrible, fleeting thought that she had been captured—by a Lich.

2

ONE DOES NOT FUCK WITH THE LICH

She awoke to find herself in a stone room, confused and disorientated at the change in location and the fact that he had not killed her; realising that was always a pleasant surprise for someone like her.

The Lich was smiling at her, though it was not the nicest smile she had ever seen; he was gleeful at his capture and she... well, she was not.

He had bound her with more gold chain, her arms outstretched as wide as was possible, her legs secured, but at least she was able to stand on her own.

"What are you?" he asked her almost curiously, like a child finding a strange bug on the ground and contemplating whether it was worthwhile to keep, or if stomping on it might be more entertaining.

At least she had the forethought to stick to a continent that she knew the language of; it got difficult when she was captured and could not understand the language of the one trying to question her.

The memory brought the hint of a smile to her lips; his violet skin, his golden eyes, and his screaming. She had not understood a single word he had said, something he did not seem to consider before he stuck a knife in her chest. She had killed six of the people from his village though—fair was fair, after all.

The Lich seemed confused by her smile and she jerked back to herself when his hand tapped her face. He was trying to get her attention, and when she looked up at him again, he repeated the question. She chose not to answer him, playing dumb or foreigner, whichever worked best for her current situation.

Maybe he would fall for her not understanding his language? It had worked before.

His jaw clenched as he stared into her face, and she could almost see the wheels turning in his brain, trying to come up with something that would explain her.

Instead, he bent down close, and she jerked back. He was sniffing her, her hair and her skin, her breath and the expression on his face showed his confusion. Lich were entirely too creepy for her liking.

"I know you can understand me," he said, his smile meeting her frown as she squinted up at him, irritated at his cleverness. "You responded to what I said in the alley. You stopped struggling when I told you to."

Considering her response carefully, she licked her lips and opted to deny the whole damned thing.

"Go jump in a volcano," she said, using her native tongue instead.

Let him make what he wanted from that.

He frowned at her, sudden doubt flicking across his face, and she felt a vicious stab of glee at the sight of it. She knew only two languages, the common tongue spoken by those on the southern part of that continent, though the language was spreading, and her own native language. She could not read the common language, but she was fluent in speaking it, a fact she was not going to be telling him any time soon.

He seemed to be torn, trying to figure out either what she had said, or if she had understood a single word he had said, and so she decided to punctuate her point by lifting her index and middle fingers to him, showing him the back of them.

He looked up at her hand, and then back to her, his lips parted in fascination.

"Interesting little beast you are," he hissed.

She had to admit she was having a little bit of fun with the monster;

she could not help herself. She had been on her own for so long that it was not often she got to mess with anyone.

He made a thoughtful sound and moved away from her, allowing her to study the room more carefully. It was entirely made of stone, with a large number of metal rings on the walls, ceiling, and floor. A large, heavy-looking wooden door was directly across from her and to her left was the Lich, bending over the table that was heavily laden with supplies and a book that he was writing in.

Tilting her head slightly, she saw what he was writing, but the scribblings had no meaning to her, as she could not read. Pursing her lips in consideration, she watched the man for a moment before she turned her attention to the gold chains, twisting her wrists to try to get herself free. There was something odd about those chains. They were not normal metal but something else, indestructible.

Frowning, she gave the chains a little tug but, while they flexed a little, they were not going anywhere and after her first attempt to pull her hand free resulted in the chain tightening on her, she opted to not try that again or risk her recently regrown arm.

IT WAS that arm in which he took an interest when he returned to her, though she suspected he had already looked her over before she had come to, given she was now naked and had been cleaned. The blood was gone, the dirt was gone, and her pale peach skin was a rather surprising sight to her. It had been so long since she had been genuinely clean.

"Why is it you smell so strange?" he asked her, but she made no indication that she heard him, too busy studying her nails. Pink, perfect ovals with little white crescents at the top set into long, slender fingers and small hands. He had even washed her hair, and she tilted her head enough that one long curl fell down over her shoulder. It was not simply crimson but streaked liberally with gold to give it a look of fire when it moved. The colour was another thing she had not seen in quite some time, nor the perfect ringlet. Her hair had been tangled for so long, matted with leaves and twigs and mud.

She looked from her hair to him as he stood before her. He touched her arm, pushing down on her bicep and then watching as the pale skin turned white, then back to peach.

He studied her face for a moment and then frowned, trying to figure her out, it seemed. He was not going to have any luck; she looked at least mostly human. She had made sure of it.

"Very well, if you won't talk, we will see how else you can understand..." he said with a scowl. Turning away from her, she tracked his movements back to the table where he picked up a very long, very sharp-looking knife, returning to her side where he pressed it against her forearm, just below her elbow, and looked to her face.

"Shove it, Lich," she hissed at him, refusing to let him know she could understand him. He only smiled slightly, and the blade hissed against her skin.

Biting hard on her tongue to keep from making a sound, she tried to pull away, but the restraints kept her in place, trapping her there.

He held his hand under the dripping blood, catching it in his cupped palm and lifted his hand to his nose, inhaling the scent of her blood before he licked the drops from his palm, his expression thoughtful.

"Odd taste..." he murmured to himself, catching more and licking it again before he returned to the book and added more notes. Glancing at her arm, she watched as the bleeding slowed and then stopped, the skin pulling back together and the angry red of the swelling eased down to leave nothing but a pink scar that would fade to white in a matter of hours and, if she put a little effort into it, would fade to nothing in a month or so, although she never bothered. His interest piqued as he saw the scar and he squeezed the skin, pulled it lightly and then shook his head.

"What are you...? You're not human," he said thoughtfully, his grey eyes sweeping down over her form where he took in all the other scars on her body. She was utterly covered in them, each one different and each telling the story of another fight, another run-in with a strange creature she tried to eat.

Pressing his index finger against the point of the knife, he spun it slowly as he watched her. She, however, was more interested in plotting her escape, regardless of how impossible that seemed right then. Sacrificing her hand was not that big of a deal, but opening doors without hands was difficult and the more she studied the door, the more she thought that the handle was made of iron. She and iron did not go well together at all.

The thought of trying to open an iron door with no hands had about as much appeal as kicking a dragon on the nose, but she had spent too long in that city already; the Lich was not her biggest concern. The other one was, and he would not be far behind her.

The Lich was growing impatient and when she did not seem to be afraid of the knife, he went for a different tool. She had no idea what it was or what it was for, but it looked unpleasant.

A short wooden bat with stubby spikes, the bat itself being quite thin. She was not keen to find out what part of her person that thing was to be used on.

THE LICH TURNED TO HER. She arched her brows in defiance but still flinched as he lifted the bat above her and brought it crashing down on her regrown arm, her scream echoing around the room as the bones splintered. He was still as he looked at her arm, his lips parting as he studied the skin. Something had his attention, and she looked around.

A small crack had appeared in her skin, not like a cut, but more like someone had dropped a porcelain doll. Inside the crack was pitch black, though it did not ooze or bleed at all and she cursed internally. That was not good; she was dehydrated and while he had only hoped to break her body, he was also breaking her shell. How long had she been unconscious that she had become dehydrated?

It was not that much of a surprise really. She had been lax in looking after her body for a while.

He grabbed her arm, squeezing the flesh painfully to watch as the split spread, but when he pressed the edges back together again, they stuck, and the crack was gone as though it had never been.

His head turned slowly towards her and his gleeful smile made her stomach twist in fear. No, she did not want him to figure out her secret.

He was far too happy for her liking; a happy Lich was not a good Lich. The only good Lich was a dead Lich, and he certainly was not dead.

Looking back to her arm, then down at the bat, he contemplated where to hit her next, lifted the bat and pain exploded at her side with the sound of breaking bone and something else, a sharp cracking sound.

He bent over and studied the cracks in her flesh, pulling the cracks further apart until she whined in pain. He was pulling her skin apart, and it was terribly, horribly painful.

Letting go of the skin, he watched as it snapped back into place and sealed, sticking back together like glue.

"Fascinating..." he intoned, his attention creeping up over her body to her face and then up to her head, where his grin grew wider, feral.

He gripped the bat between both hands and lifted it slowly above his head, his intent clear, and she hoped desperately that he would miscalculate the pressure and kill her. Closing her eyes tight, she prepared for the blow.

The sound was revolting, her screech of pain joined with the crunch of her skull breaking, the crack of breaking porcelain and she could feel the splinters growing, tiny lightning-shaped lines spreading down over her face.

"What are you?" he demanded as her eyes opened and she blinked hard, her right eye seeming to have stopped working, though she thought it was open.

She could not have spoken even had she wanted to. Her head was agony, and she was so very certain the pain would make her vomit but that did not happen.

He dropped the bat to the floor and reached for her, hesitating before his fingers touched her. She could not breathe, she felt herself suffocating inside the shell. The cracks were spreading, and each new split sent a shockwave of pain through her mind and being.

He stared at the crack, though she did not know what it was he saw in it; her, perhaps? Movement? She did not know, and she did not care. She had to keep the cracks together, she had to protect herself.

"What are you, creature?" the Lich screamed so suddenly that she jumped. He was looming over her with long fingers clenching and unclenching, not yet touching and yet so wanting to.

Pain ripped through her body as she felt her face splitting, cracking open as her ability to grasp onto the seams of her shell slipped. Her magic was slipping, her very being was giving way to reality.

Unable to speak, she screamed a terrible cry of pain and writhed, the metal chain biting into her flesh as she attempted to rip it free.

"Reveal yourself!" His voice boomed, and he reached for her face. Grasping her cheeks between his thumb and fingers, he forced her head towards him.

"You are no human woman, no simple mythical creature, are you...?" he crooned, sadistic grin widening as he studied the cracks that spread across her forehead and down under her right eye.

It throbbed in pain, throbbed in time to her racing heart and to her utter horror. She saw his hands lifting, his fingers digging into the cracks and his arms flexed as he pried apart the two fragments.

Agony, pure and perfect, ripped through her skull, and the sound she made was not one that a human could make. He was prying at her, digging his fingers in under what should have been her skull but was not. She had pushed herself backwards, not wanting him to touch her.

He was ripping her apart, ripping her shell into shreds, and her vision blackened to nothing as the pain escalated to something so high and perfect that she could not process it.

When her vision cleared again, she could see the cracked eggshell appearance of human flesh in his hand, the peach skin withering into red-brown clay, and then it crumbled to dust before his eyes and when they returned to her, cold filled her soul.

He grinned maniacally, knowing the truth and his frenzied hands grabbed at her, ripping great strips of what looked so perfectly like normal flesh, only to have it shatter on the floor and she felt herself falling, the shell no longer able to contain her, the gold chains no longer able to contain her. They had been holding her shell. Clay pattered down over her body and what was left of the thing collapsed in on itself, leaving a pile of clay and dust to flow around her.

She knelt huddled on the floor, naked and aching, with her arms wrapped tightly around her middle, trying to protect herself from his eyes and his touch. Looking down, she saw the remaining strands of crimson and gold hair, mingled with long black strands that had not been there before.

"Stop..." she whispered, her body on fire, and she was left feeling terribly exposed. Her body felt heavy, having spent so long floating in the nothingness that was her shell. It felt as though the world were pulling on her, dragging her down, and yet the air felt wonderfully cool on her skin.

The Lich was silent as he watched her, taking in the shape that was left when the shell was removed. He had been so savagely gleeful to rip it apart, so vicious and cruel, and now he was only confused, staring down at the small, pale creature that was left.

"Stand up," he breathed. Her head tilted slightly to look at him, though she did not lift her eyes up past his knees and her hair provided a shield between his gaze and her face.

How long had it been since she had seen her hair? Long and obsidian, perfectly straight and wonderfully thick. It covered her body somewhat, but not enough.

His hand was colder than she expected when he bent down, taking her by the arm and pulling her to her feet.

Keeping her head bowed, she saw that her hair had grown down past her knees, heavy and wild around her. She felt more fragile in her natural state than she ever had in that shell, her host.

He did not release her arm and when she refused to look up, he took her face between his thumb and fingers, jerking her head up.

Still, he did not speak, staring at what he could make of her face before she finally lifted her eyes to him, meeting those dead grey eyes through a small part in her hair.

His lips parted slightly as he took her in, though no matter how many times he looked away from her face, taking in what he could see of her body, his eyes returned to hers again, captivated.

"Well then, enchantress, what exactly are you?" he said. It was a rhetorical question. She knew it. They both knew he would find out for himself and he would enjoy discovering it on his own far more than if she simply told him.

Pulling herself from his grip, she staggered and caught herself against the wall, her muscles struggling to remember how to work without the host to contain it. It must have been longer than she realised since she had taken on the host. Her body was no longer used to being on its own.

He did not try to grab her again, simply watched her as she touched the wall, feeling the texture of the stone. It felt different from when she was in a host, given the clay shell muted most sensations; now she truly could feel it with her bare flesh. It was so rough and cold, lifeless.

"What do you want, Lich?" she asked finally, giving up the game of pretending to not know his language.

HE MOVED FORWARD, his grip tight on her arm as he pulled her around to face him and thrust her back against the wall. Releasing her with one hand, he brushed her hair back from her face and took a firm grip on her jaw, turning her head. In her host she had been on a level with his chest, almost a foot shorter than him but now they were nearly eye to eye, with him being only around five or six inches taller and yet he still looked down his sharp nose at her.

He turned her head first to the left and then to the right, taking in her features, letting go of her face to run his finger slowly along the length of her ear, long and pointed. Catching several strands of her hair in his fingers, he rubbed them together slowly and then lifted them to his nose, inhaling deeply before he let go again. His attention trailed down over her throat to her collarbones and shoulders, taking in the pale skin with a very carefully schooled, neutral expression.

She could not get a single hint of his thoughts; he made no sound and there was not so much as a twitch from his face. He pinched her skin between his index finger and thumb, testing the elasticity of her throat before he let go again, pulling the skin tight against her to examine the blue of her veins, and then his eyes dropped. His hands were uncomfortably rough as he cupped her breasts and squeezed them, feeling the weight before he moved on with little interest. She was not as much a woman to him as she was an incredibly interesting specimen that needed to be studied.

He touched her stomach, pressing against the skin, pinching it to see how her flesh responded before he hesitated, his eyes on her groin but he did not touch her, instead going down over her thighs and then crouching before her to examine her feet.

The whole experience was so incredibly odd that she was not sure what to do, standing still and silent while he bent her toes in, ran his thumb over the underside of them and very nearly earnt a knee to the face when his finger trailed over them and she jerked back. Her feet were ticklish, and she did not like it when someone touched them. He made no response to her reaction to his touch; instead, he caught sight of her hands and he snatched at her wrist, standing and dragging her closer to the only dim source of light, a lantern on the table.

He examined her nails carefully, looking from her fingers and then down to her toes and back again. They were a match, silver in colour and perfectly oval.

Rubbing his thumb over the surface of her nail, he twisted her fingers to see the light reflecting off the metal surface, and then he pressed the tip of his index finger against the edge of her back. Hissing, he jerked his hand back and looked at his finger, seeing a small, curved cut that blood oozed from. He had barely touched her and yet her nail had cut him easily.

Finally, after what seemed like an eternity, he stepped back from her and examined the whole of her. His brows pulled together in a scowl of annoyance.

"What's the matter, Lich? Can't figure it out?" she taunted, though her low voice was a husky, sensual purr and yet he still scowled at her amusement.

"I will figure it out, woman. You appear to be some sort of wildling, fairy or similar," he said almost angrily, and she resisted the urge to laugh. She was no fairy; they were small creatures, but he was not that far off the mark and she was a little impressed by how close he was.

Lifting her shoulder in a shrug, she turned her attention from him to the door. "There are many types," she said dismissively, not giving him any clues.

He seemed to grow even angrier at her flippant response, and she frowned as she saw that same flash of gold. She did not have the strength or dexterity yet to try to dodge it, but she did jerk back. Even so, the loop fell down over her head and he yanked hard on the other end. Gasping as the chain pulled painfully tight around her throat, she staggered backwards and her muscles gave out, sending her to the floor at his feet, her hip and hands on fire where she had landed, though she did not appear to be bleeding.

The fleeting wonder of what eating a Lich would be like. She lifted her chin to look up at him, his smug smile and triumphant eyes lingering on her as he held the chain aloft.

"Don't get too bold. You forget that I control you. Whether you live or die is up to me."

Well, if that was how he wanted to play it, he was in for a rude surprise. Her flash of amusement was gone in an instant and his brows lowered in a frown as he saw only the briefest hint of it, neither of them speaking as they glared at each other, angry and both loathing the other.

How difficult would it be for her to get him to kill her? Surely it could not be that hard if she put her mind to it. But if he suspected that she was trying to force his hand, he would stop and become suspicious. Not only that, but she had to get him so angry that he would lose that vice-like grasp he had on his emotions. She did not think he would be that easy to anger, not so much so that he would risk his precious new toy.

3
___

TORTURE GAMES

The first day in his 'care' was relatively mild compared to what she expected; he only drew her blood and watched the slow pace of the liquid. Following that he listened with a small metal device to her heart, counting out the slow beats against a little hourglass that appeared to only last a minute, something she was rather curious about as she had never seen one that was both so little, and timed only a minute rather than an hour. When she asked if it was a minuteglass and not an hourglass, he ignored her.

Her heart rate was timed out at twenty beats per minute, consistent throughout the day as he timed it, again and again, mumbling that it would explain why her blood did not flow as fast as it would in any other species.

He cut her skin and watched it heal, shone an obnoxious light in her eye by carefully lifting a directional lantern to her face, covering her eye and then uncovering it over and over, watching intently how her pupils reacted to the change.

He seemed overly fascinated with her eyes, though she did not know why and when she saw the diagram he had drawn, she finally realised. Her pupils were not round like his, but slightly elongated, and she understood right then why she could see well in the dark.

Her eyes were more like those of a feline than a human.

She had not expected to learn anything new about herself, but there it was.

He moved on to testing her reflexes, her skin elasticity, and pressed an iron rod against her arm, monitoring the burning and then the agonisingly slow healing, all while ignoring her screams of pain.

She had tried to escape only once, and when she very nearly ripped his hand off his arm, he opted to wrap her chain around a ring on the wall instead of simply holding it.

The chain was incredibly odd, having been looped twice around the ring but not tied or locked at all, and no matter how hard she pulled on it, the loops refused to slip free or even so much as budge. It was infuriating that something so simple could so completely trap her.

He enjoyed watching her struggle with it, unwilling to tug at the end around her neck for fear of it choking her again, and the more she stared at the stupid thing, the angrier she got.

He refused to answer any of her questions, but if she refused to answer one of his, he would simply slap her, the blow brutally hard.

The first time he struck her she had been thrown bodily to the floor, not at all expecting the blow and certainly not the sheer force of it.

The second time she had only fallen against the wall, clutching her face and whimpering.

The third time, and from then on, she only staggered, clutching the wall to keep from falling.

He was very fond of hitting her, which was something she did not appreciate at all. Not that he tended to care what she appreciated, and what she did not appreciate.

After he had finished his examinations, he sat down at the table and made his notes, muttering quietly under his breath and asking her questions. They were all incredibly personal questions, and she was very quick to learn that it did not matter if she wanted to answer them or not, she would be answering them, or she would be hit.

"You are biologically female...?" he asked quietly.

"Yes," she had said moodily, glaring at him from where she sat on the floor.

"Were you born in Faerie?"

"Yes."

"Have you any children?"

"No."

"Are you infertile?"

"No."

"Are you sexually active?"

"No." She did not know what the questions had to do with anything.

"Have you ever had a sexual partner?"

"No," she growled.

His expression showed his interest at that. "Interesting. Do you eat human food?"

"No."

"Do you eat human meat or only the meat of mythical creatures?"

"Both."

"Do you have body functions?"

"Such as what?" she asked slowly, her cheeks flushing.

"Urinate, bowel movements? Do you menstruate?"

"No, none of those."

"How old are you?"

"Nine hundred and something. Don't really keep track."

"What is your name?"

"Etani"

On it went until he finally decided to leave, and she sighed, her arms wrapped tight around her legs as she finally managed to get some sleep.

ON THE SECOND DAY, he grew more curious, testing her saliva and blood, forcing her to eat various oddities and monitoring to see how long it would pass. They did not.

By day three he had realised that she had no normal bodily functions, even though she had told him she did not, and his interest grew. She realised that he had been testing her, monitoring, to see if she was lying. That in itself would have given him more of a hint as to what she was, and she immediately became more wary of him.

By day five he had graduated to removing her teeth, only after commenting vaguely on the odd shape of her canines. Like a vampire, yet only barely longer than any of her regular teeth. He removed two of her fingernails and attempted to break or bend them. They bent with enough pressure and finally split, but it took quite a bit to get them to break and he found he could file them down using an odd blacksmith's tool.

He broke her bones and watched them heal, marvelled over her teeth and nails growing back in a matter of hours.

By the end of day ten, he had gone so far as to dissect her. He cut open her arm and examined the internal structure. He removed a finger for ease of access, cut open her belly and noted that while she had intestines, they did not join on to her stomach. They were, in essence, simply there for the sake of it, because they were meant to be there and had exactly no practical use at all.

He was very careful, never taking her quite over the edge into the sweet death of which she so desperately craved. After the third day, she had learnt not to scream. That alone seemed to excite the Lich when nothing else did, so she remained silent. She was unable to stop the tears that escaped, and he marvelled over the inky black colouring of them. That prompted him to cut open her eyelids to study the ducts.

He was thrilled at her ability to survive, that he had to use tools to keep the flesh open even as it tried to stitch itself back together. And yet he seemed displeased.

"It's slowing!" he raged, some two weeks after the first day he had captured his new toy.

Turning on her, he gritted his teeth and glared. She could do nothing but look back at him, her arms outstretched, hanging from the chains once more. She had stopped trying to hold herself up, allowing the chains to keep her aloft.

He had hacked off her long hair, hopeful that it would grow back like the rest, yet it did not. He was too impatient to see that it grew nearly a foot in the week since.

"Why is it all slowing? You do not heal as fast. You grow weary faster. What..." he trailed off and blinked at her, studying. "You must eat." It was a cold statement, as though he were angry at her for being so weak as to need food. "Here I thought I had my equal, yet you are as weak as the humans," he sneered, resenting her ability to make him believe.

'Damn,' she thought, for she had been riding on starvation to bring her death. It would only have taken another week or so, with the rate her body was consuming energy. Normally able to survive two months between feedings if she was exceptionally careful, she was now lucky if she would see one. He was draining her of her energy, wasting it, and had not known. He was slowly killing her, all while trying to keep her alive with his extreme care.

"What do you eat? Your stomach does not connect to your digestive tract." He was not really talking to the hanging woman, merely thinking aloud.

The Lich turned to his book, every detail of her physical being jotted out there. Flipping through the pages, he muttered profanity to himself and tapped a nail on the table. Finally, he paused on a diagram of her jaw, studying the teeth, and she was rather amused to realise that he had forgotten the circumstances of their meeting. He had completely forgotten that he had stumbled upon her consuming the elf. Had entirely forgotten some of the first questions he had asked her.

"You eat flesh...?" he wondered aloud, turning to study the limp form of the naked, bloody woman. In a flash, he turned and swept across to the door. Yanking it open, he spat at the startled guards who peeked in curiously.

Lifting her gaze, she met those of one of the guards, and his face paled. She could not really blame him. He would see nothing more than a pale woman, her right eye removed with blood staining her face, her torso cut open from navel to collarbones with her organs spread out onto a table before her like some morbid display, while she was very much alive and alert. Turning away, the man vomited on the ground.

"Bring me meat, all forms. Fresh and uncooked. Bring a human if we don't have human meat." Ignoring the retching guard, he slammed the door and turned back to his companion.

"Which do you prefer?" He began to laugh then, highly amused at his game as he approached her, and started putting her back together again, humming some merry tune while he tried to match the parts to the empty spaces in her torso.

. . .

It was an hour before the guards returned; the vomiter had been replaced by another who made a valiant effort not to look at the helpless, bound creature that she was. They dropped a platter of meat on a small table and she gave it only a passing glance. The smell divine but it was not enough to sustain her anymore. It was the other thing that they brought with them that had her attention, and she watched as they shoved in a bound man and then hustled back out, the door slamming loudly behind them.

Unable to resist, her eye latched onto the man, her mouth watering at the delicious, utterly breath-stealing smell of him and his terror. She could not help herself, she was starving, desperate and needing food, even if it meant the Lich would see.

The man began to scream at the sight of her. He was an older man, his clothing and beard suggesting he was homeless, the smell of alcohol wafting off him. So perhaps not homeless then.

An odd sound filled the room, a low growling sound punctuated by a soft mewling whimper. It was a shock for her to realise it was her making the sound, her entire body straining towards him.

How had her willpower so completely escaped her? She did not know, but she was burning for him.

The Lich had not moved, watching her as she struggled and pulled against her chains to try to get to the terrified food and he smiled as he listened to the pitiful sounds she made.

The man scrabbled against the door, his nails breaking and the smell of blood hitting her like a physical blow. A snarl escaped her, and she pulled harder, her wrist popping as it dislocated. She was going to rip her arms off if that was what it took, but that would not help her. She had to decapitate herself if she was to be free of the chain around her neck. Pride be damned!

"P-Please..." she finally mewled, her voice high and desperate. The Lich laughed, a high, cold sound, and approached her. His face split into a wide grin as he stood before her, forcing her head up to face him when she tried to see around him to the human. Finally, she looked at the Lich as he drew nearer. His fingers dug into her jaw, his eyes burning.

"What will you give me if I let you have him?" he whispered.

The feral part of her was screaming, desperate for food, and she knew she was turning feral, bloodlust and need driving her wild.

"Anything," she pleaded, her entire being drawn to the smell and sound of the human man.

"You will be mine. Mine to command, mine to control. My toy, my tool. Mine," he murmured, lips barely an inch from hers.

The demand barely processed in her mind, and she did not give it as much as a second thought.

"Yes!" she hissed, uncaring of what the deal might entail. It did not matter; she wanted the human.

His grin grew wide again, and he lifted his free hand, pressing the pad of his index and middle fingers against the centre of her chest, over her heart.

Cold seized her and she gasped, her exhaled breath showing as mist in the air.

Without a word, his eyes still locked with hers, he reached out and freed first one hand, then the other. He reached behind her and released her throat. Stepping back, his voice boomed out in a laugh as she lunged for the man, slamming him against the wall with the weight of her own body.

The last thing she heard as she gave in to the hunger was the Lich's triumphant cry of victory. He had won, and they both knew it.

She knew, even as she fed, that he had stopped laughing and was studying her every move, every action the human made, and taking mental notes. She knew it was a terrible piece of information to give someone such as him, yet her need had taken over. She had been like a drowning person and the air just out of reach. She had lost her willpower and, with it, her freedom.

Even after the feeding she was studied, the Lich circling her like a buzzard and she watched him back, that feral part of her. She was wondering what the Lich would taste like, buzzing on the high of the feed and hungering for more. She watched him and did not think he was aware of her watching. He was so oddly animated, bending to examine the blackening of the veins that littered her body, studying the blackness of her eyes and assumed her blind, studied the mulberry colour of her lips. She felt the touch of his index finger there, and snapped at him. He jerked back, and she smirked. She had tasted him, his skin and the coldness of him. She felt it there, hovering on her lip, and she licked it away.

The taste of dead blood filled her senses, and she felt her head sway at the toxin. He was not edible, he was dead. Yet the part of him that she could consume, she was sure he still had that. She was certain he still contained a soul, and she wanted it very badly.

He asked her questions she did not care to try to understand, for when she was in control no language mattered, she cared only for the hunt and kill, only for the next meal.

She only knew he was asking her questions by the way his voice tilted upwards by the end and yet none of it made any sense, none of it mattered. She was still contemplating the likelihood of eating him before he ripped her in half when she felt her control begin to slip.

'NO!' she hissed inside herself, hating that other. That her that resided always, only retreating to relish in the meal, to absorb the food and grow stronger. She had been weak, so near death and yet there she was, clawing her way back like some rabid beast.

There was no fighting it, she knew that. And yet she wanted to fight, to crush that other her who dared to press her away and contain her.

They both knew she had no option, and yet she went down fighting, leaving scratches on their joined psyche that would take days to heal. Worth it.

4

BATHS, AND OTHER HUMAN INVENTIONS

*W*hen she came to, she found she had been sitting on the floor, a blanket around her shoulders and the lich beside her, silent and pensive, with eyes still focused entirely on her.

"Welcome back," he said dryly. It seemed he made an effort to blink after that, as though his eyes had not been shut that entire time.

"How long?" Her voice was a croak, unused or perhaps overused.

"A few hours," he replied, still staring at her.

She met his gaze for a moment and then stretched out her arms before her, flexing the muscles that at first felt tired, and then flooded with energy.

She sucked in a breath as she stood, the sound hissing past her teeth. She could feel the strength returning to her, feel herself healing rapidly.

The lich stood too, staring with rapt attention as her body seemed to fill before his eyes, her skin glowing with life and her hair becoming shiny and smooth once more.

"Interesting..." he murmured as he moved away, finally daring to take his eyes off his prized toy.

"You are eating the essence, the soul. Aren't you." It was not a question so much as his wanting confirmation of fact.

She considered lying, but decided there was no point.

"Yes. I eat their soul," she responded finally, turning to look at him.

"Soul eater..." he whispered, as though that were some great wonder to him.

There was no such creature, though the humans believed otherwise. The creatures they thought to be soul eaters were little more than her own people, but she was not going to tell him that. So, she shrugged, turning away from him and looking to where the man had fallen. He was gone now, nothing left of him at all. Now that she looked, she found that nothing remained of the lich's fun with her. The blood gone, the tools gone, the room spotlessly clean once more and when she glanced back to him, she found him observing her.

"There is no point in studying you for now. There are only so many soul eating species in this world."

She quirked an eyebrow at him, amused that he would assume she was from this world. But she would not enlighten him to the truth.

"What now?" she asked, bending to pick up a blanket that she wrapped around her body and tucked into itself, making herself a makeshift dress.

"You sound remarkably calm for someone who has been... experimented on," he said calmly, eyes hooded in suspicion. She tilted her head slightly, meeting his dead gaze with her own.

"There will come a day, Lich, where it will be your soul that I consume," she replied, not a hint of bravado in her tone. She too was stating nothing more than a fact. Something akin to fear flickered across his face for only a second.

"Yes, about that..." With that he strode towards her, reaching for her.

She moved in an instant to leap backwards, landing crouched against the wall to ensure he could not get behind her and allowing her plenty of time to escape him when he came for her.

"There is only so far you can run, soul eater. There is no escaping this room," he sneered, turning to approach her again, and she bared her teeth at him, ready.

He lunged, his long arms reaching for her and she spun, dancing out of his reach. She did not want him to get his hands on her, she did not want to know what would happen if he got a grip on her now.

After a few minutes of their game of cat and mouse, he had managed to back her to the far side of the room, and they were at a stalemate. She could not get out, but he was not able to catch her and so he decided to change tactics, his grin wide.

"Guards!" he bellowed, and the two men piled in. Taking in the situation in an instant, the taller of the two closed the door quickly, locking it and slipping his key into his pocket. Glancing between the two, she noted dryly that one of the two guards was the vomiter, his mouth agape at the sight of her intact and moving freely.

The Lich swiped for her and she curved her spine backwards, avoiding the grab and she took advantage of the opening, ducking out to the side but she knew she was in trouble, three would be much harder to get past than one and she had to get that key off the tall guard.

Turning to them, she paced slowly around the edge of the room, the three of them spreading out in an effort to cut her off.

She could see their silent planning, catching the hint of a movement of the Lich's hand as he directed the men, and she watched as the two guards stepped sideways, cutting off her escape to the left and right. She was trapped, and they all knew it, it was just a matter of how much damage she could cause before they managed to get her down.

She had no intention of going down without a fight and when they lunged for her, she moved with them. Hands closed on her arm and she used that to yank the man closer to her, gripping his head and guiding it into the wall with a thud, the man staggering away as she turned on the other but the Lich was on her as well and his long fingers clamped onto her arm, clenching painfully tight.

Turning on him, she brought her knee up but before she could connect with his ribs, her legs were unceremoniously yanked out from under her and she shrieked as she went down.

The guard she had introduced to the wall jumped on her bodily, knocking the wind out of her but even so, she drove her foot into the face of the guard who had caught her feet.

The guard straddled her stomach, her arms pinned under his knees, when the Lich released her and he yelled in fear as she jerked herself up, her teeth closing on the fabric of his pants, right at his groin but she missed his flesh and to ensure she could not do it again, he gripped her hair and forced her head down.

With the other guard taking the same measure and sitting on her knees, she found herself very effectively pinned.

"Hold her down! Don't let her go!" the Lich said excitedly, moved to her side and lowering himself slowly to his knees. Leaning over her, he smiled widely even as she wriggled and squirmed, desperate for freedom.

"Stay still, lass!" the guard on her chest cried, his face pale as he struggled to keep her down; even with both of them sitting on her, they were barely containing her.

The Lich reached down and placed all five fingertips against her chest, around the spot he had touched when she had agreed to his deal and, reaching with his free hand, he grasped the shoulder of the guard who was sitting on her legs.

The Lich began to speak, the words unintelligible, and the guard went suddenly rigid, his back arching and mouth wide in a silent scream but it was her voice that filled the room in a terrible scream as a cruel, savage and biting cold dug itself into her skin and flooded through her system until she could feel nothing else.

"Should I die, you too will die. For as long as I live, so shall you," the Lich called, and the guard slumped. The coldness retreated from the rest of her body and into her heart, leaving it burning.

The second guard rushed to help his fallen companion, and she rolled onto her side, curling into a ball around her heart that felt as though it had been doused in ice and shoved into her chest. She did not flinch or try to move away as the Lich slowly bent down over her and a new chill went through her as his lips brushed her ear.

"And now, you truly are mine. Forever," he whispered, pushing himself up, and he swept from the room.

She did not move at all, her clenched fists pushing into her chest over her heart in a vain attempt to try to warm it up again, but it was not working, and it was burning like iron, constant and terrible.

He had cursed her, cursed a member of the Fae. She had never heard of a Fae being cursed before, it simply was not done and yet there she was, whimpering on the floor as she tried to push even a shred of warmth into herself.

Soon after the Lich had left, the remaining guard dragged his dead companion from the room and she was locked in again, unable to move for the pain.

IT WAS SOMETIME LATER that she finally pulled herself upright and sat huddled against the wall, her arms wrapped tightly around her knees. The burning of her heart did not ease and first one day, then another passed with her simply trying to remain calm, to exist while her heart burned on and on without reprieve.

What would the point be of taking all that effort to contain her and then just leaving her there? She did not think he had forgotten about her and yet the days had ticked by with no changes.

It was on the third day, however, when she picked up the faint sound of footsteps in the distance, something she had not heard since the guard had left.

Lifting her head slowly from her knees, she looked in the direction of the door and listened, the footsteps growing steadily louder and then louder still. Those were not the footsteps of a Lich, or even the footsteps of a normal man. Those were the steps of a large being, a massive being and her eyes widened as she pictured the creature, some great monstrosity come to destroy her.

Those steps belonged to a giant, fifteen or twenty feet tall and they crashed down on the stone, making her think they should be cracking the floor with every fall.

The footsteps slowed and she could almost see the enormous figure as it stopped outside her door. Could it smell her? Was it going to hurt her or just kill her? She did not know, and she shrank back, making herself as small as possible.

The door slammed open with such force that it bounced off the wall and crashed to the floor, knocked clean off its hinges to send dust flying around her, her hair tickling her face and she squinted, trying to see what it was that had disturbed her peace.

The cloud of billowing dust revealed an enormous form, wide and tall though not quite as big as she had imagined and with a head that was surprisingly small.

He stepped into the room slowly and she found herself face to face with the biggest man she had ever seen. Just shy of seven feet tall and easily four feet wide, with massive shoulders and arms but then the image began to change in her mind as the scent of him hit her.

He reeked of metal, sweat, and man. That was the only word she had to describe that odour, 'man,' all testosterone and anger with his cloak billowing around him, silent as he looked around the room.

Lifting her chin slowly, she took him in through the strands of her lank hair and she was utterly confused by the sight of him.

He was just so very chunky looking and his head was almost square, but after a moment the confusion clicked, the shape of him and the smell of metal coming together to tell her that the man was entirely encased in armour from head to toe.

The dust settled, and she saw his head turning, his eyes scanning the room, and then he found her. She felt an odd sensation inside her chest, an almost-twitch of her heart and a feeling as though he were pulling her towards him. His eyes were the colour of liquid gold but not the gold of the coins the humans worshipped, but the gold of the setting sun on clouds, shining and almost glowing with a radiant warmth that sucked her in so completely, captivating her.

He was silent as he looked at her in return, contemplating the tiny creature huddled against the wall and, after a moment, he came towards her. She realised then why it had sounded like he should have been so much taller; that armour would be so incredibly heavy that it dragged his feet down and she had to wonder what the man inside looked like. How strong was he to be able to move in all that metal?

He knelt slowly down before her, his armour clanking and rattling as his hands lifted, not for her but to himself, pulling the helmet off over his head.

He was not at all what she was expecting. His skin was a deep olive tan with deep blonde hair that was streaked liberally with golden brown, those eyes that looked as though he had stolen the sun and was keeping it inside him, wide and glowing. Full lips and a nose that had been broken at least once and scars... Scars everywhere. She tried her best to look at the whole of his face, but she could not keep her attention from returning to those eyes, they were just so... beautiful.

WHEN HE REACHED FOR HER, his movements were slow and gentle, tender almost, and he scooped her up off the floor. She tensed in anticipation of the pain but there was no burning as she expected and as she leant against his body, she lifted her hand and pressed her index finger lightly against his chest, fascinated by the dark grey metal that was not iron though it looked exactly like it.

"Silver alloy." His voice was booming, deep and resonating and her eyes flicked up to him. He watched her as he carried her from the cell and down the corridor that she had not seen before.

"Is that normal?" she asked, curious all the more for this odd, giant man.

"My brother told me you did not tolerate iron," he said simply.

That was such an odd thing to say, that she was left stumped for a moment. It was not until he had carried her from the dungeons of the building that she got an inkling of what was going on. Those they passed paused, bowed and murmured something she did not catch over the clanking and ringing of the man carrying her.

She was dumbfounded, unsure of his intentions. The man carried her through the halls of what she suspected to be a castle, stopping outside a door that seemed to be tailor-made specifically for him.

"Inside you will find a bath and clothing. A servant will bring you to me when you are ready, do not rush." With that, he set her down and turned, stomping his way back down the hall to leave her standing by the door, utterly confused and alone in her blanket. She had not paid much attention to the castle itself and as she looked around, she frowned.

It was an old castle, ancient even. Large narrow windows and heavy, enormous stones stacked neatly to form a shell. The ceiling was high above her, shrouded in darkness. The place was lit by little bunches of candles all along the walls and when she looked down, she found she was standing on a thick crimson rug though the floor itself was made of stone.

Around twenty feet from her stood a suit of armour, and a little way beyond that was a pretty statue of a woman carrying a large pot with a plant growing out of it.

Turning slowly, she found that only a few feet from her was another statue, a man this time with a proud face and when she looked down, she blushed to find that he was entirely naked. The woman statue was naked too, but that had not bothered her like the man's nudity did.

Turning back to the door, she considered it and her situation. It was so very strange that he had gone all the way down to the dungeons only to dump her by the door and leave. But the promise of a bath drew her in, and she stepped forward slowly, pressing the door open and was immediately hit with a blast of warm air that smelt deliciously of lavender.

There was no resisting that, and she hurried inside, inhaling the addictive scent, her hand lingering on the door as she pulled it shut.

Her muscles immediately began to relax as she took in the large room, a huge bath sunken into the floor that was full of steaming water, strewn with sprigs of lavender that wonderfully perfumed the air.

Dropping the blanket where she stood, she hurried forward towards the bath only to jerk as something moved in the corner of her vision, whipping around in alarm and catching sight of the thing. It looked like a bog witch, dirty and stained with a mass of matted hair. But when the witch moved with her, she frowned. The witch frowned too, mirroring her perfectly.

It took her way too long to realise that the thing in the mirror was her and she looked the thing over slowly, utterly horrified at the sight of herself.

Her hair was tangled and lank, matted with blood and dirt to form a revolting cloud around her head with long strips hanging down around her face. She was covered in old blood that had turned brown and cracked, adding to the dirt and grime that had built up on her skin over the days of sitting on the ground. Her stomach had healed, a long pink line running down the length of her torso and she inched closer, staring at the thing.

She had only ever seen herself once before, when she had given her baby sister a mirror in celebration of her birth. Her twin had given a lovely silver hairpin to go with it and they had been delighted to see the joy on her face.

SHE HAD BEEN DELIGHTED to shock them both when she had then turned the mirror on them. She had always assumed that because she and her twin had been twins, that they would be exactly the same, but they weren't. Her twin had deep green eyes, and she had been startled to see that hers were in fact blue. Their faces were similar, remarkably so and yet she had a spattering of little spots on her skin, only five or six on her face, while her twin had none. Similar lips, similar noses, the same ears. But she had felt a stab of disappointment when she had learnt that she did not have those green eyes. She had wanted the green eyes, the blue of her eyes was... eerie.

The memory was a little sad, but she was simply glad they were safe and after a moment, she hissed angrily at the creature in the mirror and turned away. She would look more like herself once she bathed.

Exploring the room, she found an odd handle on a wall towards the back of the room, hidden behind a short wall. Looking at it, she gave the handle a turn and then shrieked as water sudden pounded down on her head, soaking her and flooding dirty water and hair into her eyes.

Staggering back from the thing, she pulled up her hair and watched as water poured out of a little slit in the stone, cascading out like a water-fall. She had never seen anything like it before and after she tested the water, it was frigid and yet remarkably good at getting rid of the vast majority of dirt and blood on her and when she turned it off again, she decided to finish cleaning in the bath that had been prepared for her. She did not want to waste all that hot water.

Still, the waterfall was a curiosity, and she spent the hour of peace wondering how that sort of thing could possibly work. She had to suppose that it was much like the water that came out of the taps in the bath, only set up higher but she did not know how the baths worked either.

It was a relatively new thing to her, having only learnt about it ten or fifteen years previously. She had spent most of her life needing to fill a bath using buckets and the first time she had learnt that one could simply turn a tap to get hot water, she had immediately fallen in love.

It seemed that the humans had outdone themselves in the invention of the waterfall.

Scrubbing herself clean and then again, washing her hair three times and then applying a sweet smelling oil to the entirety of her person that left her smelling very faintly of some unknown flower, her skin and hair so incredibly soft she could not stop running her hands over her arms or through her hair.

She had never in her life felt so absolutely pampered, and she took full advantage. Evidently, she had taken too long, as the door opened and a tiny little grey-haired human woman came bustling into the room and looked down at her disapprovingly like she was a naughty child.

The woman was wearing a pressed and starched black and white dress, her hair pulled up into a neat bun with a little cap on top, an apron and smart little black shoes that peeked just out from under the hem of her dress. She looked incredibly formal and smart, leaving her to think that she might be looking at a royal servant. It made sense, given they were in a castle and she had an inkling that the armoured giant might be someone important.

"If you stay in there much longer, you'll get pruney," the woman said in a matronly voice that she immediately liked. "Your clothes are on the bench here. Hurry along or you'll leave the King waiting. A Lady does not leave a King waiting."

The woman bustled from the room before she got a chance to even open her mouth and she scowled after the woman. She did not want to get out, but the woman's businesslike tone suggested that it would be impolite to do otherwise, and she sighed, dragging herself reluctantly from the water.

Picking up a large white sheet of fabric, she looked it over and touched it, finding it to be oddly fluffy with a dryness that immediately stripped the moisture from her finger and deciding that it must be the whole point of the thing, she used it to dry herself off, looking around at the room to find the clothes that had been left out. She did not much like the look of them, but it was better than going around naked. Turning to the little table with the mirror, she dried her hair quickly and combed it out, the sheer length of it making this almost impossible. It had grown almost entirely back to her knees, and she dug through the drawers until she found a pair of scissors, lopping it off so that it hung to just above her backside and she smiled as she looked at it. She had always found it amusing, something she and her twin had found out at a very early age, that if they did not want their hair cut and it was, it grew back within hours. But if they wanted it cut, it did not grow back until the natural passage of time. It had driven their parents crazy.

The thought of her parents brought a slightly sad smile pulling at her lips and she shook her head, not wanting to think about that.

PICKING UP THE DRESS, she pulled it on and turned back to the mirror, somewhat more satisfied with her appearance. The dress had been designed for someone with less hips and bust than her, but it was an overall acceptable fit, tight without being revealing with narrow sleeves and a modest neckline that dipped in just slightly at the front. Flowing down to the floor to just brush the ground though the little black shoes had a heel she was not overly fond of were skipped; she opted to go barefoot as was her preference and really, what were they going to do? Make her wear shoes?

Moving silently across the bathroom on her bare feet, she paused as she considered her appearance. She was a Fae in a human city, she needed to dull things down a bit if she did not want to draw attention. With that in mind, she returned to the mirror and leant close, squinting at herself.

The magic they called a 'glamour' was fairly simple and most of her kind had it. It was simply taking what was there, and changing it to match what she wanted to be there. People saw only what they wanted to see, and she wanted them to see a human. Well, humanish. Tilting her head, she studied her ear and imagined it to be rounder, shorter and more curved and as the image changed in her mind, the image in the mirror shifted as well. It was reality bending to her will, to the will of those trying to bend it. Next came her eyes, making them just a shade smaller and her perfect skin less so, giving her the hints of human imperfections that her kind lacked. It was hard to remove the inhuman aura, but she could dull the shine a bit.

Deciding it was good enough, she studied her face and frowned, wishing for the millionth time that she could at least be half as pretty as her twin, but it was not to be and she turned from the mirror, crossing the room and slipping out of the door.

The woman was sitting patiently on a small bench that she was sure had not been there before, neither had the guard who was eyeing her suspiciously.

"Hello..." she said cautiously to the woman who nodded and stood, hustling her along the corridor.

"Come along dear, we have a meeting with the King," the woman said in a harried voice. Hurrying to keep up, she almost needed to jog, which was surprising, given her legs were longer than the human's.

"Why?" she asked bluntly, not sure what some human King could possibly want to talk to her for but her companion did not reply; instead, she simply quickened her pace and Etani sighed, hurrying to keep up with her while ignoring the stares of those they passed.

Finally, they reached a large set of doors, easily fifteen feet tall and ten wide. Why anyone needed doors, that big was beyond her.

"Go!" the servant woman hissed and gave her a little push at the small of her back.

Stepping through the doorway slowly, she looked around at the mass of people, humans and mythicals mixed together with such a calm that she was momentarily stunned. She had never once in her life seen the two together without fighting.

As she made her way slowly across the room, the crowd grew silent, moving apart to allow her to approach the throne on the far side of the room. They were watching her, studying and gauging her to the point that it made her a little nervous.

Forcing her eyes from those around her, she saw the throne and as the last few courtiers moved aside, she stopped dead in her tracks, staring at him sitting on the throne.

It was the same man who had taken her from the dungeon.

5

THE INVITATION TO DINE WITH MONSTERS

*H*is face was so calm and relaxed, almost distant as he looked down at her, that she was thrown, wondering for a moment if she had imagined the whole thing; but no, she was absolutely certain it was him, the same golden eyes, the same hair, the same tense expression.

Staring at him unflinchingly, she sized the man up as he did the same to her, contemplative and cool before his lips turned up into the faintest hint of a smile.

"Welcome to Ayathian, Lady Etani. We are pleased to welcome you to our city," he said in that same booming voice.

The room was silent, watching with curiosity as this strange woman stood before the King, looking very little like any Lady they had likely seen in their lives.

A movement caught her attention, and she flicked a glance towards the Lich as he sidled into the room, trying to go unnoticed though that was difficult given the aura of death he carried around with him everywhere he went.

His gaze swept the room and then doubled back to her, blinking once in confusion and then evident interest, uncaring of the sudden coldness that came over the room and while those in the room did not seem to like the Lich very much, they still bowed or curtsied to him, a move she was certainly not expecting.

"Brother!" the King bellowed and stood, moving to embrace the Lich and clap him on the back. She had started to suspect the situation, but it was still a surprise to see the Lich and the giant together, to see their embrace though the Lich looked as though he would have been happier without the hug.

"Brother, I'm sure you have already met Lady Etani," the King said, and she thought she caught the faintest hint of a threat to his voice.

"Lady Etani, please let me introduce you to the Prince Epharis, my brother."

Her eyes met the Lich's, and he smirked slightly, his eyes flicking down towards her chest which gave a painful lurch and burned for an instant.

"A pleasure, dear Lady," Epharis said smoothly, that cruel smile growing in evident enjoyment of the situation.

"I am Emperor Alaric," the King boomed, "But here I am known as King Alaric."

He seemed outwardly to be such a pleasant man, but there was something in her that was telling her he was not quite as kind as he made himself out to be, a little bell going off in her mind when he smiled down at her.

Glancing between the two men, she was lost on what to say and the Prince's stare had turned hungry, something she was rather keen to avoid.

"My dear Lady, what brings you to Ayathian?" the King asked, breaking away from Epharis to draw her attention to him. Sitting back in his throne, she contemplated her answer for a moment before she finally spoke.

"I was travelling from the far north, looking for a place to settle," she lied smoothly, she had no intention of settling anywhere near that place with their Lich and their giant King.

She had every intention of getting out of there just as soon as she was able and moving a very, very far distance away. "I stumbled upon your city by accident and thought it wise to collect what supplies I would need." Supplies she had never carried into the city, but only the Lich would know that. "I was waylaid and required to stay for some time, however, I will continue once the opportunity arises."

The moment the words left her lips she felt a sudden stabbing pain in her chest and her eyes flicked to the Prince. His fingers had balled into fists and she realised with a terrible certainty that he was not going to permit her to leave. Not until she had done whatever it was, he wanted from her.

"However, I may stay longer should his Majesty permit it," she added, forcing her eyes from the Prince and back to the King.

Alaric was staring at her with his head tilted slightly to the side, curious and alert to the exchange between them. Had he felt the Lich's grip on her tighten? She did not know, but she was a little curious.

"You are most welcome, dear Lady. I will have a suite prepared for your stay, as my honoured guest!" the King declared and the Courtiers applauded at the statement. The applause was unexpected, but she could venture a guess at the eccentric King enjoying it when people applauded his demands.

Even so, the fact that the King was eager to keep her close was alarming, she did not like the idea of both men trying to control her, or was she being paranoid? Was the King just trying to be kind to her? She really did not know; she did not have the information she needed.

Lowering her eyes demurely, she considered her options but in that moment she did not have a lot of room to move, she would need to remain for the time being and serve the Lich, but after that she would make the attempt to leave.

THE NOISE in the room rose, and she glanced around, unsure if she was permitted to leave the room, but Alaric seemed to have other plans for her and he was quick to invite her to a private dinner, to which she graciously accepted. She was curious about the man and wanted to know more about him and his Kingdom. He had called himself an Emperor and recalling what she knew of human culture, that meant he had conquered more than one Kingdom, joining the two into one. Or was it that they were still separate but ruled by the one monarch? She could not recall exactly, and she would need to learn it again.

Regardless, it was clear that the man believed himself to be a great ruler, and she was fascinated by him; she was fascinated by the entire place.

Excusing herself, she left the hall and found the servant woman who looked considerably more relaxed now, and led her up to the second floor and to a door that had been left slightly ajar. Opening the door slowly, she stepped inside to find a small sitting room behind a wall that was elaborately painted in green with a lovely golden tree for detail. There was a door immediately to her left and to her right, the wall simply stopped, and the room opened up.

There was a young girl standing in the room, possibly only fifteen or so with big, pale blue eyes and a shy smile, her red-blonde hair pulled up into a bun. She was wearing the same dress as the older woman, though hers was dark grey and not black.

Offering the girl a wary smile, she glanced about the room and found that the suite led off to two other rooms, one a bedroom and the other a bathroom.

Taking it in, she opened her mouth to speak when a loud bang pulled them both around and Epharis stormed into the room.

Spinning away from him, she grabbed the first thing she could find for a weapon and turned back to the Lich.

His fingers clenched around her throat and he forced her backwards, but her hand was already moving, slamming the metallic thing down against the side of his head. It turned out to be a lovely golden candelabra, which was now dented.

He did not let her go, however, and his free hand reached for her wrist as she swung the candelabra back again. Her backside hit a table, and she lost her footing, dropping back onto the top of it as his fingers curled around her wrist and he squeezed, digging his fingers into the tendons until she was forced to release the weapon.

Crawling on top of her, he squeezed her throat until she could no longer speak, bending over her until his face was only an inch from hers, furious with eyes that had begun to glow a toxic green. Her fingers clenched around the wrist that gripped her throat, her nails digging in, but he did not seem to notice at all.

"You are not going anywhere, soul eater. You belong to me, you are mine! If you try to flee, I will find you and I will drag you back here and ensure you can never escape again." He was talking through his teeth in a barely audible whisper, almost hissing the words at her. "If you defy me, I will kill you and bring you back like me, I will make you exactly like me." His nose nearly touched hers and his fingers clenched even tighter, cutting off her air while her nails left long gouges down his shin, unable to get him to release her. She nodded quickly, desperate, and he released her throat only enough that she was not in immediate danger of suffocating.

"Yes... Yes," she gasped, sucking in sweet, precious air while still trying to pry his fingers off her. He stared down into her eyes, his teeth bared.

"Don't tempt me. You are worth more to me as what you are right now but if I no longer feel that, you will be worth more to me as my Lich bride. Dead or alive, you will never escape me." He smiled then, dangerous and feral, to make her quiver, utterly terrified of him. "Do you understand me, woman?" he snapped.

"Yes, Epharis," she whimpered. He jerked slightly as she spoke his name and he leered at her for a moment before he released her throat and got off her, standing at the side of the table while he straightened his robes and hair.

"I have my first task for you, my little Etani. You are to consume this man," he said in a perfectly polite voice, as though none of the minutes before had happened, and she managed to drag herself up into a sitting position, clutching her bruised throat.

He was holding a slip of parchment between his index and middle fingers, his expression smug and superior.

"You want me to kill him?" she asked, somewhat curious. It was not like it was the first time she had killed someone, and not the first time she had killed someone under the orders of another. She had spent several years doing that, in fact. She had developed a fairly substantial name for herself in another land for being a hired killer, but the fact that this man, this mythical creature, would want her to do it for him utterly baffled her.

"Yes, you have one week," he said, and with that, he swept from the room.

THERE WAS a moment of silence and suddenly the servant girl was upon her. She sobbed uncontrollably and tried to pat at Etani's throat, wailing about being a coward and not being able to defend her against a monster like the Prince.

The thought that a little blonde human girl was upset at not being able to defend her against a Lich was a little funny and she made the attempt to soothe the girl, but it was still some time before the poor little blonde was able to stop crying. She had never in her life attempted to comfort a human before and she was not entirely sure what to do or say in order to be successful, but her awkward pats on the back and a hug seemed to be doing the trick though it still took a few tries to get the girl to be able to tell her what her name was, it turning out to be Sasha.

"I did not hear what he said, Lady, what does he want from you?" the girl asked when she had finally calmed down, sitting upon a small couch and hiccupping.

She was one of those girls who looked all the prettier for crying, her tears giving her eyes an inner glow and turning her cheeks pink. She was such a small little thing and her delicate fingers crushed the fabric of her apron as she sat, staring up at Etani with wonder in her eyes.

"The Prince and I have an agreement," Etani said evasively. What was she going to do? Was she ever going to be able to escape him? She would have to wait and see; she didn't like it, but she had little room to move right then.

"You made a deal with the Lich Prince, oh my poor Lady," she cried again, for a good hour before she finally calmed down enough to start preparing Etani for dinner and Etani was a little confused.

She had thought her black dress was perfectly suitable to be worn to dinner, but Sasha said it was both a terrible fit and entirely unsuitable. Aside from that, it seemed to please the girl to have her done up, and she did not want to stop her from enjoying herself.

Sasha had exceptionally skilled fingers, and she made quick work of Etani's hair, pulling it up into an elaborate series of braids that drew the mass away from her face and left the vast majority to trail down her back. She was given a lovely emerald green dress that was made of some sort of fuzzy material that Sasha informed her was called velvet. The shoes were completely ignored, tucked under the vanity table and, given the dress was long enough to cover her feet, Sasha did not notice.

The dress was a much better fit for her though it had a lower cut on the bust, something she was not overly fond of. But with the sleeves stopping at her elbows and the skirt bunched at her hips before cascading down, she thought it came together quite nicely. It made her look somewhat feminine and when she had seen the evil-looking device that had been designed to go under the dress, she was glad her figure made it unnecessary. She had seen women putting those on before, crushing their waists down until they were blue in the face, it looked horrible.

Finally, to complete the outfit, Sasha gave her a delicate silver bracelet, and she spun it on her wrist. She had never worn jewellery before—it was dangerous for someone like her when such ornamentation could be grabbed and held onto, or pulled to strangle her. She knew her sisters liked such things, though, and as she thanked the sweet human girl and made her way out the door, she found herself smiling a little sadly. Letari would have loved the pretty sparkly thing, but it might be quite some time before she got to see her twin again. All Fae loved shiny things, but she never allowed herself to give in to that aspect of herself.

A guard bowed to her as she stepped out of the door and she followed along behind him, her mind going over what had happened in the time she had spent in Ayathian. Captured, tortured and experimented on, threatened, and now she was little more than a slave, forced to work and never allowed to leave. Now she was being kept in a pretty cage and given pretty things in a hope of making her feel better about her situation; it did not make her feel better, she did not like it at all.

THE GUARD OPENED A DOOR, and she looked around in confusion, lost to her thoughts and having no idea where they were in the castle, but she stepped into the dining hall and paused at the assortment of people who were standing around the room. She had thought it would be more private but no, there were several people in there plus the King who was seated at the end of the table.

Two men caught her attention first, all sorts of alarm bells going off in her mind as she took in their dark skin and fashionable, elite attire, their curious faces turning to see who the newcomer was. She could not look away from them, horrified by the fact that she was in the room with Drow.

The Drow were considered to be the lower-class cousins of the elves, the violent and cruel offspring of elves breeding with demons and leaving them unable to commune with the other fae. They had been banished from Faerie, stuck under a rock, and the rest of the mythicals had hoped they would have died off, but they had not, and they were angry about the rejection.

The worst part of it all... Drow could see through enchantments.

The pair had frozen as they found her, saw through the glamour to what was underneath, saw through to what she was, and they may never have even seen the image which overlaid her form.

They were incredibly attractive, perfect faces and dark skin. The taller of the two was quite a bit more attractive than the other, grey-purple skin and long black hair. His eyes were so dark red as to nearly be black and his ears had been pierced multiple times. The shorter of the two, only an inch shorter, was considerably softer looking though still stern, his skin a dark violet with striking, bright silver eyes and white-silver hair.

They both stood with rigid, strict postures, with one hand tucked neatly behind their backs, though she was very aware that in such a position, knives would likely be nearby.

The King was watching her with a curious expression, his head tilted very slightly to the right before a woman captured his attention. She was a very pretty, wild-looking woman with dark chestnut brown hair and deep blue eyes. There was something primal about her, animalistic, and as the King waved his arm, a shock of alarm went through her. The woman was a werewolf, a loner by the smell of her.

Werewolves were vicious and violent creatures when it came to packs, but the loners were less so, much quieter and more reserved.

Her distraction towards the werewolf woman had allowed the Drow men to move, and she glanced at the silver-eyed one, realising that he had crept closer while the other had drifted to her right, trying to trap her in the corner, but she was not having any of that.

Throwing them a knowing glance, she swept across the room to approach the King who stood so suddenly that he knocked the table, sending the cutlery to rattling that no one paid much attention to. He strode quickly towards her, his face showing his pleasure at her arrival and that was somewhat of a rare expression to be directed her way.

"Lady Etani!" he boomed, drawing the eyes of the remaining people to them.

There was another set of men towards the back of the room, lingering back far enough that it was hard to see them with their forms shrouded in darkness.

Slowing her pace to greet the King, she curtsied respectfully, catching an exchanged glance of amusement between the two Drow as she lifted her skirt and they likely saw the fact that she was not wearing any shoes, something that was incredibly improper.

He bowed politely in return and positively beamed at her, offering her his hand. Taking it, she found that he was unusually warm, almost hot to the touch, with his dry lips brushing a delicate kiss upon her fingers before he turned her to introduce her to the woman.

"This is Catherine, Captain of the royal guard," he said in a proud voice.

The woman had stood, and she bowed, her eyes alert but not unkind.

"It is a pleasure to meet you, Catherine," she said, returning the bow with a curtsy. The more she looked at the werewolf, the more she saw just how lovely she really was. Skin that was almost brown with an oval face, low brows that gave her a smouldering stare and a warm smile that lit up her face. She was wearing slacks, a white blouse with suspenders and she had been wearing a cap but had taken it off and left it on the table. Knee-high boots and a black jacket that bore a series of colourful wide ribbons that she could only assume were military.

"The pleasure is all mine, Lady," Catherine said politely; her voice was rich and smooth, adding to her air of animalistic beauty.

6

TWO VAMPIRES, TWO DROW AND A LICH
WALK INTO A BAR...

"*I*zziahnordia, Drizdan, let me introduce you to the Lady. She arrived at the Court today and I'm sure she would be delighted to meet others of her status," Alaric called and her heart sank as the two Drow eagerly approached. They had been much closer than she liked and they both appeared from behind her, bringing with them the scent of blood and something else, the odour making her nostrils burn.

The silver-eyed man lifted his hand to her politely, his smile seeming to be genuinely curious, and she reluctantly placed her hand in his. His free hand immediately closed on it, drawing her hand up to his face but rather than kissing it, he inhaled deeply, taking in the scent of her skin to make her cringe.

"It is a pleasure, Lady Etani. My name is Izziahnordia, but I am called Izziah." He lowered her hand and swept one out to place it on the other Drow's shoulder. "This is my brother Drizdan."

Turning to the black-eyed man, she found him staring at her intently from less than a foot away and while she really did not want to do it, she accepted his offered hand. Her entire body tensed as he lifted it to his mouth, utterly repulsed to feel him lick it.

Jerking her hand away from him, she glared at him as she wiped her hand on her dress, the King utterly oblivious to the two men's keen interest in her.

"And finally, we have the two lurking in the back and silently judging us. Kai and Jaia," the King said, either ignoring or unaware of the death glare she had levelled on the two Drow that was met with a returned glare from Izziah and a hungry, feral grin from Drizdan.

The two men bowed politely but did not come out of the shadows, though they did seem rather amused by the comment on their judging everyone.

"Please, now that everyone has been introduced, take a seat. Epharis will be joining us shortly and we can eat," the King said, and she wondered if she imagined his glee at having them all there together.

They all approached the table, and she quickly found herself trapped between the two Drow, unable to escape without making a scene and they were gleeful about that fact, delighted by her being unable to get away from them.

Conversations started up and the two Drow men immediately started in on her, demanding in quiet voices to know who and what she was but she refused to respond, her chin lifted in defiance.

Things were relatively calm between the three of them until Izziah decided to try to touch her hand. Moving on impulse, she snatched up a knife and spun it easily, slamming it down into the table between his middle and index finger, the serrated edge a mere millimetre from the webbing between the two fingers.

The entire table went silent and Izziah stared down at his hand, his face pale and eyes wide in alarm.

The King's laughter boomed out into the room and she clenched her jaw and stared straight ahead at the wall, very aware of Drizdan who was half out of his seat, furious and trembling while Izziah was entirely frozen in shock, not knowing what to do.

"That's what happens when you try to touch a trained woman Izziah-nordia!" the King was nearly crying he was laughing so hard and there was a low chuckle from the other three.

Curling her fingers around the handle of the knife, she yanked it from the table and set it back down gently, the three of them falling into a tense, awkward silence. She could feel Drizdan's anger, his tension, and she had to wonder how close she had been to ending up with a knife in her.

Allowing her eyes to drift down from the wall, she found that a set of twins were sitting directly across from her, her head tilting very slightly to the side as she took in what they were. They were a perfect match in height and had the same black eyes, the same exquisitely handsome face, and the same full mouth that turned down just slightly at the corners. They were identical twins, very similar though the one on the left had slightly curly hair while the one on the right had straight hair.

She could not stop looking between them, picking out miniscule details that most people would not have noticed, although she did, and she had to assume it was because she was a twin herself.

They both wore incredibly high-class black suits and black leather gloves, a flash at their throats and wrists showing they wore a white shirt underneath. Broad shoulders that were slightly rounder on the left twin, both with incredible posture but the right twin had movements that were much more controlled. She took a stab at the right twin being military, the left however she did not know, and they stared right back at her, unblinking.

SHE THOUGHT she knew what they were, it seemed obvious to her. Pale skin, utterly devastating to look at, quick movements. She knew it but it was not until Epharis arrived, his nostrils flaring angrily as he saw her trapped between the two Drow and settled himself down across from his brother that she had her suspicions confirmed.

The two men were given pristine bowls of a rich red liquid and judging by their reactions, it was fresh. The smell of it reached her and she swallowed. Human blood, fresh and tantalising. The twins were vampires.

The meals each of them were given were curious, the sight of the enormous steak that was set down before Catherine nearly made her laugh and she caught a fond, amused smile from the twin to the left as he glanced at the woman, that glance almost adoring, and she had to wonder if there was something between the two.

The Drow brothers were given a salad made of an odd vegetable that she had never seen before and she was still looking at it when her own plate was set down, the smell of it immediately filling her mouth with saliva.

Looking first at her plate, then to her right at Epharis, she found him watching her with a curious, almost innocent wonder on his face rather than the smug glee she had expected. He had delivered her a fresh human heart, neatly diced and served on a bed of salad.

She hated that he was toying with her like that. She was playing the part of a human woman and yet there he sat, tempting her. Did he know that a fresh human heart still had the shreds of essence clinging to it? Did he know that it was so incredibly delicious that she wanted to devour it and lick the plate? She did not know, but she slowly began to eat the salad around the meat, refusing to give him the satisfaction.

After they had finished eating and she politely declined whatever the lump of white substance was that had been offered to her for dessert, they dispersed into small groups to talk and she immediately tried to make her escape, finding the path out of the dining room barred by the Drow brothers.

"What do you want?" she finally hissed at them, irritated that so many were trying to get to her.

"We haven't seen a Fae in centuries, we want to get to know you," Izziah said gently, but by the way Drizdan's eyes lingered on her breasts, she did not think the two of them wanted to get to know her in the same way. Drizdan's idea seemed to be less verbal and more carnal.

"I don't converse with Drow," she shot back. Izziah looked genuinely hurt, and she felt a little twinge of remorse. The Drow did not really deserve to be treated the way they had and she of all people should not treat others badly simply for being born. Besides, they had done nothing to her and for all she knew, they were decent men.

"We aren't the bad guys here; we only want to be friends," he said after a short pause.

"Yeah, friends," Drizdan said, unable to tear his eyes from her breasts.

"I'm up here," she said dryly, but he did not seem to be listening, not until Izziah jabbed him in the ribs with an elbow. "Clearly you are interested in being friends," she said angrily, Izziah's face falling slightly but then his eyes lifted to something behind her and she turned, finding herself face to face with the other person she did not want to talk to.

"I come bearing a peace offering," Epharis said, his attention flicking between her and the two Drow. Glancing back, she noted that Izziah was glaring at Epharis while Drizdan's attention was pointing down, at her backside.

"Keep it," she snapped, trying to sidestep him without making it obvious to the rest of the room that she was attempting to escape. She could feel those lecherous eyes on her, and she seriously contemplated introducing the red-eyed creep to her elbow.

"Don't be like that, my little kitten," he cooed.

What could she do with the Drow behind her and the Lich trying to play nice? She could cause a scene but that was not ideal, or she could just accept whatever it was he offered her and be done with it.

"Very well, what is it?" she asked slowly, taking his gift as the lesser of two evils, three if she considered the vampire twins who were watching the four of them curiously. Alaric was too busy talking to Catherine.

Epharis seemed a little taken aback by her acceptance but then he smiled and reached into his coat pocket, took out a small black velvet box, and offered it to her.

This had to be some sort of sick joke, she was sure of it. Why would he be giving her something that came in a box like that?

CONTEMPLATING THROWING it out the window, she let out a slow sigh and took it, opening it with the same feeling she had when she was trying to tell if Letari had crushed a spider she had found in with her socks.

Inside the box she found a very delicate silver chain, strung with a little small gem of some sort. It really was quite lovely, and she was more than a little confused by the thing. It was a necklace, a very expensive looking necklace and while it appeared quite simple, it was elegant, very fine and incredibly well made.

"Thank you, Your Majesty," she finally said, unsure of what else to say to him or what to do with the gift. Why was he even giving her gifts?

He plucked the chain from the box and moved around behind her, the two Drow immediately moving away, and she caught a glimpse of the Lich's smile.

"Beautiful and discreet, just like you," he murmured in her ear, holding it before her as he undid the clasp. Setting it gently against her chest, she looked up to find the Drow pair watching her intently, their faces a mixture of confusion and alarm.

The chain fell against her neck as he placed it down and she shivered at his touch. Once settled, the gem rested between her breasts and she realised that had been the point, all three sets of eyes dropping to the little clear stone nestled safely in her cleavage.

"You're a pig," she hissed at the Lich, as his eyes shifted from her chest to her face and then back down again as though it was impossible to look away.

"Well, if you're showing them off, you should expect us to look," he countered.

Turning away from the three of them, she held her hand over her chest and the strangeness of the necklace felt heavy on her skin and she immediately wanted to take it off, but when she tugged the chain around to find the clasp, it had vanished.

Looking down, she ran her fingers slowly along the length of chain from one side of her neck to the other, then down both sides; there was no clasp.

Turning to look at the man, he was grinning at her, apparently delighted to see that she had realised the trick. The Drow were whispering furiously at each other and the King had stood, ready to leave. "I'm afraid that not even a King may be excused from his duties," Alaric said, offering a deep bow to the room at large, the five guests returning the gesture while Epharis remained still, not taking his eyes off her, and it was not until the vampire twins and the werewolf had left that he moved to approach her while she moved to meet him.

"Remove it," she demanded immediately.

"No," he said calmly, watching as she tugged at the thing and even tried to get it off over her head, but it seemed to shrink when she tried to lift it towards her chin.

"Remove it now or..." She had no threat; it was not like she could kill him.

The Drow pair had not left, and they watched in fascination as she brazenly tried to order the man around while Epharis seemed not to mind.

"Are you two married?" Izziah asked.

Shooting him a furious glance, she looked back at Epharis and his expression was considering.

"Remove it," she repeated, her anger rising as he shook his head.

"I'm not removing it," he said as he reached forward and slipped his fingers into her cleavage, plucking the gem out and holding it between them.

"A pretty little collar for my pretty little pet," he purred, enjoying her disgust and then horror as she realised what he was saying. It was a collar? He had collared her.

Slapping his hand away, she ignored his flash of anger and turned, planning to head back to her room when his fingers caught in her hair.

A low hiss came from one of the Drow as the Lich pulled her back against him, her head tilted.

"I think you have some fans," he said in a low, taunting voice as he turned her head to look at the two Drow men.

Gripping his fist in her hair, she gave a low growl of warning that he ignored, sliding his free arm around her waist.

"I did not know Drow had sexual desires outside the family," Epharis taunted the two men.

They were watching carefully, Izziah's face showing concern but Drizdan's seemed to show what she thought might be jealousy, his jaw clenched and face furious.

"I don't really blame you, she's quite pretty. Even with the human skin on."

The two Drow exchanged a glance and Epharis laughed, delighted even as his hand started to creep upwards and he hooked his finger in the front of her dress.

Drizdan's eyes had locked on her chest as the Lich pulled the fabric down just slightly, teasing the man, while Izziah looked confused.

"Drow can't see glamours, idiot," she hissed at the Lich, reaching up to dig her nails into the back of his hand, forcing him to let go of the front of her dress.

"Oh right..." Epharis said gently, and he turned his face towards her, licking the tip of her ear to make her shudder.

"Let go," she demanded, tugging at his hand, but he refused to release her hair.

"No, I don't want to," he said petulantly.

Why were men so utterly incapable of keeping their hands to themselves?

He took advantage of her irritation and dragged the flat of his tongue up the side of her face, making her almost gag. Drizdan looked about ready to breathe fire and she realised that it was not her the Lich was taunting; it was the Drow. He was taunting the Drow with his claim on her.

She had, had enough, and she lifted her foot, slamming her heel down on the toes of his shoe. He grunted in pain and as his grip on her released, she twisted and drove her elbow hard into his jaw, sending him staggering away from her.

She was going to pay for it, she knew it, but she was not his plaything, she was not just some toy he could wave in front of others.

Rubbing at her cheek, she moved back so that she could see both the furious Lich and the furious Drow, Izziah, however, was looking rather impressed, having stepped back to keep himself out of the impending fight that seemed likely to erupt at any moment.

"You little bitch!" Epharis yelled, rubbing his jaw. She had been called worse, but his anger was something she was concerned about. Lich were dangerous creatures, however, her defending herself against him did not go against any deal they had and at no point did she say he could touch her.

"I'm not some pretty trinket you can wave around," she hissed back at him, that hint of green flaring in his eyes once more.

"You're whatever I say you are," he snapped. "I own you."

The two Drow watched the furious conversation, curiosity and the chance to learn more about them too much temptation for the brothers.

"I would like to return to my room," she said carefully, her mind going to what she could do to disengage herself from the situation.

"You are going to stay right where you are. I'm not done with you yet," the Lich said angrily. "I need to teach you some manners."

He started forward for her and she lunged for the table, snatching up one of the knives that had yet to be cleaned up and he did not seem overly concerned by her being armed.

Spinning back to him, the knife flashed, and the Lich snarled as a large crimson slash appeared on his hand, dripping blood.

He paused only for a moment, knowing the flesh wound was hardly worth the effort of considering.

His fingers caught the front of her dress as she backed away and he jerked her forward towards him. Her mind raced, taking drastic non-lethal measures, driving the knife to the hilt in his chest.

He was still for a moment, looking down at the knife and then back up at her. She had hoped he would have responded in some way, but he only looked angrier.

His hand flew and her cheek was suddenly on fire; she caught herself against the chair to keep from falling but he was not done with her yet.

His fingers caught her hair, and he pulled her back to him, his fist clenching and drawing back.

"Your highness!" Izziah cried, alarmed at the sight of the Lich about to punch her full in the face.

"What?" Epharis hissed back. "Please, you can't hit her!"

"Of course, I can, she's my property, and she stabbed me in the lung."

Shaking her head to try to clear it, she looked up at the Lich as he bared his teeth at her but then he smiled, glancing sidelong at the two Drow.

"Don't worry, I won't break her too badly," he taunted. "Get out."

The two Drow hesitated but then left the room, unable to resist the direct order of the Prince.

Turning back to her, he grinned savagely. She saw his fist coming and then there was a flash of white light, blinding pain, and everything went black.

7

TUTORS AND ASSASSINS

*W*hen she woke, she was confused to find herself sitting in her own suite and the low, slow breathing of someone who had propped her up against them. Night had fallen, and the room was filled with the warm dancing light of candles, which threw moving shadows across the floor and enhanced the warm colours of the room.

Shifting slightly, she looked at Sasha, about to thank her for being so kind in looking after her only to find that it was not Sasha, but Izziah who had been holding her.

While jerking away from him and off the couch, she tripped over the hem of her dress and almost fell, whipping around to find him sitting still, his hands in the air in surrender.

"What are you doing here?" she hissed at him. She was furious, but also there was a hint of fear for what he might have done to her while she was unconscious. She felt battered and bruised though there were no signs of marks on her body.

"I was waiting outside the dining room when Epharis left, he said that if I was hanging around, I might as well make myself useful and take you back to your suite before one of the guards found you and... well, he suggested unpleasant things may happen," he said, his cheeks darkening slightly. "Your maid was busy, and I did not wish to disturb her, so I offered to stay with you until you woke."

He spoke rather stiffly and formally, nervous about her reaction and the fact that he was alone with her.

"And you thought I would be agreeable to your holding me?" she demanded.

"You seemed comforted by my touch."

Staring at him for a long moment, she considered that. Why would she find comfort in his touch? She did not know him, and she did not trust him. But he had helped her, and she owed him at least some gratitude.

"Thank you for helping me," she said finally, confused, but willing to play nice. "I apologise for my rudeness; I do not usually buy into the discriminations that are common amongst my people and had no right to be cruel."

"You're welcome, and there is no need to apologise. We are strangers, and this is a new place for you. Aside from that, my brother can be... intense."

"Perverted you mean..." she said, her brows lifting.

"I was trying to be delicate." He smiled, and she had to wonder about the man. He was not at all what she was expecting, and she was a little surprised to find that she did not mind talking to him. He was pleasant and even a little charming.

"You're not what I was expecting," she said gently.

"Neither are you; I was expecting some stuck up, spoon-fed Fae brat," he said with a wicked grin.

Eyeing him, she bit her lip and then smiled back at him. An odd thing happened in that moment. His lips parted slightly, and his pupils expanded before shrinking back. She tilted her head, curious about his reaction.

"Are you going to kill Epharis?" he asked, seemingly unaware of his physical changes.

"That would be impossible, he has bound my life with his. To kill him would be to kill myself."

He stood suddenly and approached her, his hands taking hers gently. A spike of alarm went through her mind, but she did not pull away.

"You are Fae, if anyone can wriggle their way out of an unfavourable deal, it is you," he said, a burning certainty in his voice. He had a point; it was not like she was some helpless piece of fluff.

She could get out of that situation and she would survive. She always did.

As he moved back, a small splash of colour caught her attention and she looked at his chest. The jacket had fallen open and there was a smear of blood on the white undershirt.

He looked down and cursed, clutching the fabric and frowning at the blood.

"Sasha can fix that," she said, glancing in the direction of the girl's room. "If we get it to her now, it might not stain."

Glancing back to him, she flushed as she saw him remove his jacket and release the long row of buttons, his fingers moving easily. She could not help herself from looking. That slow reveal of his dark skin had her swallowing in a mingled alarm and... something else she did not know. She had never been in the same room as a man who was getting undressed and the thought had her frozen in place, panicked and enthralled.

The shirt and jacket had not done him justice, and she found that he was incredibly well-toned, not the soft man she had originally thought him to be. His muscles stood out sharply against his skin, giving him a chiselled look. His entire body was covered in scars. They stood out darker against his already dark skin, and she studied them all. Most of them were straight, clean cuts, but there were many that looked jagged and brutal.

Shaking her head to force herself back to her situation, she took the shirt and moved away from him to the door to Sasha's room. Knocking gently, she offered the girl an apologetic smile as she showed her the blood.

"Are you all right, my Lady?" she whispered. "I was not sure, but he is said to be quite a gentleman."

"Yes Sasha, I am fine. Thank you for your concern."

Sasha nodded and took the shirt, frowning at it before she closed the door again. Standing there for a moment, Etani had to wonder at her own ability to look after things like that. It had never bothered her before. If her clothes got too dirty, she would simply steal new clothes, but now? She would have to learn everything she could from Sasha.

RETURNING TO THE DROW, she found he had sat down and was carefully looking over the fabric of his jacket. When he found no blood, he pulled it on over his bare chest and buttoned it up, leaving a hint of bare skin at his collarbones that she found entirely too distracting.

"I had not realised I missed any blood," he mumbled, glancing up at her as she approached. "I knew you were bleeding, of course, the Prince had..." He trailed off and shook his head. "I thought I had cleaned it all."

The thought of him kneeling over her prone form, carefully wiping blood from her skin brought a flush to her face, and she dropped her eyes, embarrassed that he had been forced to tend to her like that. She had not needed to be looked after since she was a child and here he was, a total stranger and a Drow, doing it for seemingly no reason.

"Why would you do that?" she asked slowly, uncertain of him.

"I would have considered myself a coward had I so much as hesitated to come to your aid. Regardless of the histories between our people, you were injured and unable to protect yourself, I would not be a man if I simply left you there to be taken advantage of." He sounded stiff and proud.

"I am glad that you were there to help me," she said slowly, still not entirely certain about his intentions. She was willing to give him the benefit of the doubt. He had kept her safe when he had little reason to do so. "I owe you for your kindness."

"My dear Lady, you owe me nothing," he said as he stood, offering her a smile. "It was an honour to be of service to one such as you. All I hope is that you might look more favourably on my kind in the future."

Well, when he put it like that...

Crossing to him, she took his hands gently and leant forward, pressing a single, gentle kiss against his cheek. As she drew back, his dark skin flushed darker in a blush that she found rather endearing, but she did not linger.

It took him a moment to recover. He cleared his throat, seemingly lost for words and after a moment he managed to get his brain back in order.

"I should not linger for too long, my Lady; my brother will be wondering where I got off to and we do not want there to be any rumours about my presence in your rooms," he said, glancing towards the door. Sasha stepped back into the room, holding his shirt that she had neatly folded.

"My Lord," she said politely, giving him a curtsy before she moved forward and offered the shirt to him. The stain was completely gone, and the fabric was once again clean and dry.

"Absolutely perfect," he said in a delighted tone. "I don't suppose you're looking for a new posting?" he asked her, his smile turning sly as he glanced to Etani. "A young woman of your talents..."

"Sasha is staying here with me," Etani said defensively, her hands resting on the girl's shoulders. Sasha was an exceptional young woman, and she was not about to give her up to the Drow brothers.

Izziah affected a pout that left Sasha blushing prettily, looking between the two of them shyly.

"Well if you're going to be selfish about it." He pouted and then smiled. "Please excuse me for a moment ladies." He turned and moved into the bathroom to put his shirt back on. Sasha grinned, proud of her work.

"I shall leave you to talk." The pretty woman said and hurried back to her room. Looking around slowly, she took in the space properly for the first time, the walls covered in an odd square pattern that she realised were wooden shelves, all of them empty and clean. A balcony stood to the left side but before she could move to it, Izziah had returned.

"Ah, if only I could open a door to this every day," he said wistfully. He was getting bold in his statements and she eyed him warily. "I will leave you now, my dear Lady. It has been a pleasure speaking with you this evening."

Accepting his hand, she curtsied. He bowed over her hand, placing a gentle kiss against her knuckles.

"Thank you for your assistance Izziah," she said and then she paused. "I never found out your rank."

"I was a Prince in our lands, but I was banished, and my title removed; here I am a Lord." He said it with such a cool tone that she could immediately tell that it still hurt him deeply. "You are a Lady?"

"Only because the King granted me the title. I hold no title of my own, I am not of the royal family."

"THE WINTER COURT?" he asked, and his expression made her realise that he knew far more about her than he should.

"I am not of the Winter Court," she said, only half-lying. Technically she had not aligned herself with any Court. Her father had been Winter Court, but that did not make her part of it.

"Right," he said doubtfully, his eyes trailing down her form and then back up again, not believing her at all.

It was an odd moment; for most of their kind it was easy to tell which Court one belonged to, especially with the Fae. Those of Winter tended to be paler with bolder, sharply cool colouring while Summer tended to have warmer tones, rich and healthy. But that was not always the case, especially if there was a defection. It was not unheard of to see the striking, coldly pale beauty of the Winter Court in Summer, though it was uncommon. Even so, she had known there to be redheads in the Winter Court, something that would have normally belonged to Summer.

Regardless, she was only half Winter since her mother had been born to the Celestrials. She was not a Winter Court Fae, she was unaligned.

He sighed slowly, stretching with an almost feline grace that sent his muscles rippling and bulging in a way that made her heart skip a beat, captivated by him now that she knew what lay under that jacket. "It will be morning soon; I will leave you and returning to my home before my brother wakes to find me missing," he said, a hint of amusement on his face as he caught her watching his chest.

Dropping his arms, he bowed before her and she felt a slight pang of disappointment that he was leaving. It was odd, feeling like he was a trusted companion or even a friend. She did not know when that had happened, but it confused her immeasurably.

"Thank you Lord Izziah, you have been incredibly kind and greatly appreciated," she said slowly, moving with him towards the door.

"Until we meet again dear Lady," he said.

Bowing once more, he let himself out. She watched the door for several seconds as she contemplated her mind and body.

She had never felt that before; she had felt something similar a very, very long time ago, but she had never felt that. What was that anyway? A blush crept up her cheeks as she realised that it was desire, a desperate longing to run her hands over his skin for the simple sake of feeling him under her fingertips. She had never wanted to know what someone's lips tasted like. To kiss had always been to eat, to devour and yet when the thought of his lips against hers flashed through her mind, there was no hunger... at least, not that kind of hunger.

The hunger she felt then was a little more carnal, and she wrapped her arms around her middle, lost in her thoughts.

She had never given another the opportunity to get close to her like that, to simply exist with them. She had never met another, who was outside of her family, who was eager to spend time with her. It was confusing for her to think that he might actually enjoy conversing with her.

Her mind flicked back to watching him remove his shirt, and she bit her lip, doing her best to hide a smile as she imagined exploring those scars with her hands... her lips...

Shaking her head, she scolded herself for her improper thoughts. She was not some lovesick girl. And yet, she found herself wondering how any man could so thoroughly win her over and she realised in that moment that he had enchanted her with his kindness. She was enamoured.

Shaking her head, she ran her hands over the back of her neck and found the chain, looked down at it. She had forgotten all about it and she growled softly, pulling and yanking at it.

Trying to pry it off did nothing; a knife had no effect at all either, and trying to beat it with a candelabra did nothing; stretching, burning, lifting... none of the ideas she had worked. Even Sasha's assistance had no result and she seriously considered decapitating herself. It was not worth it, as she was not keen to let the Lich bastard know any more of her secrets.

"I don't know what to do, Sasha, this has me concerned," she said finally, looking at the girl as she worked with twin sets of pliers, trying to twist the links themselves apart without touching her with the iron tools.

"Surely it is a mistake, my Lady; surely he did not intend to do this." Sasha's voice was uncertain and when Etani glanced down, she saw that her face showed just as much doubt. They both knew the Lich had intended it.

While they worked, the two talked quietly over the situation, and what Etani's plans were. Sasha had been rather surprised to learn exactly what Etani was, given the glamour, but she accepted it without fear or complaint. The girl knew a fair bit about the Courts and had been happy to share her information. When Etani asked that she be shown how to clean the blood and other stains from clothing, as well as repair them, she had been utterly delighted.

The subject of names came up when Etani asked the young woman to stop calling her Lady, and Sasha asked her what her name represented.

IN TRUTH, the names of the Fae were entirely random except for a few rules.

The firstborn usually had the most names, and their first name commonly ended with an 'a.' It was not every case, but it was so common that it had become a running joke that one could usually tell who the firstborn was by their name alone.

Sasha had been delighted to learn that Etani's name was simply a nickname and that her full first name was actually Etania. She loved the fact that they shared a secret that no one else knew and it had not cost Etani anything to make the girl happy.

The subject was always a touchy one with the Fae, given the level of power that could be gained from owning a name. To know the true, full name of a Fae was to own them in full for an eternity. An order given after their name was spoken could not be denied for any reason and there was nothing the Fae could do to stop it. They would obey, without hesitation. Even siblings and parents did not know the full name of their kin, it was too risky.

Etani's name consisted of seven names in total, while her mother and sisters all had five each. That was more common than her own, the sheer number was rare for it meant she was safer than most and, as such, she was not going to complain.

The girl feared that the Lich would try to get Etani's name, but she was not concerned; it was incredibly hard to get all of a Fae's names out of them and even then, she could just give a fake name and pretend it was her real name until she escaped.

Trying to get the subject off of her own name, she pulled the slip of parchment out of her pocket and offered it to Sasha. It had gotten a little crumpled in that time, but the writing was still clear.

She had not wanted to admit to the Lich that she could not read it. "What do you know of the person to whom this name belongs?" she asked, hoping the girl would know him, or at the least read the name out to her.

"Jacob Carriger?" She paused, frowning as a thought passed through her mind. "Lord Jacob Carriger? He is a merchant King down near the city centre." Sasha lifted a brow slightly, offering the paper back. Looking down at the name, she tried to piece the symbols to a spoken word, but they did not make any real sense to her.

"Does he come to Court? Would you be able to point him out to me?" Etani asked, wondering if the paper was upside down. She really needed to learn how to read that language...

"Certainly, he usually comes in every few days to speak with the others of his standing or press for lower taxes. If he's not there today, he will be there in a few days."

Nodding, she considered what tools she had and decided it was best to go into the city with the young woman to collect supplies. She did not have any money; instead, she took two of the gold candelabra. The man was not at Court that day and so they headed out into the city. They exchanged the heavy golden candelabra for a large pile of little golden coins and several silver ones. The gold ones got her quite a lot, the silver was good, but it took ten silver to make one gold, or so Sasha told her.

Buying herself several sets of knives and some new clothes cost her five of the gold coins and nine silver. While Sasha had been terrified that Etani had simply stolen and sold the King's possessions, Etani had found it amusing that no one seemed to care where she got the candelabra from. She supposed that a Lady and her servant could sell whatever they wanted. She was contemplating what else she could steal as they headed back up towards the castle.

Loud cheering caught their attention, and they both looked around to see a carriage that had been folded out into a large stage. There were people atop it in large bright masks, dancing around and making bawdy jokes. Etani had not been able to resist watching even though Sasha was a little embarrassed. She found she rather enjoyed the show, slipping five of the silver coins into the little dish that was handed around afterwards.

The two women returned to the castle in good spirits, enjoying a quiet lunch and dinner, while Sasha patiently showed her how to sew in a way that was so clever that the fabric would pull together and the seam wouldn't be noticeable unless one looked very hard.

8

WHEN YOU FIND YOURSELF WITH THE
TASK TO KILL SOMEONE

*W*hen the man had not appeared on the second day, they retired back to Etani's suite and Sasha continued the lessons, delighting in the fact that her skills were so valuable to someone else. In return, Etani taught the girl how to wield a knife for self-protection. They continued making trades, Sasha teaching Etani how to remove stains from fabric in exchange for Etani teaching her how to make a smoke bomb. It was not hard, just a couple of commonly found chemicals that were quite content on their own when inside the jar, but when thrown to the ground, the chemicals would interact violently and the moment they came into contact with the air, they would erupt into smoke. Then came an exchange on how to embroider in exchange for Etani teaching Sasha how to turn her braid into an elaborate rose. It had been something Letari had taught her and it did not take long, but it looked incredibly pretty.

When they arrived at Court in the afternoon on the third day, Sasha pointed the man out, smiling a little anxiously before she hurried away. Watching the girl go, Etani noted a heavyset woman staring after her, a pale hand touching her own hair with longing. Perhaps the rose braid would become popular.

Lord Carriger was a tall man, slim and gaunt with sharp grey eyes and a little pointed black beard that sat perched on the tip of his equally pointed chin. He was older than she expected, perhaps in his late forties and she watched the man for a time, curious as to why the Lich would want him dead.

He was wearing a scrumptious pearl grey suit with a ruffled neck and little heeled black shoes. It was a funny look at first, but it appeared to be quite fashionable. He left the men he had been talking to as soon as Alaric appeared. Etani smiled in amusement as the King made a valiant effort to keep his annoyance from his face. The conversation did not appear to go very well, and the Lord stormed from the throne room in a rush.

Excusing herself from the small group of ladies who had been trying to coax her into a conversation, she followed the man out of the castle and into the city. With her quick pace and balled fists, it wouldn't be hard for her to be passed off as just a stuck-up noblewoman forced to go out into the city and handle some chore, or perhaps she was off to find her cheating husband. It did not matter, after the first glance, she would be otherwise ignored.

Modifying her glamour as she moved, she added fine lines to her features, reduced the overall appearance of her lips and applied just a few streaks of silver to her hair. At a glance, she would become an older aristocrat, annoyed and uninterested in dealing with the common filth in the city. It worked well as she saw eyes dropping, those around her not wanting to catch her eye and draw her stern, angry glare to them.

Carriger seemed to be in a hurry himself. He was quite easy to follow, his smart little shoes clacking merrily against the cobblestones as though those around him were applauding him as he rushed by. The thought that he might have modified his shoes to ensure they made that sound almost broke her scowl.

He was unobservant, and she was not being careful to go unnoticed; he did not once look around to see if he was being followed. She glanced around in search of street signs as though she were lost while examining the faces of those dawdling around in the late afternoon sun.

When they reached the central marketplace, however, Carriger's posture became tense, and she was fascinated to see his attempt at going unnoticed. It was having the opposite effect. He glanced around, trying to look subtle, but he did not use any of his peripheral vision. Instead, he looked up at a stall, and his eyes moved around freely, looking all around him while he rigidly tried not to turn his head at all.

It would have been comical had it not been so strange. Those around the market only shook their heads as though that was a common occurrence before returning to their tasks. The man slipped inside a side door to a shop she could not read the name of, and she cursed herself for failing to learn the stupid language.

Unable to resist waiting for him, she stepped into the alley and loitered around, exchanging a silver coin for a large square of incredible lavender fabric. She had no idea what she was going to do with it, but the colour had caught her attention.

She and the shop owner had exchanged a cheerful conversation while she positioned herself to watch the shop out of the corner of her eye. The shop owner had been quite a polite man, and he seemed to think he had won a prize at having the attention of the older noblewoman she was pretending to be.

FINALLY EXCUSING herself from his presence, she thanked him again for the cloth and informed him that she would have her servant come by for more soon. He had been a little disappointed, but still pleased that she was happy with her purchase and wanted more of the fabric. Tucking the cloth safely away in her skirt pocket, she made her way down the alley and paused, making a show of looking first left and then right as she came to the end. There was a handful of homeless in the street and they watched her curiously while she silently cursed at their presence. It would have been easier if they were not there.

When no street signs were evident, she exchanged a silver coin to a dirty young man, asking him for directions back to the castle. He pointed back the way she had come and told her to cross the square and take the main street down to the far end of the city. The castle would be to the right but she would see it as soon as she was on the right street.

She thanked him and turned back the way she had come. She scanned the building from that side, searching for windows or any form of pipes that she could use to get on top of the building. There were three windows, all of them high up on the second floor and with one quick glance up as though she were checking the weather, she knew she could get across from the building to her left. The overhanging rooves from the two buildings made the space less than two feet. That would be easy to jump... were she not in a dress.

Letting out a slow sigh of irritation at the formalities of the Court, she had to wonder how Catherine got away with wearing pants while Etani had been expected to wear dresses. Was it because the werewolf was in the military?

'Well, that just was not fair...' she thought dryly as she made her way around the building. She skipped the next alley, but the third alley appeared to be empty and she headed into it.

Glancing around quickly, she noted she was alone, and while still grumbling to herself about the unfairness of men getting to wear pants, she reached down and hitched up the stupid, lovely dress. She pulled it up around her knees and to her front so that the skirt was tight against the back of her legs and then tucked the whole lot in between her legs. Taking the tail, she split it into two sections and pulled them around to the front over her hips and tied them neatly into a bow. It left at least two-thirds of her legs exposed, but she had full manoeuvrability.

Crossing the alley to a pipe, she gave it a firm tug and when it did not jiggle, she lifted her foot and planted it against the ceramic, hoisting herself up and beginning her climb. A small sound caught her attention, and she looked down to find a young boy staring up at her with huge, fascinated eyes. She stuck her tongue out at him after a moment of consideration, and pulled herself up onto the roof of the building. Even if he did tell anyone he had seen a noblewoman climbing a wall, no one was going to believe him.

From the roof, she could see much of the city. It lay like a blanket of uneven platforms that made travelling easy. She would simply have to avoid the taller buildings in case anyone was looking out, but even then there were a huge number of chimneys and if one was not expecting to see a person walking on the rooftops, they might simply believe the smoke had played a trick on their eyes.

Turning her attention to the shop she needed to get to, she set off at a run and leapt across the narrow alley and onto the roof of the next shop. It was a thrill to run and leap and move, and it was exhilarating to feel free again.

Moving to the edge of the building, she sank down onto the tiles and looked across to the wall she needed to get to. She was not tall enough to reach the windows from the top, but she thought she could probably jump down and catch the windowsill.

Glancing down, she noted that the homeless people had either left or seemed to be asleep, so she decided to take her chances.

Rising and taking a few steps back, she ran forward and jumped off the side of the building, her nails digging into the soft wood of the windowsill. She pulled her legs up, landing in a crouched position against the wall, her feet hitting the wood with a soft thud.

Pushing the window open, she peeked inside and looked around. No one ever thought to lock their windows on the second floor, and it made the job of people like herself so much easier.

Pulling herself up onto the windowsill, she looked around. The sound of laughter caused her to freeze. A couple of guards strolled past, talking quietly. Turning her face towards the window to hide the paleness of it, she waited for the guards to pass before she moved again. Then she turned and slipped her legs in through the window, setting her feet down onto the boards.

Moving slowly, she lowered herself down onto the boards, her movements ever careful not to make the wood groan as her weight came down on it.

AFTER A SOLID MINUTE of crouching on the wood, she edged her way along towards a light she could see across the room, her arms stretched out to disperse her weight. Moving slowly, she crawled on her hands and feet.

Around halfway across she realised she was on the roof of a storage space above the second floor of the shop. She heard muffled voices from below and tilted her head. She could make out the occasional word as she inched closer to the stairs. The word 'risk' was being used frequently in relation to importing costs. It was curious, and she had to wonder what they were importing that would involve substantial risk. Something illegal most likely but it was shining a little light on why the Prince would want the man gone.

Still, it seemed to be beneath the man, something that a Prince should not really care about unless it was something dangerous or otherwise threatening to him or the crown.

It did not really matter why the Prince wanted him dead, she was more curious than anything and as the conversation seemed to be nearing its end, she started back towards the window, her mind jumping from conclusion to conclusion on what they could be importing. She slid out of the window and looked down at the alley. Finding it empty, she flipped over to hold on to the windowsill and swung herself to the side before letting go and grabbing onto the pipe that ran down the side of the building.

Climbing up onto the roof of Carriger's building, she leapt easily across and turned, looking down at the door the man had gone through earlier.

It was not long before he appeared again and she saw that he looked furious, his face red and shoulders tense.

As he started down the alley away from the market, she followed after him from above, half of her attention on him and half on the surrounding buildings in case someone decided to find out what she was doing up there.

The building they came to was prettier than she expected, a large townhouse with a six-foot wall wrapped around it, a small yard and a garden. The wall was inconvenient, but she could work around it.

A loud squeak pulled her eyes down as she settled herself in the shadow of a chimney. The man opened his gate and closed it again, taking a moment to lock it before he stormed into the house and slammed the door. What was the point of locking a six-foot gate? Half of the mythicals would be able to see over it and the other half would be leaning on the top of it. If one wanted to keep mythicals out, they needed at least ten-foot-high walls.

Mythical beings were tall, at least most of them. There were the fairies and pixies, gnomes and other common mythicals who were all considered to be mutants if they were taller than five foot. Certain breeds of elves were rarely taller than six feet. Then there were the rest of them, who considered anyone under six foot to be laughably short. She fell into the latter category and one of those lucky beings who were supposed to be tall and graceful and elegant, but hers and her twin's bodies seemed to have not gotten that notice and stopped growing before reaching the 'acceptable' six-foot mark.

She was just shy of six foot and as a result, she had been teased mercilessly by any mythical she had come across in the past nine hundred years.

They only teased her once, and if they survived that, they did not tend to try to pick on her height again. She was a little sensitive about it.

Watching the pretty house as the sun set and candles were lit, she hummed faintly to herself and tapped out a tune on her thigh. The breeze felt wonderful on her skin and each slow breath told her she was still alone, at least from anyone upwind.

The hours trickled by and finally, the curtains were drawn on the windows of the house and she exhaled slowly, pushing herself away from the warm chimney as she watched. There were two people in the house she had been able to see while observing the building. There was the tall man upstairs and a smaller woman downstairs. What interactions she had observed through the windows had been perfunctory and that made her think that the woman was most likely his maid. It was not surprising; he was a wealthy man and would have live-in staff. She assumed there was a gardener as well, she doubted he would tend to the garden himself.

HER OBSERVATIONS TOLD her that he did not tend to leave the top floor and that was not surprising either, a man like that would want to be above his staff, and so he would reside on the top floor.

It made life easier for her, as it meant she would only be dealing with a single person since there did not appear to be a wife or children.

It was closer to midnight before she finally stood from her spot and made her way towards the edge of the roof, easily sliding down to hang from the edge of the tiles before letting go.

Landing silently on her feet, she bent her knees to absorb the impact and straightened, turning around to glance first left and then right before she crossed the street. She trailed her fingers over the wall as she walked, ears and eyes alert to who might be around, but there was no one. Curfew was in effect and the only ones she would run into were others up to no good or guards. Guards were easy to hear, though; they jangled.

An adjoining wall that connected to a smaller fence of a neighbour made it incredibly easy for her to scale the wall and drop down onto the soft grass.

The man had done well for himself; she could not deny it. His house was huge and very well maintained, made of expensive white stone and dark wood, decorated with statues and marble. Crossing the yard, she followed the plan she had made up in her mind while waiting for the time to pass. She was so relaxed, she could almost hum to herself. She had the main plan, a backup, and a backup for the backup. The final plan would be to simply kill everyone in the place and then go off and hide for a while. But she did not want to do that. She might not care that much for the humans, but the maid did not deserve to die just because Etani had agreed to work for Epharis.

It was not hard to get up to the top floor, stepping up onto the sill of the bottom window, springing up to catch the next, pulling herself up with the assistance of the decorative cross-shaped beams and repeating the move until she was at the window on the third floor. If she ever had her own home, she was going to make sure it was difficult to get to her. The humans never stopped to think how easy it was for mythical assassins to get in, even the humans would have managed this house.

The curtains were lovely, made of thick and lush velvet that made her want to stick around just to touch them. Added bonus, they would block out noise, or keep it in.

Smiling to herself, she pressed the window open... of course, it was unlocked... and peeked inside.

The room was dark and warm, and smelt of a musty cologne that made her nose burn. It was oddly rich, as though it had been sprinkled all over the carpet. Her eyes began to water. Forcing herself through it, she slid down from the windowsill. The carpet was incredibly thick.

Thick enough that she could have slept on it comfortably. It felt like a massage on her feet. She wanted carpet like that in her room, very badly.

Listening to the slow, deep breathing of the man, she tilted her head and after a moment, she counted only one breath. This confirmed her thoughts that the man was indeed unmarried.

Crossing to the bed with careful steps, she noted irritably that he was one of those people who slept right in the middle of the bed. Rolling her eyes, she slid one knee up onto the mattress and eased her weight onto it. He stirred, frowning, but he did not wake. At least not until she was kneeling over him, a mere foot from him, her hands reaching for his face.

His eyes snapped open, and he made to strike her, but it was too late. She grabbed his head and pulled his face up to hers, her lips meeting his with a firm pressure. She pushed that tendril of her mind out of herself, through his lips and down into him.

She found him there, warm and blue, flickering beautifully. Her fingers curled around the blue light and she pulled him up to her, pulled him out of the shell that was his body and into herself. Her eyes slid shut as his corpse collapsed to the bed, her body humming with the taste of him.

She did not dare linger and slinked back across the room and out of the window once more.

Throwing one last glance at the carpet and curtains, she slid from the window and was gone.

9

KINGS AND OTHER MINOR INCONVENIENCES

*B*y the time she made it back to the castle, it was getting close to dawn and only the servants were about. They paid little attention to her. Given the oddities of those in the castle, it was best to keep your attention to yourself. Once she was sure she was safe, she dropped the glamour back to the human version of herself. She was at least somewhat known there; they wouldn't think it that odd that she was around.

Taking the square of fabric she had purchased, she draped it over her head like a shawl, and tried to smooth out the creases of her skirt before she slipped inside the front doors of the castle. She paused when she spotted the two vampires. They seemed just as surprised to see her as she was to see them, and they did not try to greet her. They simply watched her for a long moment while she decided what to do. She offered them a faint smile and slipped away, relieved when they did not try to follow her. As attractive as they were, vampires creeped her out. They were so still and quiet and there was the added issue of her blood being highly addictive.

It was not just her blood; it was Fae blood that they would become addicted to with even a single drop. It was said to be the magic that the blood possessed, something the vampires themselves lacked. They were only modified humans. They were given incredible strength and stamina that made them ageless and enhanced their physical attributes. They never needed to sleep, never needed to eat, and were, in essence, perfect. But they had no magic and when they got a first taste of it, that was the end of their freedom, they would be trapped for the rest of eternity being unable to sustain their bodies on human blood. They would only be able to drink from that same Fae.

Heading back to her rooms, she took a long bath and settled herself on the balcony to watch the sunrise over the city, her skin and mind buzzing with the energy of her kill.

She had killed for Epharis without really stopping to think about what that might mean for her and her life in the city. She was now the royal assassin to the Prince Epharis of Ayathian. The thought made her lips turn down into a frown before she let out a slow breath. Well, if she was going to do anything in that city, it might as well be something she was good at.

The news of the dead Lord spread like wildfire through the Court and it seemed as though everyone was aware of it by lunch time. When she arrived in the throne room, Epharis was nowhere to be seen. She was not bothered, it meant she did not have to deal with him, and any time without his presence was a good time.

Loitering in the hall on her own, she watched a small group of young men as they eyed her. They tried to get closer without making it obvious. Their attempts to flirt silently with her from several paces away made her want to laugh. Then something else caught her eye. Someone with dark skin and black hair moved through the crowd, talking with a small number of other mythical beings who seemed pleased to see him.

Seeing her, he made a beeline for her. He was beside her before she could decide if she wanted to run away or punch him.

"My Lord," she said coolly, looking him over in his smart black suit and tall boots.

"Lady Etani, I see you have enchanted my brother with your Fae magic," he said in an accusatory, almost angry voice.

"I have no intentions of enchanting anyone, least of all your brother. I am grateful for his kindness; however, I have no interest in a mate." Her eyes met his calmly while he glowered at her and she could not help but think that she had insulted him in some way.

"In this world, it is not always the choice of the woman," he growled, unreasonably angry at her.

What did that mean? 'It was not always the choice of the woman?' Of course it was her choice; she was not going to let a man touch her whom she did not want to touch her. As she pondered the oddity of the human world and its rules, the Drow stalked away. She was left alone once more, fascinated by him. He was so easy to anger and then he would simply leave.

Dismissing the strange Drow, her attention was caught by a flurry of movement near the throne as a group of men barged their way forward, the one in the lead looking particularly furious.

"You had him killed!" the leading man screamed, and the crowd parted to give him access to the throne. "It's always the same with you monsters! You kill what you cannot control!" The man was short, with a round belly and very little hair. He was dressed in rich blue fabrics and had a round, very red face.

HEADING in the direction of the screaming man, she slipped through the crowd until she came to a stop a few feet behind him. She was captivated by the accusations, and amused by the fact that he was accusing the wrong brother.

"I had no reason to kill Lord Carriger. He brought in many resources to the city on which we rely." The tired-looking King replied, slouching in his oversized throne and looking moody.

"Liar! You only want to put more of your freaks in power!" The balding man bellowed. "You and your monsters do not belong in this world! You should all be exterminated!"

A shock went through the crowd and the King's brows drew together. Etani's gaze lowered, watching as the man reached to his belt for a long knife. It did not matter if he was going to use it or not, he had made threats and was now armed; he was dangerous and irrational.

She moved forward without thinking about it. People screamed as the guards attempted to shove them aside in an effort to defend the King. Alaric had not moved, his eyes lifted at her movement and locked on her. He was unafraid of the human, but curious about her.

Three steps put her behind the man, and she drove her heel into the back of the man's knee, dropping him with a cry of pain. Reaching out, she wrapped her fingers around his wrist that held the knife while her free hand went up around his throat. With one foot pressing down on the back of his calf, she kept him easily on his knees and she jerked his head up straight, her nails a very prominent threat to him.

It had taken only a second. The man yelled in pain as her nails left a trickle of blood rolling down his flesh.

Without a word, she lifted her gaze to the King, her expression impassive. The question hung between them, neither needing to speak in order to communicate.

The man blubbered below her, the knife clattering to the floor and he pleaded for his life, begging her and the King for his release.

"Why should I spare you?" the King asked slowly, finally tearing his eyes from Etani's to look down at the man. The man had not come alone, but it seemed that none of his companions were overly keen to try to help him. "You threatened the crown, a crime punishable by death. Not only that, but you also threatened a large number of my people." His voice was calm, almost bored.

"Your Majesty, please! I never intended for this to get out of hand!" he squealed.

"But I am a monster, am I not? Do I not deserve to be killed?"

The man gasped as the nails bit deeper and blood began to trickle freely, staining the front of his shirt.

"An example will be made of you. No zealots are welcome in my city," he said calmly and his eyes lifted to meet hers, his head dipping once in a nod.

She did not hesitate for a second. In an instant she moved, her body turning to face the opposite direction. Her foot stamped down again on his leg to make him howl in agony; arching herself back, her arms reached over her shoulder and she grasped the head of the man. Leaning forward again and straining her back against the movement, the man's body was pulled tight, his back arching over hers and his neck seemed to stretch impossibly far, and then her nails dug in. Giving a jerk the head ripped free and blood splashed the floor and her clothing.

Turning back to hear the body thump to the marble floor, she grasped the head by the straggling hairs that clung to his scalp, holding it out to the King.

The King remained silent, staring down at the bloody sight before him. The bloodied woman who had killed on command without so much as a blink. She felt the blood running down the side of her face and neck, soaking her hair and the shoulder of her dress.

The room was so silent that the sound of blood dripping from the stump of the man's neck down into the pool that spread around him was incredibly loud.

THE KING TURNED his head away, the sight before him displeasing him. A second later, the head hit the ground with a thump. The traitors were not worth his attention; they belonged in the dirt. Servants hustled to clean away the mess, and she left the hall to get cleaned up. Not a single Courtier spoke for the rest of the day. Most were not human, and it was not uncommon for a death to happen in a place like this, but it was rarely that quick and the scene had left them all rattled.

She was glad that at the time, she had appeared as a human and not her full self, but she made a mental note to have a new host created. She needed a different face to show when she was not ripping humans in half for the pleasure of the Court.

Slipping back into her room, Etani had clay ordered through Sasha with the stipulation that it be delivered to the cold room in the kitchens. It was several hours before the delivery notification reached her rooms, and she had used the time to bathe under the waterfall. She flopped onto the couch, lounging while she watched Sasha sewing up the damage that had been done to her dress. She had ripped the seam tying it around her waist. It was hypnotising to watch the girl's fingers working, the tear becoming nothing at all. Sasha was quick to give instruction about how the stitching on the torn seam was different than the stitches used to repair any other part of the fabric.

A knock came at the door and both women looked up suspiciously. Etani was wary since Epharis still had not turned up, but she doubted that the Lich would knock.

Sasha moved quickly for the door. After a moment, she returned with a distressed expression on her face.

"My Lady, it is requested that you join his Majesty for dinner," she said slowly, her face anxious.

"I would be delighted," Etani responded, curious but not surprised that he would want to see her after what had happened.

Within half an hour, Sasha had dressed her. She stepped out into the hall, clad in a modest black gown that cut across her chest in a straight line and trailed the floor, hiding her still bare feet. It was pretty, but it was still too big for her liking, with layers of frothy black scratchy material underneath, and fat, round sleeves that hung off her shoulders.

Following along in the wake of the guard, she considered what he might have to say to her, and what she was going to say to him. She was chewing on her tongue by the time they crossed to the opposite side of the castle where she was ushered through a tall, unusually wide door.

She had expected to find a private dining room, but she was momentarily thrown off guard by the sight of a large sitting room that looked fairly similar to her own.

In a flash of panic, she realised that he had invited her to his private suite. She froze in the doorway. She was in the King's rooms.

"Come in," a low voice said. The King was not wearing his armour this time and even without it he was tall and incredibly broad, with massive shoulders and legs. Wearing a simple shirt, pants and boots, he looked strange to her, shrunken almost. He was less like a walking fort and more like a man.

The man was incredibly muscled and toned, with arms that bulged and biceps that were bigger than her waist, enormous thighs and a chest that most women would have drooled over. His hair reached just past his shoulders and had been tied back at the nape of his neck. Several strands had escaped and fell down around his face.

Turning around to her, he held two large goblets of red liquid. He made a slight motion to one of the two overlarge couches. She obeyed quickly, crossing the room and sitting down where he had indicated, her mind reeling on what he could possibly want from her.

The scars that covered his exposed skin enhanced his masculine appeal, brows pulled low over those incredible eyes that she could easily have gotten lost in. He looked rather grim, crossing to the couch opposite hers, and offering her the goblet.

Accepting it, she cupped it carefully between both hands, feeling a little silly. Her hands were tiny compared to his, and the goblet had been made for him, leaving her feeling like a child trying to hold an adult's drink for them.

"Your Majesty..." She stared warily, but she stopped as he gave a wave of his hand, downing a good half of the goblet in one gulp.

Swallowing slowly, the goblet hung from his hand between his knees as he leant forward, resting his elbow on his thigh to study her.

"You are not human," he said simply.

"Neither are you," she replied, earning a cold and calculating smile from the man.

"MY BROTHER HAS A HOLD OVER YOU," he said, another statement of fact. She decided not to answer, simply watching him. "What does he have on you?" he asked finally when she made it clear she was not going to reply.

Lifting the goblet to her lips, she sniffed it warily for a second before she took a careful sip, buying herself time to come up with an answer. The rich wine left her tongue feeling numb. She did not drink, not ever, and she did not much like it.

"Your brother is a clever man. He knows how to capture creatures and how to keep them alive until they are no longer useful," she said carefully, giving in to the tense silence when he refused to let her ignore the question. "How did you know I was in the dungeon?"

"One of the guards told a story of a woman being kept there by the Prince. He was experimenting on her and yet she was still alive for weeks while he tried to figure out what she was. He spoke of her being opened from navel to throat, with her innards being strewn out on the table before her." His eyes drifted down the length of her torso and then back up to her face.

She did not reply; instead, she stared back at him and pretended to take another sip. She was not keen on the sensation it caused at the back of her mind. It was like someone had set a fire, and was trying to heat her body up for slow roasting.

"He spoke of her trying to escape, and then of the Prince cursing her. Sacrificing a guard in order to curse her."

Swallowing hard, she set the goblet down on the table between them. She lifted her eyes to him as he downed the last of his wine and stood. He moved away from her to refill his drink.

"What was the curse?" he asked, his back to her but she could see a very slight tremor in his hands.

"That I should not be permitted to live if he is killed, and that we would be bound for eternity," she said slowly, shifting the goblet slightly further away from the edge of the table before leaning back and resting her hands in her lap.

The man had stomped his way back to the couch and sat down heavily, glowering at her as he rolled the goblet between his fingers.

"What about the deal?" he pressed, but he had only barely finished speaking before there came a polite knock at the door. A guard opened the door for a young woman. She wore the same black servant's dress that the others wore. She set down a large covered tray on the table between the two of them, and then hurried back out of the door, her face down. The guard was quick to close the door behind her, returning them to their privacy.

"What are you?" Etani asked, her eyes lingering on the door for a moment before turning back to him.

"I am the son of a titan and the Mother-Goddess Tiamat," he said with a strong note of pride in his voice.

The statement left her mind frozen. She tried again and again to process the information. It was not at all what she had expected. Sure, he was a huge man, but the son of a titan? Her eyes dragged down his form slowly, taking in all the bulging muscles and his height, those golden eyes and the fact that he seemed to simply radiate strength and power. It was not entirely impossible, if his mother had been of average size. The thought made her very aware that he was likely even more powerful than his outward appearance would suggest.

He had been watching her while she tried to wrap her brain around the information, an amused smile on his face at her confusion.

"Not a common mix, no," he said, almost as though he had read her lagging mind.

"Your brother is a Lich," she said, her tone suggesting the two made no sense. Lich had to be human, did they not? Was it possible for a mythical, or half-mythical being to become a Lich?

"Lich are not born, they are made. He is my half-brother to different mothers. She was human and died in childbirth, my brother was greedy and wanted to be the strongest and, in the end, he thought that being a Lich would give him that." His tone was almost oozing disgust. "I will admit, he was not wrong that it would make him stronger."

Her gaze turned from him to the window, birds flying in the distance as the sun began to dip down towards the horizon and it gave her time to take in the information he had provided.

"Now, you tell me what you are," he said finally.

Turning back to him, she considered the question and what she was. She could not deny that being honest with the man was in her best interest. Given he had been so open with her, she could not come up with a valid reason to lie to him.

"I AM ONE OF THE FAE," she said simply. It was not a lie, but it was not the whole truth either. He seemed just as dumbfounded by her statement as she had been by his, and she waited patiently while he took in the information.

"My brother captured you?" he asked, his eyes dipping down slightly to the silver chain about her throat.

"He got lucky," she replied coldly.

"Indeed, he did. How did that come about?" Regardless of how casual his tone was and how passing the question seemed on the outside, she could not help but notice that his muscles had tensed as though he were excited by something. He reached for the tray.

"I was feeding and distracted when he came upon me. He used some strange magic to subdue me." She was careful, not wanting to inform him that the gold chain was what had captured her, just in case it gave the man ideas.

He lifted the cover off the platter, offering the tray to her first. It was covered with a layer of toasted bread with little strips of spiced chicken and lettuce. Accepting one, she bit into it and chewed. The chicken tasted rather pleasant.

He had been watching her with a clear fascination. She doubted he was done questioning her, but she was patient and she remained silent, returning his stare as she swallowed the bite.

It tasted quite good, but it would do very little for her. She could gain no nutrients from it, and eventually it would simply dissolve in her belly.

Taking a second piece, she settled back into the couch and looked around his sumptuous room. It was decorated in dark colours, the woods all stained deep tones. While it came off as a little brooding, it was quite aesthetically pleasing. Against the wall in a corner was a sword that was taller than she was, resting comfortably in a cradle designed for it.

"Why did you come to my defence?" he asked suddenly, having already eaten several of the little snacks.

Chewing slowly on the second half of hers, she examined the sword for a moment longer before she turned back to him.

"I do not know, really," she said, her mind going back over the scene while his frown grew. "I acted on impulse, to protect the crown. I do not know you, but I do know that your brother should never be King. You must not be permitted to die until you have an heir." She spoke bluntly and the man's head tilted as though she had said something odd.

"How do you know I have no heir?" he asked curiously.

Her brows lifted slightly but when he did not say anything, she motioned to the room around them. Remembering she had the snack in her hand, she took a bite out of it. She could not tell what the spices were, but they were delicious. Swallowing, she looked back at him.

"You either have an illegitimate child you have not recognised, or you have none. You are unmarried, you lack a ring. Your rooms are very distinctly masculine, suggesting you have no mistress or fiancée. There is only one throne, and there is no indication that a woman has ever come into these rooms unless it's to be gone again in a matter of hours." His brows lifted and so she elaborated. "No combs, no perfume, no softening of your appearance or the appearance of your rooms, there are no women's shoes, and no woman living here would be thrilled by the colour scheme long term." Dropping her eyes to the piece of toast, she touched her finger to the sauce and touched it to the tip of her tongue before she spoke. "You are very clearly a bachelor, same as the Prince and if I'm not mistaken, you have both been in that state for some time."

10

HOW TO INSULT A KING IN FIVE EASY STEPS

"*O*bservant," he said dryly. "I have not needed a wife, had no desire to burden myself with such things."

"And as a result, should you die, your throne will pass to a Lich. A Lich King, in fact. I have a feeling those don't turn out too well." She said it as though it were only a passing thought, but she knew the history of the creatures. Very few people tended to survive when they were ruled by a Lich.

Looking at the sauce, she found that it had left her tongue tingling. She glanced up at the King, amused at his irritation. She did not often get to talk with someone like him so openly.

"Perhaps I should consider getting one," he said with a sigh, scratching his jaw before he picked up another of the snacks. He chewed the whole thing at once.

"That would be advisable, unless you don't mind all of your work being destroyed," she said, examining the sauce after dabbing a little more on her finger. It was pink and there was very little of it, just enough to hold the chicken on the lettuce.

"What is it my brother has you doing? It is not often he takes this much effort to ensnare someone."

Looking up at him, she was sure he had sounded a little sulky for a moment.

"He has yet to tell me. However, so far it would appear that I am simply his pet assassin," she said, smearing the sauce on her fingers and squinting at a little speck of red, trying to think of what spice would leave her tongue tingling that was red. Chilli peppers? Those were supposed to be spicy.

"You killed the merchant?" he said sharply, his eyes seeming to glow fully from within.

"Yes," she said simply, popping the last of the snack into her mouth and looking up at him, alert to his growing anger. She was very aware that she may need to escape, and that could be a little tricky given his size.

"Why?" he demanded, face turning a little red under the strain of his fury.

"I am not privy to the reasons, Your Majesty, I am only told who." She spoke carefully, trying to soothe the beast, and he took a moment to calm himself before he gave a bark of laughter.

"He's not even here, and the man enrages me," he said. She noticed the mask he pulled over himself. He was good at playing nice, but she was aware that he was dangerous, exceptionally so.

Pushing herself to her feet, she moved away from the couches to a small bowl of water where she could rinse her fingers of the oily sauce. Once finished washing, she dried her hands on the small towel beside it. She could feel his eyes on her, watching her every move.

"You do not look like the Fae," he said, his tone accusatory.

"And you do not look like the son of a God," she countered, turning back to him. He stood slowly, approaching her calmly.

"Why is it you do not look like them?" he asked, stopping a few feet away from her to study her face.

"I look the way I wish to look, as do many of us when we are in this world," she said cautiously, unable to help but feel that he had cornered her.

"How do you do that?" He paused, squinting slightly. "Isn't that what they call a 'glamour'?" he asked. She was amused to find him trying to see through it.

"Only a handful of species can see through a glamour, usually only those of Fae heritage. I have never heard of a titan being able to."

He looked disappointed by that and for a moment she thought that she had been worried for nothing.

"Take it off." It was an order and the silence that stretched between them was tense.

"No," she said finally, as politely as she could manage.

"I am your King!" he boomed, and she took an unconscious step back from him, her back bumping into the counter as his face turned red.

"You are not my King, Your Majesty," she said gently, trying her best to soothe the situation once more. "You are a King, but I have no King." She was tense, ready to move in an instant.

He was fuming, his golden eyes glowing. A flash of lightning whipped across them, brightening the room for an instant.

He reached for her and she took a quick step to the side, then pivoted on the ball of her foot. She spun towards the door, but he was faster than she had ever imagined he could be given his size. It should not have been possible.

His FINGERS CLENCHED around her forearm and his hands were so big they enclosed her arm and then went half again around. Jerking to a stop, she turned back. Her fingers clenched around his, trying to pry them off without hurting him.

"Let go!" she cried, hating the heat of his skin on hers. He refused, gripping harder and, with a sharp jerk, he very nearly yanked her off her feet.

"Obey me, woman." He was no longer shouting, but instead, he spoke in a low and lethal tone, giving her a little shake that pulled her even closer to him. She was only a foot from him. She hated the heat that radiated off him, it was like standing too close to a hearth.

He shook her again, roughly, to make her shoulder ache while his free hand lifted to curl his fingers in the hair at the back of her neck, gripping tightly and pulling her closer, higher until she was barely able to stand on the tips of her toes. Her head was forced back to meet his glowing golden eyes.

She did not respond, instead, she bared her teeth at him. The slap came out of nowhere. One second her arm was in his grip and the next her head was ringing. She tasted blood.

Using his grip on her hair, he threw her to the floor. She gasped, lying on her side, her face on fire. She refused to cry out at the pain.

He stepped over her, picking up the decanter of wine and drinking from it, watching her as she pushed herself up onto her hands and knees and then sat back on her heels.

Touching her lip, her fingers came back crimson and wet. Her lower lip had split and the inside of her cheek had cut against her teeth.

Lifting her gaze to him, they were both silent for a long time before he finally spoke. His voice was that same deadly calm though it was barely more than a whisper.

"You belong to my brother. You live in my city; you kill my citizens. I am your King and you will obey."

The silence stretched between them again and she felt the blood trickle down her chin, dripping onto the carpet.

"Take it off," he said.

She did not move, and he closed the distance between them in a flash. This time his hand closed around her throat and he lifted her off the ground, his free hand rising.

Her attempts to block the second blow did nothing, and she crashed through a table, lying in the splintered remains. She could feel her eye would soon be blackened. Her ears rang, but she heard his approach. Rolling, she locked her knee under her and, using the momentum, lifted herself off the ground and onto her feet. The action took him off guard, but he adjusted for it. He did not attempt to grab her a third time, since she was prepared for that.

Lifting her hand, she used the back of her sleeve to wipe her mouth, her eyes never leaving him.

"I will ask you one more time, woman. If you do not comply, I will kill you," he said simply. Epharis would know when she returned to life; it may be worth letting Alaric kill her and so she could return to kill him after. But no, that was too risky.

"Yes, Your Majesty," she said stiffly. It was not worth it; the Lich would know of her immortality and possibly even what she really was.

Standing before the man, she considered her options. She decided to see how far she could push the issue. She did not let the glamour drop, instead, she changed it. The creature standing before him was not what she was. She looked more like her youngest sister Avadari with white hair that hung to her thighs, alabaster skin, and pale blue eyes.

She still wore the dress, but it had been glamoured to appear more fanciful than it was. The bruise on her cheek bloomed, yellowed, and faded in the time it took him to study her. The cut sealed, and the scar disappeared.

When he reached for her, there was no aggression, but she still had to resist the urge to bite his fingers off. She allowed him to cup her face and run his thumb over her full lips. He drank her in, studied every inch of her face. He touched her ears, tracing the shape of them.

Leaning down, she thought for one horrible second that he intended to kiss her. But instead, he inhaled the scent of her hair.

Wondering what was going on, she allowed him to be so close for only a few seconds more before she drew back and out of his grasp, angry at him for his actions.

It had worked, the man looked almost drunk as he took in the form, she decided to show him. She was gleeful that he did not know that it was a trick.

"Forgive me. I should never have struck you," he said finally, still unable to take his eyes off her.

She made no response, instead, she gathered the energy to change the glamour once more.

He did not attempt to stop her as the change shimmered onto her features like a mirage. He seemed to be entirely lost for words now and he sat down.

Remaining where she stood, she glowered at him and dusted off the back of her dress. Wood stuck to her clothing and her hair, and a tear marred the back of her bodice.

"Are you satisfied? May I be excused?" she said finally, now unable to look at the man. He had struck her twice, forcing her to do his will. This place was not a place where she wanted to be, where men could be so cruel and have no repercussions.

She had wanted to kill him; she could have possibly killed him. But then what? Epharis would be in control and her punishment would be worse than a simple slap to the face.

"Yes, go," the King replied as he stared down at his hands, clenching, and unclenching his fingers.

Turning to go, she crossed the room only to pause at his shout. "Do not forget, you may belong to Epharis, but he belongs to me. And thus, you by extension," he said slowly.

Turning to look over her shoulder, she considered him for a moment.

"I owe you no allegiance, King. I will obey, but I am not yours."

With that, she left the room and returned to her own. Sasha lamented the dress and expressed her concern, but Etani did not deem it worth telling her the events of the day.

She sent Sasha out to order her several pairs of pants and blouses. To enjoy the rest of the evening, Etani changed into her most basic dress, and headed to the cold room where she heard the clay had been sent.

UPON REACHING THE ROOM, the servants were ordered out and one was given orders that were to be sent to Epharis. She would be changing her appearance, he had no say in the matter, and she would kill them both if he again destroyed her form.

The response he gave was apparently so vulgar the servant would not repeat it, claiming it was improper to speak in such a manner before a Lady, but that Epharis would come to her in the morning.

Thanking the man, she dismissed him and set to work.

She had ordered enough clay to make two hosts, and she planned to use all of it.

It was morning by the time she finished one of them. A small, slender woman with a mass of crimson and gold hair who was very similar to the form she had worn when first she arrived in the city. The second would have to wait for a time as she had a meeting to attend.

Leaning down, she pressed her lips to that of the host and felt herself being drawn in. Gasping, her lungs expanded, and she looked up at the ceiling. Everything was green for a few seconds, the paint was sinking in and permeating her iris.

Only once the green had faded and she wriggled her way into comfort inside the host did she sit up. Flexing her fingers, she tested to ensure they were working properly. Everything seemed to be in order, and she hopped down from the table, picked up a dress she had set out for herself and pulled it on. It was too long for her, but it would do.

Hitching it up so as not to trip over it, she bustled her way through the castle to her room. Her appearance garnered her some very odd looks, but no one deemed it worth interfering with someone potentially important.

Back in her rooms, she bathed to remove the residual clay dust from her skin and stood before the mirror, inspecting every inch of the form.

She stood at five feet, five inches with proportionate hips and breasts. Her arms were slender, her belly flat, and her legs lightly toned. Her hair fell in ringlets to the middle of her back, glittering gently. While she was a very pretty human, there was no doubt that she was, in fact, a human.

It was a while before Sasha awoke, but Etani did not remain dormant while the girl slept. Instead, she worked on her sewing skills by mending the dress. Sitting naked on the couch, she splayed the violet garment across her lap and set to work. It would be a day or so before she had her ordered trousers, and she needed something to wear.

Sasha nearly jumped out of her skin at the sight of the redheaded naked woman sitting on the couch with a pair of scissors in her hand. But the laugh that burst out of her did not change, and she beckoned the girl to join her. Sasha was happy with the sewing work, watching as Etani continued along the seam and then tried the outfit on.

Nudity around her had been commonplace, as her sense of modesty did not extend to fellow women. Women had all the same parts she had, mostly. And thus, their seeing her naked did not bother her in the slightest. It had bothered Sasha at first, but she grew used to the eccentricities of the woman she cared for.

The dress fit well enough and Sasha made the final adjustments, snipping off the remaining threads and nodding her satisfaction.

"You look perfect!" she said happily, packing away her sewing kit. She had just returned the kit to her room when the door to the suite burst open and in swept the Lich. He took one look at Etani and scowled as though her appearance had personally offended him. "You look better as your natural self," he said coldly, giving her a once-over.

"Glamours require energy to keep up. This form does not," she replied, her voice somewhat muted by the difference in vocal cords.

The Lich crossed the room and grasped her jaw, turning her head left and right to better examine her.

"Worthless, a human is worthless to me," he said, his fingers cool against her warmed skin.

"Well isn't that too bad? I'm wearing what I want to wear, and be damned your desires." She swatted away his hand and turned from him. But his fingers on her upper arm stopped her.

"I heard what happened with Alaric," he said. He did not sound like he much cared, yet the grip on her arm was gentle. "I will not allow him to lay hand on you again."

Looking back at him, she gave a light shrug. She was his property; he did not want her damaged.

"One brother is much like the other in this world," she said finally, giving her arm a tug and managing to pull away from him. He had not been trying to detain her, really.

MAKING A GESTURE TO THE COUCH, she crossed the room and fetched herself a mug of water, offering him one over her shoulder, and his grunt of affirmation was all she needed. Filling him one, she returned to him, and handed him the mug before she sat down across from him.

"You did well, the task I set you," he said after taking a long drink of the water. She mimicked him and set the mug down on the table.

"Will this be a frequent task? It would do no good to become a glutton and killing without eating is wasteful." Setting her hands in her lap, she studied the man before her. He did not change at all, his hair was the same length, his face was just as thin and his eyes had that same eerie silver-green glow that seemed to suck light from the air rather than radiate it as their colouring would suggest. He wore a matching black and grey robe every time she saw him, though it was clear they were not the same robes every day.

"What else would my little pet assassin be good for?" His voice was a sneer at that, and she recalled using those exact words.

"Were you spying on our meeting?" she asked, not entirely surprised that he would, but still irritated.

"In a sense. I can watch you due to our bond, but I must be in a trance of sorts." He had no shame in his voice, as though this were entirely normal, but she was seething.

"I would prefer it if you wear this form only when necessary," he said suddenly after a long stretch of mutinous silence.

"It is not so easy to climb in and out of these things. It causes wear, it uses a lot of energy and is demanding on the psyche. The mind can only adjust to a new shape so many times in a short period." It was not entirely untrue. It did take energy to remove it, but it was more the wear on the host itself. It took a long time to patch up the cracks that formed each time she removed it.

He looked annoyed at that, but said nothing more on the subject.

After a time, he stood and moved to the balcony. Hesitating for only a moment, she followed after him and they stood watching the city as it came to life.

"What were you before you came to this world?" he asked slowly, contemplating the city and his own thoughts.

"I was still a girl then," she replied, her eyes lifted to the sky. "We came here when we were still young."

"We?" He turned to study her face; his expression frustrated.

Blinking once, she looked at him, and a delicate flush covered her cheeks.

"My sisters and I; we came together and went our own ways some years back." They had deemed it wise, giving the scouts more targets to hunt.

"I see," was all he said. She did not want to talk about her sisters. The thought of them out there free made her sad. She missed them both terribly, but still, she knew it was better for them not to be there; and yet they were still in danger and she could not forget that.

"What were you before coming here?" she asked. It was clear that he and his brother had not been born into royalty. Neither of their parents were royalty.

"I was a scholar. I studied immortality and the beings belonging to that category. Alaric was the adventurer. He got it into his head that a man of his heritage should be a ruler, and so we came here. He killed the King and his son. Without a ruler, Alaric took the throne. I was named heir apparent, and we have been here since."

"How long ago was that?"

"A few hundred years, I did not keep track." Epharis turned from the view and looked up towards the castle turret above them.

"Why did you turn yourself into a Lich?" The words escaped her lips before she could stop them, and yet she did not try to take them back.

The Lich settled cold eyes on her once more.

"I was not strong, or powerful. I was mortal. I am no longer mortal, and now I am both strong and powerful," he replied simply.

She did not know why he was being so honest with her, but she pressed for more information while he still had the desire to talk.

"Why a Lich, though? There are any number of immortal beings out there that you could have become."

It was a long time before the Prince replied, his eyes locked on her and lips pursed.

"I wanted to be feared," he said simply. "There are few w do not fear me. One is my brother, and the other stands before me."

Etani was unable to pull her gaze from his, trapped in the silvery orbs.

"It is stupid not to fear a Lich."

"Not for a soul eater," he said simply, and tore his gaze from hers. He left her then, sweeping from the balcony and out of the suite without a backward glance.

11

ELVES AND MURDERERS

*W*atching him leave, she had to wonder what he had been thinking. Why would he believe that she would not fear him? She had spoken the truth, she did fear him. But in another way, she did not. She did not know how to reason it out in her own mind so she let it go, turning back to the city to watch it come to life. She stayed silent as her mind flicked from thought to thought.

A flash of movement caught her attention, and she squinted at it. A figure moved swiftly across the rooftops, taking smooth, inhuman leaps.

The figure made a beeline for the castle and the sight was fascinating. His movements were so clean and easy, as though he had done it a million times.

He appeared to be dressed in grey from head to toe, including his boots and hands. As he drew closer to the castle, she had to think that it was male. He had not noticed her, and she leaned forward on the balustrade to watch as the figure made the final leap from the outer wall onto the side of the castle itself, clinging to the stones like some great spider.

He had chosen his launch site well. Her side of the castle was quite close to the outer wall. She shook her head as he began to scale the wall at a surprising pace, finding handholds with ease. Before she had the chance to take five breaths, he had moved around to the curved side of the castle and she lost sight of him.

Who was he? Or was it even a 'he?' He had her undivided attention. She placed her hands on the balustrade and leant forward, out over the edge of the balcony to try to find him. He turned his head in her direction. He was dangling from the tiles of the roof, inching his way around towards a window that had been left open. He froze as his eyes met hers.

Her brows lifted and her lips parted. She pushed herself back from the balcony and out of sight. He was certainly male with that brooding glare and those heavy brows. She did not know his species, but she knew that he was like her, a killer. Who could he possibly be there for?

Heading back into her room, she pressed the doors to her balcony shut and locked them carefully. She locked both the standard lock and the larger ones at the top and bottom that had been designed for combatting storm winds. She left the curtains open in case the grey man decided to join her. She would be able to see him easily. It was another full day before she found out who he was.

Sasha had informed her in no uncertain terms that a Lady was not allowed to spend her days moping around alone in her rooms. It was rude and impolite, and not at all how a Lady should behave.

With that scolding ringing in her ears, Etani had been banished from her room. She headed down into the throne room, still licking her wounds after the meeting with the King. She wanted nothing more than to curl up in her bed and sleep the hours away.

The first thing she noticed was that Alaric was blissfully absent. Her tension eased. The Drow Lord Izziah was present, and he had evidently been looking for her. He immediately started towards her with a purposeful stride.

She was curious to know how he had become aware of the appearance of her new host body and if he could see her inside it, or if the host would block his view of her. Heading for him, her lips parted to make a polite greeting when another body blocked her sightline.

Lifting her eyes, she frowned at Epharis. Stopping dead in her tracks, her light mood melted into irritation which seemed to amuse him. He bent forward until his lips were near her ear.

"I would tread carefully around those two, they seek to know the

100

truth of you," he purred. He swept around behind her, his hands resting lightly on her upper arms so the two of them could see the Drow. Izziah's smile slid off his face at the appearance of the Prince, and he watched the two of them warily. "They are finding things out, Princess. You wouldn't want word to reach unwelcome ears. They cannot be trusted, do not forget who it is in this place that you can trust."

Well, that distinction did not fall on him, she was certain of that. She turned her head, but the Lich had slipped away like the snake he was. She frowned after him as Izziah started forward again.

Maybe the Lich had been a snake in another life... or a slug...

"WHAT DID THE PRINCE WANT?" Izziah asked in way of a greeting.

"Reminding me of where my loyalties lie," she said dryly, more curious about his words than alarmed. She was getting really tired of the pet names.

Looking back at Izziah, he was scowling at her, but then he shook his head and his expression eased.

"We must talk as soon as you are able," he said urgently, his words so rushed and unguarded that his accent shifted. She bit the inside of her cheek to keep from smiling. The Drow all had very thick accents unless they worked to hide them. It was quite endearing when his slipped out during moments of stress.

"Join me in my suite this evening. We can talk," she said, unable to even guess at what he could possibly have to speak to her about.

"I have tried, repeatedly. Your Lich has made it so I can never enter again without his express permission." His eyes hardened as he studied her face. "He is very protective of you," he said slowly, squinting as though he were trying to see through mist.

"Then I can come to you. Where are your rooms?"

"I do not live in the castle. My brother and I have a small townhouse on the northern edge of the city. It's called Nordia House."

Her brows lifted, and he gave her a sheepish smile and a shrug. "Drizdan's idea of a joke. He thought it was funny." He was looking rather tired of his brother's antics.

"I will come at sunset and we will talk," she breathed. There was a stir towards the front of the room. The heavy footsteps announced that the King had made an appearance. She tensed, glancing in his direction.

The King looked over the room, taking the lot of them in as they bowed or curtsied in greeting. Her tension eased as his eyes found her and then moved on without much of a pause.

"New costume?" Izziah asked, watching her face. He would have seen her tension as she looked towards the King.

"Sometimes it's easier to hide in plain sight," she said slowly. "I shall see you tonight." Moving away from him, she allowed herself to become lost in the crowd. After an hour or so, she spotted the grey man again.

It was by pure chance she noticed him at all. She had been conversing with some faceless man, but she had not been paying attention. All she had to do was agree with him, and he would waffle on for another ten minutes, seemingly without the need to take a single breath. People like him made pretending to be a Courtier so much easier because she could stand around for hours and not listen, while they did all the talking for her.

She had been keeping the King in the corner of her eye, wary that he might take an interest in her when she saw his posture shift. He tensed, his head tilted to the side.

He was talking to someone. While he was making an effort not to move his lips, she caught the occasional shift when it could not be helped.

Excusing herself from her companion, she inched her way closer to the throne. She noticed a narrow gap in the wall that the throne sat against. It was hard to see, and she likely wouldn't have noticed it had the King not directed his ear towards it. She could see the shift of movement inside it, the grey fabric and a hint of pale skin. The man must have seen her curiosity as his head tilted, and the King's eyes swung in her direction. She had been so fascinated by the sight that she had allowed herself to be caught. She turned her eyes quickly to a small cluster of Courtiers, pretending to be engaged in their conversation though she was still watching the throne out of the corner of her eye.

The King gave a slight shake of his head and murmured something.

She knew she was caught when the man's eyes turned back to her and narrowed.

Cursing, she decided it was a good time to make her exit. She offered her companions a cheery wave that they returned without question. She headed towards the exit, touching the folds of her skirt as though she needed to go to the powder room and freshen up. She did not have that little pouch thing that most of the female Courtiers had, but they did not need to know that.

As soon as she was out of the hall, she caught a glimpse of Izziah. His face showed concern but when she saw that he was the only one who was watching, she bolted.

IT WAS NO GOOD, the grey man had secrets of the castle that she would have gladly killed to learn. She doubted he would be interested in giving them to her.

Rounding the corner that led to the stairs, she almost shrieked as she found him standing there. She skidded to a stop and considered her options.

"Pardon, good sir, I appear to be lost!" Her attempt to make her voice as flowery and sweet as possible generally worked, but he did not seem to be falling for it. So, instead, she tried to step around him.

"Who are you?" he demanded, taking a quick step to the side in order to place his short stature between her and freedom.

"Emma," she said immediately. It was a name she and Sasha had come up with. The name of a silly, hapless young Courtier who probably did not have enough brain cells to rub together. "It's a pleasure, I'm sure. Please, excuse me."

Again, he blocked her path, and she considered giving him a good boot to the shin, or maybe she would even scream. But she did not want to draw any more attention to herself.

"I don't believe you." He said it in a low, heavily accented voice. It was thick, even without a mask over the lower half of his face. She could not tell the origin of it. It tickled the back of her mind though, leading her to think she had likely heard it before.

"That isn't my problem," she snapped, putting on airs of a young woman harassed by an unwanted suitor. "Guar—!"

His hand snapped up to cover her mouth, silencing her cry for assistance. She jerked back from him, indignant that he would dare to touch her. He made no attempt to try to grab her. He had only meant to stop her cry.

"Stop this pretence, I can smell you."

Well, that was slightly offensive...

She gave him a withering look, knowing full well she smelt of nothing but lavender. It was not like she produced body odour. Very few of the mythicals were capable of that, and she was a tad affronted by his suggestion.

"Excuse me?" she said, giving up on the frilly tone. She revisited the thought of booting his shin.

"You smell like clay and magic," he shot back, his voice dropping into a threatening growl.

Well, damn. The bastard had a nose like a basset hound.

"My father imports pottery, and I spent the entire day in the company of mythical beings," she countered, knowing she was caught but just trying to make his life difficult.

"I did not know your kind could lie..."

His words hung between them as though formed into sharp icicles above their heads, ready to plummet down on them at any second. How could he possibly know what she was? Was he capable of sniffing out the differences in her magic compared to other mythical beings? What was he?

Neither of them spoke, the silence stretching on as they both prepared for the fight that seemed imminent.

The man was taller than her, but only by three inches which made him quite small for a mythical. It also narrowed down what he could possibly be.

Her eyes swept down over his form and she was beginning to suspect that perhaps he was some breed of elf, not a Drow but something different.

Under normal circumstances, they would have had no issues with each other. The elves and the Fae were distantly related, and quite friendly, unless they came from opposing Courts.

Given he was in Ayathian, it seemed likely that he was unaligned like her, so why was he so uptight about her presence?

HE MOVED FIRST, his right hand shooting out towards her chest, but she caught it, ready for him. Using the momentum to twist her upper body, her fingers clamped around his hand and yanked him off balance. Her hair flew, distracting him, while her left foot slid forward. She planted it against the floor between his feet, sending him stumbling. He caught himself easily, spinning back on her.

It was her turn to move. She did not give him time to fully turn around, but lifted her left leg up in a vicious kick aimed towards his head, hoping to knock the observant bastard's head right off his shoulders.

His arms came up in a cross before his face, blocking the kick. It shoved him back a good foot, and he rebounded on her, coming after her with punch after punch. He scored a few times, but the rest of the blows she blocked or dodged, returning the hits with her legs just as many times as he scored on her. The man was incredibly fast. It was as though he could read her mind with how easily he was able to get his arms up to block her.

Finally, she managed to score a kick to the underside of his jaw, following the motion with a second kick as her body arched backwards. She caught herself with her hands and then flipped, landing back on her feet. He was sent flying into a wall.

He was not dead. It had been a love tap, but he had shattered a vase and the marble plinth it sat upon, ripping the curtain which fluttered down over his head.

The fight had lasted a few minutes, and while he was struggling to free himself, she made herself scarce. Only her low, throaty laugh and the whisper of fabric indicated she had ever been there.

It had been exhilarating to be able to fight again, her muscles aching in a way she loved. Her body stung where he had struck her, with bruises blooming and fading by the time she got back to her room.

She knew it had been a temporary win, and that he was going to try again. She welcomed that, glad for the chance to rub his face in it. But she did not know who he was or why he was in the city, she only knew that he had something to do with the King, and he saw her as a threat. They had been closely matched at hand to hand and she knew he would only underestimate her once.

"Sasha, I have to tell you something," she called out as she entered her room, still smiling and buzzing from the fight. There came no response.

Curiously, she turned back and made her way around the hall to the girl's room. There was silence for only a moment before someone started screaming.

She did not realise she was the one screaming until the guards burst into the room. Their hands were on her, dragging her back from the doorway, yelling for more guards while they tried to quiet her.

Sasha lay in a pool of blood on her bed, her throat slit from ear to ear. She did not appear to have been harmed any other way. She had been staged, her arms stretched out at shoulder height, her feet together, and her dress spread out around her, the fabric smoothed. The killer had even put her little cap back on her head.

Her scream continued as the guards pulled her from the suite.

She did not resist, allowing the tall man to turn her towards him, his hand against the back of her head to comfort her.

Sasha was dead and had been for quite some time. The smell of decaying flesh flowed out into the hall with them. The human had been her friend and companion, someone she had been able to rely on. She had been so incredibly kind that she had started to shift the way Etani saw humans. She was so sweet, so small, and now, she was so very dead.

Finally falling silent, Etani sat down on the bench with the guard at her side. His hand clenched on hers as men moved around her. Her eyes locked on the carpet and watched the feet.

She did not flinch as the King arrived and then the Prince. She remained silent, watching the floor as tears streaked her cheeks.

The guard let go of her and the Lich's fingers curled around her upper arm, pulling her to her feet.

Looking up, she saw the King was watching them with narrowed eyes, making the connection of who she was and why she was there.

Epharis half-dragged her along, his robes billowing around her. His grip released only to wrap his arm around her shoulders, and she found that the long sleeve was oddly comforting, shielding her from the gawkers.

They entered a room that was packed with books and scrolls. She obediently sat down when he pushed on her shoulder. She remained still, unable to see anything, but the terrified, pain-filled face of the first friend she had ever made.

The Lich shoved a drink into her hands, and she held it limply, the liquid in danger of spilling out onto her lap but the Lich placed two fingers on the underside of the cup and lifted it. She drank the strange-smelling liquid. It was only after her eyes started to droop that she realised he had drugged her with a sleeping aid. With a gentle pressure on her shoulder, he pushed her down onto the couch and before her head hit the cushions, she fell into a deep sleep.

12

THE FAMILY SECRET

*W*hen she woke, the sun had risen, and she found herself wrapped tightly in a heavy blanket. She was still on the couch, her head resting on a cushion she did not recall being there when she fell asleep. Across from her on the opposite couch sat the Lich, his head bowed over his steepled fingers, his fingertips resting against his forehead and his elbows on his knees.

"I forgot how slow your heart beats," he said almost too quietly for her to hear. "It took a long time for the drug to clear your system." He was not looking at her, instead, he appeared to be watching the floor. She felt confused, groggy, and unable to really focus on him.

"I don't understand," she mumbled, her tongue sticking to the roof of her mouth.

Looking down, she noticed that her skin had dried and tiny cracks had opened in the joints. She must have been out for days if her host was cracking already.

He did not reply; instead, he stood and crossed the room to fetch her a mug of water. She took it from him eagerly, gulping down the liquid. When she finished it, he refilled it.

She did not much like that he seemed to be able to read her mind, but she let it go for the moment, trying to get her sluggish brain to start working again.

"What happened to Sasha?" she asked finally. She kept her eyes lowered as she flexed her fingers to get the cracks to stick back together.

"She was murdered by an unknown entity. Whomever it was appeared to have killed her out of spite," he said dispassionately.

The bottom dropped out of her stomach. She might have been able to save Sasha had she been there, but she had been out socialising and playing around with the grey man.

"Had you been there you would have been lying dead alongside her," he snapped, glaring down at her.

She could only shake her head, sipping the last of her water from the mug. She set it in her lap. She could have protected Sasha. She knew it.

"Whoever this was, they were an assassin. Powerful both magically and physically. The stench of magic was all over that room, and it was not your magic. It was similar but tasted different."

She did not know magic had a taste, the thought almost made her laugh. Perhaps she was delirious.

"Rest for now, you are safe in here. No one can enter these rooms without my presence. Not even my brother or the guards."

Lifting her eyes from the mug, she took in the room. After a moment, she realised that he had brought her to his own suite. It was packed with books, everywhere. On every available surface, in towers and piles, on chairs, and she was alarmed to see that he had even stacked them inside the empty hearth.

His suite was the same as hers though bigger and it did not appear to have a room for a servant. His bedroom door was open, and she shivered at the sight of his bed, not entirely comfortable with that. He had threatened to make her his Lich bride. Besides, did Lich sleep?

"Whoever is after you knows where you live, so, for now, you will stay here. There is no arguing on that matter. You are too valuable," he said, cutting off her attempted protest.

He did not wait for an answer. He left the room and shut the door firmly behind him. She was left alone in the fire hazard that was his room.

She did not like the idea of someone being after her. Someone had been after her for the last nine centuries, but she hoped it was not him. She really did not want to think he was that close.

How long had she been in Ayathian? She thought it had to be close to a month. That was plenty of time for him to track her down. But would he be bold enough to attack her inside the castle? She did not know, but she did not want to find out.

THE HOURS TRICKLED by in Epharis's absence. After she had refilled the mug three more times, she felt somewhat better, enough that she moved slowly around the room, examining the books and picking one of them up. She had it upside-down at first, but she quickly realised that and turned it up the right way, looking over the strange plant on the page. It looked like a waterlily leaf, but the words made no sense to her.

Setting the book down, she continued her examination, but boredom was getting the best of her, so she started to build.

Stacking the books around the couch in piles of matching type, she successfully set the last book down on the roof of her little house and wriggled inside. With a faint smile, she held a large book on her lap.

Epharis finally deemed her worthy of his presence. He came and stood for a long time staring at the book house she had built. He watched her fingers trace over the illustration, but she could not figure out what it was. It was some sort of device with a glass cylinder and a large amount of wood for the frame, but she could not make heads or tails of it.

"What do you think you are doing?" he asked, sounding shocked. "Reading," she said sheepishly, glancing up only enough to see

his legs through the doorway.

He did not speak at first. He crossed the room to her, snatched the book from her lap, and turned it on its head. The device was a tank of some sort. She felt the blush creep up her cheeks, but refused to look up.

"You can't read," he said flatly. No judgement, no condescension, just a statement of fact.

She did not reply, looking down at the page with the hope that if she stared down at the words for long enough, they might simply divulge their secrets. They did not.

With a sigh, the Lich picked up a quill and parchment, swept the books off a small table, and placed the paper and quill on the surface. When she did not hear a crash, she looked at the books and found that they were simply hanging in the air, floating in the exact height of the table he had swept them from.

She stared at them for so long that he coughed to get her attention. She looked back at him, eyes wide. He had written a long string of letters on the page. First, she looked down at the black, spiky looking characters, and then up at him.

"This is the alphabet," he said curtly, taking on a lecturing tone. His hands clasped behind his back and when she looked back down at the letters, he gave a long-suffering sigh and turned the page around so that the letters were at the top of the page. "We will begin with this. Follow after me."

And so, began her long and exceptionally painful lessons in reading the common language.

It was a lot harder than she had realised and she found it was easier to speak it than it was to read it, especially given the words seemed to change meaning when coupled with other words. She had never realised that the two were spelt the same way, though spoken entirely differently. Not only that, but each new generation of humans seemed to add to the collection, and that made it even harder to keep up with.

But the lessons did help her with her grief, and that seemed to be his main purpose for teaching her. Not to educate her but to distract her, and if he caught her with tears in her eyes, he shoved a book at her and demanded that she read the first chapter by a predetermined time or he would use the book to hit her on the head.

For weeks they remained in the room. He drilled her on how to spell words, and when he was satisfied, he graduated her to full texts. The weeks turned into months, and then into even more of them.

He seemed quite pleased with her progress, and she was glad for her newfound ability, perhaps even a little grateful for his efforts though she was not going to tell him that.

Whenever she grew hungry, he had food brought in. He would watch her clinically as she killed the men and women. The one time he brought in a child, his eyes watched her, wide in fascination.

She reacted violently when she saw the little boy, perhaps nine or ten, and very dirty. One glance at the boy was all it took for her to launch herself backwards as though she had been bitten. She crammed her body in between the hearth and a bookshelf to ensure the boy could not so much as see her. Her reaction had Epharis scrambling to kick the boy back out of the room. He had said nothing about the incident. It was the one and only time he had brought in a child, and she never offered him an explanation for her behaviour.

It was an unspoken law for her people, not to kill children. It was taboo in the extreme. It was not done, ever. If you were found to have killed a child, then you would be immediately executed by the first mythical to get their hands on you. It did not matter how dire the circumstances or how close to death you were. You did not kill an innocent child. There were supposed to be no side effects to killing a child; it was like any other soul. But the mythicals were weird when it came to children. They revered them and they all knew why, though no one mentioned it. It did not matter the species of the child, they were never, ever to be touched.

After Epharis decided she was competent enough, he moved her on to experimenting by following the instructions in the books. That was when she started to get nervous.

He had given her a large supply of tools and ingredients, all of them stored in the spare room that had been empty up until that point She skimmed through the pages to find one that she thought looked interesting. It was the same potion he had given her to help her sleep. She set to work.

It was not hard, though she occasionally had to ask him for clarification on a word she did not recognise. In the end, she felt the potion had turned out quite well. So much so that Epharis offered to consume it himself, and when she offered it to him, he drank it without question.

It was two days before he woke up. When she saw him jerk upright from where she had dragged him into the sitting room, she laughed at his confused, angry expression.

"A bit strong for you, Lich?" she taunted. She ducked as he pelted a book at her, something he had done to her on many occasions. He had a tendency to throw things at her if she made a mistake. It was a very effective means of stopping her from making the mistake again, especially after the first time a book had smacked into the side of her head causing her to drop acid on her legs.

It had taken over an hour for the muscles, tissue, and part of her kneecap to regrow. She had not spoken to him for a week after that.

BY THE TIME he allowed her to leave, she had lost track of time passing. She was at first confused by the people in the castle who were wrapped up in thick furs and heavy coats. That struck her as odd, but it was not until she passed a window and saw that the world had turned white that she made the connection. It was winter, and that meant at least three months had passed since Sasha had died. She was entranced by the little spots of white that fell from the heavy clouds above.

She had never seen anything like it though she had heard that the world turned white with winters in the south. She was so captivated by it that the low voice took her by surprise.

"Beautiful, isn't it?" he said gently, standing a good foot back from her in case he startled her, and she attacked him. She could not tear her eyes off the moving world outside the window, but she had caught the scent of Drow and she recognised the voice.

"What is it?" she asked, leaning so close to the glass that her nose nearly touched it.

"Come and see," he said evasively.

Turning away from the window, she followed him out of the castle. The world was surprisingly cold and yet it was not unpleasant. Stepping out of the castle doors, the air was starkly different, and she had to wonder if the castle had been enchanted to keep the interior warm.

Lifting her hands, she watched the tiny spots landing on her skin and melting away, leaving a tinted spot of moisture on her skin. It was ice, falling from the sky.

"They call it snow. It happens when it starts to get cold," Izziah said gently. She could feel his eyes on her, watching her as she stretched out her arms and smiled at the little pats on her skin. "Have you never been this far south before?"

Shaking her head slightly, she blinked as a shower of white flakes fell from her hair, dusting her skin and clothing in white that quickly turned to water.

"We did not have this in Faerie, nor in the north where I lived." She had spoken without really thinking of the words, but he was not surprised. Most of her kind were born in Faerie or had at least lived there for a time.

"You were born in Faerie?" he asked casually, but she thought it sounded forced.

"I was. My family were outcasts," she said to cover up her slip. The snow felt like kisses on her skin and the chill was delightful, waking up her senses and her body at the same time.

"Etani, I know who you are. You do not need to lie to me."

His words hit her like a physical blow and she dropped her hands, turning to look at him slowly.

"Who I am?" she asked. "I am nobody Izziah." It was mostly the truth; she had been a nobody for her entire life. At least, she was nobody important to a man like him. To her people, she was simply a problem that needed to be dealt with. To the Prince, she was a valuable tool, and she was just another half-breed to the Winter Court. To Alaric, she was a valuable collectable that had slipped through his fingers, but she could not fathom what value she might have to Izziah.

"Etani, you're a Princess of the Winter Court," he said. It took her several long seconds simply to take in his words.

"What?" she said, her manners forgotten, and she almost laughed, that was utterly absurd. All of the Princesses of Winter were in Winter, they did not leave the place.

She half-smiled, but at his flat expression, the smile melted away like the snow on her skin.

"Your father Lutheral, he was the Prince of the Winter Court, the only child born to the Queen. He could not rule because he's male, but you are his child and you're female. You're in line for the throne." Her head was beginning to spin, and she shook it slowly. He picked every word carefully, making sure she did not miss a single one. "The Court doesn't know you exist, he never told them. But if they find out who you are, they will take you back."

How did he know her father's name? How could he possibly know any of that?

"How do you know his name?" she demanded, defensive and growing angry at this horrible, cruel game he was playing with her life.

"IT WAS NOT ALL that hard to find if you knew what you were looking for. A Fae Lord who decided to dilute the species without permission? No, that was so rare as to be almost laughable, the Fae don't procreate outside the species unless it's to ensure there is no loss of magic or risk of inbreeding. There had been a rumour though, the Prince who was said to leave the palace for long periods at a time without leaving Faerie. It was assumed he had fallen for a Summer woman and was off with her. But he made a mistake and had made an enquiry as to the validity of a half-breed daughter taking the throne. How he could protect her from being eaten alive by the Court. How he could protect her from his mother. The Queen never believed the rumours, she believes all men to be liars and inconsequential outside their ability to bring more female Fae into the world. She did not ever believe or even acknowledge that he would be so stupid as to displease her by breeding with another species." Izziah could see her anger and disbelief. Her cheeks flushing as she considered the consequences of ripping him apart. He swallowed hard. "There was a portrait found in his rooms. A white-haired woman with grey eyes, and two girls with midnight black hair. Twins, one with vivid green eyes, and the other with blue."

Her legs gave out, and she plopped down into the snow on her backside, her head spinning. He rushed to her, but she shoved him away when he attempted to comfort her. This was impossible. It was a lie. How could he possibly know? How could he know any of that? Her father's name? What her mother looked like? That Letari had green eyes?

She felt like she was going to vomit as she tried to process it all. How was it possible that she...? The Princesses were the most valuable, precious commodities to the Courts. They were beyond valuable. They were the survival of the Court. If there was no Queen, the Court would die, and the human world would die with it. Everything would simply end. There had to be a Queen in all four Courts, there was no question about it. So how was it possible that they would allow a single one of those precious creatures to escape? They wouldn't. There was no way the Queen would ignore the rumours that her only son had produced a female child. There was no way she would ignore the possibility of a direct descendant. Would she?

She was breathing hard, hyperventilating. Her fingers had gone numb, her mind reeling as she recalled a memory of her father.

He was so handsome and strong, with vivid blue eyes and a huge smile that showed off tiny little sharp canines. Pale with a shock of black hair that was wild around him.

"Now Etani, you need to remember who you are, my little Princess. You're everything to me, you're everything to all of us," he had told her, but she had only been five and had not understood. He had told her what she was. She had just thought he was being playful, being the adoring man that he was.

Izziah pulled her to her feet and helped her back inside. Her body trembled as she tried to come to terms with this information, tried to come to terms with how much danger she was in.

"You can't tell anyone, Izziah," she said as the shock began to wear off and the realisation of the threat sank in. Reaching for him, she grasped the front of his jacket, staring up into his bright silver eyes. "Not your brother, not anyone. No one can know this; you must destroy all of the information you have. They can never know of me; the King must never find out."

He nodded quickly, seeing the panic in her eyes.

Should she kill him? That seemed like the best option. But no, it would draw too much attention to him and then to her. She could not have more eyes on her. Besides, she liked him, he seemed to like her, and she thought that he would likely be useful in the future.

"I will say nothing to anyone," he breathed, his face close to hers.

"Thrice," she said as her fingers slipped into his hand, her gaze a challenge.

He knew she was demanding his silence, that if he promised it three times that he would be physically incapable of sharing the information, and she refused to let go of him.

He met her eyes, and she saw the fear. He knew what it meant. Even if he was not a member of the Fae, she could bind him just as effectively as if he was one. His wrist twisted as he clenched his fingers around her hand in a grip that was almost painful.

"I will not speak of this," he whispered three times, his eyes locked on hers.

A warmth spread through her, starting where their hands touched and creeping up her arm until it filled her body. The promise was there. It was sealed, and he would never be able to break it. She could release him from it but she wouldn't, and they both knew it. Letting go of him, her fingers tingled, but she ignored it.

"Thank you, Izziah," she breathed, confused for a moment when he did not let go of her. Instead, he shifted his grip until their fingers were linked together.

"Anything for you," he murmured. She saw his desire to give her the title she deserved, but his tongue refused to form the word. His smile turned wistful, but then he released her.

13

CORPSES AND KINGS

*S*he had been about to turn away from him when a thought struck her, a low hissing whisper of a word that had her frowning.

"Epharis knows," she said finally, making the connection between that day months ago, when the Drow wanted to speak to her, and Epharis called her Princess. He had known... He knew that whole time she was in his suite and had not said a word.

"How could he possibly know?" the Drow demanded.

"He watches me. He might be watching you also. He called me Princess that day in the hall."

The Drow looked concerned, but they knew there was nothing that could be done about it. The Lich would not be so quick to bind his tongue as Izziah had.

"He won't say anything, it would be too much of a risk," he said finally, taking several long moments to think over the situation.

"You suppose so?" She sounded a little desperate, clinging to this tiny shred of hope. She could not just up and leave like she normally would have done. She was trapped in the situation.

"He values you; he made an effort to ensure you could not escape him. He would not make that effort for just any creature. Even more so now, knowing who you are. You are precious and valuable. He won't risk the King trying to take control. He will do whatever it takes to ensure the King never finds out."

It took her a moment to process his words, and finally, she nodded her agreement. He was right, Epharis would not want anything to happen to his prize. The Lich would protect her secret better than anyone.

"You're right," she said finally, noting the slight fading of his eyes at the confirmation. She did not understand it, but he seemed less than happy at her words.

Glancing in the direction of the throne room, she bit her lip and considered what to do. She had planned to return to her suites, but the stabbing reminder of what had transpired there gave her pause. She did not want to live in those rooms anymore, but was not sure where else she could go.

"Etani, I do not feel it is entirely safe for you here in the castle," Izziah said after she lingered a beat too long.

"I am able to defend myself, Izziah," she responded, a little hotter than she had intended. She was more than capable of defending herself.

"You cannot watch your own back, you need protection." He seemed to regret it the moment he said it. Anger flashed in her eyes, and she took a step back from him.

Without a word, she stalked away from him and towards the throne room. Hearing him follow, she ignored his attempts to apologise and swept into the hall.

The King's golden eyes found her instantly. She made no move to show she had noticed, instead she shook the Drow off and allowed herself to be lost in the crowd. Joining in on a conversation with a group of young women, she was able to pass the time in peace.

She was not stupid enough to try to leave, though. The King, the Drow, and who knew who else were all trying to catch her eye, and she knew they would be eager to try to speak to her. She ignored them all. The one time she glanced up at the King, she thought he looked impatient, but she did not feel that it was for her. The reason for his impatience made itself apparent within the hour.

· · ·

TRUMPETS BLARED, and a man came striding into the room. He was puffed up with great self-importance and strutted his way across the hall. A path was quickly made as the Courtiers shuffled back.

"King Alaric, I greet you on behalf of the Weorene Empire. I have come to offer gifts to ensure our continued allegiance in these troubled times." The man wore a rich red doublet with a white sash across the chest. His scabbard was empty, and Etani assumed the sword had been forced to remain outside the throne room or even the castle itself. His pants were dark brown, and he wore knee-high riding boots. Grey hair was expertly quaffed, and his chest was thrust out. He looked like a red, old peacock, and she struggled to hold in a giggle.

All eyes in the room turned to Alaric to see what he would do. Many people seemed to be having the same difficulties she was having in trying to keep a straight face.

"Welcome, emissary of the Weorene Empire. We thank you for your generous offer of gifts on behalf of the Weoreneian people."

Was it just her, or did the King have an oddly hungry look in his eyes? Glancing around her, she saw nothing concerning.

A great gasp filled the room as six men marched in with an enormous gold plate filled with an even bigger pile of gold, jewels, and precious gems. It was impressive, but that was not all. Following behind the plate was a parade of strange and exotic animals. There was a bird with gold and red plumage, the sharp beak had an odd golden colour. The tip of its tail was engulphed in flames.

She gasped along with those who could see it: a unicorn. The poor beast was tethered with a golden bridle. Tears unconsciously welled in Etani's eyes at the sight of such a radiant creature bound and treated like some common mare. Behind the unicorn followed a beast with the body of a lion, and the front legs, head and wings of a great eagle. A string of colourful fairies in jars hung on a stick between two imps.

Indignation filled her at the sight of the fairies, but she made no move to free them; what could she do when her mind kept telling her to keep her head down?

On and on the line went, the creatures getting stranger by the second until the last, a real-life dragon. It was small, a baby by the looks of it, but people were still quick to press back from it.

A muzzle tied its mouth shut, and its wings were bound to its body. The poor thing crawled along behind the giant man who led it.

The entire show was repulsive. Etani could see the disgust on the faces of the mythical beings in the crowd, though the humans were thrilled. She had been about to step forward when a large carriage came into the Hall. It was made of gold, encrusted with gems and silver decorations. The sight of it was so incredibly odd she paused. There was a carriage inside the throne room of the castle, drawn by two snowy white horses.

What stepped out of the carriage was even more bizarre. It was a woman. Her face was veiled, and she wore a long ivory and cream dress. Approaching the King, she dropped into a deep curtsy before him, bowing her head.

"Presenting the Princess Nayishma, daughter of Emperor Varsas. The King wishes that in order to maintain peace, the Princess remain present in the city of Ayathian."

The woman had not moved from her curtsy, almost prostrate before the might of the King.

This surprised the King; he had not expected to be facing one of Varsas's daughters. And what was worse, the creature would be staying long term.

"How generous of Emperor Varsas to offer his daughter in such a manner," Alaric said after a pause.

Etani could see he was attempting to contain his rage. Thankfully he was keeping it under control.

The Princess stood slowly, her chin lifted. No shred of her appearance was visible to anyone in the room.

"We graciously accept these gifts," the King said through gritted teeth.

The emissary did not stay long after that, preferring to escape while he had the chance and declining a dinner invite. This seemed wise to Etani. The Princess accepted with a nod of her head, not a word spoken.

The strangeness of the Princess intrigued her to no end and the need to meet this girl itched at her mind. She could not figure out why it would nag at her, but the need was there. The easiest way was to get herself invited to the dinner. With that goal in mind, she set herself in a position closer to the throne for the remainder of the day. The Princess had brought three older ladies with her for company, and they hung around her like a miasma, making it impossible for anyone to get near to her. But Etani was patient, and she was too curious to give up her chance to meet the strange, foreign Princess.

JOINING in on the conversation near the front of the hall the King was most likely to exit by, she made as though she were there by chance, her eyes meeting those of the King as he moved to leave the room. Acting as though it had been accidental, she immediately looked away again, pretending to not want his attention. He decided he was going to give it to her, whether she wanted it or not. Approaching the small group, he loomed over them all. The women curtsied, the men bowed, and Etani remained upright, staring at him with a defiant set to her jaw. Her defiance seemed to amuse him more than anything.

"Would you do me the honours of joining my party for dinner, kind Lady?" the giant man said. She thought she registered a note of mockery in his voice. They both knew it would not be easy for her to refuse given the sheer number of people who had heard the offer. Clenching her jaw in feigned anger, she nodded once.

"It would be an honour, Your Majesty," she responded in that high voice she had adopted for the host.

"Excellent," was all he said before he departed the hall. People bowed as he passed, whether he acknowledged them or not.

The group tittered at the scene and Etani headed out of the hall, inwardly pleased at her success.

Making her way back in the direction of her old suite, she found the door had been barred off.

"Lady Etani, your rooms are now in the East wing. Please allow me to take you there," a guard offered. She glanced at him, confused, and a little worried.

Accepting his offer, she followed after him. She had never heard of the East wing before, but she soon realised where he was leading her. Back in the direction of Epharis's rooms.

Much to her disgust, her rooms were right next to his. After thanking the guard, she headed for the Prince's door and gave it a hearty kick with the ball of her foot.

The door swung open and there stood the Lich, looking mildly annoyed at the interruption. His expression changed to one of smug amusement at the sight of her.

"It is one thing to protect me, it is quite another to ensure I am right at your side at all times."

The Lich gave a slight shrug and stepped out of his room. He grasped her by the arm and pulled her along towards her own set of rooms. He thrust open the door and almost threw her inside, following in behind her.

"It is only fitting that I keep my little Faerie Princess safe," he said in a sarcastic voice, speaking again before she could snarl at him. "These rooms have the same protection as my own. Coupled with the increased number of guards this wing possesses, you will be safe."

Gritting her teeth in frustration, she knew she could not argue with that logic.

"I am not your Faerie Princess, Lich," she spat at him, tugging her arm free and looking about the room. It was then she realised there was another figure across the room, and she froze. Sasha stood there, grey skin and eyes white with death.

The colour drained from her face and she staggered backwards into Epharis's chest. His fingers curled around her upper arms and he leant down to speak directly into her ear.

"Do not for a second forget what I am, Princess. I tolerate you because you are useful; the moment that is no longer the case, I will turn you. Or I will give you to my brother. I know how badly he wants you, and it's not as part of his collection of freaks anymore... He wants other things from you." His suggestive tone told her what he meant, and his lips were cold on her ear, his jaw firm against her head. His grip tightened for an instant before loosening again. "You will be mine, dead, or his."

With that the Lich released his hold and left the room, the door slamming shut behind him with a sound of terrible finality. She knew then, with a terrible certainty, that she was never going to escape him. Any attempt to escape would be pointless. He would never let her go.

She had forgotten about the dinner, forgotten about the King and the news of her heritage. All she knew now was that Sasha was standing there, or rather her corpse was standing there. Her throat had been neatly sewn shut, her body cleaned and dressed in a tidy uniform and apron.

It was her hat that tipped Etani over the edge, however. It was slightly askew, and it was known to have been a quirk of the girl when she had been alive. The corpse had dressed herself.

Etani's screams and sobbing lasted hours. Unable to enter the room, she curled herself into a tight ball in the furthest corner away from Sasha. The corpse did not move, it only stood in perfect silence, oblivious to the suffering of her former friend.

THIS TIME no guard came to save her, no King or Prince was there to rescue her, no Drow to pull her away. She was alone with the corpse, and it was fracturing her mind.

She did not know what she was going to do, she could not think clearly, she could not breathe or move. Her legs were clutched tightly to her chest. She had made herself as small as was physically possible.

Finally, she began to calm down, her screaming stopped, and her crying eased. She started to think again, cataloguing her situation and what she needed to do to survive this world of monsters.

Slowly, with the precision of someone snuffing out a candle, she began to snuff out her emotions. Her sorrow, her pain, her loss, her loneliness. One by one she shut herself down until all that remained was the slow burning hatred and cold determination. If what the Prince wanted was a heartless creature to do his bidding, then he had succeeded.

Slowly she pushed herself to her feet and crossed the room, heading into the bathroom to bathe. The corpse followed. She ignored it. It picked up the clothes she dropped to the side; it arranged a towel. She pretended it did not exist, just like with any other servant.

Finally, she shed her host body, and left it floating in the bottom of the filled bath. Then she finished her routine.

She wore no glamour and the ethereal creature that stood before her was said to be appealing. She did not see it.

Her eyes were slightly too large and were the colour of those shockingly blue butterflies. They started out ice blue in the middle and darkened to midnight blue at the outer edges. The colours blended, and they were incredible to look at, but did she find them pretty? No, her sister's moss green eyes were much nicer.

She had an oval face with a small, pointed chin and alabaster white skin, sharp and defined cheekbones, a small nose, and dark mulberry-coloured, full lips. Long, tapered ears and naturally defined brows, and full lashes that seemed to touch her cheeks when she closed her eyes.

Her body was not proportionate; her breasts were a size too big for her delicate frame and her nipples were small and dark pink, her hips slightly too wide and her waist was narrow, giving her an odd shape that she had known women to try to mimic with corsets. Small shoulders, slender arms with a hint of muscles, small hands with long, slender fingers. Each one was tipped with a metallic silver nail.

Her collarbones were defined, her ribs only just visible, and her stomach flat. Her backside was annoyingly round, and she had toned thighs and long legs that ended in small feet with those same silver nails. Her skin was smooth, with only a tiny smattering of freckles and her waist-length straight black hair shone blue if it caught the light in just the right way.

In all, she had been called beautiful and exotic, enchanting, or whatever else they tried to tell her, but she only saw a freak. No glamour, no host, no illusion, just her. She hated the sight of herself, and she could see the contempt on her face in the mirror, her eyes dragging down the form and picking it apart, noting all the things that were wrong and disgusting.

Why did it feel so odd to be naked in this world? It was as if the air rubbed her skin the wrong way.

Turning away from the mirror, she found herself a simple, plain black dress. Was it the one she had worn on her first day in Court?

Perhaps it was. She did not know, nor did she care to remember.

She needed a break. She needed an escape. She locked the corpse thing out as she headed into the bedroom. She crawled onto the bed, collapsed onto it, and gave herself over to sleep.

When she woke, she did not feel any better. She dragged herself back out of the bed, her mind working sluggishly as though she had been drugged again. But she did not think that had been the case; she was simply drained. She was beaten down, and she had to work to keep herself from hurting.

What she really needed in that moment was to get out of the castle, to be alone for a time, and to think. She knew there to be gardens nearby, she could smell the flowers from the balcony window of her old rooms. The thought made her heart lift just a tiny bit.

14

THE PRINCESS OF WINTER

*S*kirting around the corpse to stay as far away from it as possible, she slipped out of her room and pulled the door shut. She did not want to see the thing anymore, knowing she had let her friend down by not being able to protect her.

She found four guards in the hall. They were all watching her curiously, given a redhead had gone into the room the night before and now a brunette was leaving it. Oh, the rumours were going to be glorious.

"Get rid of it," she said flatly. The guard looked confused at first before starting forward with a curious expression.

Shaking her head, she tried to orientate herself. She started down the hall, her mind on the gardens but she did not make it past the door to the Lich's room. He pulled the door open and swept out, looking remarkably like a vulture in his sweeping black robes.

"What is that stench of Faerie magi-" he broke off as he caught sight of her, blinking hard for a moment, and then clenched his jaw. He was not angry; he was trying to control his sadistic glee. She could feel it radiating off him in waves.

"Your Highness," she said after a moment. Her voice low and husky, belonging to a lover who whispered in your ear as you lay in bed, hungry for more sinful pleasures. It was a voice that promised all of the darkest, most depraved pleasures a person could offer. It was not intentional. She could not control that purring sexuality that seemed to ooze out whenever she spoke. It was annoying because people thought she was flirting when she was not.

"Princess, how delightful it is to finally see you," he said slowly. He knew something in her had changed, and now he had to be wary of her. At least when she had felt fear, he was mostly safe. Now she would kill him simply because she could, her own life be damned.

"Join me for a stroll in the gardens?" she asked, polite as you please.

The man seemed to be contemplating the question as though it were some great philosophical dilemma. Why would she have invited him out into the gardens? What was her plan? Was she going to kill him? No, she did not really intend to do anything to him, but he did not need to know that.

"I would be delighted," he said finally, deciding on something she could only guess at.

Accepting his arm, she linked hers with his and allowed him to guide their way.

People stared openly; they couldn't not stare. The Lich was arm in arm with this strange, riveting creature that many of them would never have seen before. The other half would know immediately what she was.

"Is it still snowing?" she asked politely. The curtains in that corridor had not been opened yet.

"I believe it is, yes." While their questions seemed calm and relaxed, internally they both seethed. She was seriously contemplating the deal she had made with him and the curse he had placed on her, weighing it against her own immortality. Would the curse keep her from being able to be reborn, or would it vanish with the death of this current life? Was she willing to risk it?

For the time being, the answer was no, and that was enough for her to let the thought of killing him in the gardens pass.

Apparently, the Lich had other plans for their little stroll, for instead of leading her outside, he tugged her in the direction of the hall.

"This is not the path we agreed upon," she said as he pulled her unresisting towards the archway.

"We will go for that walk, but for right now I want to see his face."

The Lich sounded horribly gleeful and their appearance caused the stir she knew he had been hoping for. Thankfully for them, the Court was a lot emptier than usual. Most Courtiers did not wake until noon. Those that saw her fell silent, causing their companions to do the same. The group nearby looked around at the abrupt change in noise. The wave of silence started at the back near the doors and reached the throne after two breaths.

The King had been occupied, finally looking up only once the room had fallen completely still.

She had to admit, his reaction was rather enjoyable.

First, she felt his gaze on her. She knew his pupils would shrink to the size of a pinhead. He sucked in a deep breath to fill his lungs as though he might get a hint of her perfume or the scent of her hair. His face reddened and his jaw fell slack. His eyes raked down her form, retreating from her hips and up to her arm, curled snugly around the arm of his brother. His jaw clenched and lightning flashed in his eyes. He knew who she was. He knew she had tricked him in his rooms. He was livid.

To make matters worse, Epharis extended his free hand and turned her jaw. Cupping the curve of her jaw with his fingers, he lifted her head just enough and leant down, planting a firm, cold kiss upon her forehead.

An odd crunching sound came from the hall, making everyone in the room jump. The King had crushed the wooden arms of his throne beneath his enormous hands.

Finally, the Lich took his grand finale and stepped forward. He bowed low to the King, his hand still possessively on Etani's arm as he drew her forward two steps.

"Your Majesty, might I introduce the Princess Etani of the Winter Court."

Her heart stopped beating and her mind went blank while the room exploded with voices, cries of shock and alarm. No one could remember ever seeing a Fae, let alone a Princess of Faerie.

This was bad... This was so incredibly, ludicrously bad. The son of a bitch had outed her in front of at least twenty people, and to the one person she did not want to know. And the Lich was loving it. It was a game to him, playing with them all like some great chess set, moving her around and waiting to see what would happen. Then he would laugh and laugh like it was all nothing.

She would not make a scene; rather she gave her very best curtsy to the throne where the King sat visibly shaken, his expression one of abject horror.

"I have graciously agreed to introduce the Princess to our beautiful gardens and humbly ask that you please pardon our rapid departure." Without waiting for a response, Epharis pulled her from the doorway and out into the gardens.

She was patient enough to wait until the guards were well out of earshot before she turned on him. In an instant she grabbed him and slammed him up against a wall, her nails at his throat. Feeling the slight pressure at her waist, she glanced down to see he had a knife against her, one made out of a dark grey metal that sang with the promise of pain. At a stalemate, she pressed herself against him, pinning him to the wall.

"What are you playing at, Lich? Why would you tell him?" Her voice was a low hiss, her anger showing through her calm facade. "Every Fae within a hundred miles looking to make a name for himself will go running to the Court with this information."

"You will be hard-pressed to find a Fae in that range, my dear girl. And I cannot fully keep you safe on my own. Now you have the undivided attention of the King, there isn't so much as a bug that would dare bite your pretty skin for fear of what he would do to it. I have given you the best protection in either world. I do not do things on a whim."

Staring into his dead eyes, she pondered his words, unable to deny he had some points.

"You have taken an enormous risk, and for what? To keep your pet alive?"

"Think, Etani. The King is obligated to protect you, to treat you well. He can do nothing to you for fear of retaliation from the Court. He cannot pursue you, cannot hurt you, and he will see to it that you are given everything you could possibly need." His voice was low, threatening. The knife had cut through the fabric of her dress, a small stream of smoke coming from its feather light contact with her bare skin.

"What I need is my freedom. I cannot evade these people when I am forced to remain in one place," she said finally, her grip on him loosening him just enough that he withdrew the knife a fraction of an inch.

"You do not need to evade them when you are under the protection of the most dangerous man in this world."

"The most dangerous man in your world is a child when compared to the most dangerous men of my world, Lich. You have signed my death warrant." Shoving him hard into the wall, she backed away from him. Still, she was not stupid enough to take her eyes off him when he had that iron blade.

"I have ensured that no one will ever find you again," he said after a moment. He dabbed at blood that streaked his skin, the result of her nails.

"And how is that?" she snapped, wiping her bloodied fingertips on her dress.

"The city is bound. If the King demands an order of silence, no one will be able to speak a single word of your existence outside of it." Cleaning his own fingers off on his robe, his eyes lingered on her fingers for a moment in contemplation.

"And of course, he will want something in order to give that order."

The lich looked up into her face and blinked, momentarily blinded by her.

"Of course, but we will get it."

"We wouldn't have needed it if you had kept your damned mouth shut," she snapped, turning away from him.

"Lovers quarrel?" A voice called from the distance and both Etani and the lich turned to see who had spoken. It was the Grey Man; he was stalking towards them in the snow. She could not help but notice that the man walked on top of the snow, leaving not a single footprint.

"Mind your own, ghost," the lich barked, irritated at the interruption.

"Now, now. I haven't been formally introduced to the Princess." There was a definite sneer in his voice and once he had closed the distance to the pair, his hand thrust out for hers.

"How's the face?" she asked dryly, accepting his hand and allowing her own to be touched only briefly by what she realised was fabric, not lips.

"Healed fine, you have quite the kick," he said in an equally dry tone.

Even in the brightness of the snow reflection, his hood hid his face, but she pieced it together. He used fabric and illusion to keep the hood dark regardless of the light.

"And you have quite the right hook."

The lich seemed to be stumped by the conversation, his teeth clenched in anger. Reaching for her, he snatched her hand from the gloved grip of the Grey Man and wrapped it protectively around his own arm, possessive.

"Now that you have been introduced, please kindly excuse us." He gave her a tug in the direction of the path, and she followed, her eyes lingering on the compact man.

"That's no way to treat a Lady, Your Highness," the man called out, clearly laughing without uttering a sound.

The lich made no response; instead he tugged her along the path until they had rounded the corner.

The last she saw of the man, he had turned to the wall of the castle and was staring at the spot she had pinned the Lich, his chest expanding as he inhaled.

"Who is that?" she finally asked after a time.

"Aelen, given the name of The Ghost. He is Alaric's pet assassin," he said finally, deciding not to ignore her question. The implied 'just as you are mine' hung between them.

"Interesting, he is not human," she said after a moment of thought.

"No, he is an elf of some sort. He keeps his hood up at all times, but was forced to reveal his face during my brother's method of control. He requires your face to be visible as well as a lock of hair. With those, he can ensure you obey him."

Blinking once, she compared that to the far more effective method the lich had used. But perhaps the King was not so skilled in magical manipulation.

"The Ghost. Who came up with that?" she asked.

"Lady Catherine, the werewolf bitch my brother keeps. She said he swooped around the castle like a ghost in that grey outfit of his. It stuck."

Letting out a low breath, she nodded. She could see why that would be the case, given his knowledge of the castle's hidden inner layer and his ability to pop up at any moment.

"Why is he so interested in me?" she asked after several moments of thoughtful silence.

"Those my brother has him hunt are never human. He is scoping you, looking for a weakness for when Alaric decides you are no longer useful. It wouldn't be the first time my brother has had one of our kind assassinated because they no longer mattered to him and they knew too much."

Coming to a slow stop at a bench, she withdrew her arm and crossed to a small, frozen rose bush. She had spotted something. Feeling the lich watching her, she bent down to part the leaves and found a small, perfectly blue flower.

Carefully, she pinched it from the base and turned. Without a word, she approached the lich as he sat down, tucking the flower behind his ear.

She did not know why she did it, only that the cold, frozen thing seemed to match him so perfectly. Brushing back his long, lank silver hair, she found that his ears were pointed, very similar to those of an elf. Taking note of that, she stood calmly between his knees and tucked the flower in place, pressing it down gently to catch the stem in his hair. His eyes had been locked on her face the entire time. Neither of them spoke.

Smoothing down his hair, she cocked her head to the side to examine her handiwork. Adjusting a lock of hair on his shoulder, she gave one nod and moved away from him, only to be stopped by his hand catching her wrist. Glancing back at him, she met his burning gaze with her own. Silent words passed between them, ones of hatred and want, of distrust and yet total, complete trust.

She could not help but wonder if the man had ever had someone like her in his world. She doubted it, and yet she did not feel sorry for him. He had brought it on himself, he had earned his title.

With his hand light on her wrist, he lifted her arm. To her shock, he pressed the palm of her hand against his cheek, feeling the slow beat of her heart against his jaw.

Neither of them moved for several minutes, the Lich listening, while she stood frozen before she finally relaxed. Her thumb ever so gently caressed his cheekbone.

She understood him, they were one and the same. Yet she knew his feelings for her were generated by control and dominance. She did not try to pull away from him, but rather granted him that small shred of comfort that she doubted he had felt for centuries.

Sometime later the protesting screech of a gate made them jerk apart, his fingers releasing hers as though stung. Without a word, the two moved apart and headed back in the direction of the main doors.

IT WAS several days later when she finally heard from the King. She had, half expecting him to demand a meeting with her on that first day of her introduction, but it was nearly a week before he came.

He did not come quietly either. The boom of his knock on the front door of her suite made her jump.

She had been sitting comfortably on a little day bed beside the open door to the balcony, her eyes lowered to a book on reptilian anatomy. She had noticed a marked increase in the reptilian species heading through the city, making their way north in order to escape the cold, and she had been curious about them.

Naga, lizard creatures she had never seen before, dragons, and it was even rumoured that an enormous turtle had been seen in the ocean. All heading for warmer weather and stopping in only to collect more supplies or offer news from further south.

From what she knew of the continent, there was not a whole lot further south, only swampland and a small city that no one wanted to go near. Ayathian was as far south as most people would ever venture.

The boom came again, the door quivering under the strain of the blows that came in threes, mere seconds apart.

When she did not open it fast enough, she got an odd sense of warning. She threw herself into the bathroom, just in time for the door to be summarily kicked down, taking part of the wall with it.

Rubble rained down, the door slammed into the wall that she had just hidden behind, and dust filled the air.

"Where are you?" the King bellowed into the room.

Peeking around the door, she saw the man was glowing with anger, lightning crackled around him, and his eyes found her in an instant.

He moved in a flash, lunging across the room, and making a grab for her head.

Scrambling backwards, deeper into the bathroom, she managed to escape his grip though only barely. Had the man grown bigger? His head nearly scraped the ceiling, and she was certain it was around ten feet high.

Hitting the counter with her back, she found herself unable to move any further back as the man leaned down to peer at her from under the doorway.

What on earth could she have possibly done to earn this level of fury? She did not know. She had been so quiet and patient, not making a stir and remaining in her rooms.

The man's face vanished as he stood, his fingers appearing a moment later on the top frame of the door. He was going to rip it off.

"Your Majesty, stop!" she yelled, watching as cracks appeared in the wood, the wall screaming its pain. "Please stop!"

Slowly, the man's head came into view and he glared at her, reaching in with reflexes no one his size should have. Grabbing her leg, he yanked her from the room and into the main room of the suite.

Her voice rang out in a scream as she felt the bones break under his grip, but he did not loosen it.

He lifted her up, and she hung from one leg before him, her entire world suddenly upside down.

Inwardly glad she had decided to wear pants and not a dress, she tried to right her thoughts even as she dangled there. Her foot brushed the ceiling as he lifted her higher, yet her long hair still touched the floor below her.

"Who do you think you are?" he bellowed. Normally the raised voice wouldn't have bothered her that much, but the man had semi-transformed. The voice made her eardrums vibrate and caused her face to screw up in pain. There was no denying the man was, indeed, half titan.

Reaching up behind her with both hands, she gripped the handle of two long blades she had stashed in sheaths that ran crossed against her lower back. Holding them tight, she heaved herself up and used the knives to cut the tendons in his arm.

His fingers released her instantly, and she hit the ground hard on her back. Breath gone from her, she rolled and flung herself back up onto her feet.

He roared at her, but they both knew full well the git would heal in a matter of seconds.

His blood was hot and smelled strongly of copper, filling the room with a heady scent that made her mouth water.

Backing away from him, she slid her right foot back, her arms moving into a defensive posture as she leant forward, ready for another attack. It came, and the man was blinded by fury as he tried to grab her torso.

Her blades flashed; silvery metal turned red as she quite simply lopped off his middle finger from the first knuckle.

Again, he bellowed and swiped. Her body was airborne, flung sideways and crashing into a wall.

Plaster crumbled down around her as she attempted to catch her breath, looking up in time to see his hand.

15

NO HONOUR AMONG ASSASSINS

She cursed him, his fingers curled around her head. This time when he lifted her, she felt certain he was simply going to rip it from her body. He lifted her off the ground, her neck on fire.

Stabbing both knives up into the side of his hand, she knew she would miss the tendons, but it was worth the effort.

Unable to breathe with his palm crushing her face, she ripped the knives out and stabbed again and again. His ring finger released, tendon cut, and she was able to gasp in a breath and scream for him to stop.

"Brother!" a voice bellowed from the hall. Everything tilted horribly sideways as the titan was thrown off balance. He released her, and she crashed to the ground. She spun to see that the titan was missing a good chunk of the back of his knee. The lich had hacked it off with a long black sword she had never seen before. She made for the Lich only to find the titan's hand coming for her again.

She crouched and sprung up into the air and somersaulted over his grasping hand, landing on an uneven piece of plaster on her barely healed leg. She stumbled into the Lich who caught her. In the next breath, the world went black.

Air crushed from her lungs, the grip around her shoulders and back was so tight she thought the titan had them both in his grip. But a second later, the world lightened. The air was bitterly cold. The Lich released her. She staggered back from him and fell onto her backside in the snow.

Gasping for air, her eyes were wild as she looked around her, unable to place where she was. Behind her, a good few hours march, was the city of Ayathian.

"How?" she gasped. Her lungs were reluctant to expand.

Without a response, he was on her and before she could react, he had punched her in the chest.

Skidding back in the snow, she remained on her back but was suddenly able to suck in a full breath of sweet air. Wheezing slightly, she stared up at the cold blue sky, unwilling to get up. The snow was soft, the sky was pretty, and she was hurting. Maybe she would just stay there for a few minutes... hours... maybe she would think about getting up tomorrow.

Her view of the sky was broken after a moment by the livid face of the Lich. Why was he so angry at her? She had only been defending herself!

"Can you breathe?" he asked, restrained fury tinging his tone.

She nodded her response, sucking in air through her teeth while her body attempted to heal whatever damage his punch had caused, along with the damage from the fight.

"The living should not be taken in such a way; their lungs do not usually expand again. That is why I punched you. I ruptured your lungs and forced them to heal."

She gave another nod, knowing full well she would have told him to stick his explanation up his arse had she been able to. But her lungs were inflating again, and she was able to breathe normally.

Accepting his arm, she pulled herself up onto her feet and without asking, used his shoulder as a means of support as she leant forward, wheezing.

"What... was... that...?" She managed to speak between noisy exhales.

"I think he's a bit upset you refused his invitations to dinner," the man said, sarcasm oozing from his tone.

"What?" she asked again, lifting her head enough to see his face. His jaw was set, his eyes on the city in the distance.

"I was blocking his invitations, then his demands," he said with only a hint of guilt. "I assumed he would be told it was me and not you."

Rolling her eyes, she pulled herself straight and stepped away from him, her hands prodding experimentally at her chest.

"You are... by far the most... dysfunctional family I have ever heard of..." she said finally.

The Lich gave a snort and picked a piece of plaster out of her hair. "So, he threw a tantrum? Because of you...?" she said finally, at last able to breathe normally.

"Basically," the lich said after a pause. He began to laugh and, unable to help it, she began to laugh as well. The entire situation had been impossibly ridiculous. The man was a child who threw a tantrum when he did not get what he wanted.

"We will head back, by the time we return he will have calmed down."

"Or ripped apart half the castle. Why did you bring us out here?" She lingered only long enough to use the snow to clean off her hands, leaving it crimson.

"I will admit that the place was not a priority at the time. I only thought to get you out before he ripped your head off your shoulders."

"I'll admit, I had thought he was going to do that also," she said, hurrying to catch up with the lich as he started towards the city.

BY THE TIME they reached the city, the sun had sunk low on the horizon and the pair were glad to be out of the snow. Some of it had been deep enough to reach their middles, but finally they made it back. The city was subdued, seeming oppressed by the low clouds and heavy snowfall.

She noticed the Lich slowed down as they moved, and she slowed her pace as well, wondering at it. Perhaps the cold affected him after extended periods? She did not consider it prudent to point out his weakness, but she catalogued it for future use.

Once they reached the castle, the Lich burst in through the doors and headed for the throne room. It was deserted, aside from the King, who had clearly been waiting for them.

"You took longer than expected," the man said slowly, his control over his physical appearance back in check, and his voice no longer a booming that made her ears vibrate.

"I see you have gotten your temper back under control," Epharis retorted, crossing the room with Etani following along a few steps behind him.

Alaric's eyes fell on her and his jaw clenched.

"I was the one rejecting your attempts to meet with the Princess. She is still under my protection," Epharis cut in, stepping to partially block her from his angry glare.

"Did you know of her rank?" the King asked, his fury turning on Epharis.

"Not until recently."

"How did you figure it out? Why would she hide this?" They were speaking about her as though she was not even there, and it irked her.

"I have my ways, brother. She did not know herself until I told her," Epharis lied smoothly, leaving out how Izziah had been the one to find out the information.

She had no idea why he would lie about it, but she decided it was best to let the lie stand.

"I see. I have a right to meet with all royalty who set foot in my castle. You will cease this attempt to block her." Seemingly calm now, she felt more confident to step out from behind Epharis and look at the King. She was surprised to see just how angry he looked, his jaw set. She knew he was protective of her, but for him to go so far out of his way to keep her from his brother's attention had her more than a little curious.

"If that is what you wish brother," Epharis said with a deep bow, as though all the King ever had to do was ask.

Turning, he swept from the room and left her alone with the King.

Feeling suddenly abandoned, she looked to the King, who seemed just as surprised.

Glancing around the room, she realized then why he had agreed to this, but not a dinner. They were not alone in the Hall. Guards were stationed around the room. In a dinner, she would be entirely alone with him.

Crossing the room, she decided to play nice and curtsied before the

King, though it was somewhat ruined by the fact that she wore pants rather than a dress. To compensate, she lifted her right hand to cover her heart in a fist, bowing her head.

"Your Majesty," she said calmly, schooling her face to one of complete calm. She might be running mostly on a lack of emotions now, but there was still a strong sense of self-preservation, forcing her to be ever wary of the man before her.

"Your Highness," the man retorted, almost chewing on the words as they came out. The air was thick with anger and distrust, but she remained calm.

"I find it interesting that you did not know of your heritage," he said finally, weighing his options of what to do with her.

"As I am sure you can imagine, it was a shock." Perhaps she was being a little flippant, but the entire situation was ridiculous.

"Why did your father not tell you, or your mother?" he asked.

"My father was killed when I was but five, and my mother two years later. They did not have time enough to tell me." Though she could vaguely recall her father calling her his little Princess. She had not thought anything of it except that her often gone father was giving her his attention and she was revelling in it like the attention seeking little monster she had been at the time.

"Is that right...?" Doubt coloured his words, but she merely shrugged her response, having nothing more to offer him. She had spoken the truth. "As a member of a royal family, I am obligated to offer you my protection. As my guest, you are obligated to adhere to the laws of my Kingdoms. You will keep the rooms Prince Epharis has set out for you. However, the protections will be removed. You will join me whenever it is asked of you."

Eyebrows lifting, she could not help but smile at the man, darkly amused.

"I am the property of Prince Epharis. His law supersedes the laws of your Kingdom. I obey him." Not entirely true, she obeyed when it suited her, but he did not need to know that.

Fingers clenching on the arms of his throne, he thought carefully. "We have two options here, Princess. Either you can obey me, or I will ensure that your people know exactly which room in which to find you," he said simply.

The threat hung between them, thickening the air until it was hard to breathe.

"You will not stop until you have what you want. You are a child, a little boy who wants the toys of all the boys around him, who throws a tantrum when he cannot have them, and will break them to ensure they cannot be played with by anyone else." Her voice was low and calm even though she was angry at him for trying to threaten her.

Standing, he stepped down from the dais and approached her; the approach appeared non-threatening, but she knew better. She was ready for him this time.

"My brother will not be able to protect you forever, little Winter Princess. When that day comes, I will be there to take control." His voice was a low growl, making sure the guards were unable to hear from their posts.

"I will die before I allow you to control me," she said just as low, her chin lifted in defiance.

"That remains to be seen. Death will not save you."

His hand lifted, and he grasped her jaw gently, directing her face first left and then right.

"I vaguely recall you once mentioning my not having a wife, Princess. Perhaps we can have that rectified. Before you were but a commoner, but now?" He leered at her, eyes raking down her form in a manner that made her flesh crawl.

"I will not be the one to die if you make that attempt." Horrified, she began shuffling through her knowledge of laws surrounding such things. Was it possible for him to do that? To force her into marriage? It was not unprecedented, especially when a Kingdom had been conquered. She had no Kingdom to conquer, that meant she was vulnerable.

The amusement in his eyes confirmed her suspicion, and she slapped his hand away as hot fingers trailed down the delicate lines of her throat.

"I am not yours to marry off to any man, King. If you have not forgotten, I am not yours to command." She could not hide that hint of panic, the sudden, terrible fear that yes, yes, he could. Just because she was not directly under his control did not mean he could not claim her as a political prisoner.

Swallowing hard, she stepped back from him, unable to tear her eyes away from that sadistic grin on his face. She was in trouble. She needed help.

"I'm afraid you are, Princess. You were in my command from the moment you stepped foot on my lands."

A flash of movement dropped down on her right. She lunged away from it, missing the swing of a knife by a mere inch.

Spinning, she lifted her arms in defence as her attacker came at her again. The grey man, the King's royal assassin, had come for her. The knife sliced along her forearms, pain ripping through her body as white wisps of smoke rose up from the cuts. She bit down a scream of pain as the iron seared her flesh.

Throwing herself backwards, she parried another slash from the knife, using her bleeding arms to shove his thrust upwards and to the right, deflecting the blow.

"No lich here to protect you this time," the Grey Man purred, delighted at the chance to take her on again after what she had done to him in the hall.

She did not make a reply, but rather aimed a side kick to his ribs as he rebounded from a second failed attempt to stab her in the chest. She did not think he was out to kill her, only severely wound her.

Desperately, she tried to figure out what to do in that situation. Turning, she bolted across the room away from both King and assassin, only to be barred by one of the guards. They were in on it too.

Aiming a kick right between his legs where she knew he would be less protected, she snatched his spear from his hands as he fell, spinning and lifting the spear in time to use it in another block.

He shoved her back into the wall. Her head thumped against the stone and her vision spun horribly. She was prepared, even with the nauseating movements of the room. Spinning the spear, she flicked the point up as the assassin came at her, scoring him across the chest, but allowing him to capture the spear in his free hand. Holding it out and away, he slammed into her and the blade of the knife sunk into her shoulder.

SCREAMING IN PAIN, she adopted the same method on the assassin that she had used on the guard, bringing her knee up between his legs.

His now empty hand dropped to deflect most of the force, but he still staggered back from her, clutching himself. Remaining in the middle of the room, King Alaric merely watched the fight, amused.

Ripping the blade from her shoulder, she went after the assassin, taking advantage of his moment of weakness.

Using her off hand, she threw the knife at him, point first. The knife missed him by an inch as he twisted to avoid it, but she was on top of him before he could balance again. Using her weight, she crashed into him and he fell with her on top of him. Straddling him, she forced the shaft of the spear against his neck to press down, crushing his windpipe.

He was not idle, his fingers curling in her loose hair and yanking her head to the side. Falling off him with a gasp of pain, she found it was now him on top of her.

Aiming a punch for his throat, her knuckles connected, and he fell. Twisting her hips, she managed to knock him off her and she stood, delivering a solid kick into his ribs. She was certainly not above kicking a man while he was down.

The guards were not above cheating either, for she had not heard the guard sneaking up behind her. The spear whipped around, catching her just below her navel. The guard gripped the other end, leaning back and heaving. Effectively holding her in place, she wriggled and squirmed in his hold, her nails screaming against the metal of his armoured stomach.

Pinned to his chest, she watched the assassin stand, his arm covering his bruised ribs as he came for her again.

Prepared, she lifted her leg and planted her foot in the middle of the assassin's chest, both thrusting him back and forcing the guard off balance, tipping him over backwards.

Falling with him, she used the momentum to somersault backwards off the guard and back onto her feet, panting softly and backing away from the men.

Lost in her surroundings for an instant, she placed the King a few yards to her left, the guard and assassin directly in front of her. Six more guards were stationed around the room, but they looked more content to simply watch the show.

"Slippery little snake, aren't you...?" Ghost said, his hood askew and posture hunched.

Not deigning to give him a response, she tried to place where the knife or spear had landed, but could see neither out of her peripheral vision. Daring to flick a glance to her right, she spotted the spear and lunged for it, sweeping it off the ground and spinning in time to see the guard barrelling down on her.

Having only a split second, she spun the spear and drove the point into a join in the marble, using it to pole vault over the man and land crouched on his other side, searching for the assassin.

He was nowhere to be seen. Cursing, she turned. The guard backed off her, panting hard in his heavy armour.

Damn, where had that monster of an elf gotten off to?

She did not hear him coming up behind her, and felt only the faintest brush of fingers against the middle her back. Everything went black.

16
———

IRON BLOOD AND A MONSTER

*W*hen she awoke, there was a buzzing in her ears, irritating her more than anything. Rolling her neck, she attempted to rub her ear with her shoulder, only to find that her head was strapped down and it was not going anywhere.

Trying to push herself up, she found she had been bound at multiple points to a chair. Every finger, her wrists, elbows, and upper arms were all tied down. There was a strap across her chest and stomach, and across each thigh and calf. A strap across her neck and one across her forehead, all keeping her unable to see what was restraining her. She could only feel where the pressure pushed against her skin.

"Damn this city, and everyone in it," she growled. She attempted to bend her fingers enough to start carving into the wood of the chair, but her fingers had been tied down at the second knuckle, leaving her unable to flex them enough.

"Now that's not very nice," a low voice said from somewhere behind her. Turning her head as much as she was able, she tried to see who it was and where she was being held.

Before her there was nothing but a blank, nondescript stone wall. Above her, a blank nondescript stone ceiling. Left, and right?

Same thing. The floor was made of wood planks, so it was not as boring as the rest of the room, but there was not much to keep her interest.

"Who are you and what do you want?" she asked, straining at the bonds that held her.

"My name is Aelen. I am called The Ghost around here." The voice held that same thick accent, but it was not what she expected. It was smooth and light like honey yet had dark, sensual undertones that she found oddly tantalising. He stepped around her holding an oddly shaped lantern, and she could finally see him.

He was definitely an elf of the high or dark variety. His hair was jet black and hung thick and straight to his lower back. His eyes were a deep blue she had never seen before. His skin was the colour of inner tree bark, soft and warm. His ears were long, pointed like her own. The clothing he wore left nothing to the imagination. The black fabric was so tight it appeared to be painted on, and she could see every single muscle, including very pleasant abs. His pants were also black, and tight. They clung to his legs, giving her a good view of how toned his thigh muscles were.

He also wore black knee-high boots and a single gauntlet on his left hand that was made of some strange black metal. The finger guards were sharp like talons, each joint individual, pointed and dangerous-looking.

The lantern he held put out a light that was pure white, nothing like the warm yellows a normal lantern emitted. It was a thin cylinder with an elaborate dragon wrapped around it, yet the metallic dragon did not seem to block the glow at all.

Watching him place the lantern on the ground, she pondered what was going on.

"So, Princess. I am sure you have heard of what I do for the crown. I am, however, not here to kill you tonight. I am here to perform the same ceremony on you that is performed on all of those under the service of the King." He sounded so completely calm and matter of fact, as though this was entirely normal.

"I'd prefer it if you did not," she replied, borrowing from his calm.

The man's lips flicked up into the shadow of a smile before he caught it and gave her a flat, emotionless stare.

"I'm afraid you have no say in the matter. King Alaric has decided that you are too much of a risk, and given your allegiance is to the Lich Prince Epharis, the King has decided that taking things into his own hands is necessary. You are too much of a threat." He spoke with a touch of bitterness, leaving her to think those were not the words Alaric had used.

"I am not a threat to the crown. My allegiance is to the Prince, and the Prince is under the crown." She knew trying to reason with him was pointless, but she had to try.

"Prince Epharis is a man unto his own. He has loyalties to the King only because he chooses to right now. If the Prince were to leave, or try to take the throne, you would follow his lead. You would likely kill the King." As he spoke, the elf crouched down and laid out a small leather roll of tools which he withdrew from a pocket on his thigh. He carefully released the ties and unrolled it to reveal a long row of needles, bottles, and other tools of the trade.

She had never thought of the Prince leaving before. She had always seen Epharis and Alaric as inseparable, brothers and royalty. The Lich and the titan God King. But as she thought of it, she realised the lich was there only because it was convenient, or entertaining for him and if it was no longer that, he would leave without a word, pulling his assassin Princess along behind him. And she would go, there was no question of that. Her loyalty was to him, not this place. Her loyalty was to him only because he made it that way and he would ensure it stayed that way until he no longer needed her.

PICKING UP A SMALL SYRINGE, the elf turned a bottle upside down and stuck the needle into it, pulling the plunger and sucking a healthy dose of the substance into the barrel. He set it to the side, preparing a second syringe and placing it beside the first.

"What did you do to me, during the fight?" she asked finally, a morbid curiosity growing in her about what that first syringe contained.

"A simple spell that knocked you out for a few hours. You are a far better fighter than I gave you credit for. It only required three taps on your skin to work, and thanks to the guard, I was given that chance. Without him I might have had to turn to other alternatives."

"What is this ceremony going to entail, and what will happen after?"

He was kneeling beside her now, using a scrap of gauze soaked in alcohol to rub at the corner of each elbow, his brows knitting as he attempted to find a vein.

"The ceremony requires we take your blood and hair. It will be stored somewhere secret by the King. Should you attempt to leave without his permission, he will throw them into a fire, say the magic word, and kill you. If you have been given permission to leave, you may destroy them at your own discretion." She was surprised at how informative the man was. He worked carefully to ensure that he did his job without harming her in a way outside of what was demanded of him.

"What's the first syringe for?" she asked, watching as best as she could.

"Given your ability to heal at an unprecedented rate, I have deemed it necessary to dose you with diluted liquid iron to ensure the blood does not clot until I have a large enough sample."

Cold flooded her system, and she jerked, straining back from him.

The chair groaned under her.

"I am sorry, but it was the only way. We will ensure you are returned to Epharis for treatment after." He ignored her attempts to struggle for freedom, tying her left arm with a tourniquet until her fingers began to thrum with her heartbeat.

"Please, don't do this... please," she whimpered, fear flooding her system.

He ignored her, pretending he had not heard her. Moving to her right side, he picked up the iron-filled syringe and methodically slid it into her skin and into the vein below. It stung a little, but it was not terrible. Then he began to push down on the plunger.

Her entire arm felt as though it had been thrust into fire, the vein immediately turned purple and then black, the colour moving down and up her arm with each beat of her heart until it reached her fingers and shoulders. Her nails turned from silver to black, the base an unpleasant purple colour that darkened her fingertips. At her shoulder, the black branched out, headed across her chest, up her neck and down under the neckline of her clothing.

She was gasping now, trying desperately to fight through it but it was growing more intense. She was certain her arm would burst into flames, but it did not. As the blackness crept up her neck, her jaw clenched, and she felt a crack as the tightness of her jaw cracked one of her teeth. Tears had started to fall as the black reached around her elbow, staining her cheeks and dripping onto her chest. Her vision went black, then returned with a bloody red tone to the world. Her ears began to scream in a high-pitched tone. Blood began to dribble down her upper lip, following the curve to her jaw. Circles of darkness formed around her eyes, so dark that she could see them, bruised and ugly. Her other ear joined in the squealing as its twin and her legs went numb. By the time it reached her heart, she was screaming, unable to stop. She had no idea what the elf was doing. She had never felt the prick of the needle or the tug on her hair. She could feel nothing but a burning flame that seemed to intensify with each pump of her heart.

Finally, it reached her brain and her whole body convulsed. The wood under her palms splintered. Her hands reflexively balled into fists until her nails dug into her own skin making it bleed freely. Her ability to heal was gone.

Her screaming had been blood-curdling, but the silence that followed was worse. She was no longer able to scream, the muscles in her throat had stopped working. Every muscle had locked up, turning her to stone. Inside her head, a mad cackle started as she was crushed under the weight of the pain. Her primal self took her chance.

SHE AWOKE in a bed that smelled strongly of Epharis and she inhaled sharply, breathing him in.

She scanned the room, but he was not there. She was a little annoyed he was not there to see her wake. Crossing the room, she pushed the door open and strolled into the sitting room to find him sitting there with a pile of books around him.

"Epharis..." The tone of her voice, slow and seductive, made him look up. Instantly he knew something was wrong, his face going guarded.

"Etani, I am surprised you can stand," he said slowly. Her lips pulled up into a savage grin.

"Don't worry about me, little Lich. I'm just fine." Her voice was wrong, her tone off and without another word, she headed straight out the door. She had a bone to pick with two men.

The Lich followed after her, curious and wary in equal measures.

She did not so much as pause as she headed in the direction of the throne room, stealing a sword and a knife along the way from guards who were barely conscious at that hour of the night.

The room was empty, not surprising, but she turned and headed in the direction she knew the royal suites to be.

Walking towards the door, she quickly cut down both guards, blood splashing over her. Without pause, she lifted her right foot and slammed her heel down on the door, just above the handle.

The door opened with a bang and she strolled in, the maniacal, feral grin still on her face.

The King jumped to his feet and turned to see the bloodied, manic Fae in his doorway. Her nightdress was blowing in the wind. The lich followed several steps behind her.

She stalked into the room and headed straight for the King. The King stood his ground, ready to defend himself.

"Give it back, Kingling," she said as she approached him, her blades held aloft.

"Etani, you are unwell," he said warily, backing across the room towards his sword.

She cocked her head like a sparrow, her eyes wide and her mouth pulled into a grin that would give him nightmares for years.

"Last chance, little King, give it back now or die." The King hit something on the wall, sidling away from the weapons, even as she bore down on him.

"It is for security, Etani," he reasoned.

But she was no longer interested, she could hear racing footsteps, and she turned in time to see the elf come running into the room.

Screaming her fury, she turned on him. As one knife slid between his ribs, she turned and threw him out of the closed balcony doors.

Her head tilted back, and she turned, looking at the King upside down.

"I'll be back for you momentarily. Don't go anywhere," she crooned.

Ignoring Epharis, she crossed over the broken glass of the doors and took a running leap off the balcony.

Her hair and dress billowed out behind, and her furious scream filled the air as she fell, feet first towards the body of the elf below.

He was not dead, seeing her and rolling suddenly to the right. Landing hard, her knees flexed and absorbed the impact. The recoil gave her momentum she needed to launch herself at the assassin. Using the sword, she hacked at him, swinging wildly. Again and again she swung. The elf dodged and parried her frenzied attacks as best he could, using only his arms and hands.

His kicks to her body went unnoticed, his punches nothing but touches on her skin.

She was going to hack him to pieces. Then she was going to do the same to the King, and retake what was hers.

Eyes black as sin, she swung and stabbed at him until she was able to run him through.

Panting hard, she pinned him to the side of the castle, her forearm pressed against his throat, her bloodied face inches from his. "Payback. You stick something in me... I stick something in you." With that last word, she drove the sword through his stomach with enough force that it stuck in the wall of the castle behind him.

Her rapid-fire, frenzied attack had beaten him. Blood escaped his mouth in a flood as he coughed.

Crooning at his side, she licked up the side of his face, growling happily before she turned and walked away from him, leaving him to die. Tilting her head up to the balcony where Alaric and Epharis stood, she grinned at them and headed back into the castle for round two with the titan God King.

By the time she reached him, he was ready for her. Epharis stood off to the side, watching her as though she were back in the dungeon with him again.

"What's the matter, lich, want to join in on the fun?" she leered at him, his face remaining impassive.

Turning her attention to Alaric, she leant down and picked up two large shards of glass, clenching them so tight her fingers bled.

"I asked nicely, so I am no longer going to be nice." That was her only warning before she went for him. She only made it two paces before a hand on her arm stopped her.

The Lich curled his other arm up around her shoulder and pressed two fingers gently against her chest. Her entire body went rigid and locked into place. That maniacal grin, those wide, empty black eyes, all locked with greedy intent on the King.

"Epharis?" Alaric asked, lowering the sword he had been raising to defend himself.

"Alaric, this is not the Etani I know. Give me a chance to reason with her," the lich said, his arm remaining over her as though he was protecting her.

Alaric glared at his brother, uncertain of whether or not this was some kind of game. The lich could never be trusted fully.

"You have three minutes," he said finally.

Stepping around her frozen body, he leant forward until he was whispering in her ear.

"Etani, I know you're in there. While this state fascinates me, you are not allowed to fight Alaric. He might not seem like much now, but he can obliterate you. I know what threats he made, and I will not allow him to force you into an arranged marriage, especially not to him. If you return now, he might give you leniency. You must come back, I demand it." He spoke so fast she could barely keep up, yet every word sunk in through the fog of anger and primitive instinct.

Turning her eyes to meet his, she knew he would be unable to tell where she was looking, given her eyes had no pupil, iris or sclera. Only bottomless blackness that glittered gently in the candlelight.

Why should she fight? She did not want to fight. She was in pain and so incredibly tired, it was easier to simply give in and let this numb side of her endure the agony of the iron coursing through her system.

Yet that last order, she felt it tugging at her, forcing the primitive her down. She did not even struggle this time, her primitive mind understanding the alpha, the dominant in their dynamic.

The blackness bled from her eyes and as the magic hold on her eased, she collapsed forward into his arms. She tried so hard not to scream, and instead bit her tongue.

"Epharis," she gasped in a tiny voice. His arms tightened around her protectively, clutching her to him.

"If you ever poison her with iron again, brother, I will kill you," he said, curling his arms around the back of her knees and hoisting her up into his arms.

Clutching the front of his shirt, she clung to him. She shuddered with each beat of her heart. Another tooth cracked under the strain of her clenched jaw. Her fingers contracted in the fabric of Epharis's robes, tearing them, and still the brothers stared each other down.

"If there is no need, I will not have to do so again," Alaric said finally, acquiescing only a fraction.

Epharis nodded, turning to leave.

"You should get someone to fetch your little assassin. I'm sure he's getting bored down there." With that, Epharis carried the suffering woman from the room and back to his own.

Setting her down on the bed, he made quick work of setting up a device she had never seen before. It had two empty canisters, a lot of tubes, and a little rubber pump. Unplugging one of the canisters, he allowed the tube to dangle down into a bucket and he gripped her arm, forcing it down from its position curled against her chest, absently trying to press the pain from her body.

Inserting a small needle into her arm, she watched as he began to squeeze the pump repeatedly, setting into a slow rhythm in time with her heartbeats which he felt by holding two fingers against her wrist.

Watching with a morbid fascination, Etani saw black-red blood move up the tube, drip into one of the canisters, and then drain out into the bucket.

"This may not work, but at least if you are unconscious from blood loss you will not feel so poorly. Your body should replenish the blood, though whether or not the iron has damaged your veins is unknown at this point." He spoke calmly, giving her something to focus on. "If it has damaged your organs beyond what your body can handle, you will die. But if we can siphon enough of the infected blood, the clean blood should trigger healing."

17

NEVER TRUST A DROW

*A*n hour passed and still he pumped, still he drew out her blood. The bucket had to be emptied twice. The blood in the second bucket seemed clearer, but her eyes were struggling to focus so she could not be sure.

At some point she began to sing, halting and low, under her breath. He did not speak any more, simply listened and worked as best as he could.

Another hour went by, and she wondered if his hand was tired. She wondered if a lich's hands could get tired. She did not really know, and she was left watching his fingers as they squeezed the little rubber thing that drew out her blood.

By the third hour, her blood flowed a rich crimson, and the lich finally stopped. Glancing up at her face, he was startled to see she had been staring at him. For over an hour she had been watching him, her cracked lips moving in a slow rhythm of a song that was barely audible.

He glanced down over her body; she knew she must be almost emaciated. The sheer amount of energy it had taken to rid her body of the poison and produce fresh blood had drained her. Yet she did not feel hungry, she only felt as though her brain were floating two feet above her head. She could not take her eyes off him.

He stood and headed out the door. She blinked hard as her body tried to pull her down towards sleep. He had been keeping her awake, and without him, she faded towards unconsciousness. It really was an unpleasant way to die. It was not quick or easy, and it was not elegant or brutal. It was just long and slow. It was by far her least favourite way to die.

Glancing down, she traced her fingers gently over her ribs, each one sharply visible against the fabric of her dress. Her hip bones looked odd, protruding from sunken flesh.

Her fingers looked like a skeleton's, and she saw that her nails were still black.

She could count out only four beats per minute, her lungs feeling like they had become weighted, not lifting enough to keep her alive. She was dying, she knew it. At least the Lich had made an effort to save her, even if her dying meant he was going to learn her secret.

A smell hit her like a slap to the face. She looked around, seeing first the Lich, and then the eyes of a young man.

The sight was confusing. The young man was pale, though she thought that was from fear. His warm, honey brown eyes were huge as he took in the scene.

The Lich did not speak, he only dragged the struggling man into the room. With one hand on the back of the man's head, the Lich forced him into a bow over her.

He was what smelt so incredibly good. He was all sunshine and life, rich and deliciously alive. Her mouth had begun to water, and she licked her lips, wanting him so badly.

A cool hand slid tenderly under the back of her head, lifting her gently while he forced the man down.

She had begun to growl, animalistic and hungry. The food was so close, but she was so weak she could not even lift herself to him.

He had begun to cry, his warm tears dripping onto her face. With a brutal shove, the Lich forced the man's mouth down onto hers.

She was not gentle with him. She ripped her way into him, and snatched that precious blue light from his being, not caring if she damaged it, not caring that she left fragments. She only cared that she got what she needed, and she devoured him mercilessly.

The Lich threw the limp corpse away, his eyes locked on her, as the energy of the man's life flooded into her. Her eyes slid shut.

Her next breath was sharp and sweet, her heart started to speed up until it was thudding steadily in her chest. Her body sang, and she knew what Epharis would see. Her body would fill in, muscle and tissue replenishing, leaving her healthier. She was still pale when her eyes opened again, still weak and tired, and too thin.

She was still so very hungry, and he was standing right there.

Reaching for Epharis, she dragged him down towards her, her lips tilting up as he moved. He did not realise what her intentions were, and he allowed her to draw him closer.

By the time he realised, it was too late. Her arms had locked around his neck, her face turned to his. He went rigid as her lips met his.

Immediately she felt the rebuttal, a wall of protection he placed around his essence. She tried first to poke at, and then clawed at it in anger. She wanted it, and she beat against the wall that blocked her from what would satiate her hunger.

Attempting to distract him from his concentration, her fingers trailed over his neck to his collarbone, feeling over his chest. It did not work.

His fingers curled in her hair and he pried her face away from his. Her arm tightened around his neck, attempting to both pull him back, yet he was stronger. Using one hand, he managed to pry her arm off him. He threw himself away from her, his back hitting the wall.

She remained lying on the bed but it wasn't long before her stomach roiled. She rolled onto her side and grabbed the recently empty bucket, vomiting into it. Her head seemed to recoil as though someone had stretched her brain out and then let go.

She had never in her life had someone capable of denying her.

The tendrils of herself that had reached into Epharis snapped off and recoiled into her own mind, causing it to spin and her stomach to heave.

What came out of her stomach was black and thick with the dark grey of the iron mixed in.

THE VOMITING CONTINUED for several minutes. Epharis remained a healthy distance from her as he attempted to put his thoughts back in order on what had happened.

He knew what she was capable of, and yet he had allowed himself to get close enough that she had been able to grab him. Had he not possessed such abilities as he did, he would be dead. She would have followed him, but he would have perished.

Slowly, he crossed the room to her. Keeping his distance, he stroked her hair.

Finally able to settle her stomach, she slid off the bed and crossed the room to a small basin to rinse her mouth and splash her face.

Gasping softly, she stood with her arms braced against the basin, breathing slowly.

She was ravenous, but she had to keep herself under control. What she had done with the lich had been desperate, but she was thinking now.

"Why is it, any time I am in this position, you bring me here?" she asked finally, her eyes focused on her nails. They were still black, her fingertips discoloured.

She had not rid her body of all the iron, but it was thanks to the lich that she had survived at all.

She knew she was valuable to him, but why was he intent on saving her life, and for what? What was his motivation?

Clicking her nail against the bowl, she straightened and turned to look at him over her shoulder.

"You needed help," he said simply, still standing beside the bed.

She remained silent, watching him for a time. It was hard for her to decide what he was. He was a Lich, but he was also gentle at times.

He was a monster at other times, cruel and sadistic. He was controlling and domineering, yet he gave her freedom she would not normally have expected. What did he want from her, really?

She was not going to press him any further, her mind whirling as she tried to process what was going on.

"Did the elf die?" she asked, having only vague thoughts of the elf being involved in some manner. She did not know why, or how he had been involved, but there was a sense that something had happened.

"No, he will live. Running an elf through is not often fatal," he spoke slowly as he came around the bed to her side.

Cupping her jaw, he lifted her head to examine her face better. "You still look ill." Pressing his thumb lightly under her eye, he stretched the skin to see how it rebounded. It seemed as though she was dehydrated.

"I'm lucky to be alive," she said slowly, the words hanging between them for a long time.

"Yes, well, let us get you someone to eat," he said, dismissing her words as though they were nothing. He was not about to let her thank him.

Clasping his arm around her thin shoulders, he pulled her towards the door and out into the hall.

Finding a meal that night was more of a challenge than she had found before, given the cold, and the news of an 'incident' at the castle. People decided it was better to hide in their homes.

As a result, the odd pair had been forced to head down into the docks; even many of the homeless had found a place to hide.

The man they found had been curious enough to follow the hooded pair into an alley. He was stunned into silence by the appearance of the inhuman woman. He did not put up a fight, but embraced her as an old friend, giving himself up to her as though that had been his intent all along.

She did not understand why, nor did she care. It was so odd, for his willing surrender had made him taste almost sweet.

Lowering his limp form to the ground, she bundled him up in his cloak and the two left, leaving his corpse there to be discovered later.

She felt better after that, the tips of her fingers were no longer discoloured, yet her nails remained blackened and felt oddly brittle.

Her skin had regained most of its colour, but she was still paler than ever. The dark circles around her eyes had eased, but had not vanished.

Her body filled out and her veins appeared to be their usual blue, but the site of the injection was blackened with a dark bruise that refused to leave. It was possible she would have to remove the arm, and had been saying as much to the lich when something moved ahead of them.

The sight of Izziah and Drizdan was quite a surprise.

"Princess!" Drizdan boomed as the two approached, Izziah followed along behind him as though he expected to be in trouble.

"Lord Drizdan, Lord Izziah. What brings you out on this fine night?" Etani asked, her attention switching between the two men, before finally settling on Izziah. He looked horrified at the sight of her, and then refused to meet her gaze.

"Just exploring the city, these places are so very fascinating. It is an honour as always, Prince Epharis." Drizdan had a silver tongue, and bowed deeply to the Prince, yet his eyes returned to Etani.

"Pleasure," Epharis responded, though his tone suggested it was anything but.

"What brings you both out this evening?"

Before she could respond, Epharis cut in, his eyes locked with loathing on Izziah.

"We are out here for the Princess to recover from her injuries. She was quite ill, you see. She nearly died." The level of anger and hatred that hung in the air after that statement was so thick you could almost cut it with a knife. Izziah seemed to have found a pebble on the road that was extremely interesting.

"Is that so? Well, I am glad to see you in such good health Princess," Drizdan said, his lips pulling back into a malicious grin. "My brother here was just telling me about a conversation he had on this same matter, with the elf."

Her confusion vanished like a soap bubble as it clicked. Izziah...? He had betrayed her. She was not the one that moved this time, but rather Epharis, thrusting Drizdan out of the way and grasping Izziah by the throat. The lich lifted the smaller Drow up, his feet dangling and kicking.

Etani tried to follow after and drag Epharis back, but she found a warm arm had slipped around her waist. Drizdan held her firmly against his chest, keeping her from intervening.

"Give me one reason why I shouldn't kill your worthless Drow self, right this instant," Epharis snarled, his eyes glowing a hypnotic green, emitting an unpleasant grey smoke.

Izziah could do nothing but choke, attempting to kick the lich, but he was unable to get in a solid blow.

"Let this happen," Drizdan whispered in her ear as she attempted to wriggle free of him. Then she fell still again, uncertain.

"I've always wanted a Drow remnant; you would make the perfect addition to my collection. Let Alaric have one brother, I'll take the other." Epharis seethed, the air around him crackled and the temperature dropped even further.

Etani spun around, driving her elbow into Drizdan's ribcage. She threw his arm off and ran to put herself between Epharis and the hanging Izziah.

"Epharis, stop! You can't, he belongs to Alaric!" she cried, tugging at his free arm. "Stop and think what will happen if you decide to kill him on something he said."

Epharis' attention turned down to her, their eyes locking. His teeth were bared in a feral snarl, ready to rip the man apart.

"Epharis, please, don't do this now. You can have your revenge later, but not here." She did not dare blink for fear that he would lose interest in her. His eyes turned from her eyes to her bruised arm and then back. The sounds behind her were terrible, the man was spluttering and choking as he tried to free himself from the grip of the lich.

"Fine," Epharis said finally and let go, leaving Izziah to fall into a heap on the ground, gasping for air.

Wrapping his arm around her, Epharis pulled her away from the Drow men. She glanced back over her shoulder at the two. It was such an odd sight. Izziah stared after her with an expression of abject shame. Drizdan's was one of pride and a deep, insatiable desire.

She shivered as she turned away, allowing herself to be ushered from the scene. Stopping at the gates to the castle, he turned on her and seethed.

"You knew perfectly well what he did, yet you stopped me? Are your feminine desires such that you would allow a traitor to be at your side?" he snarled.

Eyebrows raising, she absorbed that information. Did he think she spared Izziah because she desired him? Was he out of his mind? He was a Drow, and had betrayed her. She would not so much as consider him a prospective mate, let alone think of him as anything less than a traitor.

Anger flared in her, and she glared up at him. His expression one of surprise.

"I would no sooner take a Drow as a lover as a horse. Do not assume that my actions are ever derived from something so low as sexual desire," she snarled at him, furious that he would even consider her to be so weak.

He hesitated for a long moment before finally nodding.

"Very well, I will leave his punishment up to you," he said finally, turning away from her and heading inside.

She stood there, confused and uncertain. She was so angry and disappointed at the Drow that she was left unable to decide what to do. So she followed after the Lich and headed back to her rooms.

THE NEXT DAY, the lich revealed his lie. On a small slip of parchment was the name 'Izziahnordia'. He had ordered her to execute him.

Cursing him, she tried to come up with a strategy to get out of the order, but nothing she came up with seemed plausible. She did not deem it wise to approach the lich himself, nor to go to Alaric with the news, so she let it nag at her for days.

Even as she tried to ignore it, unwanted thoughts returned to her, and she began to grow paranoid. Had the lich himself ensured the words would return to her, in case she tried to back out? But she told herself she was worrying over nothing and gave herself time to fully recover.

A week had passed since the incident in the street and she had run out of excuses not to do her job. Finally setting out, she dressed herself and stood before the mirror to search her attire for any hint of something that might shine, or pull in a way that would make it difficult to move. She wore black pants and a black long sleeve top, covering her from neck to wrists and down to her toes. Her arms were covered from elbow to fingertips in soft leather gloves with the fingertips removed. This made it easier for her to pick locks. Inside the gloves were two long knives, her weapon of choice.

Her hair was braided back in a long coil that she tucked into the back of her hood. A mask covered the lower half of her face. A leather corset around her middle allowed her to hide a large number of knives on her person. She wore boots, only because it was more convenient for her. With weapon storage and soles that were soft to not make a sound, they were perfect for the job she had to do. Against her lower back she had a small pouch of several different concoctions she had developed. It contained several poisons and a smoke bomb. All she had to do was shatter it. Her belt held a small array of throwing knives, a pouch with a garrotte and a length of rope for scaling. A second rope hung from the balcony to her room, giving her easy access to the grounds below without having to pass through the castle.

Picking up a small vial from the counter before her, she sprinkled a splash over her clothes. It was designed to neutralise her scent to most beings. It was supposed to be effective on Drow, according to her books, but she had not tested it.

Every buckle and strap on her attire had been dulled down with black paint, her fingertips dipped in a dark dye to ensure the paleness of her skin did not show through.

She looked like an assassin, there was no denying it. Pulling her hood forward to cover her face better, she let out a low sigh and headed out onto the balcony.

Climbing over the railing, she made her way down the rope. Her gloves were a bit slippery at first, but the abrasiveness of the rope roughened them up.

She reached the bottom, and headed across the grounds and out into the city, her mind on the task at hand.

18

ASSASSINATION OF A TRAITOR

*I*t took her a good two hours to reach the residences of the Drow brothers, given she was moving slowly and carefully.

The residences themselves were huge in comparison to the rest of the city. The house backed up to the interior wall of the city, spanning at least a block on its own. The gardens were overgrown and wild with plants she had never seen before, and the buildings were low and dark with strangely sharp angles. She had to wonder if the brothers had them built themselves.

Using a rope attached to a small hook, she was able to climb over the wall that kept their home private. She dropped down in the weirdly springy grass. She hated the feel of it under her feet as she hurriedly crossed the garden, jumping over a path of stones and ducking behind a tree.

Thankfully there was not a full moon, but there was enough light for her to see without being seen.

She could see a candle flickering in one of the windows, but the rest of the residence was dark.

It was not one building, but a series of smaller buildings clustered together and linked by little stone pathways. She did not have a clue where either man would be.

Deciding to try to see what was going on in the room with the candle, she flitted her way around the garden, her eyes locked on the ground, her ears sharp.

She did not trust any of the strange plants and made an effort to avoid them, just in case. She stuck to the grass, and used the trees for cover.

Inching her way around, she was finally able to see inside. She hid behind one small building set off to the side. She was able to see most of what was happening in the curtain-less room.

Drizdan was staring off into nothing, his eyes unfocused as though he were thinking hard about something.

The man wore a black shirt that remained unbuttoned, his long black hair was unbound, and his dark skin shone in the candlelight, his sharp features giving him the look of a God.

Shaking her head at the sight of him, she turned and started along the wall in the opposite direction, trying to get a layout of the house.

That room was Drizdan's, so where was Izziah's?

She could not hear anything akin to snoring, and she silently cursed the man for being so considerate of his fellow sleepers. No, this would not be that easy for her.

Deciding that she was going to have to get inside to try to hear anyone sleeping, she made her way across to the main cluster of buildings.

The main building appeared to be a cluster of twelve rooms set out in a large square formation that was divided evenly into quarters. Each quarter was divided by a path that led to a garden in the centre, and she could hear a small waterfall, leading her to think that the garden in the middle likely had no roof.

Drizdan was in the corner section closest to the city; with that in mind she reasoned that Izziah should be somewhere on the opposite side of the square. Given their personalities, it was likely that they split the buildings down the middle and each took half, giving them both about six rooms. Her issue now was, which side of the square was whose half?

Each side also had a large gate blocking access to the inner garden. She was betting that the hinges had not been oiled.

Deciding against going through one of the four gates, she opted to go up and over the building instead. She gauged that she could do that fairly easily.

Circling further away from the room she had seen Drizdan in, she found a small pile of wooden crates conveniently piled against the wall, out of the weather.

She did not linger on how handy that was; instead, she used them to help her reach the overhang of the strange roof. To her dismay, the tiles were of a strange substance and they made a noise as she moved them. But she had no other option, so she moved as slowly as she dared, her body low to the tiles, making her way up and over. Lowering herself down over the other side, she slid the last few feet and cringed as the sound of rattling tiles broke the quiet of night.

SHE FROZE, feet braced against the roof, but nothing happened. No one came out, and no one stirred in the room below her.

Deciding she was the luckiest assassin in the world, she lowered herself down and pressed against the wall, the overhang of the roof giving her the shadow of darkness.

Inching her way along the stone path, she found a window and pressed her ear close, listening hard. Nothing. She continued on.

Scoping out her surroundings, she was momentarily shocked by the layout. In the middle of the little square garden, was a flower bed filled with flowers so similar to the colour of her eyes that she momentarily lost her train of thought. Who had planted those? Where had they found them?

They were large flowers with four big petals, four smaller ones filling the gaps between the bigger petals and a strange frill circling the black centre. They were exquisite, and the colour was beyond anything she had seen before.

Shaking her head to clear it, she considered her options. She could go to her left or to her right. One way would take her further along the row, the other ended in a corner and headed off at an angle to her position. From what she could tell, she was opposite and down two rooms from where she had seen Drizdan.

Realising her mistake, she pondered the size of the rooms around her and shook her head. The room she had seen Drizdan in had been large, but not that large.

She had been wrong; the rooms comprised a ring that formed the outer four walls of the complex. Inside that ring, there was one large room, meaning in total there were around twenty-four rooms—assuming none of the outer rooms were elongated and took up more space than she calculated.

The question was now: which one of those rooms was a bedroom?

Turning, she attempted to look inside the window of the large room nearby, but she was unable to see through the curtains.

Cursing, she tried to decide where to go. She was either going to find the right side of the complex or she was not.

Letting out a slow breath, she decided to try for the side she was currently on. She would try to get into the cluster of six rooms before her. If that did not work, she would try the next six to her right. Then the six to the left of her current position. After that, she was left with the cluster of rooms directly across from the one she was at then, and Drizdan was there.

Shaking her head at the irritation of it all, she sidled along to a door set into the wall. Opening it slowly, she slipped inside and turned to examine the darkness. She could not make out much, but the floor under her feet was made of wood. Stretching out her arms, she came into contact with a counter and, confirming her suspicions, she moved along to find a chair. Damn, she was in a kitchen.

Trying to map out the situation in her mind, she did not think there was enough space for there to be a corridor that separated this room from the five smaller rooms, suggesting those rooms led straight off the one she was in now.

Deciding that it was best to test that out rather than assuming, she crossed slowly and slid along the back wall until she found a door. Opening it, she was immediately hit with the smell of food.

"Damn..." she hissed and closed the door again, her mind racing.

So that corner of the complex was an eating space of some description. What were the rest?

Deciding to risk it, she headed back across the room as slowly as she dared, doing her utmost to remain silent.

Slipping out the door, she looked to her left and then headed that way. Even as she approached, she knew she was correct, the slow sound of breathing reaching her as she passed the pathway leading out to the gardens.

She could still see a slight glow coming from the windows across the way, so she knew Drizdan was occupied.

Testing the door, she was annoyed to find it locked, along with all the windows. She was starting to resent the man for his forethought in keeping himself safe.

She returned to the door and crouched down before it.

She was going to have to pick it in the dark.

WITHDRAWING her tools from under her glove, she set to work picking the stupidly complicated lock. Her eyes unfocused as she tried to go by feel.

A nerve-wracking five minutes passed, and finally the lock clicked softly. Slipping inside, she knew she had found the right room.

His scent was everywhere, warm and rich. The sound of breathing came from deeper in the room to her left. The flooring in that room was carpet, and it muffled her steps as she approached him.

She had decided not to kill him with her usual method. Her talent was too good for that; instead, she was going to stick a knife in him, much as the elf had stuck a needle in her.

Approaching the bed, she listened to his slow breathing. She slid one knee onto the mattress. Moving fast, she pounced on top of him, straddling him and pinning his arms with her knees.

Pulling at a string in her gloves, her knives sprung free of their pockets and into her hands, both lifted high above him.

With a cry of surprise, the lights in the room burst into flame as one, illuminating the scene.

He wore no shirt, the blankets bunched up around his middle, silver hair a mess, his eyes wide in fear. She took in what she could of his room.

Everything was done in dark browns and reds, including his satiny sheets.

In a second he saw her eyes and he realised who was atop him. His cry for help turned into a scream of pain as she drove her knife into his chest.

Something hit her from the left side, and she fell to the ground.

Someone climbed on top of her, and her second knife went flying.

Drizdan had come to the rescue of his brother. He gripped her arms and pinned them to the bed. Izziah struggled to his feet, the knife sticking out of his chest.

How he was still alive? She had been sure she hit something vital.

As she attempted to buck him off the Drow laughed, wriggling himself down lower on her hips to ensure she could not. She drove her knee up into his back. He jerked forward but did not fall off her.

Gripping both her hands in one of his, he yanked the mask off her face and smiled, delighted.

"Welcome to Nordia house, Princess."

She growled her response and wriggled, trying to inch him back up her hips. He obliged, comfortable at the sight of her trapped under him.

"Get off me Drizdan," she hissed, driving her knee again into his back. He took the blow without a grunt.

"Now, now. You come into our home, try to kill one of us and then demand to be let go? Tut, tut Princess. That's not how a Lady behaves."

Izziah had pulled the knife from his chest, and picked up a shirt to stop the bleeding. His voice came out in a wheeze, suggesting she had stuck the blade right through his lung.

"Don't hurt her Driz, you know she's only here because of the Prince."

Drizdan's vicious grin only grew wider at that news.

"So, the lich just hands her up on a platter, how kind of him. I can think of so many things I'd like to do with his precious Princess." He leered at her.

"Don't be repulsive. Bind her and help me," Izziah scoffed, turning away as Drizdan rolled her onto her back and bound her hands behind her with the length of rope she had tied to her belt.

"This won't be the last time I tie you up," Drizdan whispered in her ear before he stood and moved to help bandage his brother.

Turning her head, she looked over to the two men. She had been bound wrist and ankle, though they had not bound the two together as they should have done. Immediately, she rolled onto her side to hide her hands from them, her nails going to work on the bindings.

"She got you good Izz," Drizdan said as he tied off the bandage and adjusted it, ensuring the pad was in place over the wounds.

"Well, you saw what she did to Aelen, and he was prepared for it."

Drizdan gave a grunt and turned to look at her. Her nails had cut halfway through the bindings. She went still, not wanting them to notice.

"Help me move her, she'd be better off in my rooms. They're more secure," he said, crossing back to her.

"You can't keep her Driz, she belongs to the lich." Izziah looked terrified at the prospect.

"No, but I can have my fun with her until he gets here. Oh, don't worry, I'm not going to do anything like that." Drizdan rolled his eyes and grabbed her ankles, lifting them.

Izziah moved behind her and lifted her up, his arms under hers. Attempting to kick Drizdan with both feet, she bared her teeth at him. He laughed.

"That's my girl, I like it when they fight."

She knew he was being crude to disturb her, but still, he was a Drow and they were savages.

As they left the room, she cut through the last of her bindings and made her move, jerking herself forward. She swiped at the bindings on her feet, and managed to score Drizdan's navel at the same time.

They dropped her, and she spun, crouching to see Izziah had bolted. Grinning, she went after him, Drizdan unable to give chase with his belly sliced open.

Izziah led her out into the gardens and into a small meadow. He turned and put his arms up to defend himself.

Skidding to a stop, she reached behind her to draw out two more knives.

"If you have to kill me, do it with your kiss," he said, his eyes forlorn.

Lifting a brow, she lowered her arms and considered him in the moonlight.

"Why should I let you go out like that? You betrayed me. I should be able to choose the manner in which I kill you," she replied after a breath, feeding her anger.

"It was an accident; I did not realise he was planning to do that to you. It was academic," he pleaded, too afraid to move a muscle.

"You expect me to believe such a stupid lie?" she asked indignantly.

"Please Etani, you have to believe me. I would never intentionally harm you like that." He sounded desperate. He started towards her, stopping when she backed up.

"Please, just grant me the death of my choosing. I will still be dead."

She considered that for a moment, torn. On the one hand, she had her orders, which she did not want to perform. On the other hand, if she was going to kill him, should she give him that choice?

"Very well," she said finally, sliding her knives back into their sheaths.

With a gasp, he dropped to his knees. She approached slowly, kneeling before him.

Without a word, he reached up and pushed back the hood of her cloak to see her face in the dark.

Kneeling there, she studied his face and felt the first drops of rain falling.

There had not been a single flake of snow anywhere on the compound, not one. Something had been keeping the snow out.

Shaking her head at the realisation, she jerked as he reached out and took her hand in his, clutching it tightly to himself.

Placing her free hand on top of his, she leant forward, hesitating a mere inch from his face.

His eyes were wide in fear, his fingers tight on hers. Leaning forward to meet the distance, his eyes slid shut and his lips met hers.

Doubt filled her as she tasted him on her mouth, the kiss tender and slow. She expected this must be what it was like to kiss another for no other reason than to kiss them. It was an odd sensation.

Her own eyes slid shut as she sank into the kiss, releasing the tendrils of herself that reached into him, grasping and greedy to encircle the little fiery ball of his essence.

She got only a lick of taste when something around her neck crunched in a sickening way, and then she felt nothing at all.

19

HOW TO TELL YOU'VE BEEN KIDNAPPED

*W*hen she woke, she found herself lying naked on her back. She was in a spotlessly clean, barren room with nothing in it but a single lantern hanging from the ceiling.

Rolling onto her side, she groaned at the pain in her neck. She reached up to find it swollen.

Had her neck been broken? Who had broken her neck? One name came to mind, and she burned with resentment.

She was unable to get up yet, rolling over had been the best she could do, so she curled her arms under her and remained still, letting her body repair the damage.

As time passed, she found herself listening to the sounds of the house, trying to figure out where in the compound she was being kept, but she could not place herself. She had to surmise that she was perhaps underground, that or the Drow men had come up with a very effective means of blocking sound.

The sounds of boots came from somewhere nearby. Was that above her? She rolled onto her backside and pushed herself backwards until she was pressed against the wall. It took her longer than expected as her legs only wanted to work sometimes. She had to assume that whomever it had been was skilled in anatomy. He had caused severe damage without injuring her enough to fully kill her. For the first day, she would be entirely paralysed from the neck down.

The Drow brothers entered the room. She huddled and watched them warily, her legs hugged to her chest. She had crossed them in order to protect her modesty. But someone had to have stripped her, so they had probably seen it all already. They were both wearing white fabric headdresses over their heads. They covered their faces and hair, which left her unable to tell them apart. She was surprised at just how similar the two were in body shape and size. She assumed the masks were to both hide their identity and keep their mouths protected from her.

"Glad to see you're awake, Princess," one of the brothers said. She could not gauge which one had spoken, though it sounded like Izziah.

"You know, you can only keep me here so long," she replied with false bravado.

"Not necessarily. We can keep you here just as long as we desire. The lich is keeping his distance for now." That was Drizdan. She frowned, trying to work out which of the men before her had spoken.

The one on the right turned and locked the door behind him, the left one started towards her.

"What exactly are they planning to do?" she asked, warily. She tried to decide if keeping her modesty, or allowing them to touch her was the better option. She was torn.

Neither replied, and she watched calmly as the man approached her. He came to a stop a few feet from her. He was just inside kicking range.

She looked up at the anonymous head, and raised an eyebrow in wonder at how he could see through that thing.

"Do you really think Epharis is going to let you keep me here long term?" she asked, turning her attention to the second man as he approached.

"Probably not, but we have time to play." That was definitely Drizdan, and it was definitely coming from the man on the right.

Letting out a slow exhale of frustration at her situation, she drove her heel into Izziah's knee. The bone crunched, and she threw herself sideways to avoid any retaliation.

Izziah's screams covered the curse Drizdan had made as he went after her, only to find her sprinting for the door.

He barrelled after her, but she reached it first and grabbed the handle. She screamed in pain and jerked back, lifting her hand to see raw red skin.

The man slammed into her from behind and pinned her in place. His breath was heavy in her ear as he grabbed her hand and forced it down. Pressing her wrist against the door handle, she heard him laugh through her screams and the sound of sizzling skin.

"So, you do have a weakness..." he purred and jerked her back from the door, tucking his foot under hers and tripping her. She landed hard, face down and he landed on top of her, driving his knee into her lower back.

Izziah was up again, hobbling over to the two as she attempted to get her breath back and wriggle out from under him.

Her spine was working only barely, and he had just driven his knee into it. She had lost feeling in her legs for a good three seconds, but finally, the feeling had returned.

"Iron, she can't stand iron," Drizdan said, reaching down to grasp her unbound hair. He used it to hold her head down, even as she attempted to lift herself up off the ground though her arms were shaking.

"Right..." Izziah said and left the room.

"Struggle all you want princess; it's just getting me more worked up. Just as soon as Izziah is gone, we'll get to have that fun," he crooned above her, deliberately grinding his knee down into her back.

Grunting in pain, she went still, panting softly and trying to figure out what to do now.

"Aww, don't submit now. I like it when my women struggle."

Ignoring him, she considered the room around her, but there was nothing she could use to defend herself.

Returning after only a few moments, Izziah came in. Drizdan gave a snort of disgust.

"Such a gentleman," he sneered, gripping tighter on Etani's hair and forcing her head up.

"See, Princess? He's going to look after you even after you tried twice to kill him…"

Letting go of her hair before she could make any sense of the situation, he reached under her and grabbed first one wrist, then the other.

She expected to feel the bite of iron, but instead, she felt fabric.

Sliding the sleeve of something onto her arms, he lifted it up over her shoulders and tucked it down over her back to where Drizdan was still leaning on her.

Hearing the sound of metal, her stomach dropped, and she clenched her jaw. She must not scream.

But it was so hard when the sizzling started. Closing the cuff around her wrists, Drizdan got off her, moving away as Izziah took a moment to tug the fabric down to rest midway down her thighs.

Grabbing her arm, he lifted her up enough to pull the robe around her. He tied it off around her waist.

"I'm sorry, but we can't let you loose to come after me again," he whispered as he brushed her hair back from her face.

"Go jump off a cliff," she hissed back, struggling to her feet.

A steady stream of smoke was coming from her wrists, the sizzling sound loud in the silence that followed. So much iron in so little time, she did not know how she had managed to survive this long.

Turning away from them, she headed deeper into the room, settling herself with her back against the wall to ensure she could see them at all times.

The two men left soon after that, locking the door and leaving her there alone once more.

She knew she would not be able to kick the door down, but perhaps she could get the door open?

Grabbing the hem of her robe, she tucked it carefully into the gap between the shackles and her blackened skin, sighing at the relief it brought. No, it would not stop it completely, but the lack of direct contact eased her suffering.

She had no idea how much time had passed before they came down again; this time it was only Izziah.

"I have come to take you up for a bath. If you fight, I will drug you and leave you down here," he said in a matter of fact tone, lifting a large syringe out of the pocket of his pants to show her, then tucking it away again.

'Well, thank you for showing me where it is...' she thought dryly, allowing him to help her to her feet.

She felt dirty, having remained in that room for an unmeasurable amount of time. She had been correct about it being a cellar. He led her up into the brightness of day.

Squinting, she saw the garden was overgrown but beautiful, filled with exotic plants, trees, and flowers.

She turned to look in the direction of the castle, wishing without end that Epharis was about to swoop in and pull her out. For one fleeting moment, she had been sure she saw something, but she could not tell what it was. It was too far away.

THEY PASSED through the Courtyard and into the side of the compound that housed Izziah's room. He did not pause, instead, he led her into one of the offshoot rooms—into what had to be the most lavish bathroom she had ever seen.

Everything was white and black marble with gold fixtures. A huge chandelier hung above them and she pondered how it was possible that something like that was able to fit in the room. She had barely needed a leg up in order to get onto the ceiling of the building, yet that chandelier was easily seven feet.

"It is designed to look bigger on the inside than the outside. Fae aren't the only ones with magic." Izziah said when she had stopped to look up at it.

He gave her a warning look as he removed one of the cuffs, tugging the robe off her shoulders and allowing it to hang loose around her waist. Then he returned the cuff to her blackened wrist. He did not so much as look at her nudity, and she was grateful for that if for nothing else. He was even kind enough to cuff her hands before her rather than behind.

Able to undo the sash of the robe, she moved away from him to the bath that was issuing little jumping balls of steam, yet the room itself was clear of steam.

Shaking her head at the oddity of Drow, she climbed into the sunken bath to find it perfectly deep. She could sit with just the tips of her shoulders above water. Groaning aloud at the heat, she set to work cleaning herself as briskly and thoroughly as she could, her hair giving her some trouble, before she simply basked in the deliciousness of the bath.

"I wanted to bring you here sooner, but Driz said you were still too dangerous. He wants to wait until you are weaker," Izziah said, sitting nearby and handing her liquids as she pointed them out to him.

"Your brother is a clever man," she said, unable to deny it was a brilliant plan. The cuffs would speed up the process now, meaning it would only be a matter of time before defending herself was out of the question. "What exactly do you plan to do with me?" She handed him back a bottle after sniffing it, and he picked one out himself and offered it to her.

"He believes that we can use you as a means of buying our way back into the Under Dark. Our mother would accept us back without question if she could get her hands on a Fae, let alone one of the Princesses. You can buy us back into her favour."

Looking to him as she opened the bottle, she frowned as she considered that. Drow worked on a matriarchal system just like the Courts. They had female rulers, and the women ruled the household. It meant that the men were quite submissive and would do anything asked of them. Having the displeasure of their mother must have been agony for him.

"That's quite a plan, really, I'm sure your Queen would be ecstatic to get her hands on a Winter Court Princess." She sniffed the bottle and lifted a brow, turning the bottle to try to read.

"It's a skin oil," he said when she frowned at the language.

Making a sound of pleasure, she began to apply it liberally. The warm smell of pine and jasmine filled the room.

"Mother would be very happy." He accepted the bottle back and returned it to the shelf, watching her face as she enjoyed the bath.

"I never thought of what it must be like to have a mother like that. My mother was considered one of the most beautiful, kind and brilliant to have ever been born. Then there was the Fae thing, and everything went downhill from there. If I was even half as brilliant as her, I would have been happy."

Pulling the plug out from somewhere around her feet, she stood and accepted the towel he offered her, wrapping it around herself.

Stepping out of the bath, she crossed to the mirror and picked out a comb, watching her hair as she brushed it out. It had become tangled, but not unmanageable.

"You don't seem to be too angry at what we plan to do with you." He sounded perplexed. She found him in the mirror, watching her hands as they moved.

"If I were in your situation, I might have done the same," she said after a moment. The comb moved freely through her hair now.

"You are too forgiving," he said, standing to approach her. "You should be angry; you should hate us."

Turning to face him, she rested her backside against the counter and pulled her hair over her shoulder to braid it with skilled fingers.

"We all do what we must, to survive. For you, survival is the Under Dark." She dropped her eyes to see what she was doing and paused when his hand reached out, taking the thick stands from her and turning her so he could braid it himself.

"FOR MY BROTHER IT IS, but not for me." His breath was cool on her shoulder and suddenly she was forced to recall the moment their lips had touched in the meadow.

He had been thinking of it, too, for as he finished the braid, his hand had lifted to brush over her shoulder. The touch made her shiver, and she was left wondering about the reaction.

The door burst open and Drizdan stalked into the room, his eyes nearly alight with fury.

"Get her back in the cellar Izziah. She is still dangerous!" Reaching forward, he grabbed the chain that linked her hands and jerked her from the room. Nearly having to run to keep up with his furious pace, she followed him back out into the night and again glanced towards the castle. She did not see whatever it was she had seen that first instant, and she wondered if it had been an illusion.

Drizdan thrust her into the room. She spun to see him as he threw in the robe that Izziah handed him. She would not be able to put it on with her hands bound, but she did not think he really cared.

He slammed the door and locked it, and the two men left.

Left to wonder at the events of the bath, she settled herself down in her normal spot to the back of the room. It was only a matter of hours when the door opened and Izziah walked in.

"I am being sent as a scout to our people, we are going to be taking you to them in a few weeks if we can arrange a meeting with mother," he said, excitement in his tone. He crossed to her and undid one of the cuffs to help her into a new robe he had brought with him, taking the one she had wrapped around herself.

Returning the cuff to her wrist, he paused and traced a slow finger around the outside of her burnt skin.

"I am sorry for this, but Drizdan wants to drain your strength as fast as possible. It was this or his repeatedly breaking your neck."

"I have to say, this is a better alternative," she replied, already feeling the effects of the iron draining her.

"I must go, he is waiting. But I will be back in a few days." He gave her a hopeful look and hurried from the room again, leaving her to wonder at his excitement.

It was the next day when Drizdan came down into her room with the promise of a bath. She could go willingly, or he would drag her.

She opted to go willingly and stood on shaky legs to follow him out of the room and back upstairs.

This time he took her to his room and his was the opposite of Izziah's.

While Izziah's had been rich and warm, Drizdan's choice of style was all silvers and greens. While it was not as filled with life, she had to admit she liked it.

The bathroom was less ostentatious as well, the walls and floor made of a dark grey marble and the counter made of granite. The fixtures were a dark silvery metal she did recognise. It was not iron, but it looked similar.

Drizdan approached her, and he removed the cuff long enough to help her out of the robe. Unlike Izziah, Drizdan had no issue looking her over as she undressed and climbed into the bath after he had cuffed her again.

There was no denying the bath was wonderful, somewhat shallower than Izziah's but no less pleasant. Her knees appeared above the water if she bent them, but it was long enough for her to sit with them stretched out.

Drizdan picked what she used to clean herself, yet she was not displeased at his choices.

"Did he tell you what we are doing?" he asked after she had taken the time to thoroughly clean herself.

Accepting the bottle of hair oil, she rubbed it into the long strands, letting the bulk of her hair sit on the side of the bath to absorb the oil.

"He did. I did not expect your plan to be so clever," she said, tilting her head back to enjoy the bath.

"Why not?" he asked, seemingly offended.

"Do not get me wrong, I do not think you are unintelligent. Only that it was so simplistic and yet entirely genius. There was so little room for mistakes and, had you not managed to capture me, the plan could still have been used at a later time. Were you the one the snapped my neck?"

Staring up at the ceiling, she found that it had nothing at all. The candles that lit the room were lined around the walls to give the room an intensity she found appealing.

"I was. I need my brother; I could not let you kill him." Toying with the bottle of oil, he watched her without embarrassment.

"Need him for what?"

"He is Mother's favourite. If I did not have him, she would never accept me back, even if I had a Queen as my prisoner. With him and you, I can get back." He did not sound ashamed at his plan, only irritated that he was not the favourite of his mother.

Turning so that she could rest her chin on the edge of the bath, she looked at the man as he sat cross-legged on the floor. His feet were bare, and she had not noticed. It was such an odd thought to have, but the fact stuck in her brain.

"I suppose that is a valid reason to keep him safe. I assume that is why you sent him instead of going yourself?"

20

MONSTERS AND MEN

*H*is eyes met hers and he gave a slight nod.

"In part. I cannot trust you not to try to kill him again while you still have the strength to do it. That, and he is more diplomatic than I."

She nodded slowly and turned away, tilting her head back to rinse the oil out of her hair.

After she was sure all of it had been washed out, she gave herself a few more minutes of soaking before she pulled out the plug and stood.

He stood with her, smiling slightly as he held the towel. He did not offer it, instead, he studied her. Her hair was sticking to her, and she stood dripping, her chin lifted in defiance. She made no effort to cover herself, knowing full well he would only force her hands away if she tried. She did not want him to touch her if she could avoid it.

He offered her the towel, she took it and wrapped it around herself, following her actions of the previous bath and borrowing one of his combs in order to brush her hair. Thankfully it only took a few minutes. She could feel him behind her, close enough that his breath tickled her skin.

"You are so incredibly beautiful," he murmured, her muscles tensing.

It was his touch on her arm that broke the moment and she turned, reaching behind her to grab the razor he used to shave. She slashed it across his face, and he howled. She slipped past him, heading for the door.

He was after her in a second, her exhaustion allowing him to catch up with her. First by the towel and then by the hair. Ripping the towel from her body, he managed to halt her just long enough to shove her forward. She landed hard on the floor; her arms crushed under her and her hair splayed out up above her head.

Dropping to his knees beside her, his hand settled down on her side, feeling along her ribs and down to her hip.

She shuddered at the sensation, remaining still as she considered what she could do. Being chained meant she would be less likely to be able to defend herself.

He settling onto his elbow, his front touching her back, and she could feel his eyes on her as his hand traced back up, coming to rest against her waist.

"Don't worry Etani, I'm patient enough to wait for marriage," he murmured in her ear, leaning down to gently catch the tip of her ear between his front teeth and lip. He bit gently on the sensitive cartilage.

He gripped her waist firmly, squeezing her, and she could feel his hair tickling the back of her neck, blending with her own.

He traced his way down the length of her ear with one sharp canine until he reached the lobe, nuzzling the side of her face and lifting his nose to her hair, inhaling deeply.

She was repulsed, even more so when he jerked her hips so that her backside was pressed against his groin.

He growled in enjoyment, and she tucked her arms deeper under herself to better protect her chest from his hand when it began to slide up once more. Her attempt to protect herself was wasted as he forced his hand up under her arm. His fingers dug into the soft flesh of her breast.

He bit down hard on her earlobe, earning a gasp of shock and pain. He released the lobe and licked away the blood, following along the line of her jaw as far as he could reach.

The Drow inched his way down to her neck, his hand lingering on her breast when the door burst open. They both looked up.

"Epharis!" she cried. The lich stalked into the room. He took in the scene, and the air crackled in his fury.

Stepping past him, two guards entered the room, long and slender swords gripped in their hands.

The Drow threw himself away from her and stood, his posture defensive.

The instant Epharis moved away from the door, Drizdan bolted and disappeared into the night. None of the three men made an attempt to go after him, their intent only to scare him off, not harm him.

Etani pushed herself up on shaking arms, and the two guards turned away as it seemed they only just realised she was naked. Epharis had already seen it, so he did not look away. Instead, he swooped down on her and pulled her to her feet.

He reached down and released the locks of the shackles with a touch of his fingers. His actions were slow and gentle as her skin stuck to the toxic metal, peeling away as he released them. She did not care if it hurt, but he was concerned for her blackened skin.

HE WRAPPED his arms around her protectively, making a silent gesture to the guards who quickly left the room to do whatever it was they had been told to do.

"Hush now, you are going to be all right," he said, running his hand down her hair and settling himself down on the bed to keep her company until she had gotten her breath back. She had not even realised she was gasping.

His eyes trailed down her form and lingered on the red marks on her chest and on her hip, but he said nothing right then.

He bundled her up in his robes, wrapping her in them so no one could see her.

Carrying her as tightly against him as he could, he left the room. "Where?" he asked, his arms tightening around her form and lifting her slightly higher against his chest.

"Not here, Your Highness. The compound is secure. I have found her belongings." One of the guards had a soft, almost low voice. It had a soothing calmness to it that she drew upon in desperation.

"Very well, my brother must have good reason to keep them both alive. For now, we will return to the castle." She felt him moving again, heading along the path in the direction of the main gates. Peeking out, she could see that there was a very large hole where the gate had once been.

"How did you find me?" she asked after they had crossed at least a third of the city.

"I thought you had seen. I had scouts monitoring the compound. I was not permitted to go in until I had seen proof." He spoke quietly with the guards keeping a respectful distance behind them.

"The black shadow?" she asked, her head resting against his chest. It was dark and pleasantly warm; the lich increased his body temperature to comfort her, or shock was making her feel colder.

"Yes, they look a lot like flying cats. But as soon as I saw you, I started preparing. Alaric blocked me again, demanding that I take those two specific guards with me, so we had to wait for dark—that was the only way we would be permitted to go. But conveniently, they had been off on a mission and did not return until this evening. We left immediately after their return." The lich sounded livid, clenching her so hard it hurt but she did not care. "Damned vampires," he snarled under his breath.

"Just in time. They planned to take me to the Under Dark and sell me for status and forgiveness."

The lich stopped and looked down at her, wrapped up as though in a cocoon in the darkness of his robes. The guards had stopped as well, remaining back.

Lifting her eyes to meet his, she gave a slight shrug.

"I wouldn't be the first Princess sold off for political reasons," she said, making the lich grunt in agreement.

"I have to wonder what Alaric's plan was, letting them take you," he said, setting off again.

"Perhaps he plans to start an alliance with the Drow. Even if they planned to return to the Under Dark, they are still bound to him. They would have been forced back, eventually."

"True, perhaps you are right." He fell silent then, both of them thinking hard.

The events of the evening remained unmentioned, neither wanting to bring it up and neither wanting to have to deal with it.

As they reached the castle, she noticed that Epharis had begun to make a sound very akin to growling as they passed the gates.

"Alaric," the Prince said as he mounted the stairs, followed closely by the vampire guards. Even as he stopped, they continued on to come to a stop behind the King, turning to face Epharis.

"Epharis, I hope it all turned out well?" the King said, sounding cheerful.

"Yes, I managed to free her right in time," he said angrily. "Excellent, I look forward to seeing you both at dinner tomorrow."

Unable to see the King, she was left with the expression of Epharis to gauge the situation, and he looked angrier than she had ever seen him.

"It would be a pleasure," Epharis said coldly, moving past the King.

"Oh, Epharis. Keep a closer eye on your pet Fae, we would not want her to fall into the wrong hands. It would speak badly of everyone involved if she were to disappear," the King said.

"Don't rise," she whispered, feeling the arms under her tense.

He stalked inside and headed straight for his own rooms, leaving her on the couch to collect clothing for her to wear.

While he was gone, she made her way into the bathroom and took another bath, trying to wash the smell of the Drow from her skin and hair.

HE CAME into the room after only a few minutes, dropping onto a small bench and leaning his back against the wall. He had no care for her modesty, and she did not care to be modest in front of him. He was not a man, he was Epharis, the Lich Prince.

"He knew," she said as she used an oil mixed with sand to scrub at her skin.

"Yes, he did. You are right, you were valuable as a political sale." He set her clothes on his knee and watched her as she bathed. His staring while she bathed no longer bothered her, she was not a sexual object to him, simply his property, much like a pet dog.

"What are we going to do?" she asked, picking out her favourite forest scent and using her nails to scrub at her scalp.

"I do not know at this stage. We will have to wait and see what we can learn."

Neither of them seemed happy at that, but they had no other choices.

She rinsed out her hair and soaked in the water while watching him even as he watched her.

"Are you all right?" he asked.

She was about to give a flippant response, only to realise that he was genuinely asking her.

She stopped and considered that.

"I had never thought of myself as a prisoner until then, or as someone that one could trade for a value. Up until I came here, I was my own person, but now I am not a person, I am a commodity that has a high price at auction. What if you cannot find me next time? What if you are too late?" She met his eyes with her own, hating herself for sounding weak.

He gave no response, but she could tell he was thinking hard on the subject.

"I will be fine. I will need to eat soon."

He nodded and stood, leaving the pile of clothes for her. Getting out of the bath, she stopped to look at herself in the mirror. This time she really looked, trying the find what it was about her that had driven the Drow to such an action.

Digging past the self-loathing and prejudice, she found that if she looked at herself from the perspective of an outsider, she had a beauty that she had never seen before. She was gaunt, and sickly-looking, yet she had an inhuman perfection and a radiance about her. She truly was the Goddess of beauty and life. She had been called once before, so long ago.

Shutting that thought down fast, she scowled and allowed the prejudice to return. She was not; she was a black-haired, white-skinned freak.

Turning away from the mirror, she dried herself and dressed in a pair of simple slacks and a dark grey blouse with a stylised corset that did little more than give the appearance of her accepting fashion in that age.

Walking from the bathroom on bare feet, she peeked around the room to find the lich standing at his books. He had clearly been studying for some time.

"Did he force himself on you?" he asked bluntly, his back to her. While he sounded indifferent, she could see the tension in his shoulders.

"No, what you saw was the first time he touched me," she said honestly, heading for the couch and settling onto it, her legs crossed under her.

He made a soft grunt of acceptance and then turned to look at her.

"I had been thinking on your needs when it comes to food, Etani. I believe it is possible that we could fabricate it."

"Fabricate a human soul?" she asked sceptically, watching him. "Yes, we can fabricate a human soul."

OVER THE DAYS THAT FOLLOWED, she told him of the fruits she had eaten while in Ceress, not bothering to hide many of the truths about her people that she had kept hidden for so long.

He asked if it was possible to steal and grow the fruits in the human world, but she told him of their inability to grow in a world with so little magic.

Disappointed, they turned to the work of fabricating a soul, while he also worked on another project that he had forbidden her to see.

She did not care as it gave her time to experiment and learn, all of which provided her more time to recover from what had happened to her in the recent months.

From her calculations, she had been in Ayathian for around four to five months, though she could not be entirely sure. It was an odd thought; it was by far the longest she had ever stayed in one place and she was growing anxious about her sisters. It was not like they could not cope without her, but going that long without a visit from Ceress was unnerving, and she was worried that he would make a move against her sisters.

Her attempts to fabricate a human soul were all failing, one by one, and she could not understand why. She had followed his notes to the letter, and still, nothing was going right for her. It was infuriating.

Throwing down the gloves, she ran her hands through her hair and looked up at the Lich. He seemed quite happy that she was unsuccessful, pushing her to try again and again, but she was convinced that it was impossible to do. He, however, kept telling her she had simply done it wrong and needed to try again.

It had been days since he took her from the compound and any attempt she made to try to stop was met with his insistence that she just was not trying hard enough.

Her demand that he do it himself, if he was so sure it could work, was ignored. Repeatedly.

Glaring at him while he picked out several items from the storage cupboard, he hummed softly to himself.

"I can feel you glaring. If you are glaring, then you're not working," he said after a moment.

"This is not working. I've made it at least ten times and it's not working," she snapped, infuriated at him and at herself. It should not be so hard to make. It was not wrong, she knew it was not wrong.

"You must be doing it wrong then," he said for the hundredth time.

She seriously considered throwing something at him, but she knew she would only be cleaning up the mess and remaking all the damaged stock if she missed him.

"It's not wrong," she hissed back at him.

"Is that a tone I detect?" he asked in a perfectly reasonable voice.

"No," she snapped.

"I think it is. I do not like it." He was talking to her like she was a child and she clenched her jaw. As far as she could tell, he was younger than her, he had no right talking to her like that. But telling him that was not the smartest idea, so she kept her mouth shut, and just glared at him.

"Stop glaring," he said after a few more minutes.

"What are you doing? Why aren't you helping me?" she demanded.

"I am working, which is what you should be doing."

"It's not working, it's not!" she cried, "I have followed your instructions over and over again and it doesn't work."

"Do it again." he said and she could tell he was getting angry at her now.

"I've done it repeatedly!"

"Do it again!" he yelled back, turning on her.

She shook her head and stalked from the room. She knew it was not going to work, she was not going to try, and fail, to make the stupid thing again. She was going to go out into the city and find herself some food.

Something pricked her neck, and she jerked slightly, the world giving a sudden, violent lurch. She staggered, feeling nauseatingly like she was trapped in a boat in the middle of a storm.

"What..." she gasped, resisting the urge to vomit all over the carpet.

Turning slightly, she saw a syringe with an odd yellow-brown liquid inside. Blinking hard, she followed the hand holding it up to him and it took a moment to process what she was seeing.

"Epharis?" she asked, not understanding why he would have stuck a needle in her.

"I'm sorry Etani, this is our only choice." He sounded regretful, and he caught her before she could hit the ground when her legs gave out.

Cradling her gently, he laid her out on the couch, and turned away.

"This is the only way I can keep you safe," he whispered, as he collected supplies. She watched as first one, then four, and then two, and then six of him started moving around the room, picking up items and setting them down in a neat pile.

Squinting, she frowned as the two Lich picked up an amulet, she was sure she had seen it somewhere before, but she could not put a name to the thing. Then her consciousness faded to black.

21

THE LICH PRINCE

*W*aking, she found herself strapped down onto a long table in the middle of the Lich's sitting room, a place she had come to see as a safe place for herself in the Lich's rooms. She had to note that the Lich was just as talented at binding her down as the elf had been, except for her fingers. But the table under her was metal, and she could not scratch her way through it.

Letting out a huff of frustration, she stared up at the ceiling, trying to figure out what she was going to do from there. Distantly, she had a vague recollection that they had plans for dinner with the King at some point in the recent past that they had blown off without a thought. A small twinge of amusement went through her at the thought of Alaric's rage over not being able to touch her when Epharis was around.

At least she was able to lift her head, turning it to see what was around her. To her surprise, she was not the only one in the room. To her right, there were three men bound and gagged and sitting against the wall. They were all conscious, and they looked right back at her.

"Well, this can't be good..." she said to the men, leading one to snort and roll his eyes.

Looking to the other side, she found a smaller table covered in various tools of the trade, alchemical compounds, and that amulet that she still could not place.

It was the Lich's return that made the amulet's origin click into place. A dawning horror fell upon her.

"No. No, no, no!" she strained against the bindings, the leather groaning but refusing to give.

Her sudden alarm had set the men to terror, for if she was alarmed, it was likely they needed to be as well.

"Calm yourself, everything is going to be okay." He sounded wrong, as though he were convincing himself as much as her.

"You can't do this, Epharis, not this." He was going to turn her into a Lich, just like him.

"It is the only way to protect you." Turning to the table, he picked up the amulet and crossed to the men who were struggling valiantly to get away. But the Lich had already begun his work, placing the amulet around the first man's neck and drawing a knife from the sleeve of his robe.

"Please, Epharis think about this. You know this rarely works, you know what will happen, we do not even know if this works on mythical beings. Please stop and think. There are other ways." Twisting her wrist in the strap, she was able to start attacking the leather with her nail, but even as the first one snapped, her inability to lift her forearm off the table blocked any other attempt.

Cursing him, she tried to think of how else she could escape.

"This is the only way, Etani," he said, drawing a strange arcane rune on the man's forehead in what she could smell to be her own blood.

The man was crying, too frightened to try to move, though his fellow sacrifices were doing their best to escape.

Realising she had no other option, she traced the line of her body and what she was able to reach with her hands bound like that.

She curled her wrist under and stabbed her nail deep into her palm. Blood began to flow, oozing slowly and then faster as she found the vein she was looking for.

Death was an easy escape.

Jaw set in determination, she used her nail to dig and scrape across her palm, cutting veins and then cutting them again when they healed.

She had not fed since her time in the cellar and that made her healing weaker. Concentrating, she focused on keeping her heart rate as fast as possible, which was not entirely difficult given the circumstances.

To her side she could hear the murmured words, sobbing, and then an unearthly keening.

Looking around in alarm, the man went limp, eyes still open and empty while the amulet glowed a soft blue-white and the Lich removed it from his head, turning to the second man.

His struggles and attempts to dodge the Lich's hands bought her a few precious seconds as she worked, keeping the veins open with blood pooling under her and dripping off the table.

She had to wonder at the insanity of the entire situation, the string of events that had taken place since her arrival and now, suicide to escape becoming a Lich by a man who had run out of ideas on how to keep her alive. Why he was so intent she would never know.

The man began to scream as the amulet fell around his neck, the murmuring starting up again as the arcane symbol was again drawn.

Her head was beginning to hurt, she felt somewhat lightheaded, but it was not enough. She would not bleed out fast enough.

Cursing her ill-luck, she started up on the strap on her still-trapped hand, deciding that speed trumped discretion at that point.

THE LEATHER SNAPPED, and Epharis turned at the sound. His growl of anger sounded loud, but he could not stop his work.

Whimpering, she set to work on her second palm even as the Lich raced to finish his incantation that stripped the second man of his soul, leaving him to slump forward.

Turning to her, he moved to bind up her hands tightly with a strip of gauze. He stared down at her.

"You mustn't do that. I am doing this for your own good, Etani. You have to trust me," he said, his fingers tracing her jaw.

"Please, Epharis. Why are you doing this?" Tears had begun to form tracks down into her hairline, wiped away by a gentle finger.

"I cannot lose you," he said simply. Ensuring that her fingers were wrapped tight enough that she could barely bend them, he returned to his work.

It clicked then; that look of cold tenderness in his eyes, the fury at seeing what Drizdan had been about to do to her, his determination at getting her back.

Was it possible the Lich loved her? Was it possible that a Lich could love?

Her mind reeled, her palms healed over, and she was out of ways to try to escape.

Epharis had moved on to the third man who seemed to have come to the realisation that there was nothing he could do; instead, his chin was lifted high, determined to die as a man. Tears still fell, but he was not going to go out a coward.

The amulet was moved to him, her blood drew the symbol on his forehead, and the Lich spoke the words. The man was looking at her and she stared back at him, an odd understanding coming between them.

She had never felt sorry for a human before, but in that moment, she felt pity for him. He was dying to keep her alive.

Her eyes slid shut even as the life left him, his body going limp. Epharis lifted the amulet from the man and moved to her, standing at the top of the table by her head.

Opening her eyes to look up at him, she saw nothing but grim determination on his face.

Lifting her head gently, he placed the amulet around her neck and slid her hair free of the chain; the other necklace, the collar, was removed without comment. He placed the amulet gently between her breasts where it would remain for eternity.

Her breathing had become slow and even once more, knowing there was nothing she could do to stop it.

The blood under her was used to draw a symbol against her forehead, his fingers tender on her skin.

"Epharis, I don't want to die," she whispered, giving him a moment of pause.

"You won't. I know what I'm doing," he said slowly, leaning down to place a gentle kiss against her temple.

Closing her eyes, she parted her lips obediently as he placed a leather gag into her mouth.

"So, you don't bite your tongue off," he whispered, stepping back and holding his hands out to rest on either side of her face.

Biting down hard on the gag, she was struggling to keep herself from hyperventilating as the realisation sunk in that there was absolutely nothing she could do about her situation.

Whimpering, she could do little more than look up at him as he began to murmur, his voice low and echoing in her ears. Her skin began to crawl, and she shivered in horror.

Inside her, she could feel something moving. Something that was not ever supposed to move. A cold trickle that started somewhere around where his cold fingertips pressed against her skin, his fingers splayed wide. Each point of contact crept into her flesh, burrowing down into her brain and neck.

She was gasping, the cold freezing her skin and leaving her brain feeling numb. Biting down harder on the gag, she did her best not to scream as the tendrils of ice dug and pushed, spreading out through her system and encircling her racing heart. It felt as though it were going to explode inside of her chest.

THE LICH'S voice rose in a scream, the sensation of otherness filling her, and then the first exploratory finger touched her heart. It was almost curious in the way it extended a tiny finger to brush her. It was the oddest sensation she had ever felt.

She was having none of it, swiping at it in her mind and pushing it back from herself a fraction.

But then it touched again from somewhere behind her. Turning on it, she swiped again, but it was already gone, dancing back and reaching again.

It was playing with her, this darkness and icy magic. It wanted to see how she would respond, it wanted to play before consuming her. But there was a troubling edge that the creature seemed to emit, the little licks of taste were wrong. She was wrong.

Manifestation of the thing took only an instant, and it stood there in her mind's eye. It was the shape and height of a child, amorphous and yet still shaped. It had no hands or feet, the limbs ending in curves.

"You are not human?" the voice was high, sweet and so very much like a child that she recoiled impulsively.

"No, I am Fae," she thought to the thing. The thing poked at her.

"Not human? Why then?"

"The Lich wants to change me." She tried to draw back, but the thing poked again, seeming to stretch in a way no creature should.

"Lich wants change? Lich King Epharis? Why no change human?" Everything the thing said was a question, but she did not have an answer. Instead, she thought over her relationship with the lich.

"Ah, Lich loves? Lich cannot love?"

The pitch of its voice was making her head ache, but it seemed more curious than ever.

"I do not know," she finally replied. "What are you?"

"We are demon? Power of all Lich to possess another? We come for essence?"

"You can't have it," she retorted.

"We take essence? Essence feeds us?" The voice was as sweet and gentle as ever, frustrating her all the more. "You do not fear us?"

"No, I can protect myself," she said, but was not entirely sure if that was still the case.

"We take essence, it feeds us now? We hunger." Those last words were said in a feral snarl and it stabbed at her.

There was no dodging it; instead, she exerted her own will to shove the thing back, even as it found her and ruptured her thin protective layer.

That touch was enough to set her entire being ablaze, and the thing poured itself inside her, filling her with the cold emptiness.

Forming a self there, she looked around and found a small glowing blue figure behind her. She knew instinctively that it was herself, small and whimpering.

Hushing it, she moved to cradle it in her arms. It had been damaged, blue light leaking out of a spot on its arm.

Patting the spot gently, she looked around to try to make out anything that would be helpful.

Nothing appeared to her as it would have done in her mind. But this was not her mind, this was her soul house. The place in which the purest, most naked essence of herself hid. This was the part of the human she crashed through to get to the soul. The glowing figure was her soul.

How she had been drawn down to that point, she had no idea. But there she was, her consciousness stuck next to her soul.

"Tsk-tsk. I did not think you would be able to get in this far," a voice said. She turned to see what could only be a demon.

He was enormous, spikey, and covered in a thick black carapace. He had eyes that glowed red and his teeth all came to points. His voice was deep and gravelly, making her insides vibrate.

"Well, whose fault is that? You should never underestimate me."

"I'll keep that in mind, Fae. Well, since we are here... I am Abraxas. And you are?"

Lifting a brow at the casualness of the situation, she gave a slight shrug.

"Etani," she said simply, knowing that demons, like Fae, were able to control with a name.

"Etani? Interesting," he said with a note of real curiosity in his voice. "How did you come by the ability to enter here?"

"I do not know, I figured you brought me here." She pushed herself up, her hand defensively on her soul's shoulder.

"Not I, I have no interest in you being here. Your presence complicates matters." He pondered her for a long time, considering his options. "Nevertheless, your lich has decided to bring me here, sacrificed three souls to do it, no less."

Shaking her head, she took a deep breath and prepared herself for a fight. She was going to defend her soul against a demon.

"Don't do that girl, you'll only damage your soul and you're going to need every shred of it if you want to remain sane after."

"Don't worry, you won't be successful, and I will remain myself," she said, moving to stand between him and her soul.

"No one survives without becoming a Lich. You are one or you are dead." He was inching his way around her, trying to decide where to attack from.

"I'll be the exception." She sounded braver than she felt, and after everything she had been through, she was tired.

Smiling with shark-like teeth, he lunged forward, his arm transforming into a long, lethal-looking spike. The thing was easily a foot long and looked as though it could cut the very air with how sharp it was. She was not keen on letting it touch her. Ducking to the side, she lunged forward in turn as he was retreating and struck a blow into his side, tearing up her foot in the process.

Backing away to assess her strategy, she knew she had to draw him away from her soul, so with that in mind, she fell into a defensive posture, allowing him to come after her while she backed away and turned him.

She did not know what would happen if he struck her, and she was not willing to find out, but at least her foot healed like normal.

Managing to twist him around so his back was to her soul, she drew him further away until she felt she was in a better position to finally be able to retaliate.

She took advantage of his next attempt to cut her from navel to chin, spinning and using the momentum to lift her right leg and slam her foot into the side of his head. He grunted, falling sideways. Something had been knocked off in the blow, a large spike that she was quick to pick up. Finally, she had a weapon.

The demon turned on her, seeing the thing in her hand. He immediately went still, his eyes fury incarnate.

Turning, he saw the figure of her soul several metres behind him. Realising what she had been doing, he turned and pelted towards her like an arrow.

She was after him in only a second, but she knew that second was a second too late.

The demon reached her soul first and rather than slashing it, his hands sank into her core and sent her staggering, her image flickering as her soul's light dimmed.

Looking up finally, she could see the being had a face, eyes huge and oddly round ovals. It was crying, long streaks of glittering white making tracks on its visage.

"No! Do not surrender! Do not let him win! You cannot! You are Etania Daewen! You are the Celestrial Fae mongrel Princess and you will not give in to a low-rank demon! No matter what that damned Lich says!" She dropped to her knees, realising that her consciousness was screaming at her soul to stand up to a demon. The pointlessness of it all sank in and she crumpled, unable to catch her breath even as her soul's light flickered.

"You're better than this..." she whispered to herself, agonizing over it all.

She could only just see her soul from her position, but its light barely illuminated the area. It was staring at her as though the demon poisoning her did not matter. Then it looked at the demon, and the demon blew backwards, light radiating out from the being.

It was the demon who sputtered, trying to crawl back towards the soul but unable to bear the light.

"I'll find my way back to you, and when I do, I will be stronger, I will take you," he managed to say before his darkness sputtered and went out.

Turning her attention to the soul, the being dimmed itself and approached, helping her to her feet. They both looked down to an inky black spot that had formed on its chest. The demon had caused permanent damage.

Lifting the spike, she offered it to her soul, the being taking it and smiling, that smile burning white though it had no tongue, teeth or mouth at all.

"You'll be okay," she breathed. "I'll find a way to fix this." Touching the spot against her soul's chest, she went rigid as words and memories flooded her and she found herself lying on her back having no knowledge of how she got there. Her soul was standing over her, its smile turned into a little 'o' of surprise, its oval eyes were wide. It made a dismissive gesture at her.

"Got it, time to go," she said only after she was able to sit up again, her mind reeling.

Her soul nodded and pointed to a door that had not been there before. Offering her soul a smile, she headed back out and her eyes flew open.

22

LOVE AND THE LICH

*T*he Lich untied her after his work had been completed. He sat across the room, his sword resting on his knees and his eyes locked on her. It was not all that surprising, really. If one was lost to that attempt, it usually left their body a feral thing that would rip and devour everything in sight, continuing mindlessly until it was killed.

Rolling onto her side, she heaved, but nothing was left in her body to bring up. The sound had him moving to her side. The damned did not heave, they raged and screamed and destroyed.

"I'm alive..." she gasped, her eyes finding his feet as he came into view. He was wary, but he needed to see her. Turning on him, she found the shock and wonder on his face a little charming, at least until her foot flew and she kicked him squarely on the side of his head.

She was on him even as he fell, her hands closing around his throat. As pointless as the gesture was, trying to strangle a Lich, it made her feel better. But the colour of her skin made her pause, at least it did after her fingers had already closed around his throat.

He did not so much as try to struggle, instead, he stared up at her.

His hands lifted, and he brushed her face, her cheeks and lips.

"How could you..." she whispered, tears suddenly filling her eyes. "I trusted you..." Turning, she reached for one of the knives they had agreed to hide around the room, ripping one from its place stuck to the underside of an end table. "I trusted you!" she screamed, lifting the knife above her head.

"Stop." He did not yell, did not even raise his voice. Instead, it had been as though he had been speaking to himself. Her muscles seized mid-downward thrust. They simply stopped dead.

He was gentle as he moved out from under her, ignoring the books that tumbled to the ground. Sitting beside her, he stared at her in wonder.

"How is this possible? You're not a full Lich," he said, unable to help himself. His hands reached for her face again. He wiped away the tears that continued to fall, examining the inky blackness of them. "What happened?" he asked, making a little gesture that allowed her arms to fall free, the knife sinking deep into the floorboards.

"Your demon needs more training," she snapped, tugging at the knife but unable to pull it free of the floor. Giving up on it, she turned to him, hating that he was still staring at her. "He got his hands on my soul, but it rejected him. He vanished."

The Lich blinked at her.

"He touched it?" he asked, shaking his head in response to her single nod. "That's impossible, if the demon had touched your soul you would have changed."

"Look at me!" she raged, holding up her arms that were no longer a pristine white. They were still white certainly, but they held a weird blue-grey tint that she hated. "This is what you did to me! I am changed!"

He shook his head, reaching out to grab her wrist. She felt it too, the steady beating of her heart.

"You are alive," he said. "You rejected the change; you are only a half Lich."

"Half Lich, there's no such thing," she scoffed, yet she knew she was not dead. Still angry at him for trying to change her into a Lich at all, she glared while his expression was one of a bewildered child.

"It shouldn't be possible."

"Well, it happened. And what was that with you telling me to stop?" Settling herself on the floor, she studied her skin, hating what he had done to her.

"As the one who turned you, I can give commands like that. Coupled with my will, I am able to force you to do things like that. Minor things usually. It's not like remnants, generally it was believed it was to stop foolish young Lich from getting themselves killed."

He could not bring himself to tear his eyes off her.

"Your eyes glow when you're angry," he said in a conversational tone.

Fuming, she pushed herself up and moved away to the bathroom, coming to a stop in front of the mirror. The changes were minor at least; the change in skin tone, the definite glow of her eyes as her fury simmered. She looked otherwise normal, though. It was inside where she felt the difference.

Normally she would have felt cold in his rooms, but that was no longer the case. She felt comfortable in there, the temperature perfect. Her heart felt somehow wrong, beating slower than before but still beating stubbornly on. Her mind felt off, sideways in a sense, but she could not quite figure out what was wrong with her.

"I think you are all the more beautiful," he said, standing in the door to the bathroom.

"I think I look half dead," she growled, turning to him, the movement making her feel slightly queasy.

"Half dead, and more beautiful. Coldly beautiful, better than the rest of us mere former humans."

She shook her head, looking to the floor as she tried to right her thoughts and get everything back in order, yet it was still difficult.

"WHAT WAS the point of this? Why do you care enough to try to keep me alive?"

They both knew why, but she wanted him to say it. She wanted him to validate his actions with a proper reason.

"You know why," he said simply. "I want you to say it."

"I am the only Lich in known history who has learnt how to love," he said slowly while she remained silent, waiting. "I am in love with you. And to protect you I tried to make you like me."

The way he said it made her stomach cramp, but it was not from repulsion. The words, the news, his confession, it hung between them and she finally looked up to his face.

She thought for a long moment, considering what had happened and how she had screamed for him, how she had hoped he would save her. She had wanted it to be him who saved her. She always wanted it to be him.

"I..." she opened her mouth to try again, but he lifted his hand to stop her.

"Don't do that. I am no fool Etani. I do not require your comfort," he said, but her mind was reeling.

"I love you, too," she finally whispered, the realisation hitting her an instant before she spoke it. She had started to fall in love with the sadistic, dead Lich Prince.

There was a beat of silence between them, both of them shocked by the revelation. In an instant, he crossed the room and on impulse her arms reached for him, even as his reached for her.

Lifting her chin to meet his as his face turned down, their lips met in a brush of both desperate need and tender fear. Lifting her up onto the counter, his arms enclosed her, and she hooked her legs around his back. They remained like that for what seemed to be an eternity, hungrily exploring each other.

It was the first time since she was a girl that she had kissed another without an ulterior motive, and it was pure bliss.

When they broke apart, she opened her eyes to see him staring into nothing, astonished at the turn of events.

"Etani... You cannot love a Lich. It's ridiculous," he said finally.

Her frown was instant, her stomach dropping out from under her. "So? I'm a half Lich, this whole situation is ridiculous."

He looked at her then, her lips parted and slightly swollen from the pressure of his mouth. He reached out and brushed her hair back from her face, shaking his head.

"Epharis, don't do this now, just be glad." She gripped the front of his robes with her fingers, trying to gently draw him closer to her once more.

"Glad? My greed almost got you killed. My selfishness turned you into this." He waved his hand at her and she had to admit that it stung a little.

"You were trying to protect me. There's nothing wrong with that."

He scoffed, turning away from her but then turning back. He was angry, but unable to move away from her.

"You're a child, you know nothing of my intentions." Offended, her eyes narrowed.

"I'm older than you," she said, crossing her arms over her chest. That made him pause as he looked at her. "I'm immortal." It seemed to her like that should have been obvious to him by that point in their relationship.

"But you tried to kill yourself..." he sputtered, reeling.

"I can die just the same as any other, but I don't stay dead, a bit like the plague." Her tone was dark, not caring that she had told him that.

"That's why it failed. You cannot turn an immortal into a Lich. What other secrets do you have?" He gave her a suspicious look, and she arched her eyebrows.

"That was for you to find out," she retorted snippily. How could he do that after he had said something so important to her? She did not understand, and she resented him for it. "You cannot say that and then take it back in the next breath."

"You are still living, you deserve better."

"Better? Who is better? The Drow?" She knew it was a low jab, but did not really care. She wanted him to think about what he said, to realise that she wanted what she wanted.

He glared at her.

"We cannot be. Even if I were to believe it was right, Alaric would never allow it," he said finally.

She felt as though he had punched her in the chest.

"Very well, seeing as your brother's approval is more important." Low again, but she was angry and hurt.

Sliding off the counter, she stalked past him and he made no attempt to stop her.

She had been stupid to think the Lich actually cared, to believe he was even capable of loving her. Lich could not love.

She had been stupid for letting herself feel anything for him. She knew better than that. She had gone nine hundred years without once allowing herself to get close to another being, and now she had gone against her own rules. And he had rejected her. Ava was wrong, love was not better than safety.

Returning to her rooms, she made a decision. She was going to collect supplies, and she was going to hide out for a few days. She would give herself time to recover from this latest deviation to her life.

Grabbing a pack, she filled it with clothes, weapons and her poisoning kit. She did not know what else she would need out there, but for the time being, she felt she had everything.

Stripping off her clothes, she pulled on a fresh set only to stop at the sight of an odd mark on her wrist. It was in the shape of the amulet. Feeling her chest, she found the amulet was not there. The mark was four centimetres from top to bottom in a spikey pattern that resembled a star with four main points. It was completely white, and unless one was looking hard, it would not be easy to spot.

The mark only fuelled her anger, and she tugged on a long-sleeved tunic that covered the mark. Sliding on her gloves, attaching her belt and pulling on her boots, she headed for the balcony with her pack and headed down into the grounds. She did not want to pass the Lich in her path to escape.

DROPPING DOWN CAREFULLY, she turned and headed in the direction of the castle gates, but found her path interrupted by the vampire twins. She had only ever seen them twice and their similarities threw her off. They wore the same black long coats with black pants, black vests and white undershirts; they also wore the same black wide-brimmed hats that hid their faces. They had been looking down as she approached, and she considered just breezing past them.

She was certain they had been talking, but she could not be sure.

She hoped to slip past them, but she was not that lucky.

"Princess," one said. She could not tell which one had spoken, for their heads had not lifted.

"Afternoon, Jaia and Kai, isn't it?" she asked slowly, trying to be polite, her mood still sour.

"Yes, Jaia and Kai." They spoke in unison and their synchronisation creeped her out.

"A pleasure. What are you doing out already?" It was barely sunset, and she had to wonder if their attire protected them from the sun. They were indeed wearing gloves and their black boots vanished into their trousers. Their hats covered their heads and their clothing covered every other inch of them.

"We come out to see the last shred of day. It reminds us of what it was to be human and it is not dangerous so long as we are careful." This time it was only one of them talking, but she did not know which one it was.

"I see—"

"But we have a purpose this evening," they interrupted her together. It was making her skin crawl.

Immediately she became wary of the two, somehow sure they were there for her.

"What might that be?" she asked, her tone dry.

"We come on behalf of King Alaric. He asks that you not leave the castle grounds. For your own protection." They spoke in alternating sentences, one man speaking one sentence and then switching it. It was irritating, or perhaps it was only irritating because she herself was irritated.

"My protection?" she asked, tired of the games the royal family played.

"There is a shadow in the city that hunts you. The shadow has only one goal, it is your death."

That made her pause, thinking immediately of Sasha. "What shadow?"

"Shadow is called Cain." They continued to speak, but her ability to listen had shut down as she connected the dots. Her people had found her.

"How do you know the shadow's name?" she interrupted. Her voice sounded distant in her mind.

"Met with Epharis and said he was hunting a Fae woman. You are the only Fae in the city and Epharis asked for his name, so he gave it," one of the twins said.

Fear flooded her as she tried to take in everything she knew about

Cain. They called him Cain The Destroyer. He was the executioner for Queen Illia. Queen Illia was the ruler of the Celestrial people and about as friendly as an angry cobra.

"There are safeguards?" she asked as her eyes scanned the upper walls as though she might catch Cain creeping over like the spider he was.

"Plenty. You look different." The first voice had sounded calm, the second was curious, and she looked to see that the right twin had lifted his head.

It was the softer looking of the two, his lips slightly parted to show white teeth. He really was a shockingly attractive man, his oddly sweet, dark eyes taking her in as she did the same to him.

"Kai," the twin said. She noted that the sun had set enough that the light no longer reflected down into the grounds. He had seen her hesitation and offered his hand. After a moment, she realised he was introducing himself.

She was surprised when he shook her hand instead of kissing it, as if she were his comrade and not a Princess.

It made her feel good to be treated as something that was not royalty.

"It's nice to finally be introduced, Kai," she said honestly. He beamed at her, the pleasure on his face confusing her. Why would he be so keen to meet her?

"Kai likes meeting new people. He has been eager to meet you properly since the dinner." The other voice was lower, mellower and calmer. But he held out his hand just as Kai had done and she accepted it. He did not shake her hand at first, but then gave a slight twitch of his head and did so.

"You have changed again," he observed.

She was struck by how attractive he was, so much so that she was struggling to contain a blush. She did not know what it was about him that appealed to her and why it had happened then but not at the dinner. It was incredibly strong, and it made her aware that she had no idea how to talk to him.

"An unpleasant turn of events," she said finally. The two men exchanged a glance as he released her hand. She was blushing, she knew it, but he really was just...

Cutting off the thought, she needed to keep her mind on the task at hand and not moon over him like a hormonal teenager, especially given what had happened with Epharis.

"You seemed to have recognised the name of this shadow," Jaia said, motioning back in the direction of the castle and the gardens. Giving a slight nod, she headed that way with the two men. Oddly, the two vampires were the most normal people she had met in that place.

"Cain The Destroyer," she said in a low, bitter voice.

Kai opened the gate for them and Jaia motioned for her to enter first. She was a little startled by just how polite they were.

Stepping through the gate, she turned to wait for the two of them, and they set off again. With one of the twins at either side of her, she could not help but notice it was a defensive formation. They were protecting her while under the guise of conversation.

She found that she did not want to leave. They were friendly, and it felt good to hold a conversation with someone who did not want anything from her.

"What kind of name is that?" Jaia asked after a couple of minutes had passed and they had left the earshot of the guards by the gate.

"It was what he was given at birth. Executioners are bred and raised; they are given a name that they are expected to live up to," she said, letting out a slow sigh.

"Strange culture," Kai said, offering her a shy grin when she glanced at him.

"You have no idea," she said with a sudden exhaustion. Why did it all have to be so difficult? "How did you know Epharis had spoken to him?"

"We were spying," Jaia said unabashedly.

She stopped, looking between the two who stopped a step after her and turned back to look at her.

"You were spying on the Lich?"

They nodded, Kai looking ashamed, but Jaia met her shock with level eyes. She began to laugh then, helpless to the ridiculousness of the situation. Kai first looked shocked and then grinned.

"Told you she wouldn't be angry," Kai said, nudging his brother.

They were like little boys who had been caught doing something naughty, one defiant and one ashamed. She decided right then and there that she liked them both.

"Do you do that often?" she asked only after she had stopped laughing.

Jaia shrugged.

"Any time we see him doing something odd," he said, a previously unnoticed tension in his shoulders easing as he offered a hint of a smile.

"Does Epharis do anything that isn't odd?" she asked. The twins exchanged a thoughtful glance before Kai shook his head. "You know what he will do if he catches you," she said, fascinated by the two of them.

"We know, but we're vampires, we don't get seen unless we want to be," Kai spoke brightly and after a moment of quiet wonder, the three set off again.

"Is there anything we should know about Cain?" Jaia asked, stepping ahead to open the next gate for them. This time he stepped through first, her following and Kai coming in and closing it behind them.

She thought seriously about that question, bringing up rumours that she had heard and anything that might be useful. She looked at the two, slowing her pace and biting her lower lip. How much did she dare tell him?

"You have to understand my situation here. I am not free to leave; all I have left is my secrets."

The men stopped, exchanging another look before Kai shrugged. "We keep secrets better than anyone."

Jaia only nodded his agreement, his face serious again.

"I had heard rumours of how the Prince had entrapped you. We are sorry you must suffer." Jaia spoke with the utmost sincerity and it was doing nothing to calm her schoolgirl crush.

Motioning to a table stone set up with four chairs, she sat down and the twins sat as well, looking interested.

"I take it you are spies by trade, or is that just a hobby?"

Jaia smirked and touched the side of his nose.

"I will sell you a secret, if you can find a way for me to free myself of the hold the Lich has on me."

Kai frowned in thought, but it was Jaia who spoke. "It would want to be a big secret."

"It is enormous," she promised. "Deal," Jaia said and offered his hand.

Feeling a surge of emotion inside her chest, she took his hand and sealed the deal.

23

A GIRL MUST GUARD HER SECRETS WELL

hey both looked to Kai, waiting for his response. He nodded and took her hand, locking himself into the magical deal as well without any hesitation.

"There are four Courts in Faerie. Winter, Summer, Heathen, which was Spring, and..." she paused, the word sticking to her tongue. "And Ceress, formerly Autumn. Ceress is the home of my people, Celestrials." The silence was palpable as they first absorbed the information and then did their best to come to terms.

"Two secret Courts of faerie?" Kai whispered, looking stricken.

Jaia looked as though he was never going to be able to speak again, his eyes huge.

It was no small deal. The Courts had always been two since the first day of the world. Never four, only two. The mythicals had guarded that secret for the entire history of existence.

"That's huge!" Jaia cried, jumping to his feet and beginning to pace before them.

"How was this hidden for so long? No one has ever heard of four..." Kai whispered, watching his twin pacing.

"We live for secrets, thrive on them," she said dryly, unable to help watch the vampire pace. "Imagine their ecstasy at keeping a secret from the entire human world."

Jaia was muttering the words 'four Courts' to himself over and over.

"Cain is from Ceress too, I knew him growing up, he would tell me all the time that he was going to kill me for being a half-breed."

"Winter," Jaia said, nodding. "We could feel that on the first day. Winter Court always smelled of cold, full-blooded or not, ghoul or fairy. Always a hint of cold."

"Right, my father was a Winter Fae. Both my mother and father were pure-blooded, so that makes me half. Being half is an abomination in Ceress. Cain has been trying to kill my sisters and me for centuries."

Something she had said caused the brothers to glance at each other once more, but she was not sure what.

"This Cain is here to kill you for being an abomination?" She nodded again, causing Jaia to start pacing again.

"It will be hard to know what to defend against if we do not know the full extent of his abilities. But at this time, we will assume they are like yours," Kai said quickly.

His face fell as her cheeks flushed.

"Do you know of my food source?" Both brothers nodded in silence. "That is something he can do, and would likely do to me if he got the chance. We have the ability to move between Faerie and here." She decided to leave out the fact that she could move others and not just herself. "Fast, strong..."

"That is a lot of ability, and I assume you have others from your father," Jaia said. She nodded and gave a slight shrug. She was not about to hand them all of her secrets.

"Why are we protecting you? You should be protecting us," Kai said, eyes wide in wonder.

"I tend to believe that you are also here to monitor me," she said gently, patting his arm when he looked upset. "I would accept no less from spies. I would have been disappointed if you had not reported back to the King."

He gave her an apologetic look and nodded, confirming her words.

"He is pure-bred?" Jaia asked.

"As far as I am aware, my sister and I are the only non-pure to exist, or to have existed for generations. We do not procreate quickly."

"Twins?" he shot, now chewing on his nail.

"Identical, though you wouldn't know it to look at us now." She could not help the bitterness in her tone.

"I like your skin," Kai said brightly, smiling at her. She smiled back, heartened by his kindness.

Jaia returned to the table and stared at her intently.

"This is a lot of information to take in, Etani. We will do everything in our power to try to free you as much as possible, but it will take time."

"It's not like I can go anywhere," she said wryly. He snorted a laugh, nodding.

"Tell me a little about you two."

Leaning forward, she rested her elbows on the table and her chin in her hands, watching the pair.

"We were born around seventy years ago in a small village to the west. We were just normal men at the time, I was a carpenter, and Kai was an inventor. Kai is a genius, he really is," Jaia said. Kai blushed, as much as a vampire could blush. Instead of reddening, his cheeks darkened, and she could not help but smile at how adorable he was.

"He was selling to a vampire when the vampire took an interest in his work. The vampire decided he wanted to keep Kai as his prodigy forever. He turned Kai and followed when Kai crawled home. When he found out we were twins, he decided he wanted the matched set. Here we are," Jaia spoke slowly, as though the story tired him out.

"I'm glad it happened, if not we would be long dead and would never have come here to Ayathian," Kai said cheerfully. Jaia only looked at his brother sadly.

"At least you have each other," Etani said gently, glad they were together.

"Yes, where is your sister?" Jaia asked.

"In hiding with my youngest sister. My twin..." she trailed off, frowning. It was too much information to give them. "She has been mentally ill since we were young. Our little sister is good at masking them but cannot mask us all. I chose to leave and draw away the attention, they hid. Last I heard my twin enjoyed being a cat."

"That's awful, I'm so sorry," Kai said, grasping her hands in his.

"I hope to save her one day, but I have not studied the mind yet. I don't know if it's possible to repair her mind."

Jaia tilted his head slightly, wondering.

"I had heard there were ways of repairing a broken mind. How is it you know your sister likes being a cat? Do they write to you?"

"No," Etani laughed "My twin has abilities I do not, she can change her shape at will. Our younger sister can contact me telepathically if the need is great. But we will not risk it. Our kind can tap into it in your world. I feel that perhaps the lack of magic scatters the contact somewhat. We don't want them being able to follow the link to either end."

Jaia nodded in understanding.

"Back to this Cain. How do you think he found you?" This was stumping her as well.

"I haven't an idea on the matter. Perhaps I was careless..." She did not think it was that, but there was no way of knowing.

"If I have the chance to ask, I'll do so," Jaia said, only half-joking.

Tilting her head back to look up at the castle, she frowned as she considered what to do. Was she going to have to wait, stuck in the castle grounds forever?

Out of the corner of her eye, she saw something flicker. She glanced in that direction, her stomach dropping out. The twins had been right, and she did her best not to look. Cain stood atop the wall and was looking straight at her. He must have been circling the wall the entire time.

Making a slight summoning gesture, he dropped down behind the wall once more. How long had he been circling the castle waiting for a chance to catch her eye? How many times had he seen her?

"It has been a delight Kai, Jaia. But I feel I must head back to my room." She stood slowly, stretching her body and groaning at the delicious sensation of muscles moving.

"We will find out what we can on our part of the deal. Just be patient and we will get back to you." Kai said, though he seemed uncertain.

"We will come to you, it's best if you don't try and find us or raise suspicion."

Nodding her agreement, she let out a slow breath. It wasn't like she could escape on her own anyway.

The two stood with her, but it appeared they trusted her enough not to do something stupid, and they let her leave on her own.

Heading back along the path, she could see the shadow moving out of the corner of her eye, following her.

Rather than returning to the castle, she flitted across the main path to the gardens on the other side. Slipping inside, she followed the path until it rounded a bend and she studied the wall. Heading for the edge of it, she scaled the stairs that accessed the top of the wall.

A SECOND LATER, a white hand appeared. The man wore a long, tattered, white-lined black jacket. Its hood was pulled high over his head. He wore grey pants and a grey tunic with a sash that flowed long down to brush the tips of tall boots. He had a long, ordinary-looking sword that whispered ominously. He wore black gloves and his snow-white, shoulder-length hair was in need of a wash.

Settling herself on the parapet, she watched the man climb up. He looked around, then stalked towards her. She remained sitting, curious to see what he would do. She smiled. The idiot had apparently forgotten about the protection because he ran face-first into the invisible wall. Grunting, he fell back a step and stopped.

"Etania," he snarled, glaring at her. "Cain," she replied simply.

Silence stretched between them, as he paced back and forth before her like a caged lion.

"Come out here and talk."

She laughed, the sound making him cringe. Like all of their people, they did not like to hear it as it made her seem normal and not a mongrel.

"Why don't you come inside?" She patted the stone beside her.

The word he called her then would have made her blush in the past, but now it only made her brows lift.

"That's not very nice, Cain. You'd think you'd be politer given you want me to do something."

Oh yes, she was going to toy with him for all she was worth. He had been chasing her for so long, threatening her and taunting her, and threatening her sisters. Now she had the chance to sit around and watch him? Of course, she was going to toy with him.

He bared his teeth at her.

"Well, whore, why don't you come closer and let me look at you. It has been what? Fifty years?" The insult did not bother her, she never understood it though. Given she was an outcast, when had she had the time to qualify for the status of 'whore'?

Pushing herself to her feet, she approached the centre of the parapet. She could feel the protective shield only a foot away.

Lifting her chin, she met his grey eyes with her own.

"What happened to your skin?" he asked, tugging the hood away to get a better look at her. He had a new scar running down the side of his face.

"A Lich tried to turn me. Fun fact, you cannot turn an immortal into a Lich, did you know? It will change you though."

Cain looked as though she had hit him, his lip curling. "So, you're even more of an abomination now."

She shrugged in response, looking him over.

"You're looking a bit worse for wear, Cain. Not keeping up to palace standards when you're out here with the peasants?"

That got the response she had expected. The man was incredibly vain, and her drawing attention to his drab appearance and general dirtiness irked him.

"Better that than a whore," he snapped.

"I'll have you know, I am wearing the height of fashion for someone of my profession."

"They let a whore work in the castle?"

"Certainly, I work for the crown as a matter of fact. Thus, the shield." She smiled at him, knowing it would anger him more.

He made an attempt to punch her in the jaw, but his fist rebounded off the shield with a loud crunching sound.

She grinned, mocking him. She knew it was a stupid idea to mock the man, but he had it coming. He had been one of her worst bullies growing up, always telling her he was going to kill her as soon as the order came. She had always said he should just shut up and try, but she had been terrified of him. She might be one of the only abominations, but she was far from the first he had come after. He had been the one to kill her father.

"I'd never thought you so cowardly as to hide behind a wall," he sneered.

Lifting her eyes from his broken hand that was rapidly healing over, she gave him a quizzical look.

"You've never known me to be stupid, either."

He grunted his agreement, his attention going to the barrier in search of an opening.

"How did you find me?" she asked curiously, turning so that she could watch him as he paced. His hand trailed over the barrier, pressing against it.

"I lost track of you around fifty years back, maybe less. Last I heard you were in Ampherdon. Your pattern was erratic, but I knew you would not stray that far from your sisters, just in case. No matter how good you are, girl, you always stick within a day or two's distance of wherever they are currently hiding." A flash of concern must have crossed her face. "No, you are the bigger threat. I will find them next. A noble brat and an insane mongrel can't be that hard to find."

Her brows arched, amused. They might be exactly that, but Lee spent most of her time as some animal or other, and Ava was remarkably talented. She would not be found, not ever.

"That doesn't explain how you found me."

"Rumours, mostly. If even a suspicion of unusual disappearances of humans came up, I went there. Dispatched a handful of vampires and a ghoul, but it was worth it. How is it you managed to feed all that time without their being noticed? Vagrants?" he asked, and she nodded. He sneered. "Picking off the scum of the scum species, not only are you a mongrel whore, but you're disgusting too. Have you no shame?"

"Food is food when you're on the run, Cain." It might be considered disgusting to most of her kind. They only thought the cleanest humans were worth the death they could provide. That meant nobles, powerful merchants and the like. She had never been so picky; rich or poor, they all tasted the same.

"I'll bet you even ate children," he whispered, coming to stand as close to her as he could, his eyes alight with malice.

Repulsion filled her, and she turned to him, glaring.

"Nice try, Cain." She knew he was trying to get a rise out of her, but she was safe for the time being.

He frowned, irritated.

"If nothing else, you've matured."

She had, given her struggles throughout life. She had matured faster than most would have. Even at her age, she was still young in comparison to the rest of her kind. She was only around nine hundred, still technically a teenager if one compared it to the lifespan of the humans. From what she knew of Cain, he had a good thousand years on her, if not more.

"That tends to happen when you're forced to fight for your life." "So, what now?" He crouched before her and she backed away, folding herself down into a cross-legged sit.

"You're not getting in," she said, her hands resting in her lap.

"You can't stay locked in forever. You need to feed eventually, and you know I will go find your sisters if I deem it not worth waiting here." He spoke calmly as though discussing strategy with her was entirely normal.

She paused to think about the number of humans in the castle. There were prisoners, servants and a few Courtiers. Generally, humans were advised against lingering in the castle due to the threat of night-wandering mythical beings. Many of the servants were non-humans for that exact reason. Even if they were humans, they were generally locked away at night, or only half-human.

At best, she thought she had maybe a year's supply if she was careful. Unless Epharis agreed to bring in fresh food. She frowned at the thought.

"I'm a patient man, Etani," he said, catching the realisation as she calculated.

How long would it take for him to give her up as a lost cause? A year?

"Or you could come out of your cage and face your fate like a Celestrial."

"Celestrials are the last to face their fate, Cain." She scoffed, knowing he had pride for their kind, so much so that it made him blind to their failures. "You're getting old, Cain, what makes you think you can defeat me?" It was pure false bravado, but it sounded good to cast doubt on him, even if it only dulled his pride's shiny surface.

He glowered at her, his thumb tracing the grip of his sword.

"Not so mature after all." He sounded almost disappointed by that.

She could only smile at him, shrugging one shoulder, and shifting her weight to get more comfortable.

"It would appear we are at an impasse," she said, silently glad the King wanted to keep her alive, yet resenting him for making her feel appreciative.

"For now. I could just go find them."

She knew he was goading her, but the thought still made her stomach clench in fear.

"AND HERE I thought you liked me most." His eyes narrowed on her, so she changed tactics as her tension rose. "You won't do that, not when you're finally so close." She smiled to hide her fear, not wanting him to know how much his threat worried her.

He grunted, knowing she was right on that subject. Had he wanted to find them, he would not be there. But there they were, hanging out on the parapet like old friends.

"I will find a way in, then I can deal with you and move on."

"I'll be waiting," she said calmly. Her eyes locked on him as he stood and crossed his arms over his chest.

"Very well, until next time," he said and turned, hopping off the parapet and disappearing from view.

She waited a few minutes to see if he would return but he did not. Pushing herself to her feet, she headed back in the direction of the castle.

She needed a place to hide out, from the Lich, from the King, and from everybody.

Looking up at the castle, she made a mental note of the placement of one of the towers and set off for it. Perhaps she would find freedom there.

There was one thing to say for stone buildings like that, they were not that difficult to climb if you knew how.

Her hair whipped around her as she began the ascent, her fingers searching out grooves between the stones and pulling herself up, her boots finding even the faintest hint of leverage to keep her upright.

From halfway up, she looked out over the city, at just how huge it was. It was magnificent, if a little scattered. It was as though Alaric had taken a few handfuls of buildings and just tossed them on the ground, and said it was good. The roads made no sense, some of them doubling back on themselves or stopping abruptly around a sharp corner.

Shaking her head at the confusion that was the male sex, she began to climb once more.

Reaching the top, she pondered her position. She began to inch her way up and around towards the window, having gotten off-centre.

She climbed wherever it was possible to climb instead of going in a straight line.

Gripping the soft wood of the windowsill, she strained to lift herself up that last little bit to be able to see inside. It was empty, and that was unexpected. She had been certain there would be a wizard in there, or a bat, or something.

Finding nothing at all was quite jarring. Regardless, she climbed inside and thumped down on the floor. Had she known about this tower she might have come there straight away, a safe little hole for her to hide in.

The stairs cut a hole in the floor on the opposite side of the room, and it was large enough that she could set up her base there. The only question was, could anyone get up there?

Heading for the stairs, she started her way back down. The stairs were considerably easier than climbing around outside had been.

She could not help but wonder why she had never seen this entrance before. It did not take her long to find out.

The stairs ran in a spiral along the outer wall with the inner wall being solid stone to support the weight of the tower and room above. She was unable to see around the edge, so when she came to what should have been a door, it appeared as a solid wall.

Pressing on it, she surmised that it must have been walled off. Grinning to herself, she headed back up to her new room, safe for now.

Setting down her bag, she slipped off her boots and settled herself down by the window, and watched the world go by.

24

THE PRINCESS OF WEORENE

*D*ays slipped by and she decided to start stealing a few more of her belongings from her room, sticking to the outside of the castle. It had become more interesting and fun to her as the days passed.

She had managed to steal a broom and pan, using it to remove the spiders and sweep the floor. She loathed spiders... Though if she were being honest with herself, she was terrified of them, and any insect for that matter. All those scuttling legs triggered some part of her mind and made her skin crawl. At least the broom made it easy for her to squash them from a distance.

She had made herself a bed out of blankets and pillows. Aside from several of her books and a healthy supply of candles, she left everything else down there. It would have been perfect if she had managed to get her alchemy supplies up there, but she felt that might be pressing her luck too far.

At that stage, 'the powers that be' seemed content to leave her alone, so long as she did not leave. She wanted things to remain this way as long as possible and for the time being, they did not stop her. It would not take the vampire brothers long to find her if they made half an effort, anyway.

She spent her days reading, safe and secluded up in her tower hideaway but none of her books gave her much information. What she needed were the books the lich kept hidden in his room from prying eyes.

It was not worth getting caught sneaking into his rooms and she had to wonder if there was a main library that she could get to.

Deciding to make that her mission for the day, she set off towards the main section of the castle and slipped in through one of the windows on the top floor. She wore only a simple dark grey dress, knowing she did not look the part of a Princess, but she did not care. She was on a mission.

It took her the better part of an hour to find anything that even vaguely resembled a library in that enormous place. She found all sorts of interesting things, including a storage room containing nothing but the guard helmets and a couple in the middle of... couple things. She found a supply of linen, and a cupboard with a full suit of armour stuffed in it.

The library was small. It smelled damp and looked dingy but she was willing to give it a go.

Crossing to the first row of shelves, she picked out one, frowning at the title. It was a language she had never seen before.

Flipping it open, the pages stuck together and made a squelching sound when opened. The whole thing was filled with a strange language. It looked more like pictures than a written script.

Setting the book back on the shelf, she tried a few more, but they were all in that same writing.

Cursing under her breath, she turned away only to freeze at the sight of the Princess of Weorene.

She had not seen the ghostly woman since the first day she had been brought to the castle.

"Hello..." she said warily, unable to contain a sudden burst of curiosity about the Princess and why she was always entirely covered.

"Hello," the Princess said gently. Her voice was low and melodic, with an odd lilt Etani could not place.

"You're the Princess of Weorene, right?"

The Princess nodded, remaining perfectly still as though she were made of marble between movements.

"My name is Etani," she offered, trying to figure the strange girl out.

The veil that covered the girl moved weirdly, and Etani took an immediate step back, just in case.

"You are able to read that?" the Princess asked, ignoring the introduction.

"No, it's in a foreign language. Can you?"

The Princess nodded and moved forward, her hands lifting to see the book. Even her hands were covered with thin gloves.

"This is a book on farming in marshlands," she said, reading the cover.

Now that the Princess was close, she smelt funny. It was hard to place the smell; reptilian, almost. But it was a gentle smell, light and somehow soft. It was not unpleasant though it was unexpected.

"Is this your language?" Etani asked, and the girl nodded. "Where is Weorene?"

The Princess looked up, her head tilting slightly to the side.

"Not from here? Weorene is from the southwest, deep in the swamps." The way the Princess pronounced the 's' note made her think she was indeed a reptilian.

"I did not know the swamps had a ruler; I was led to believe it was no-man's-land." Placing the book back, she stepped away and considered the library. Odds were, this was the Princess's private library that she had walked in on.

"My father was elected King. Kings like Alaric do not consider that to be actual royalty." The Princess's tone when speaking of the King made her smirk.

"Not a supporter of the good King Alaric, I see?"

The Princess shook her head and then froze.

"Wait, I recall now. You're the Prince's assassin, correct?"

"Yes, I work for Prince Epharis." The Princess took a half step back and Etani's cheeks flushed. "I am not here to harm you Princess; I found this room while hunting for a library."

The rigidness in the Princess's shoulders eased.

"I assumed King Alaric had sent you to get rid of me. He is under the false impression that I am here in the hopes that our Kingdoms will be joined in marriage. I assume my father hoped for the same," the Princess said angrily.

"I am sorry to hear that, Princess, the men here are... Interesting," she said, feeling genuine pity for her.

"Please, call me Nayishma. Everyone here calls me Princess and forgets I have a name."

"All right, Nayishma, may I ask why you remain covered?" She could not help but ask, it was nagging at her.

"For modesty, and to keep my heritage private from prying eyes. Few know of what my mother is."

"And what is she?"

"A Gorgon."

The word hung between them for a long moment as Etani processed the turn of events. Gorgons were supposed to be legend, nothing but a legend. Everyone knew the names of the Gorgon sisters, but no one knew if they were real, let alone were capable of breeding with a human.

"Who... Who is your mother?"

"Stheno."

She did not know what to say to that; instead, she could only stare at the girl before her.

"You're the offspring of the Gorgon Stheno..." Finally, after the minutes had stretched by.

"You don't believe me?" the Princess asked, sounding hurt.

"It's hard to process. The gorgon sisters were only legend, a story." The Princess nodded and, to Etani's horror, she lifted her veil.

The Princess was undeniably exquisite with rich, dark bronze skin that melded into small patches of scales around her neck, jaw, and chest. Her hair was a glittering bronze-red that started as coils and ended in the diamond heads of snakes. She had full, pouting lips and amber eyes that were slitted like a snake's. Her tongue was human, along with her arms, face and torso. She also seemed to have the legs of a human woman as well.

"May I?" Etani spoke as if in a dream and when the Princess nodded, she reached out to trace her bare fingers down the long coil of the snake, cupping its head in her hands.

It was surprisingly light, not like an actual snake at all, and it blinked at her as though her curiosity amused it. That was both creepy and fascinating.

"You're Fae?" Nayishma asked curiously.

"Yes," Etani replied simply, utterly captivated by the incredible woman before her.

"I've never met a Fae before." The Princess seemed just as captivated by her.

"I've never met a half-Gorgon before."

"I'd be very surprised if you had," Nayishma said with a giggle. They looked at each other for a long moment and then smiled.

They had both just made a new friend.

AFTER THAT DAY she spent much of her time with Nayishma in the library, talking quietly and getting to know her. They had both been lonely, and while Nayishma had her maids, it was not the same as having an actual friend.

Etani was just glad she had someone who did not expect anything from her, someone who cared about her, and treated her like a person rather than an object or tool.

They talked about the men in Nayishma's life. Etani learnt that the Princess did not desire men. She had not ever met someone who did not find attraction in the opposite sex, and it fascinated her.

It had not bothered her at all, especially given the Fae tended to not care what the sex their lovers were. Same-sex couplings were just as common as opposite-sex couplings, and having more than one lover was considered fairly normal, especially for the Queens of Faerie. They were expected to have multiple husbands and lovers to ensure there was plenty of opportunities for female heirs. They did not tend to mind if a Queen took a female lover, so long as she was still with men as well. There had only been one case of a Queen not liking men and they had found a way to work around that, inseminating her when the time came.

She eventually gave birth to a girl, two of them in fact, and a boy. It had terrified the Court at first.

So, to meet a woman who only liked other women was an anomaly to her, and she had pelted the Princess with question after question. After the first few, Nayishma seemed to realise that Etani was not judging her, but was genuinely fascinated. She had been quick to explain the situation in Faerie and that had smoothed it over completely.

When the subject of her own sexual preference came up, she blushed furiously and managed to stammer out that she had none.

Nayishma had been stunned to learn that Etani had not ever been with a partner. Etani learnt that Nayishma had two girlfriends in her past, but neither had worked out. Given that Nayishma was the only child born to the King, it was not a good thing that she was not interested in men.

It was not like a woman like her would not be able to reproduce enough to provide an heir of her own, it just wouldn't be with her chosen lover, given her lover wouldn't have the necessary bodily functions required for procreation.

They were frank with each other, questioning the other about their histories and their bodies, the embarrassment quickly leaving them, and their conversations became rather earthy at times.

Nayishma had been indignant to find out that most Fae did not menstruate but were fertile. She had explained that the female's egg did not leave the body every month, it stayed in the womb, ready to be fertilised until conception. Sometimes the womb could be damaged, or the conception could fail, but given how low the fertility rate was with the Fae, the fact that the women did not menstruate was a good thing. Most did not even consider children until after they were well over one thousand anyway.

They had discussed what was involved with sex between two women, and the Princess managed to wheedle out the fact that Etani liked Jaia. The Princess giggled happily at the idea of Etani and the vampire, who she had said looked as though he had a rod stuck up his... They moved on from there.

She told the Princess about her sisters and then about Cain, about her history, about the Lich and the King, about everything. Nayishma told her everything about her life in return, which had not been all that wonderful.

Nayishma was the only child of an overbearing man who was obsessed with keeping his throne, though he loved his daughter dearly. It had been he who insisted upon the veil and hoped that he could get her married off before anyone found out what she was. By that point, it would be too late.

Etani had not really understood, given Nayishma was an incredibly attractive woman, a fact she had stated blatantly to make the Princess blush.

But then the Princess teased that any woman who could fancy 'metal rod enema vampire,' as the Princess had so lovingly decided to call him, was not in any position to say who was attractive and who was not.

After that their discussions turned to their future plans; neither of them knew what they were. Etani only hoped to escape and get back to her sisters, Nayishma only hoped her father would not marry her off to Alaric.

During the weeks that passed with the Princess, she had spent most of it in the tower and had quickly learnt that the stairs did not actually end in a dead-end but rather in a trick door that was hidden behind a tapestry. She had found it purely by accident when a spider dropped down on her. She had fallen backwards down the stairs, landing in a heap, upside down at the bottom of the stairs. She had looked up to see a small indentation in one of the stones.

It opened the wall, and she peeked out, finding the hall empty, and then she closed the wall again, delighting in her find. The wall, not the spider.

Nayishma found the story highly entertaining, especially when she learnt of Etani's deep-seated fear of all things in the category of 'insect' and had laughed, given that Weorene was in a swamp and insects were everywhere. The thought made her cringe in horror.

A MONTH PASSED since they had accidentally found each other and she was surprised when the Princess came stalking into the room, her posture irritated, and thrust a small envelope into Etani's hands.

It was an invitation addressed to 'Her Royal Highness, the Princess Etani' and had been delivered to Nayishma, to be given to her.

"It would appear that Alaric is aware of our friendship," she said dryly, confused as to why the Princess would be given the invitation.

It was written on very heavy parchment and really was quite pretty, with gold lettering.

"He is trying to make me jealous," Nayishma said, settling herself down on one of the cushions, her veil flipped up over her head to reveal her striking face.

"Jealous of what?" she asked, holding the heavy envelope between two fingers away from her body as though it were going to bite her.

"He is trying to show he favours you over me."

Meeting the eyes of the Princess, the two exchanged a 'men' roll of their eyes.

"Does he see himself and his Kingdom as such a fine catch?" the Princess asked, looking down at the invitation. She took it back and slit it open, her expression waspish.

"Apparently so," Etani said in amusement.

Nayishma opened the envelope and pulled out the letter, giving it an expert flick to open it up.

"To the Princess Etani. You are cordially invited to the Masquerade Spring Ball. The ball will be held on the full moon of this month." The Princess read aloud, inflecting a pompous voice that made Etani laugh. "The full moon is only a week away, isn't it?"

Etani nodded, looking at the invitation with distaste.

"Short notice," she said. "Maybe I was not originally invited and Epharis made him?"

"No, I only got mine today as well, they came together."

She made a soft 'hmm' sound as she dropped her attention back to her work.

"Why a masquerade ball? It's not as though everyone won't be able to tell who everyone else is," she said finally, frowning as she shifted her weight. Holding the handle of the blade between the arches of her feet allowed her to get a better angle, but the blade was stubbornly refusing to slide into the groove. It was an invention of her own and she was not even sure it would work.

"I believe it is for the fun of pretence. Courtiers get off on games. Will you go?" Nayishma asked, her attention caught by what her friend was doing.

"I doubt it. I have better things to do than prance around being groped by strangers, if I wanted that I'd just go to dinner with Alaric."

Nayishma laughed, low and husky.

"I get the feeling it's not that much of a choice. We could go together, really rile up the savages."

Etani looked up from her work. Her eyebrows lifted.

"Two women? I'm sure they will be foaming at the mouth." She thought about that for a moment, considering the reactions. "All right, let us go together. What shall we be?"

Nayishma frowned, tapping her finger against her full lower lip. It was a gesture Etani found endearing.

"I'll have my ladies make us something and surprise us both. Come to my rooms to get measured? I'm sure they'd love the challenge."

Etani was not so sure the ladies would be as eager as the Princess suggested, but when they arrived the ladies were ecstatic at the sight of her.

"We have heard so much about you, come in, please!" they cried.

There were three of them, two dark elves of some form and one reptilian.

They were all dressed exceptionally well, all smiling and bright-eyed at the turn of events. Etani had never felt so welcome in her life.

The tallest of the ladies was names Sthiss. Her skin was an exotic green with white and brown stripes. She looked very much like some species of tree goanna, sharp teeth and a very, very long tail. She stood on her back legs, with long fingers and even breasts, a narrow head with black eyes, and a flat snout.

The other two looked remarkably similar to one another, and it turned out that they were sisters. Venorth and Odvihe. They both had deep blue-purple skin and bright red hair, big silver eyes and even bigger smiles. All three were dressed in neat black uniforms and the two elves wore black boots, which Etani found unusual until she realised that they lived in a swamp and tall boots were probably wise.

It seemed that Sthiss was the leader of the trio.

As THEY BEGAN to contemplate what they were planning to do, the two Princesses were ordered to strip to their undergarments.

Obediently, they did so. Etani's were simple, made for function, but the ones Nayishma wore were both beautiful and seductive.

"Where did you get those?" Etani asked, flushing when she saw Nayishma staring at her form with a hint of jealousy.

Taking a moment to examine the Princess, she noted that the patches of scales covered her from head to toe and glittered very slightly in the light coming through the windows.

She was not overly well-endowed, but she was perfectly proportioned. Slender, streamlined and curved just enough to catch the attention of any man, or woman in her case. The patches of scales only added to her air of exotic beauty. There was no denying the Princess was exquisite and that left her wondering at the jealousy.

"I made them." Sthiss said gently, coming up beside Etani with a long and knotted measuring rope.

She was an efficient woman, murmuring the measurements to her fellow ladies who were quick to jot them down.

Lifting her arms obediently, Etani looked to Nayishma. "What do you suppose the point of the ball is?

"I don't know, but knowing King Alaric, it can't be all that good."

"Perhaps he just wants to enjoy a night of festivities." Venorth said gently.

"Perhaps so, but I doubt it," Nayishma said, exchanging a doubtful glance with Etani, who had to agree. She did not see Alaric as the type to waste time like that.

"So long as his plans don't include us, I am fine with it." Etani said, watching as her bust was measured, and then her waist. "I'll be glad for more time to avoid the politics around here."

"Have you seen the Prince recently? He's been in a right mood prowling the halls day and night," Nayishma shared, smirking when Etani threw her a dirty look.

Stepping to the side obediently, she allowed her inseam and thighs to be measured.

"Don't be mean, Nayishma," Odvihe said, the Princess looking put out by being scolded.

"He can prowl around all he likes. I like my hiding spot and I am not sharing. I might be his pet, but I insist on a bit of privacy. I will not be kept by his side like a well-behaved dog."

"Good for you, men need to be put in their place, or they'll get all big-headed. We women rule this world, regardless of what the menfolk think," Sthiss said.

The two Princesses exchanged a grin as Etani's arms were measured and she dropped them back to her sides. Her head and neck were measured last, and she was permitted to get dressed again.

"What of King Alaric, what has he been up to?" Etani asked, pulling her pants back on, watching her friend's measurements start at the chest, just as hers had.

"He is as polite as ever, but I get the feeling something is going on behind closed doors. He has to struggle a lot with his anger." She was then poked in the belly and told off for trying to hold it in and she giggled.

"You mustn't do that, you are perfectly proportioned, stand natural-ly," Sthiss said.

"Perhaps I should start joining you in your exercises." Nayishma said, looking at herself in the mirror.

Etani gave her a more critical look, blocking out the bias for the woman being such a precious friend.

"I do not claim to know the male brain, but from what I have observed, the men in this city prefer the plumper woman," she said slowly. Nayishma looked crestfallen. "However, you are not a particularly tall woman and your weight is proportionate. If you wish to become more toned, then I welcome you; however, it seems men are sometimes intimidated by a woman with muscles. You are a Lady; you are beautiful and you have exquisite colouring. Any man would be ecstatic to be your husband. As for women, I do not know what they would prefer when it comes to a mate. But I think you are gorgeous." She had spoken clini-cally; the three ladies had first exchanged conspiratorial glances and then smiled.

"Well said, Princess," Sthiss said happily.

"That was lovely," Venorth agreed, her smile soft and warm.

Odvihe was looking at Nayishma with concern, but the moment passed and Etani skimmed over her words to try to find what bothered them. She could not place it.

Letting it go, she smiled, and waited for the work to be done.

"I am thinking mostly black for the Princess Etani. It will enhance the colouring and eyes. We can counter with silver and white for the Princess Nayishma with her warmer tones. Do you feel you can stand to be without a veil, Princess?" Odvihe asked, giving the two Princesses a sly, conspiratorial smile.

They wanted hints, and the Ladies knew it, but she was not giving up any information, and when Nayishma agreed, the plan was set.

The two Princesses finished getting ready and headed back out into the castle, Etani about to head for her tower.

"Come with me to dinner with the King." Nayishma blurted out, fidgeting with her veil now that she was hidden again.

"Yish, you know I can't stand the man." The nickname slipped out, and the two stood in silence for an instant, watching each other. It had been the name she had called the woman for weeks, but only in her own head.

"Please? Then we can spend the evening making fun of him."

Grateful that the name had been ignored, she affected a pout and shook her head.

"Pretty please? I'll get you a present if you do."

Etani narrowed her eyes at her friend. That was low. Lower than low, that was cheating. Nayishma knew full well of her weakness for gifts. She had not received a gift since their mother had been with them, and she cried when Nayishma gave her a small brooch Etani had been pining over. After that, she had to explain, and the girl then took to bribing her. It was also part of her Fae heritage; Fae liked shiny things.

"Cheater..." she said finally, and Nayishma clapped. "Go get changed and meet me outside the hall."

Grumbling, she obeyed nevertheless, swapping out her pants and blouse for a nearly black modest dress that covered her from collarbone to toes and wrists. It fit her well. She pulled her long hair up into a messy knot. She slid two sharpened sticks into it and pulled on a pair of black sandals with gold painted vines that Nayishma had given her. Deciding she was ready, she headed back out.

Slipping out into the hall, she froze at the sound of yelling. It was none other than Epharis himself, and she took off at a run in the opposite direction, leaving the curtain to fall still as she fled.

25

THE KING AND THE BIRDS

*E*tani met Nayishma, and the two linked arms. They headed for dinner, enjoying the silent companionship the other offered. Nayishma giggled at Etani's telling her about Epharis.

Pushing open the door to the private dining room, Nayishma trilled to the irritated-looking man who sat at the end of the table.

"I hope you don't mind that I brought a friend, King Alaric."

The man's face lit up at the sight of the straggler and he stood quickly, coming over to greet them properly. Etani gauged that he did not do that anymore, judging by Yish's tension.

Allowing the man to take her hand and brush his lips against it, she put on her best fake smile.

"It is my utmost pleasure to see you again, Princess." he said, his voice low and growling.

She wondered if he realised that he had been rude from Nayishma's perspective. The Princess only gave a slight tilt of her head as if to say 'See? Told you so.'

"The pleasure is all mine, Your Majesty," she replied, resisting the urge to yank her hand back as he lingered, not wanting to let go.

Finally, he did so and greeted the Princess politely, but his tone was bland.

"Have a meal prepared for the Princess Etani," the King called to a serving-man who stood to the side of an inner door. The man seemed to melt, he vanished behind the door so fast.

The King pulled out their chairs for them, one on either side of the table next to his chair at the end. They sat and Etani placed her hands in her lap, feeling awkward.

"Where have you been hiding, Princess?" Alaric asked, watching her while making an effort to seem like he was not.

"I go from place to place, testing the area for secluded places to hide," she lied, knowing Nayishma would have a huge grin on her face. She had wanted to ruin Etani's night, she just knew it.

"I see, why do you not return to your rooms?"

"It's harder for people to find me if I'm not in my room." She met his eyes, the remark a pointed reference to him and his brother.

The moment drew on for a beat too long as she and the King stared each other down.

"You're an insolent little beast, aren't you..." he growled. Her eyes narrowed.

"And you're a megalomaniac, we all have our faults."

Nayishma choked on her water and gave a delicate cough as though it were unintentional.

The man looked like he was going to explode, while Etani looked back at him calmly, almost begging him to have a go.

The door opened and three servants entered, each bearing a large tray. Setting them down, their meals were revealed. The King got what appeared to be cow meat, cooked and seasoned with a variety of vegetables. Nayishma got an assortment of odd-looking meats and various roots. It was apparently good, as she eagerly started eating. Her own plate, however, held a large crystal bowl filled with a reddish-brown liquid that glistened ominously.

She looked at it doubtfully and then up to the servant who looked apologetic.

'From the Prince,' he mouthed, and left.

If nothing else, she was sure he did not want her dead yet, so she picked up her spoon and took a sip. Energy zinged through her, and she looked down at the liquid in confusion.

Had the Lich actually managed to synthesise a human soul? She did not think so, but the feeling left her hopeful. He was close.

She began to drink the liquid as delicately as she could, oddly enjoying the almost hypnotic feeling it gave her. She was glad for it and considered for almost a whole minute that she could go to see him, but then changed her mind again.

After they had finished eating, Nayishma stood to leave and Etani followed a beat behind.

"No, stay and talk awhile," Alaric said, standing quickly and motioning to the balcony where two large day beds languished in the dying sunlight.

Pursing her lips, she accepted Nayishma's hand, and the two women led the way out onto the balcony, the King following close behind them.

Settling themselves close together on one, the King was left to sit on the other and the three looked out over the city. Between them, her fingers clasped Nayishma's tightly, their hands hidden by their dresses.

"You should join us regularly from now on, Princess," he said, and Etani squeezed Nayishma's hand.

"That is very kind of you, Your Majesty," Etani replied, not giving him a real answer. "Are you looking forward to the ball?"

"Very much so, I hope you both will attend."

"We will," Nayishma said happily, and the King smiled.

The remainder of their time was left to mild conversation that got no one anywhere but left them all feeling rather irritable, but Etani was too stubborn to give in.

When the women left, she made a quick promise to meet over the following days.

It was three days before she got to see the Princess again, the woman kept busy with Princess's duties, but finally, they met in the library. "You need to come to fittings!" Nayishma cried, flustered.

It was only two days before the ball and she smiled, embracing her friend and then allowing herself to be dragged off.

Neither woman was allowed to look during the process, to the point where a strip of fabric was tied around their eyes. Laughing, the two women felt their way around the room, bumping into each other and various objects. Finally, willing to obey the orders of the maids, she stood still and then stepped into the dress.

It was lighter than she expected, the dress lifted over her naked form. As far as she could tell, the dress was quite tame, made of an inner slip and only one other layer. The bodice was hard, and she knew it would cinch around her, even before it was finished being laced. She slipped her arms into the small sleeves that only covered her shoulders and dropped her arms. It was satin, soft and smooth.

Lifting her arms when she was caught trying to feel her gown for clues, she pouted.

Something was placed around her neck and something soft tickled her cheek. She tried not to jerk away, but it was hard. She thought they might have been feathers.

A heavy mask was placed over her head, and the thing fell down to cover the top half of her face. It covered her head in something she could not feel.

Around her wrists two soft cuffs were placed, but they felt incomplete.

"With markings just down her cheeks, darken the lips?" The maids were whispering to each other.

"Do you have ear piercings, Princess?" Venorth asked, and she shook her head, her head moving weirdly at the movement.

"No, but you can if you need. It will only heal as soon as the jewellery is removed." She lifted her hand to catch the mask as it slid down her face and she felt something long that extended down away from her face to stop just below her chin in a beak-like shape.

"It won't do that once it's finished," Odvihe said gently, fixing it and holding it in place so she could be observed.

"I think patterned as we suggested, can we cinch her any tighter?" Sthiss asked.

"She's only into the lace, not tightened," Odvihe muttered and there was a pause.

"Oh right, I forgot how shapely she is..." Venorth said wistfully and Etani flushed.

"Her breasts are going to be around her ears, we might add more here for modesty." A brush of a finger traced a line over the upper curve of her breasts and there was a general murmur of agreement.

"All right, take her out of it, get Nayishma ready and we'll look at Etani's ears."

Slipping free of the gown, she was led away by Venorth and sat down in nothing but the slip.

"So, she will have a similar problem with the bodice, more for modesty," Sthiss said softly.

"I think the hips need to come in more, she looks like she's carrying around a pumpkin." Venorth added.

"Less on the neck, it's too overpowering. We can add more later, but removing them after will be hard," Sthiss murmured.

"I think otherwise it is perfect," Odvihe exclaimed, sounding far too happy.

Eventually, Nayishma joined her on the seat and the dresses were tucked away. Able to see again, the two settled into a long conversation about the ball. The maids gossiped about what the others would be wearing while working in the sewing rooms. Many of the women were having their maids work down there. Many of the costumes were spectacular, some of them were silly, but that was to be expected.

The ladies made quick work of Etani's ears, applying a pin to her lobes and slipping a small silver ring in each to keep the holes from healing shut. She did not want to mention that earrings had been a sign of marriage for her people. It would be fine.

"Stay here until the ball, the King won't think to come here," Nayishma said when it was time for Etani to leave. Etani thought it was the first place he would go, but she agreed, and the two women spent the last remaining time together locked up, being fitted again and again and spending as much time together as possible.

On the day of the ball, the two women were permitted to linger on the balcony in the sun, but by the time lunch rolled around, they were forced inside to prepare. The ball would start at sunset.

Ignoring the protesting moans of the two women, they were ushered into chairs and their makeup was applied. They were not allowed to look at each other and all the mirrors had been covered.

. . .

HER SKIN WAS POWDERED, her face decorated, and patterns were drawn on her arms and across her chest.

Finally, with her eyes closed, she stepped back into the gown one last time. It was heavy and felt odd.

"Hold onto the chair," Sthiss ordered, and a foot was planted firmly against her backside as the strings of her corseted top were pulled tight, much to her wheezing disgust.

The maid had no issue rearranging her breasts in the top before adding a few more decorations, and then the neck cuff was applied. Things brushed her cheek again, but this time they remained, fluttering up around her right side. They would partially obscure her face, at least she assumed so.

Buttons down her back were pinned into place, pulling lace around her corset and shoulders, leaving most of her upper back bare or only hidden by lace.

Turning on command, she got a sense of the mass of her dress as it rustled. She thought the thing probably added a good foot to her overall size. At least no one would be getting too close to her.

Her hair was slicked back with a sweet-smelling oil and long strands were braided down the side of her face, and allowed to dangle down her front. The headdress was applied and pinned into place.

More painting of her face and the cuffs were added at her wrists. "Now Etani..." Sthiss whispered. Venorth and Odvihe were wrestling with Nayishma who did not want to wear a corset.

"I have added pockets to your gown. It will allow you to carry weapons on your person. In order to keep them from slipping free, the inner layer is separate. All you need to do is shift it to the left and the pockets will open; the more you shift, the wider they will open, so be careful. We do not suspect anything will happen, but you are capable of looking after the both of you. We cannot protect the Princess, so make sure no man gets touchy with her."

Etani nodded, accepting the weapons she was handed and slipping them into place. Sthiss showed her twice how to shift the inner satin to open and close the pockets. She nodded again, satisfied.

"Two minutes, ladies!" Odvihe trilled and the sound of the divider told them they would soon be able to see each other.

Shifting herself to turn in the direction of her friend, her heart pounded at the excitement.

"A touch more on Etani's lips, I think," Sthiss said, and it was applied.

"Nayishma needs that to come up more, or she's going to pop out of her corset." Something was adjusted and when the maids were finally satisfied, the women were allowed to look.

Nayishma was ravishing in a white and crimson gown of frothy fabric that spilled out from her hips. Her skin was patterned with flames and feathers. Her corset was almost bare aside from a little jacket that stopped mid-way down her arms, the sleeve covered in little red and gold feathers.

Her headdress was undoubtedly a phoenix, a small bronze beak flowing smoothly into gold, silver, rose, red, and the occasional green feather that trailed down the back of her head to her shoulders, melting seamlessly into a long creamy white train that spread out behind her.

She wore armbands made of gold that were patterned into the style of flames and seemed to dance like fire when she moved.

Her face was its usual shade, her lips a deep crimson, and little lines traced down each cheek in three spikes away from her eyes, each one punctuated by a glittering red gem.

She did not wear a veil and her eyes appeared huge.

"Now turn and see yourselves," Sthiss said, sounding breathless. Etani turned, not sure what to expect.

The sight of herself stole her breath away, and she knew she was the raven.

Her dress was made of layers of satin, and the same frothy fabric as Nayishma's, except more subdued. It reflected their animals well, the phoenix being flashy while the raven was sleek and subtle.

THE SATIN WAS a deep metallic grey, covered by two sheer layers of the black frothy stuff, a pattern of flying birds starting somewhere behind her and stopping just below her bust.

Her bodice showed her black satin corset beneath, but was covered by delicate lace that covered the corset entirely, reaching up to her shoulders and spilling down only a few inches over her arms. A deep V at her chest that showed off so much cleavage she was not sure where it had all come from.

Her wrists were clad in two cuffs that were decorated with black feathers, yet when they caught the light, they shone blue.

A tight, wide choker covered her throat, long feathers rising up out of one side to cover a small section of her face. The top half was dressed in a mask similar to Nayishma's, except that it was long and black, stretching out past her face and down past her chin. The beak melted into glossy black and dark grey feathers that trailed down over her hair, but some stuck out, allowing her to understand why it had felt weird to turn her head. The mask had a lot of wind resistance.

She had been powdered with an odd substance that added a metallic silvery sheen to her skin. It counteracted the black wing outlines that had been traced onto her.

Long streaks of kohl had been painted onto her face under the mask, making her look as though she had cried. In her ears were large silver earrings set with sapphires and dangling tiny black feathers.

"Am I Morrighan?" she asked in wonder, turning to look at Sthiss who was crying happily. She nodded eagerly.

Morrighan was an odd figure in history that a descent few in the area knew of, believed to be the Goddess of war and destiny in that culture. But she had always taken the form of a raven and it was rumoured that she blessed a battle if there were ravens on the field.

She could not help but wonder at the choice.

Turning again to the radiant sight of Nayishma, she smiled at the beauty and had been about to speak when a gong went off.

"Oh, you must go or you'll miss introductions," Odvihe squealed, handing the two elaborately tooled silver masks that looked so akin to lace that she had to feel it to be sure it was not.

"Your masks can be worn as just a headdress, wear these instead if the masks get in the way."

"Introductions?" Etani asked. Nayishma did not know either, for she shrugged, and they headed in the direction of the ballroom.

To get to the ballroom, one had to enter through the main doors and turn left, avoid the throne room, and instead follow the outer wall into a room that backed onto the throne room. They fell into the throng of people, or rather the throng of mythical creatures.

There was something of everything there: a peacock, a star, a woman dressed oddly as a jester. Some wore huge, elaborate gowns, and some opted for simple ones.

She knew early on that her mask was going to get in the way of her vision and she quickly slipped on the smaller mask, pushing the larger one up so that it rested on the crown of her head. She could see much better and it made her feel more comfortable.

Nayishma followed suit soon after, saying she was struggling to turn her head properly. The costumes looked amazing, and the ladies had done them both an enormous service, but they had been designed for fashion, not for function.

The line began to form several yards back from the doors to the ball-room and music drifted out to them. They were required to wait, and so Nayishma started up conversations with a man disguised as a black centaur unicorn. The horn was squishy when Nayishma asked to touch it.

His costume was brilliant, large squared off gloves, a glistening bare bronze chest, and a long mane running down his back. He wore hoof-styled shoes and had large amounts of hair coming out of his ankles.

He seemed glad for the attention, chatting happily with the Princess. Etani however, felt as though someone was watching her and she looked around, finding several staring at her costume, but there seemed to be no malice.

Slowly the line moved and Nayishma made friends with a sphinx, a rabbit, and a cyclops.

The Princess was delighted by the costumes, while Etani grew more anxious. The feeling of being watched would not leave her. She let Nayishma do almost all of the talking while she simply kept an eye on those around them.

26

THE SPRING BALL

*W*hen it was finally their turn, they stepped onto the balcony and saw that the ballroom was sunken compared to the rest of the castle. Around twenty steps led down to the floor below. Scanning the room, Etani watched the crowd while they milled around. It was difficult to tell who was who.

"The Princess Nayishma of Weorene and the Princess Etania of the Winter Court of Faerie," the announcer boomed out.

Heads turned as their names were called out, and the two exchanged a glance.

King Alaric, who was dressed as a warrior, perked up, looking towards the balcony. Another figure turned their way and her eyes met those of Epharis, who was dressed as a wizard. He stared just as hard as his brother.

Turning to the stairs, she was forced to release Nayishma's hand, allowing her to lead the charge.

With one hand on the balustrade, the phoenix descended the stairs, her free hand holding up the hem of the gown so she did not trip.

Mimicking her, Etani followed the Princess. She was glad when they reached the bottom and she could settle her dress again. The shift in weight had been pinching her side, and the pinch eased when the dress was dropped.

The Princess led the way through the milling crowd as the next couple were introduced. They stopped before King Alaric, both curtsying deeply before the man as was standard for such events, according to Nayishma's extensive knowledge of Court life.

The King dismissed them with a wave, yet his eyes were fixed on Etani. Turning her back on him, she allowed herself to be pulled into a small group of dancers, grinning when Nayishma placed her small hand against the black fabric at her waist.

"Now Yish, don't get any ideas," she teased. The woman pulled her into a dance when the beat dictated.

They moved seamlessly to the music, swapping hands and turning back the way they had come, Nayishma even going as far as to twirl her, which set Etani to laughing quietly.

Before too much longer, they were both asked to dance, she by a man wearing what appeared to be a high general's uniform. The man who took Nayishma wore a cloak with large horns sticking out of his forehead. He was a demon, and Nayishma was delighted to have a chance to dance with a demon.

Accepting his offer, she placed her hand in his, and her other hand on his shoulder, allowing him to lead her into the slow steps.

He was young, perhaps in his early twenties, with a pointed little beard she found oddly charming. His eyes were sapphire blue, and she noticed he had slightly pointed ears. Giving him a more clinical appraisal after that revelation, she thought that he might be a Halfling elf.

"My name is Rictor," he said in a low, smooth voice.

"Etani," she whispered, allowing him to twirl her and stepping back to him.

"You're the Princess that showed up without warning one day?" He seemed genuinely curious and her grin was all the confirmation he needed. He grinned back, tilting her into a dip that bent her back over his forearm. Straightening again, he pulled her smoothly into the next song as the music changed.

"You're an elf general?" she asked, falling into step with him.

"I am, I am General Leonold of Astor." His chest puffed up as he spoke, and she laughed. The man of whom he spoke had been a famously ferocious and dedicated elf that had lived some three hundred years previously. He had led his King into victory multiple times, finally to be cut down by his own King, who poisoned him.

"Let us hope you do not meet the same fate."

It took him a moment to realise she was teasing him, and his smooth face flushed.

Promising to dance with him again later, she was pulled away by another man, this one dressed as a pirate, wooden leg included. She had to wonder if he actually cut off his leg to suit the part.

His dancing was a little awkward, but it was more fun for that fact and he was quick to laugh.

"Riskal the Rascal," he boomed. The man was huge, standing well above her height. He had a big red beard, and wore a white shirt that was open to midway down his chest, showing red chest hair too. He had on brown pants and a red sash around his waist held a sword.

"Quite a pretty little thing, aren't you," he said jovially, and she 'accidentally' stepped on his foot, which made him laugh.

AFTER TWO DANCES WITH HIM, she had lost track of Nayishma. Refusing a dance to a man dressed as an angel, she invited him to join her for a drink before heading back out onto the floor and he happily followed. His little golden wings were charming, and his round face matched his round belly perfectly.

She took the opportunity of the drink to look around, locating her little Phoenix towards the back of the room, dancing with the unicorn centaur from the hallway.

The night progressed quickly, she passed from hand to hand, and stopped to locate her friend whenever she lost track of her.

Her night soured when the hands that found her next were thin and cool. Looking up, she found Epharis looking down at her.

He slid his arm around her waist and pulled her close as he began the dance. She had to admit he was an exceptional dancer.

"You have been hiding from me," he said calmly. She knew that calm was more warning than if he had been shouting.

"Hiding is a strong word, I'd say—" she cut off as he jerked her closer to him and gasped, almost falling into him. He caught her, using the action to whisper in her ear. "If you hide from me again, I will tear this city apart to find you."

Releasing his grip on her, she fell into step with him again. She swallowed, meeting his eyes. He was deadly serious, and she shivered at the thought of being alone with him.

The music changed, but no one was brave enough to try to take her from the Prince, and so she fell into step with the new pace.

He kept her close, only allowing her far enough way to twirl before pulling her close again.

Releasing her hand, he dipped her back, and she felt his fingers tracing up her throat, feeling her naked skin. The move was so incredibly sensual and possessive that she wanted to hit him, but she did not touch him. A flick of his fingers had the choker fall free of her throat and his eyes lingered.

"I have always thought your throat was beautiful," he murmured and pulled her upright once more.

Gritting her teeth, she tried to free herself from him, turning only to have her arm caught and her body pulled back against him, her back to his chest.

He moved so seamlessly that it looked entirely intentional, as though it were all simply part of the dance. Two more steps of the dance and his arm curled around her jaw, turning her face to his, her body entrapped in his arms.

His face was so close to hers, she could barely think. He released her, spinning her out only to draw her back in once more.

"Epharis, why can't you just let me go?" she whispered as his arm curled back around her. They spun in a circle slowly, their bodies turned so that they gazed behind each other though their faces were turned to each other.

"You are mine," he said simply, his fingers tracing her jaw as she was let out, both taking a step back and then moving back in towards each other.

"Only for so long as you need me," she retorted. The expression on his face gave her chills.

"You will be mine forever, Etani, Princess of the Winter Court. I never intended to let you leave."

The words resounded in her chest and she jerked her hand free of his, but he caught her again and pulled her into another twirl.

Anger built up in her, and she wanted to escape, to find Nayishma, but the woman had disappeared in the crowd once more.

"You lied..." she whispered, her heart aching for a reason she could not understand.

The lich nodded once, his eyes lifting from her to something that was happening at the back of the room.

The music cut off sharply, and the crowd surged back.

Epharis's arm went around her protectively even as she turned, trying to understand what was happening.

A scream resounded, and the sound struck a chord in her that filled her instantly with cold.

"Yish?" she asked automatically, looking around her. None of the faces were ones she recognised.

Prying the lich's arm off her, she pushed past those around her, searching for her friend.

Guards had moved forward, shoving people out of the way to get to the incident.

A GLANCE at Alaric told her the King had been watching the dancers from his throne, but he was now standing, his face pale.

Dread filled her at his fear, and she shoved harder, struggling to get people out of her way.

The smell of blood hit her like a wall, and she knew instantly that something truly awful, something life-altering, had happened. She did not know how she knew, but she did not think Nayishma was all right.

The crowd went silent as the scuffle broke apart, something or rather someone slumped to the floor, blood spilling around the figure. She tried to get closer, but people were backing away. Then she saw who it was.

"Nayishma!" she screamed. People were quick to get out of her way then, and she ran for the Princess, her silvery-white and gold gown turned crimson.

An attempt to stop her was made, but an elbow to the face was all it took to get them to back off. Slipping in the blood, she staggered to her knees and her arms went around the Princess, lifting the woman's light frame into her lap.

"Yish, you're going to be okay," she whimpered, scanning the wound and knowing it would not be okay. The blood was the distinct colour of venous blood. "I'm here, it's okay... It's okay..."

Nayishma looked up at her, her bloody hand resting against Etani's face.

"No, my darling, I'm not."

They both knew the Princess lacked the ability to heal given her heritage. Etani wanted to scream and rage that monsters like her could heal, and the good, sweet, wonderful Nayishma could not.

"Yish I'm sorry... I could not get..." She went still at a little shake of the head from the dying Princess.

"It was my time, that's all. But... I do not want to die like this, not from a knife... Please..." Yish stared up at her and through the cloud of anguish and horror, she could see what Nayishma was asking.

"I can't..." she whimpered, hating herself. Nayishma drew her closer, her eyes fluttering.

"One last gift from me to you, kiss me," she whispered, her breathing erratic.

For an instant, Etani felt a horrible terror in herself, knowing that her best friend wanted her death to be at the hands of someone she cared for.

She knew she would do this for the woman.

Leaning down, she caught the delicate jaw in her fingers and lifted her face. Ignoring the gasps of those around them, she kissed the Princess.

When she delved, she could feel the fluttering of a soul that was desperately clinging to its home, but when her tendrils reached for Nayishma, the soul turned and reached for her in return, arms wide in welcome.

When she withdrew, she constructed a box in her mind, one simple and delicate. The lid was carved into elaborate detail that showed the beautiful face of her friend. Placing the soul in the box, she pressed it shut. She was not going to consume her friend, she was going to keep her safe and warm, stored away deep in her heart.

By the time her eyes opened, the Hall had been cleared, all except a large number of guards, the King and Prince, the vampire twins, and the werewolf woman. Behind her, she heard the blubbering of the captured assassin.

Lifting her head, she could feel the blackness retreating from her eyes and they met those of Alaric, who was staring at her both horrified and intrigued. She vaguely noted that he had never seen her kiss before, but that did not matter now.

Hearing a grunt and then a scream of pain she turned, her eyes falling on the murderer. Laying the Princess down gently, she turned and pushed herself up in the same move. Epharis had known what she was planning, and he wrapped his iron-strong arm around her middle, even as she went for the man.

Screaming her rage, she tried to elbow the man in the ribs, but he merely grunted and wrapped his free arm around her chest, hugging her to him.

"Let go, Lich!" she raged, struggling and wriggling, but his grip would not budge. He let her scream profanity, hit him, and even break a few toes in her stamping his foot, but still, he held onto her.

"We need information, Etani," he said finally when she had gone still. Her breaths came in ragged pants and her eyes were locked on the man who looked like he was about to vomit in fear.

"I'll get anything you want from him," she said, wanting nothing more than to get her hands on the assassin.

"You are too emotional." He said it dispassionately, his arms tightening in response to her tensing muscles. He nearly hugged her off the ground, her back pressed into his chest.

Making an effort to relax her muscles, she turned to the King, glaring at him.

"I am going to interrogate him," she demanded. The man's brows lifted, seemingly not offended by a mere Princess making a demand of a King.

"Very well, Epharis will monitor to assure we get the information we need."

Her grin was savage as she turned back to the man and he made a squeaking sound, seeing the two of them together, the Lich restraining her.

Epharis looked frustrated, but he agreed and only after the man was led away did he release her.

Stepping away from him, she turned to see Nayishma being gently lifted from the ground into a stretcher by her crying maids.

Hurrying over, she helped them and frowned at the veil that covered her face. She removed it, throwing the wretched thing in the drying blood. As the Princess was lifted, Etani leant down and kissed her forehead gently.

"I'm sorry..." she whispered to the maids, each of whom hugged her tightly before departing with the Princess.

"Where are they taking her?" she asked, sensing the Lich had followed close behind her.

"They will have her treated so she can be returned home in a proper state as is befitting her status," he breathed. She knew that meant embalming her, a form of entombing her in her perfection.

"Don't let them veil her."

The man gave a low murmur of agreement and placed his hand lightly on her shoulder, turning her. Her eyes lingered on the retreating group, finally turning to look at him once they had vanished down the hall. She blinked at the intensity of his stare. This was the first time he had gotten his hands on her, outside of a formal setting, in months of trying to find her while she had hidden from him.

She had to think he was restraining himself from throttling her, but instead, he only spoke in a low voice, squeezing her shoulder and pulling the headdress off her, handing it to a guard to have it taken up to her rooms, and ordering the Princess not be veiled.

"We will deal with this assassin now, then we will talk."

She nodded, planning to slip away before the latter, but she wanted to get her nails into the man who had dared to touch her friend.

Allowing him to lead the way, she followed him down into the dungeons and still further down and she realised that was where he had kept her, but not which room had been hers.

They found the man in the sixth room on the right side of the hall. The Lich allowed her to open the door, watching as she pressed her hand against the centre of it.

It swung open slowly on screeching hinges. The man screamed as her feral grin turned on him, her eyes alight with malice. She was still wearing the blood of the woman he had murdered.

She was going to destroy him, and she was going to enjoy every minute of it.

He had ended the life of one of the most beautiful, kind, and gentle people she had ever had the privilege to meet, and she was going to make him pay for that.

After she made him pay, she was going to make whoever sent him pay.

Stepping inside, the Lich followed her, and the door slammed shut with a deadly finality.

27

THE ASSASSIN AND THE CHURCH

*S*he had been gentle at first, merely asking him who had sent him and when he did not respond, she punched him, clinically observing as his broken nose and bruises healed rapidly.

That got her undivided attention because the man was undeniably human.

"Can humans develop abilities?" she asked of the Lich, even as the man's nose popped back into place.

"No, they are human because they have no magic. If they had magic, they would be mages, witches and the like." He had also taken a keen interest in the man, coming closer from his position against the wall by the door. He was there to observe, not assist.

"Interesting..." she said as she leant closer. Tilting her head, her nose brushed the skin of his throat as she took a deep breath. He smelled like a human, she could not smell even a hint of anything magical about him. Straightening, she used her index finger to wipe a drop of blood off his jaw. Touching it to her tongue, she felt a zing of energy go through her, the blackening of her veins around her eyes vanishing as fast as they formed. The Lich's eyebrows rose at the sight and she shrugged. She had never told him about her and blood, and she had no intention to start now.

His blood tasted human, pure human. Shaking her head, she crossed her arms as she considered him, the development momentarily distracting her from her task.

"He is pure human. Completely and totally. A curse wouldn't leave a magic fingerprint if it were done by a talented being." The Lich was one such being. The curse he had laid on her did not so much as register on her being. That made her look to him, but she dismissed the possibility. He had no reason to risk war with Nayishma's father by having her killed.

"So, who cursed you, little human?" she asked conversationally.

The man clenched his jaw, refusing to speak. He was angry at her. She had found and confiscated the little pill of cyanide he had hidden in the collar of his shirt.

"Very well, I'm bored of this tactic, time to move on." She turned to a small table the Lich had delivered upon request; most of the tools looked horrific, but were essentially useless. They were all for show. The more mundane tools, however, were not. Picking up a pair of pliers, she clicked them twice, the sound seeming to make the room vibrate with their malice.

Approaching the man, she hooked her foot around a little wooden stool and drew it closer, dropping down onto it in front of him.

"Who sent you?" she asked calmly as she placed the pliers against his middle fingernail. She looked up to see the man both glaring at her and sweating profusely. She looked back dispassionately, and when he did not speak for twenty seconds, she clamped down on the nail and slowly peeled it off.

The man's screams were anguished, but she ignored them.

Bending down, she removed the boot on his right foot.

"Who sent you?" she asked when his screaming turned to sobs. She set the pliers against his big toe, the threat resounding. He shook his head, but he was cracking. Meeting his eyes, she slowly peeled off his toenail.

His screams were terrible, but still, he refused to name who had sent him. Losing her patience with him, she stood and planted her foot on his chest, pushing him back. As he began to topple, she caught the seat between his legs and eased him back onto the ground. She did not want him to crack his head open and make it hard for him to talk.

Picking up a cloth and a jug, she held them above him in threat. The man whimpered but clenched his jaw. She shrugged and placed the cloth over his face. Epharis moved to help without being asked, kneeling and grabbing the sides of the cloth to hold it down tight.

"Last chance," she said, and the man called her something that sounded remarkably like 'Lich whore.'

She began to pour, slowly. At first, the man did not react. Then he began to choke and thrash. The two watched with clinical indifference as he nearly drowned, only to have the cloth removed.

The man looked terrified, gasping in as much air as he could, and choking on water.

"High Priestess Amalee," he said between gasps.

The Lich moved, and she looked up. He had schooled his expression, but she knew he knew something.

"Who is that?" she asked.

"The high Priestess who worships my brother's mother," Epharis said slowly. "Why would she care enough to kill a foreign Princess?"

"The Princess was here to marry King Alaric; she would sully the Royal line. No half-human should ever be allowed to take the throne or bear a child from the God-King."

Etani looked to Epharis, who looked disgusted.

"The Princess did not want to marry Alaric," she said, not understanding.

"She did not have a choice. It was a prophecy that the Princess that came to the castle would marry the King Alaric." All three realised the error at the same instant. Nayishma had been brought, but Etani was the Princess who had come, even if she did not know she was a princess at the time. He had killed the wrong Princess.

"Did Alaric know about this plot?" she asked, ignoring the Lich who was still staring at her.

"No, we did not want him to stop us over some petty risk of war. War is nothing to the threat to the Royal line." He did not sound so sure then, studying her more carefully than she liked.

"The prophecy is about you..." Epharis said and they both looked at the prisoner. He was staring at her still with an odd, fanatic gleam in his eyes.

"Prophecies aren't real. They are vague stories made up by hallucinating drug addicts that were given the title of 'Oracle' by men. These aren't real. These things aren't set in stone and no one is destined to do anything." She stood calmly, meeting his darkening glare. "They will only happen if you follow them. I have no intention of getting married to Alaric and will never allow it to happen." She did not like that look, the one that almost screamed 'mine.'

Turning her attention back to the trembling man, she sat down beside him with her legs crossed, giving the jug a shake to see how much water they had left.

"So, you killed my best friend because of a story this Priestess told you. Who are you?"

"Joseph, just Joseph. I am an acolyte for the church," he said. She thought him a little old for the status, but let it go.

"Where is this church?" she asked, making a mental note to give this Priestess a visit.

"Underground. Centre of the city," he said, eyes lingering on the jug. A glance told her Epharis was out of commission for the time being.

"Is that right? Perhaps you should take me. I'd like to have a chat with this Priestess." She grinned at him, his eyes going wide.

"Yes, yes I'll take you," he squeaked.

TEN MINUTES later she had her new companion bound, gagged, and stumbling along ahead of her on a leash attached to his throat. It had started raining heavily, and she felt it suited her mood. She was so angry right then, but soon that anger would fade, and she would be left with the crippling loss of her friend. Until such time, she was going to make use of her fury.

She crushed the thought and focused on the task at hand. The Lich had dumped an oiled cloak on her head as they left; the thing was his, and it dragged on the ground, but it kept her dry. The Lich only glowered when she looked to his own bare head. Knowing better than to argue with him, they set off.

It was dark, and the rain made it hard to see. They had made it halfway across the city when Epharis grabbed the back of the cloak, yanking her back. She staggered, and the rope went limp; she was about to snarl at the Lich when she saw their prisoner on the ground, an arrow sticking out of his face. Lifting her eyes, she saw another one where she had been a second before. Turning, she saw the third arrow sticking out of Epharis's chest.

He looked more annoyed than anything, pulling it out and throwing it to the ground.

"Check him," she said, and before he could stop her, she dropped the cloak and ran for the wall. Planting one foot against the bricks, she pushed herself up and caught the tiles of the ceiling. Climbing up, she rolled, just in case. Staying on her belly, she scanned the rooftops.

"There..." she hissed and shoved herself to her feet. She was after the figure in a second, her hair sticking to her, her dress shredded by her nails to allow her faster movements. She heard the Lich yelling her name, but she ignored him. The figure was heading in the direction of the city centre, and she was catching up on him. There was one thing to say for supernatural strength: it made her fast.

Seeing the figure vanish, she pushed herself as hard as she could, and leapt off the roof. The figure went into a cemetery of all places. Airborne, she saw him look up and reach for another arrow. But she was faster, landing in a roll, and ducking behind a tombstone.

She peeked over it. She saw the figure notch the arrow, but he was unable to find her in the gloom. Cursing, the figure ran for a large stone tomb at the centre of the cemetery.

SHE WAS AFTER HIM AGAIN, her bare feet splashing in the rain, but he did not seem to hear her. He yanked the door open and vanished inside. Rather than go in after him, she stopped at the side of the door and listened to the sound of running footsteps.

Then she followed the figure. The tomb was large and filled with too many candles and a statue of a large woman with an elaborate headdress.

Not stopping to consider where she was, she bounded down the stairs after him. She was just fast enough to turn her body at an angle to avoid being skewered by an arrow.

"Leave this place, scum!" a man's voice called from a few feet away.

"I just want to talk," she called back.

He swore at her and she laughed. That was not very nice.

"With your Priestess, not you," she clarified. "That is, if she still wants her prophecy to fail."

It was bait, the man probably knew it, but still he bit.

"Come into the light. Who are you?" he asked warily. She peeked around the corner, saw his bow was down, and stepped into view.

"The Princess your Priestess did not know about," she said, taking a moment of pleasure in his shock.

He stared for a moment, then motioned for her to follow.

The deeper they went, the more the place began to creep her out. A few feet back from the stairs was another statue, this one screaming with a large axe at the ready. She did not know much about this Goddess, but she seemed mean.

He led her through a door and into a large cathedral. She did not have a clue how the thing existed, all silver-inlaid stone and glass. It had huge windows that depicted the Goddess, and a very odd-looking Alaric.

Turning, she found not one but nine bows pointed at her from alcoves along the walls.

"I think you cheated," she said to her companion, who made bow number ten.

He smirked at her and shoved her forward towards a door at the back of the cathedral that was glowing red. She walked calmly, her mind working on what she would have to do in order to escape. She could take out her companion and one other in a second, but then she would be dodging eight arrows. It seemed wise to just wait and see what would happen.

Passing through the door, she took a moment to wring out her hair, giving her companion a nasty look when he tried to push her along.

"Need to look good for my meeting with the woman who wants me dead," she said, giving her tattered dress a shift.

The idiot had not checked her for weapons, and she was loaded. She had even weaved two vials into her hair, checking their status when she wrung it. They were intact. The shifting of her dress had been strategic, for the move to the side had opened the pockets to her weapons. Sthiss was a genius.

They headed down yet another corridor, and she could smell the sheer number of humans nearby, presumably with weapons pointed at her.

Thinking of guiding Epharis to her, she patted down her dress and tore off a shred of fabric, tossing it aside as though she was not really thinking about it. But if Epharis managed to track them, the fabric would guide him straight to her.

The next door led into an enormous natural cavern that was teeming with people, all of them kneeling in prayer to a massive statue of the Goddess and Alaric. She was staring up at it when they were noticed. Whispers spread through the cavern.

A woman on a dais looked up from something she had been reading aloud to her people.

"What is this, Henry?" she asked, curious.

The woman was unusual-looking, with tanned skin and silvery hair, yet she was young.

She wore a steel brassiere that hung with fabric from between her breasts around her back. It left a triangle at the front of her body visible, and her skirt was made of the same material hung with wide strips of crimson fabric at her front to cover her. The fabric trailed to the floor between her feet but left her sides entirely bare. She wore a strange spikey silver patterned tiara and a necklace that covered much of her chest along with two armbands in the same pattern that covered her arms from wrist to elbow. A silver crescent moon hung point-up from the front of her skirt contraption, and a design to match her arm bands was painted onto her thighs and shins in silver.

She languidly stood and Etani had the sudden unpleasant realisation that this woman was exactly like the Queen of Ceress. They were so alike it made her skin crawl. The overall effect was odd, but also erotic even though she had overdone it.

"This woman had Joseph, and he was leading her here and so I killed him. She followed and is claiming to be the Princess of prophecy." He yelled the words, making everyone look up.

Etani had stopped paying attention and was instead looking around the cavern. Walkways had been strung up to join little platforms all around the ceiling and they were heavy with men, women, and an awful lot of arrows.

Why would a church need so many guards? Right, Goddess of War with a tyrant for a King who happened to be the Goddess's son.

They were still talking, but Etani tuned them out in order to scope out the room. She knew it would antagonise them, but it would entertain her just a little.

When the man grabbed her arm, she smiled and turned, her own hand lifting to curl slender fingers around his throat. The movement would have been missed had any of them blinked, and she strained, lifting him a few inches off the ground.

"Never touch me," she whispered, but with the silence of the room, her voice was loud.

Bows were drawn and she could not help but think she now had a very handy meat shield should they decide to loose those arrows.

"Let him go," the Priestess demanded in a husky voice. Etani considered that, and then let go. He hit the floor in a heap with a loud thud. Looking down at him, she tilted her head just enough to see the Priestess.

"So, let's chat."

The Priestess nodded once, the arrows were lowered, and Etani started forward as the Priestess motioned for her to approach.

As she walked, she felt people moving around her in a wave as though she had touched them. They withdrew and yet she felt as though they wanted to reach out and touch her. She hated them looking at her like that, but what else could she do?

As she moved, she felt an odd breeze rush over her, her hair brushed back and when it settled again, it was dry. The same happened to her dress and her skin.

The Priestess looked confused by the change, but then irritated as though something had gone wrong.

ETANI HAD NOT BEEN responsible for it, but she was not about to complain.

Stepping up onto the dais, the priestess turned, and she followed as the slender, swaying woman stepped behind the enormous statue and down another flight of stairs that turned back on itself, leading into a long corridor lined with doors. This must be where the people lived...

She followed the priestess to one of the first two rooms. Etani paused, wary, but a deep breath told her the room was empty, so she followed.

The priestess set to lighting the room. Etani lingered near the door. She was surprised by how barren the room was, only a bed, a desk, and a wardrobe.

"Interesting home for a high priestess," she said slowly, realising that it was not her room at all, but rather just one that would be empty.

"Who are you?" the Priestess snapped, turning on Etani.

"Princess Etani of the Winter Court," she said calmly, moving to the closet and opening it to find it filled with nothing but grey robes.

She closed the closet again, now out of things to keep her interested. Looking over her shoulder, she smiled at the Priestess.

"And what is your name?" she asked.

"I am the High Priestess Amalee," the Priestess replied, looking sceptical.

"Well Amalee," She was not about to give this woman any respect. "You and I have a problem. You see, your little assassin did not kill the 'Princess who came to the city.'" She used her fingers in sarcastic quotations. "As a matter of fact, he killed the Princess who had been brought to the city, and had about as much interest in Alaric as I have, which is to say none." The Priestess had opened her mouth angrily, and Etani took the opportunity to turn, her arm flinging out and sinking deep into the woman's stomach. The Priestess doubled over, wheezing, and Etani examined her hand. She had caught her knuckles on the elaborate belt the woman wore.

"That woman you killed was my best friend, Amalee, and I am not a woman who handles loss well. Do you know what I do here in Ayathian?" She waited patiently for the woman to respond, but she was still wheezing. "Well, you see, I kill people for Prince Epharis. And further, I am also happy to inform you, I am a mass murderer. In particular, I enjoy killing humans, much like yourself." The burning rage inside her was reaching a boiling point and when the woman seemed to be about ready to stand, Etani curled her fingers in the woman's hair and drove her knee up into the woman's face.

"In fact, I quite literally eat humans like you for breakfast. Your species is my food source, isn't that fascinating?" Her voice had become low and clinical once more. She let the fury build, simmering just under her skin, and she knew her eyes had begun to glow in her fury.

"You killed the best friend of a soul-eating assassin because you had the wrong name." The woman hit the floor, cradling her bleeding face and crying. "You killed her because she was in your way, regardless of whether she was the right Princess or not."

Reaching down, she grabbed the woman's jaw and forced her to her knees, their eyes meeting, blue on green.

"You killed the only person in this city that I cared about, because of a story you were told. And you did not even bother to try to find out if there was a possible second Princess, who, incidentally, was more likely to be the right woman, given Nayishma was a lesbian. She would sooner have slit her own throat than marry a man." Her rage had peaked, and she felt numb, her fingers trembling just slightly as she leant in. A maniacal laugh started up in the back of her mind as her lips parted, and she licked the blood from the Priestess's face.

"I'm going to kill you, Priestess, and then I'm going to eat you. Not your soul, you are not worth the death my kind can offer, but rather I'm going to eat your flesh, starting from that pretty face." She lifted her free hand and drew a slow, clean line down the woman's cheek with one nail, blood welling immediately. "You see, I love the taste of human flesh. That is a secret I never tell anyone, but it excites me. The question is, should I allow you to live long enough to see me eating you?"

She grinned at the woman's squeal of terror.

"I only have one question for you, Amalee. What is one reason why I should keep you alive?" she purred, having leant forward until she could see her own glowing eyes in the woman's terrified ones, see the specks of silver that had not been there before, glittering in the candlelight. "One reason, Amalee."

The woman was incoherent, blubbering and praying.

"Your Goddess won't help you this time," she cooed, and let go of her jaw. Reaching her hand back, she smiled and then shoved her hand through the woman's chest. Blood splattered everywhere and Etani could feel it, the heart fluttering madly.

"What a pity, you were quite pretty," she lamented as she curled her fingers around the organ, feeling arteries tearing.

She tugged and the woman's entire body jerked forward, her eyes huge.

"Goodbye, Amalee, say hello to your Goddess for me, I'll be coming for her next if she tries to meddle in my life again. I have no issue with being known as a God killer." With that, she pulled the still racing organ free. In the seconds that followed, Amalee stood alert and terrified, watching as Etani bit into the organ and ripped away a chunk.

As she swallowed, the woman dropped dead in a heap on the floor. A beat passed and then an alarm went off somewhere in the cavern.

Turning, Etani held the heart in her hand and left the room, leaving the corpse where it was. She stopped and turned back, removing the armbands and the large necklace. They were nice, she would keep them.

With the jewellery in one hand, the heart in the other, she made her way back up the stairs and stepped onto the dais.

She came to a slow stop as she saw who was standing in the middle of the cavern. King Alaric had come to join the party, late. Typical...

Neither of them spoke for a long moment, the sound of blood dripping from the heart was loud.

"Etani..." he growled, and she smiled at him slyly, licking blood from her lips.

"Eye for an eye, Alaric," she purred, delighting in his anger.

Finally, he saw what she was. Finally he would realise she was not someone to toy with. Her brows lifted as his sword was unsheathed.

"Going to kill me, Alaric?" she asked, only mildly concerned.

Rather than turning on her as she expected, he lifted the sword and spoke a single word she did not understand. Arrows rained down on the parishioners. Their screams of horror turned to anguish as they were all cut down, the room quickly going silent.

"You are a monster..." he breathed, his eyes alight. "Marry me."

28

LOSS AND RETURN

*O*nly minutes after Alaric proposed, Epharis arrived and collected her in her stunned state. This most recent development squashed her anger in an instant.

Halfway back to the castle, she turned, screaming and raging at him, punching him and kicking him, clawing his face and breaking several parts of him.

It lasted several minutes until she sank to the ground and screamed in pain at the loss of her friend.

Finally, the anger vanished, and all that was left was her loss. Her screams resounded in those who heard them, unearthly and broken.

Epharis wrapped her in his arms, enduring her struggles and repeated hits to his chest and shoulders. He endured everything she gave him, still holding her when she succumbed to tears and cried into his chest.

Her entire body heaved, her fingers ripping holes in his costume as she clung to it for support. Head bowed between her arms, her tears fell freely onto the cobblestones and the length of her hair that pooled between them.

"What am I going to do?" she pleaded of the Lich, unable to lift her head.

"I don't know," he said, sounding as though he were in great pain.

She did not care.

Clenching her eyes shut, she sucked in a huge breath of air and screamed her pain into the void, dissolving into crying once she ran out of breath again.

She did not know how long she stayed there, kneeling in his arms. But it was nearly morning before she finally stopped.

Empty, she curled herself into Epharis's side, her cheeks stained. The blood had long since dried and flaked, and much of it had fallen off.

Her chin lifted, and she looked up at the sky, staring up at the stars and trembling.

Arms tightened around her and she snuggled closer to the warmth of him. She no longer cared what he had done or who he was, she simply wanted someone to hold her and comfort her.

Shifting, he tucked one arm around the back of her knees and one around her back, lifting her up off the ground.

She did not budge, her eyes still lifted to the sky.

Three days later she went hunting for something, anything, that would give her something that would serve as a reminder of the Princess. But the rooms in which the Princess had stayed had been stripped clean and polished. There was nothing.

Standing in the room, tears trailed down her cheeks, and she stood wrapped in a blanket and a dress she had been wearing for days. Her bare feet padding softly.

With her hair loose around her shoulders, she hugged the blanket tighter and crouched down.

The guards assigned to her moved to see what she was doing, but she ignored them.

They had been assigned to be with her at every moment of every day by order of the Prince, and they obeyed.

"Princess, there is nothing left," one of them said, his voice echoing in the helmet.

Epharis had been smart enough to insist they wore their helmets too, after she had kissed the first guard to follow her in a fit of anger.

Ignoring the two men, she slid forward onto her knees, sitting on her heels as she looked around the empty room, searching for anything.

Even a hair from one of the maids would be enough. But the cleaners had done their job well.

Pushing herself back up, she padded into the bedroom and found it empty, blank, and sterile.

Turning back towards the guards, she stared at them for a moment, having forgotten they existed in her mini-mission.

They shifted uncomfortably, knowing the odds of her exploding into a death machine were fairly high.

But then she looked away from them and headed back in the direction of her rooms.

Walking into her rooms, she glanced at the door that the Lich had ordered be installed, linking their two suites together.

Stopping in the middle of her room, she looked around in confusion, not sure what she was looking at.

Something was different, something had changed in the time it took her to get from her room to the library and Yish's rooms and then back.

A loud growling and then two crashes had her turning slowly, her eyes falling on Cain.

He smiled at her as he stepped over the two guards, blood pooling under them.

Looking down, she watched the blood even as Cain approached her, his hand reaching to curl in the hair at the back of her head. He jerked her face to his, the point of his sword pressed against her stomach.

"CAIN?" she whispered, finally registering his face.

He blinked, momentarily taken off guard by the little girl voice and lost look in her eyes.

"What game is this?" he snarled, the point of his sword cutting through her blanket and then her dress.

"You're here..." she sighed, relieved.

The sword withdrew slightly, and he looked shocked by her relief. "You aren't going to fight?" he demanded, seeming to be annoyed more by her lack of resistance.

"Why would I?" she asked, confused.

A sound from their right made Cain jump and when the door opened, he slid smoothly behind her. The hand that gripped her hair only tightened and jerked her head back. The sword blade brushed her throat, blood welling where it touched.

Epharis stepped into the room and froze at the sight. Etani stood limply, clutching her blanket as though it would save her, her neck bent back against the man's shoulder, the sword ready to lop her head off or slit her throat open.

"Who are you?" Epharis barked, lowering his books onto the table.

He had been trying to get her back to herself by using the books.

"Cain of Ceress," Cain snapped back, pulling back his hood to reveal his face.

Recognition showed on the lich's face and he looked between the two of them.

"Very distant cousin," Etani said dryly, earning her head a painful jerk, and new blood trickled down the blade.

"I'm not related to any mongrel whores," Cain almost yelled. "What's wrong with her? What did you do?"

Epharis looked indignant at the accusation. "She lost someone close to her. This is why you are here? To kill her?"

"Yes, this mongrel has been on my list for almost a millennium," Cain replied, taking a step back and pulling her along with him.

"Is that right?" Epharis said slowly, his face going carefully blank, the look he got when he was thinking.

"Yes, now if you'll excuse us, we have to be going." He backed away with her back pressed to his chest, and she met Epharis's intense stare with her own empty one. She did not care if he killed her, she just did not want to hurt anymore. Maybe she could stay in the spirit world for a few years? No, that cursed sword, Orenmir devoured souls just like any good Celestrial. She would be really dead if he did that.

"Then we'll go visit Letari and Avadari, and maybe I'll take your head with me."

It was the wrong thing to say, and he knew it was wrong the moment he said it. Her body went rigid against his and he realised his mistake when he had not tried to restrain her.

Her elbow drove back into his ribs and she turned, ignoring the stabbing pain in her throat. The sword moved away from her neck and he staggered back. Pivoting on her left foot, she turned and lifted her right leg, slamming her heel into his chest.

He fell backwards and vanished over the side of her balcony.

Making her way out onto the balcony, she looked down and then jerked back when Orenmir was thrust up at her face. Stepping back, she looked down to see fingers clutching the edge of the balcony. The man was quick to climb up before she could nudge his fingers off with her toes, as she had been about to do.

He landed hard on the balcony and she stepped back from him, her need to protect her sisters kicking in.

"How did you even get inside?" she asked, an inkling of curiosity demanding an answer to the question.

"Been here since the ball. Security was dropped to let everyone in, so I simply walked in."

"Your brother underestimating people again," she said dryly to the Lich.

Epharis grunted his agreement. Clearly, Alaric had not expected the assassin to be so bold as to simply waltz in through the front doors when that was the only way in or out. The opening in the barrier had only been as wide as the front gates.

"Brother?" Cain asked, and Epharis nodded.

"Prince Epharis of Ayathian. Brother to King Alaric of Ayathian," Epharis said.

Reaching out, he placed his hand on Etani's shoulder and drew her back. Cain's eyes locked onto the gesture and his lip curled even as she retreated.

"Gone so far as to bed a lich, Etani?" Cain sneered, glaring at her.

"No, Cain, I have gone so far as to never have bedded anyone," She retorted, and Epharis twitched slightly.

CAIN'S FACE screwed up as though the thought of her still being pure revolted him, but it was likely anything she said would have revolted him.

"Why don't you come back tomorrow?" Epharis asked, but Cain was working himself up towards another attack.

Reaching into his robe, Epharis drew out the hilt of a sword, holding it at his side while his other hand pushed her back behind him.

She was more than happy to let the two men fight while she sat and watched.

Cain sneered at the handle and shook his head. "Going to take more than that, lich."

In response, Epharis swung the sword down, point facing the floor. As it swung, the handle grew into a large, ornate black frame and the blade began to form, chipped in places.

By the time the arc stopped, the sword had fully formed, so completely black it seemed to suck in light.

"I'm afraid you will have to go through me to get to the Princess," Epharis said.

"Very well, lich, prepare to die."

Cain lunged forward, swinging hard. Sparks flew as the two swords met, the silver sword catching in the grooves in the black sword and allowing Epharis to twist the sword out of the way and plant a solid punch against Cain's face.

Settling herself in a chair, she tucked her knees up to her chest and watched, unable to decide which would be better, an eternity with Epharis or death to Cain.

Swinging again, the tip of Cain's sword scored Epharis's arm and his fingers went slack. In response, he switched arms and struck back with a heavy blow that sent Cain staggering back.

The fighting continued for several long minutes and, though not a whole lot had happened, she decided that the two were very closely matched.

Epharis had the upper hand, given there was nothing behind Cain but open air. Epharis took advantage of that, throwing heavy blows and knocking the smaller man back time and time again. Finally, he planted a kick to the man's midriff and Cain doubled over. He drove his knee up while Cain went down, the man was flung backwards, and this time he fell off the balcony properly.

A moment later they heard the crunch as he hit the ground far below.

Making her way back out onto the balcony, she rested her elbows on the railing and looked down.

"Think he's dead?" Epharis asked, looking down dispassionately.

"I heard he's like me. Dies but doesn't stay dead," she said, sounding just as uninterested.

Watching the form below, she was irritated to see the man roll over and then limp away.

"He'll be back up here as soon as he heals," she said, watching the form vanish around the corner of the castle.

"No doubt," Epharis said dryly, standing beside her to watch. "You're quite the swordsman," she said finally, glancing up to him and noting that some of his long silver hair had been lopped off. "Would you like me to fix that?" she asked, not sure why she asked.

He looked down at his hair, then back to her and gave an awkward nod of ascent.

Leading the way back inside, she picked up a chair and beckoned him into the bathroom with her.

Opening the window and curtains to allow in plenty of light, she sat the lich down and picked up a comb.

It had apparently been a while as his hair was matted, but she worked her way through it slowly, using oil when the knots got stubborn.

Moving to stand before him, her fingers were gentle as she placed them under his chin to lift his face, tilting his head slowly so that his jaw was level.

He stared up at her, his eyes showing his confusion and then alarm when she picked up a pair of scissors.

But she did not try to stab him; instead, she knelt down between his knees and caught the long ends of his hair.

With her eyes on her work, she tugged and pulled his hair, carefully cutting away the longer pieces. By the time she looked up, his face had become a blank mask, careful and empty.

Moving behind him, she pressed her palm against his back and one against his shoulder, straightening his spine and forcing him to sit up straight so she could cut it all in a straight line.

IT TOOK SOME TIME, her need for it to be perfect leading her to take longer than the average person, but by the time she was done, foot-long strands littered the floor around them.

His hair now came to his mid-back, and she found herself running her fingers through it slowly.

Feeling his eyes on her, she flushed and turned away only to have him stop her.

Looking into his eyes, she tried to read him, but he was too good at hiding his feelings.

Leaning down slowly, ever so slowly, her nose was a mere inch from his when her body shuddered, and she gasped. Blood splattered Epharis's face, and they both looked down to see an arrow sticking out of her chest. It would appear that Cain had come back much sooner than expected.

Staggering to the side, Epharis stood and went after the man, the fight loud and angry. Etani, however, blocked them out, trying to figure out what to do with the arrow. She was certain it had hit a lung; she could taste copper.

Curling her fingers around the protruding shaft, she gave the arrow a tug and gasped in pain, unable to get it out on her own.

She could not help but feel that the situation was funny, the intensity of their moment in the bathroom, the near kiss, then an arrow through her chest.

As blood filled her lung, it was suddenly hard to breathe, and she decided that the left one had collapsed. She wheezed, trying to suck in enough air to compensate.

Looking first to her chest and then the wall, she decided that she either needed to break the thing off or shove it out; either way, she was running out of time.

Staggering to the wall, she stopped long enough to cough up a large amount of bright red blood and then turned her back to the wall. Sucking in a difficult breath, she shoved herself back against the wall and the arrow jerked forward, protruding further from her chest.

She wheezed a happy little 'Yay' before she sank down the wall to sit on the floor.

"Epharis..." she breathed, blood bubbling at her mouth as she grabbed the arrow and yanked at it again.

She thought the end of the arrow was now somewhere in the region of her lung. She gave it one last yank and threw the wretched thing to the ground.

Her body worked furiously to try to heal the damage, even as the loss of the arrow increased the speed at which she bled into her lung.

Dropping onto her side, she hacked up more blood and her vision went wobbly, the room spinning.

Gasping in air as her lung inflated once more, she forced herself to cough up the last of the blood and looked towards the door, but she could not see anything.

Shoving herself off the floor, she moved to the door and glanced around to see what was going on. Nothing, the room was empty. They were on the balcony.

Following them out, her eyes narrowed at the sight of Cain's sword against Epharis's throat.

Bending down to pick up the leg of a shattered table, she silently moved up on Cain.

Epharis must have seen her, but he made no move, even when the leg rose into the air above Cain's head.

"Sorry you won't get to taste Celestrial flesh," Cain was saying.

"There will be time," Epharis replied, leaning back out over the balcony railing.

The table leg swung, and her hands vibrated as it struck and rebounded, the man staggering to the side.

Her hand went automatically to Epharis, gripping the front of his robe and dragging him forward to keep him from falling off the balcony.

"Sword?" she said, turning to give Cain another solid beam to the head with her table leg.

"Fell," he said, touching his throat where blood had welled up.

She gave a soft huff and lifted the leg again, preparing for another blow when Cain turned on her, earning her a very well-placed uppercut to the solar plexus.

Air left her recently healed lungs, and she crashed back into the wall of the balcony. Cain turned back to Epharis, who backed off slightly.

Sucking in air through her teeth, she glared at Cain, frustrated that this man was in her way all the time.

Turning back on her, she was shocked when he caught her around the waist and pulled her close to him, her entire form going stiff.

Fingers in her hair, he turned her face to his and planted his lips down on hers.

29

YOU CAN ONLY LOSE SO MUCH BEFORE YOU GO MAD

*T*he world around them vanished as she immediately retreated into herself, shooting down through her being into that place where the glowing figure stood; all the while she had delved just as viciously into him as he had done to her.

On the surface, they would simply be standing with inky blackness spreading from around their eyes, mirroring each other, but internally, the fight had taken a more primal form.

Her consciousness guarded the door, stretching out into him in order to dig her way cruelly through the layers of protection. She found his centre, but there was no protection there, no consciousness keeping his soul safe.

She did not understand that. Even as she felt his consciousness coming to form ahead of her own, she was barred from getting in.

'How?' he thought, not understanding how she could be there and inside him at the same time.

"Haven't a clue. But it is your last mistake," she whispered, her tendrils reaching for his soul, curling around it.

The connection snapped, and they both screamed as their minds rebounded violently into their own forms.

Clutching her head, the world shuddered into focus, everything tinted a horrible black.

Cain recovered first, taking one look at the both of them and then leaping off the side of the balcony and vanishing.

"Where?" Epharis hissed, looking down, but the man had disappeared into nothing.

She could not speak, or she might vomit. Her fingers pressed into her forehead and she sat on the ground with her head between her knees.

She had gotten a taste of his soul and she found herself craving more, desperately hungry.

Shaking her head to clear the thoughts, she looked up to Epharis as he approached her, "I'm sorry, I had to stop it."

Squinting, she tried to process what he said but her mind did not want to put the words into a meaningful sentence.

"Need to sleep..." she said, her own voice sounding weird in her ears.

He helped her to her feet, and she clutched at him to keep from falling over as they walked to her bedroom.

Crawling into bed, she did not care that she was bloody. When he turned to leave, she grabbed at him, pulling him back.

"Stay," she half-demanded, and sighed when she felt him settle down beside her.

Catching his arm, she pulled it tightly around herself, and fell asleep with the musky smell of him filling her senses.

When she woke, it was to a sharp mental jab, and she sat bolt upright.

"Ava!" she cried, trying to figure out where she was.

Turning, she saw she had been asleep on Epharis's chest, the man was still awake and watching her.

"Where's Ava?" she demanded of him and he could only give her a confused look.

"What's Ava?" he asked, sitting up.

"What? Ava, Ava!" she twitched violently as another jab struck at her brain and her eyes went wide in realisation.

Staring at the lich, she felt the sense of terror and urgency. "He's got my sister!"

THROWING herself out of the bed, she ignored the shaking of her vision as she stripped out of her bloody clothes and stumbled into her usual hunting attire, ignoring the gaping lich behind her.

He was quick enough to catch the clothing she threw at him, though, finally getting up and dressing himself.

"Where... Where is Ava? Tell me where!" she called, knowing full well Epharis had no idea what was going on. She had to reach her baby sister.

An image fluttered into her mind and she paused, mid-reach for her belt as she recognised it.

Placing it in her mind, she flicked through places she had been over the last fifty years, shuffling through them as though they were a deck of cards in her hands.

Stopping, she examined one and then nodded, pulling on her belt and then turning on the lich.

She needed him, but this was an enormous part of herself. Part of her life that she did not want him to know about, and she bit her lip, weighing the pros and cons of revealing it to him.

"Screw it," she hissed and grabbed his hand. Passing through the room, she collected whatever weapons she could find and glared at him.

"If you tell a single soul about anything you are about to see, I will kill you myself, be damned the consequences," she snarled, fear making her sound almost rabid.

He looked baffled and angry at her words, but he still nodded.

Eyes narrowed, she glared at him for a moment longer. "Stay here." And then she used her small, sharp canine to bite the tip of her little finger.

She drew a line in the air and her blood hung there, lingering. When she had finished, she reached out for it and pressed against the right side.

The blood stretched, the air warped, and she slipped through the opening, vanishing from that reality into the land of Faerie. She had cut a hole in reality.

Turning on the doorway, she pulled it shut and then opened it again, just enough that she was able to stick her hand through, her mind focused hard on where she wanted that hand to go.

Feeling the grass, she found the hilt of the sword and yanked it through, tugging the door shut fast.

Looking at it, she was surprised to see it had begun to give off an evil grey-green smoke.

Not caring, she opened the door and stuck her hand through once more; this time her fingers closed on the fabric of someone's chest. Curling, she yanked the lich through.

He stumbled in and looked around, not entirely sure what he was doing.

"Welcome to Faerie," she snapped, thrusting the hilt of the sword at him.

"How?" he gasped, and she looked at him, her eyebrows shooting up.

The man looked so completely different; she did not even know where to start.

The gauntness had faded to make him look more human, and he sucked in great heaving breaths as though he had not taken a breath in an eternity.

"We all have a way to get back here if we need to," she said evasively. "You are going to see things here, Epharis. The world is not the same here and we need to move quickly. Ava, or Avadari, is my youngest sister. She is in trouble and she is looking after my twin Letari. Cain went after them, I don't know why he is going now, but we have to get to them now."

Epharis hesitated for only a moment before he nodded. "Let's go," he said quickly.

She grabbed his hand and pulled him through the trees. The trees there were massive, some of their trunks larger than the castle they had just left, and they swayed in the breeze, the bright green leaves whispering gently.

"Don't listen to the trees, they will try to ensnare you," she said, already hearing the whispers and soft feminine giggling.

Dryads lived in the woods and rumour had already spread that there was a man nearby. They had come out to try to get their little fingers into him. It was not hard to understand, given Dryads were always female, so they needed men of other species to help them reproduce.

Tugging him along behind her even as he slowed, she knew the promised whispers were getting to him.

"Epharis, come on. Oh shoo! Be gone tree witch!" she snapped at the woods.

The response was one of deep offense, and the whispers stopped. It was a racial slur, but it usually worked to get the prissy creatures to go away, at least for a little while.

Breaking into a run as they neared the edge of the woods, she threw a glance in the direction she had come to know so very well but then stopped when Epharis stopped.

"Epharis please..."

"Just one moment, I need to..." he trailed off as he saw what someone of his species would only ever be able to dream about.

THE LANDSCAPE WAS SO WEIRDLY flat that it looked like a poorly done painting. But one could see where the four Courts collided.

Winter with its low, silvery clouds fading out before coming to a sharp and sudden stop, butting heads against a clear sky and warm sun.

It was a bizarre, disturbing sight.

Turning, he looked directly away from the join between the two, because it was obvious that they were only two of the four sections.

Behind them, in the distance, sat the spiral City of Ceres, looking very much like a shell she had been given once at a coastal city. It started wide at the bottom, and then slowly spiralled up into a cone, the top of the point housing the palace in which her greatest enemy lived, plotting her death.

"What is that?" Epharis said slowly. The city was surrounded by a thick forest.

"Ceress," she said warily.

"Why is it here?"

"Winter and summer aren't the only Courts, Epharis," she said slowly. His eyes first found hers, then the joining point of the four sides of the weather. Four.

"Four..." he said slowly, staring up at the sky.

To look at, it was clear what the original four had been: Winter, Summer, Spring, and Autumn. But something along the line had changed, spring and autumn becoming corrupted. So, while the skies matched up, the people no longer did.

"I told you, you would see things," she said, meeting his blank stare when he turned back to her.

"You're from one of the two hidden Courts?" When she nodded, he swore slowly.

"We can talk about this later; we have to go."

She froze when a horn went off. She grabbed his arm, pulling him into a dead sprint.

"Damn, the hunt! Go!" she yelled as they ran. The two Courts had sensed an intruder and had come to deal with it. They were not kind to species who should not be in Faerie, regardless of which side of the coin they came from. It was the only time Winter and Summer worked together in harmony.

After a good ten minutes of running as fast as they were able, she skidded to a stop and turned, looking around to try to find the right place, panting hard.

"This way..." she said and pulled him several more steps towards the city of Ceress. Stopping again, she looked up at him and smiled faintly. "This part is going to be uncomfortable for you," she said and bit into her finger, drawing the line and shoving him through unceremoniously. Turning to see two packs of wild dogs pelting towards her, she grinned and slipped through the slit in reality, then stepped out into pelting rain.

The lich was retching hard on the muddy ground, his hands on his knees, and head bowed.

"Yeah, going there is good, but the sudden withdrawal of magic is hard. That is why most of them won't ever leave, it's too painful to lose that connection."

Giving him exactly two minutes to recover himself, she then pulled him along behind her without so much as a word.

Trudging through the wet foliage, they came across a small town that looked a little worse for wear. A scattering of houses sat along a single muddy street filled with pigs and a free-roaming cow.

She scanned the street, but it was empty, at least at first glance. Something moved and her face split into a huge grin as a small, entirely black cat with enormous green eyes came pelting towards her.

Her arms stretched out automatically and she caught the little bundle of fur, hugging it tightly to her chest and then turning to Epharis. With her hands curled under the little cat's shoulders, she held it out.

"This is Lee, Letari."

Epharis looked down at the soaked cat with an expression that made it clear he thought she had lost her mind. The cat hissed at him.

"Letari is a shapeshifter," she explained. The cat gave her a pathetic little mewl.

Hugging the cat to her chest, she looked around in the hopes of seeing another cat, but no luck.

"Where's Ava?" she asked. The cat hissed angrily.

The cat lifted a paw and pointed down the street and back out.

Epharis blinked spastically, trying to process the fact that the cat had responded to her question and then pointed the direction out to them.

"Things are rarely ever what they appear to be on the surface," she said in a manner of comfort, heading down the street.

The rain kept everyone inside, which she was glad of, because she did not need the village to see what was happening.

Following the direction the cat had pointed out, the two-headed back into the woods. After ten minutes, they found a large cave entrance in a small outcropping of stone.

Handing the cat off to Epharis, neither of whom seemed to be happy about that choice, she told them to wait. Then she headed inside.

The cave was warm, well-lit, and filled with various items she recognised as belonging to one sister or the other. What she did not see was her sister. Turning slowly, she studied the room carefully.

"Did not take you long to get here," Cain said, stepping out from the darkened space at the back of the cave that she assumed was where the two women slept.

Avadari was held tight to his chest, a large red circle of blood forming at her abdomen.

She looked terrified and all the more beautiful for it. She had snow-white skin and waist-length silver-white hair. Her eyes were a pale violet that was fairly common for their species. With her long. pointed ears and delicate face she looked like an angel. She wore a silvery dress embroidered with white and pale pink flowers.

Small hands clutched her abdomen, and silver tears stained her cheeks.

"Etani..." she whimpered, her sweet voice sounding devastated. "You shouldn't have come."

"I had to..." Etani replied, searching the beautiful face of her baby sister.

The wound was not that bad, she would heal quickly, but she knew Cain would not have trouble killing her. Ava did not have the strength or the willpower to harm anything, even to save her own life.

Outside, a scuffle sounded, and Epharis grunted at the sound of flesh hitting wet flesh.

Turning slightly, she saw Letari hurrying into the cave, followed by a scowling, confused Epharis.

"She changed... Right in my arms..." he was saying to himself, shell-shocked.

Letari was her own mirror image with the only difference being that she was slightly smaller, slightly softer and her large eyes were a deep green. Her hair had been cut short at some point, now coming just to her shoulders.

"Fleas," Letari said with a huge grin on her face in response to Etani's eyes on her hair, as though that were the best thing in the world.

Epharis looked between the three women, studying their faces and making silent comparisons.

"Family reunion. How charming," Cain said, clearly annoyed at being ignored.

Etani reached for her twin and pulled her close, protective of her damaged sister.

Letari happily burrowed into her chest, content to be back with her twin where she belonged.

"If you harm them, I'll destroy you..." Etani warned, unable to decide how best to handle the situation before them.

"Empty threat when I have this one," he sneered, his arm not holding the sword wrapped tight around Avadari's middle.

"You would kill a pureblood just to get to us?" she retorted, and Cain's sneer slipped just a little.

Ava always had the protection of her blood status before, but now it seemed that the loss of such a brilliant, perfect representation of their species was a price Cain was willing to pay in order to remove the embarrassment of the mongrel twins.

"Collateral," he snapped.

Shaking her head slightly, she released her twin, hating the loss of the contact she had missed for all those years. She needed to be able to move freely.

"How about you and I go outside and discuss the matter?" she asked, trying to think.

"How about you come over here and die, then I'll let her go?" he retorted.

Letari gave a low whine, and Epharis moved forward to catch her shoulders, drawing her back. She did not try to fight him, instead, she merely stared at her twin, ignoring everything else but the sight of her sister.

"Only if you promise to let her go," she replied, and Cain looked shocked.

He gave a slow nod, and Etani moved forward, ignoring the whimpering that came from behind her.

Coming to a stop before him, he watched her as he released Ava.

Ava started forward, her eyes wet with tears.

He moved in an instant, the sword withdrawing and then driving forward, but it was not aimed at Etani as she expected; instead the sword drove through the slender, delicate form of Ava. It protruded from her chest.

Her mind went blank as she saw Ava's back arching, her scream of pain joined by Letari's terror, and Epharis's shout of disgust.

Withdrawing the blade, Etani saw her sister fall, their eyes meeting as the life left her, snuffed out in an instant as Orenmir devoured her soul. She felt her own life ending with the quiet thump of her sister's corpse hitting the stone floor.

30

THE END

*B*efore Ava's body hit the ground, Cain turned on her, bloodied sword raised.

She did not even think, she simply moved. Turning, she drew back her right foot and drove it forward, connecting right between the man's legs and dropping him like a tonne of bricks.

He rolled away from her, allowing him to dodge the second kick that was aimed for his head and he flung himself back up onto his feet, sword at the ready.

Her mind had gone entirely blank, and she moved on instinct as Letari wailed and struggled behind her, Epharis trying his best to keep her from escaping.

She had shut down so completely, she did not even have time to process the loss; her entire focus was on killing the man who had so thoroughly destroyed her.

Following after him, she reached behind her to draw out two long blades that rested against her lower back, extending her arms out and then swinging them down together, both knives hitting his raised sword in a perfect mirror of each other. Twisting her wrist, she slapped the blade of her left knife against the flat side of his sword, her right-hand slashing across his stomach, but he was quicker.

Spinning, she used both knives to slash across his chest one after the other, and so the dance began.

She had the upper hand, being faster and trained with two weapons rather than his one, and she was in a blind state where nothing mattered. Slashing fiercely, she parried his lunge and scored again and again on his flesh.

Her agility training made her flexible and light on her feet, allowing her to dodge better, and her form of fighting made her better at close-quarters combat.

He was moving her, she knew it, but it did not matter until he had her facing away from the mouth of the cave. He turned, flying towards the sound of voices.

She was on him in a second, leaping off the ground and landing on his back, one arm wrapped around his neck, the other driving the long blade into his shoulder. His sword clattered to the ground, but he threw her off. Perhaps he had been trying to escape. She was not sure.

Pushing herself to her feet, she went after him as he ran. She turned, searching for Letari.

Epharis was unconscious on the ground, his neck twisted at an odd angle, and she left him there, knowing that while he would have an enormous headache, he would survive.

Sprinting out of the cave, she saw something that drove a spark of terror through her heart.

Letari was standing off against Cain, her razor nails bloody as she clawed his face and chest, leaving him ragged and bleeding.

Running after them, Letari turned and smiled at the sight of her sister coming for her. But then Cain grabbed Letari's head and drove a knife into the back of her skull, twisting viciously.

Letari was the next to hit the ground, the delighted smile still on her face, and Cain fled. Instead of going after the man, she skidded to a stop beside her twin and lifted her off the ground, checking her pulse to find it gone. She had known it would be gone, there was too much damage to survive, even for Letari.

Clenching her jaw, she prayed that her twin had the same gift as her, and would not remain dead.

"What's the matter, Etani, last woman standing?" Cain taunted, sounding breathless somewhere around her.

She lowered her sister and stood, turning to try to find him. She did not speak, only searched for him. He was kind enough to come for her.

He tried again and again to punch her, and she parried and blocked the blows, her mind empty, and yet all she could see was the faces of the two she had spent her entire life trying to protect.

It had been her duty, a job she gladly accepted because that was what you did for your family. A duty he had sought to rip away from her, and had now torn to shreds.

Avadari's soul was trapped in his sword, and she would never be able to escape unless the sword was destroyed. She did not know if Letari was like her, she did not know if either of them were like her, but she knew that unless she got Ava out of that wretched thing, she would have no chance of returning to life.

WITH THAT IN MIND, she let her rage and agony add force to her blows. She let her anguish at the loss of Sasha, then Nayishma, and finally her precious, wonderful sisters, fuel her rage.

It was too much, she could not handle it, and she wanted it all to end. She wanted freedom from the pain. She wanted to join her sisters in death.

But she could not do that if there was even a shred of hope that one of them would return to life like she did. She wanted nothing more than to smile as her sisters tried to understand why one moment they were dead, and the next they were underwater. She wanted to laugh with them and explain that they had been reborn, to discuss the strange place they went to upon death.

She wanted to conspire about the strange shadowy figures that lurked just off the path that would lead to rebirth, to feel that odd pull back towards life.

She wanted to tell them about Ayathian, about Epharis, the priestess, Nayishma, Alaric, Sasha, the twins... She wanted to tell them everything.

She wanted them to know how much she loved them, and how much it had broken her heart every time she had been forced to leave them behind to keep Cain busy.

She had never told them how happy it made her to come back to them and check on them. She had never told them how much she loved them because it always hurt too much knowing she would have to leave again in a matter of hours.

She had wasted her life running, but she had thrown it away for them, to keep them safe.

Tears stung her eyes as she thought over all the little things she had wanted to share with them: a butterfly wing, a shell, a rock that looked like a man's genitals. She never once got to share those with them; she never got to share anything with them.

They had been in the human world for only weeks before they realised they needed to split up. Twenty-five years together with her twin, seven years with Ava, and then nothing for the remaining nine hundred. She got to spend a total of a few hours every couple of years with them.

All because of that bastard before her; it was his fault she had lost out on so much with her precious sisters. It was his fault she had never been able to share herself with them, they had died never really knowing her, always seeing her as just that other sister who came by sometimes.

He was the reason they had to spend their lives in one cave after another, always wary and always afraid.

She did everything she could to keep them safe, and in the end it had not been enough; she had not been enough, and she would never get that chance to tell them how sorry she was for being distant, for being cold.

Her jaw clenched, she ignored the pain of each blow, as she did everything within her power, just to get her hands on him. She wanted to rip him apart with her bare hands. She wanted to eviscerate him.

He was afraid, she could see it. He was not aware of how strong she had become, not aware of just how much her anger would scream through her and send her into that anguished void of impotent rage. She blamed him, and she wanted him dead. Not only that, she wanted Illia dead.

She was going to bring an end to the Queen of Ceress for ordering the deaths of her sisters.

Her blows turned feral, her fingers and mouth bloody as she used nails and teeth to rend his flesh. When that did not seem to work, she came up with a new idea.

Reaching behind her, she felt along the small pouch of vials against her lower back and picked one out. Under the cover of trees, she pulled the cork with her thumb and the powder filled her fingers. He seemed to think she was exhausted, and he was grinning maniacally as he flew towards her. She lifted her hand, blowing the powder into his face.

The man screamed, his arms flying up to clutch at his face as the blue powder puffed up around him and she smiled, stepping into him.

Without a word, she drove her knee up into his groin and he dropped. The moment he was on the ground, she stepped over him and dropped down onto his stomach, taking first one arm and then the other, stuffing them under her knees.

He was still screaming, and she shut him up with first one punch, and then a second, driving her fists into his face over and over until he stopped making any noise.

That made her feel a little better, or at least less angry.

Looking down at him, she contemplated what it was she could do to him, and her head turned, looking at the limp corpse of her twin, looking towards the cave where Ava would be lying, beautiful and perfect in death.

LOOKING BACK DOWN AT HIM, she bent down over him and sank her teeth into his throat. He screamed, but she ignored it, ignored his attempts to throw her off him, and ignored his attempts to kick her back or twist his arms. Tearing the flesh from his neck, she spat it out onto the ground and bit again, and again, and again.

He did not deserve the peace of the death she could give him; he did not deserve a beautiful death. He deserved to die in the mud, his throat ripped out by a half-breed freak.

She bit and spat until all that was left was his spine, and then she ripped the spine apart. There was no surviving that; none of them survived decapitation.

If he could come back like she could, she would be glad of it. She would gladly spend the rest of eternity killing him over and over again, but she doubted he would. The ability was so incredibly rare now, regardless of what the rumours had been when she was a child.

Standing, she picked up the head by what was left of the spine and turned, throwing the thing into the trees, not wanting to see his face ever again. But she would, she would see him every night in her nightmares, killing her sisters over and over again.

Heading back towards her twin, she carefully wiped her bloody hands clean on the soaked grass and lifted the body tenderly from the grass.

Cradling the body in her arms, she closed her eyes and willed her sister to know how to escape the spirit world, begged her to come back, pleaded silently and screamed into the void for her to come back.

Stroking the beautiful, pale face, she began to sing quietly, a lullaby their mother had sung for them when they were young and sick, or fretting, or did not want to go to bed.

Her voice was low and soft, her tears falling freely as she stared with a desperate longing at her twin. She wanted nothing more than to do that, to just sit there with Letari and stroke her hair, to listen to her laugh and smile with her.

She could not survive without her sisters; she did not want to survive without them.

Clenching her eyes shut, she bit hard on her lips, trying to keep her face from showing her anguish as she rocked slowly back and forth, comforting the body of her dead sibling.

"You're okay, Lee..." she whispered, her smile feeling warped as a stab of pain ripped through her body. "You're okay, I'm here now."

She should have been there the whole time, but she had not been. It was her fault for not being strong enough in time. It was her own fault that four incredible, wonderful women were now dead.

How could she have been so stupid as to think she could look after them? Who was she? Just some foolish girl who thought she could keep all of those innocent lives safe? She was not even considered a full adult by her own people.

She wished she had been older, stronger, braver, better. She wished she could have been enough, but she was not. She was none of those things; she was a scared little girl trying to protect other scared little girls from the adults.

Why couldn't they have just let them live in exile? She should have asked for help, asked anyone who had listened. She should have demanded someone help her protect them but instead she was arrogant, and that had cost her those lives.

She should have gone to the Winter Court, begged the Queen to protect her sisters in exchange for herself. She would have done it without a second thought had she known, but she had never dreamt that he would go after them when he had been so close to getting her.

She should have gone there. She should have done better... She should have done everything for them...

How long she sat there she did not know, but it was long enough that the body had begun to scatter, and Epharis walked from the cave and approached.

"Etani?" he asked, looking shocked by the carnage.

She did not take her eyes off her twin, even when he joined her on the ground.

Her body was disintegrating as most mythicals did when they died, ensuring there would never be a trace of them left to be studied.

Her fingers traced her twin's jaw, and she watched as the spots she touched scattered into the wind.

"Avadari is gone," he said, sounded devastated. "She disintegrated into dust..."

"So, humans cannot find more out about us," she said gently, tracing the full lower lip, watching the flesh scattering. It was not morbid; underneath there was nothing but a swirling blackness filled with a million stars as though their insides were a reflection of the night sky.

Leaning down, she traced a soft kiss against the pale forehead and began to sing quietly once more.

She did not want to see as her sister vanished into the wind, so she kept her eyes shut even as the weight on her lap eased and then finally vanished.

She had lost everything that ever meant anything to her. She had failed to keep any of them safe. She could not even do something so simple as keep them safe.

Had she only kept Cain's attention for a little longer, she might have been able to kill him. She might have been able to spare her sisters of their deaths. She might have been able to save them both had she not left. The sight of Letari's joy at her appearance bit at her, her heart breaking.

She did not scream and rage this time, she simply sat with her eyes closed, the tears flowing freely. She made no attempt to stop them.

Epharis made no attempt to touch her either; he merely remained with her and kept guard while she suffered in silence.

How had she been so blind as not to realise he would go after them? She had assumed that he had suffered the same mental injuries as her.

Why had he not been incapacitated? She did not know, and she did not care enough to try to figure it out right then.

Finally opening her eyes, she pushed herself to her feet and turned back to the cave.

Entering it as though in a dream, she took only two things: a small black cat pendant she knew Letari had loved dearly, and a delicate hairpin Letari had given Ava for her birthday so long ago.

It was a long strip of silver with an elaborate swirling pattern on either end, and two strings of little silver beads stretching between both ends.

The little black cat had been what led to Letari turning herself into a cat at every opportunity.

She saw the sword, Orenmir, and picked it up, placing it on the bed. Reaching behind her, she pulled out a single vial and spread it over the mattress, picking out one of the larger candles. Turning to see Epharis standing in the mouth of the cave, she threw the candle onto the powder.

The cave shook as the powder erupted in flames so hot, they were blue, the sword melting in a minute with a terrible, keening scream.

Leaving the cave, the pair stood a few feet back as the fire spread to consume everything inside. Eventually the rocks themselves caught fire and evil flames spilled out, to be quenched by the rain.

Slipping the necklace around her throat, she clutched the cat tightly, the pin clenched in her other hand. They watched the burning cave, right up until it collapsed and what remained of the demonic fire was suffocated by the dirt.

There was nothing left for them in that place. There was nothing left for her in any place, and she turned slowly to the Lich, seeing his fear at her empty eyes.

She had no purpose anymore, her purpose for existing was now gone, her sisters were gone.

Stretching out her hand for the Lich, she barely felt it when he took it.

She would take them back to Ayathian and she would wait there for a time. If she did not feel her sisters, she would kill herself, and she would sever the connection to life. It was nothing more than a ribbon, it would be easy.

With this plan in mind she was glad that, if nothing else, she would be with her sisters again soon—all three of them would be dead.

Together at last, the way it should have been all along.

ABOUT THE AUTHOR

Born in Mackay, North Queensland in Australia, N. Malone's writing journey started at the age of nine. It wasn't until the age of twenty-nine that the career began.

The story of Etani had been building for nearly ten years, daydreams and forums until the character became a reality when book one had begun.
Now, with twelve books in the works, the story can continue.

"If you like writing, then write."

https://www.nmalone.net

AFTERWORD

If you enjoyed Etani, you can follow along on her adventures in book two
"Trapped Princess", available on Amazon
My Book

Your opinions are valuable, please take a moment to leave a rating.